# CURIOUS MEMORIES

# CURIOUS MEMORIES

By
Luke Sheehan

© 2023 by Luke Sheehan
All rights reserved. No part of this publication may be reproduced, stored in a retrieval system, or transmitted, in any form or by any means, electronic, mechanical, photocopying, recording, or otherwise, without the prior written permission of the author.

Starrow LLC
www.starrow.org

Printed in the United States of America
Ebook ISBN-13: 979-8-9876642-2-3
Paperback ISBN-13: 979-8-9876642-0-9
Hard Cover ISBN-13: 979-8-9876642-1-6

# Table of Contents

Chapter 1. World of Darkness . . . . . . . . . . . . . . . . . . . . . . . . . . . 1
Chapter 2. Distant Shore. . . . . . . . . . . . . . . . . . . . . . . . . . . . . . . 12
Chapter 3. New Dawn. . . . . . . . . . . . . . . . . . . . . . . . . . . . . . . . . 29
Chapter 4. Awakened . . . . . . . . . . . . . . . . . . . . . . . . . . . . . . . . . 44
Chapter 5. Calm Before the Storm . . . . . . . . . . . . . . . . . . . . . 62
Chapter 6. Exosphere . . . . . . . . . . . . . . . . . . . . . . . . . . . . . . . . . 72
Chapter 7. At the Edge of Dusk. . . . . . . . . . . . . . . . . . . . . . . . 83
Chapter 8. Momento. . . . . . . . . . . . . . . . . . . . . . . . . . . . . . . . . 108
Chapter 9. Double-edged Dagger . . . . . . . . . . . . . . . . . . . . . 122
Chapter 10. Dying Light. . . . . . . . . . . . . . . . . . . . . . . . . . . . . . 135
Chapter 11. Tall Ears, Sharp Claws, and Big Hearts. . . . . . . 154
Chapter 12. Blood and Feathers . . . . . . . . . . . . . . . . . . . . . . . 166
Chapter 13. Ignite . . . . . . . . . . . . . . . . . . . . . . . . . . . . . . . . . . . 175
Chapter 14. Paper, Honey, and Pumpkins. . . . . . . . . . . . . . . 188
Chapter 15. Rain Cloud . . . . . . . . . . . . . . . . . . . . . . . . . . . . . . 200
Chapter 16. Rising Tides . . . . . . . . . . . . . . . . . . . . . . . . . . . . . 222
Chapter 17. Eyes of the Storm. . . . . . . . . . . . . . . . . . . . . . . . . 230
Chapter 18. Emberlight . . . . . . . . . . . . . . . . . . . . . . . . . . . . . . 247
Chapter 19. The Truth . . . . . . . . . . . . . . . . . . . . . . . . . . . . . . . 270
Chapter 20. The Warmth of Home. . . . . . . . . . . . . . . . . . . . . 289
Chapter 21. Rekindled . . . . . . . . . . . . . . . . . . . . . . . . . . . . . . . 303
Chapter 22. Starlight. . . . . . . . . . . . . . . . . . . . . . . . . . . . . . . . . 334
Chapter 23. Moonlight. . . . . . . . . . . . . . . . . . . . . . . . . . . . . . . 352
Chapter 24. Snuffed Out. . . . . . . . . . . . . . . . . . . . . . . . . . . . . . 363
Chapter 25. Brightest Light . . . . . . . . . . . . . . . . . . . . . . . . . . . 372

This book is dedicated to those who need a lot of help and, even more so, love.

This story contains harsh mental health topics, violence, and sexual assault. Please, be careful on this journey.

# Chapter 1
# WORLD OF DARKNESS

*You should die*, whispered the wet, venomous lips of a lady-like voice.

Sam flinched as her cold tongue slithered against his eardrum. He pried apart his heavy, crusty eyelids to a sea of bone dust and a sky of ink. And at that moment, he thought he heard a ceramic vase crack.

"W-What?" He rubbed his eyes with the rough wipe of his wings, but the flat landscape still blanketed his vision. *Where am I?* There was a kiss of wind that curled ash from the ground. The flakes looked like shooting stars in the empty, ink sky before they swirled back and stuck to Sam's raven feathers. The air was dead cold, but the blanket of ash and bone was warm and brittle over his sunken, leathery feet.

The snow-like cushion rose like mountains between the wide weight of his toes. *Am I standing on the moon?* He raised his foot, watching the powder flutter down with an Earth-like gravity. He then squinted to the horizon, where the sharp line between an ink sky and ashen ground cut his sight. *There's nothing here. . . .*

*You belong here, for you are nothing.*

1

Icy goosebumps crept up his spine to his neck, as if a spider had found its mark, ready to take a bite. Sam veered around. Every time the voice spoke, it grabbed his head and yanked his thoughts away. "Who's there? Is this a dream?"

*It's never a dream with you.*

Sam scrunched his eyes closed and grasped his head in anguish. "Stop! Please! Get out of my head! W-Where'd you even come from?" he screeched in fear.

The voice was like a flower's petal, soft and alluring. But the way and words it spoke shivered Sam to the marrow of his bones.

"Sam?" spoke a warm voice.

Sam's heart melted. To him, hearing that voice was more valuable than gold. "Please! Who's there? I need help!"

*Asking for help again? Pathetic.*

Tears escaped Sam's eyes and soaked his feathered cheeks. Those words were needles to his eardrums, forcing him to wince with every poke.

"I'm so sorry, Sam," the warm voice spoke once more, louder, almost as if—Sam veered his head with neck-cracking speed to Hugo, who stood a few steps from him. His ruby and honey dragon scales gifted the ink and ash world with brilliant color. Sam could quickly feel the warmth Hugo radiated into his feathers. To him, Hugo looked and felt like a freshly-bloomed sunrise in the dead of winter.

"Hugo!" Sam fell forward in surprise and crawled through the sloshy powder to Hugo. But just before he stood back up, he froze when he saw Hugo's heavy tears. "What happened?" Sam's heart begged him to ask that with a pinch.

"I'm so sorry, Sam. . . . I didn't know she would come. I tried. I–" Hugo squeaked in sorrow.

Hugo had never seemed so sad in Sam's eyes. Tears and snot flooded out from Hugo and dripped from his chin. His wobbling mouth and heavy forked tongue moved with the words he wished to pour out to Sam, but only empty air escaped those lips.

"Hugo?" Sam felt a deep, heart-pinching pain. "Please, Hugo, let me fix this. I-I can help you," he begged and found fresh tears drowning his feathery cheeks and shining over his beak.

With a simple glance, Hugo's eye met Sam's. Then a sudden gravity crushed Sam back to his wings and knees. Before Sam could look up, Hugo vanished in a puff of green smoke.

"Hugo!" Sam shot his wing into the smoke to grab him. But Hugo was gone; not even his warmth remained in the air. The cold, hungry spider crawled up Sam's neck feathers instantly.

*He left because you're annoying.*

Sam grasped his skull tight enough to crack it. With every heavy thump, his heart struggled to support the rest of his body. *Please, shut up!* Suddenly, time wouldn't pass quickly enough, and it felt like an eternity had passed between each merciful breath. *I want to go home. . . .*

At that second, a distant sniffle forced his head to turn. He knew instantly who that sniffle belonged to. And once he spun around, his eyes met his mom, Mary. She was kneeling deep in the ash with her head low and her hands gently over her thighs. She had a fluffy, emerald sweater over khaki pants, and her copper hair colored the landscape like Hugo. "M-Mom!" Sam yelled with joy pounding his heart. But sorrow hung a thousand anchors under his ribs once he saw her eyes.

She was smiling, but tears welled and sank over the curvature of her plump cheeks. Less sad than Hugo, but far more painful. To him, seeing Mary cry is, and always will be, the worst feeling in the world. He carefully pulled himself closer. His body begged to help her with an itch in his chest. His wings and back numbed at the tingling remembrance of her firm, loving embrace. And his eardrums rang at the wish to hear her cheerful voice again. He missed it so much that–

*You don't deserve her love. She regrets adopting you.*

Sam froze, feeling all warmth robbed from his chest by those words.

Then Mary opened her arms to accept him. The tips of his toes suddenly tingled to keep moving forward. *But . . . she doesn't love me. How could she? I'm just a waste of a son . . . a stupid bird.*

Before Sam could open his beak to talk, Mary grabbed him and lifted him high from the ground into a great, big hug. He almost squawked in surprise. Her inviting, plump body was so soft and warm, he sank in bliss. "Don't let anyone say that you don't deserve love," Mary said. Sam's heart melted with those words and her strong arms, giving him a loving, firm warmth.

Sam looked at her beautiful, berry-blue eyes. Then, he shyly looked away. "Thank you, Mom, for always being there for me. . . . I never thought I'd feel this again," Sam murmured and began to weep. *This is all I ever wanted to feel.*

Mary inhaled a deep, snot-bubbling sniffle.

Sam looked up at her face again and nearly broke down on the spot. "M-Mom?" That word pinched its way up his throat with a squeak.

Mary leaned down until Sam's toes bent against the ground. She cupped his fluffy, feathery cheeks with her gentle hands. And without a second of delay, she gave a heartwarming chuckle. "Remember what I used to sing to you to help you feel better?" She smiled with sorrow flowing from her eyes. "You and Hugo had *the thing*, but we, had this. . . ."

> *Through the rumbling storm and the long cold night*
> *you will find . . . warmth in my open arms.*
> *Like your heroes who fall, you will rise with them all*
> *and you will see how high you'll fly.*
> *The sun will rise, and the night will set,*
> *and you will see your brightest light.*
> *My strong, and brave, Saiai.*

"Remember that little lullaby? My singing isn't concert-worthy, and the rhymes aren't the greatest, but it's special to us, right?"

Sam sniffled with a firm nod against her sweater's soft yet itchy knitting. His tears soaked each thread. *I love you more than words can hold.*

Before Sam could open his beak to say his thought, she sniffled, then vanished in familiar green smoke. He gasped, falling from her hug and slapping the ground.

"Mom! What's wrong? Let me help! I want to help!" His chest expanded in and out with every panicked gulp of air he sucked in. He tried to stand, but his knees wobbled too much to bear. His eyes stung, and his soaked vision blurred the ink sky and ashen ground into gray.

*But you can't help. You're useless. You can't even stand on your own.*

"Shut up!" he screeched just before his left knee cracked, and he collapsed back onto the warm dust. He grasped his head to squeeze the voice from his brain. "Mom . . . please, I need you. I don't want to be alone!"

But he stopped once he heard the warm snap of a wood fire. It was so quiet that Sam had to listen between each breath. But he suddenly paused and squinted as each crack became louder and louder until a noise like a branch snapping in half jolted his head. There was a distant, subtle screech of someone in agony, but Sam was the only one here, *right?* he thought.

He rolled to his other side with his wings firmly over his head and saw a young, dark flame. It struggled to stay alive in the colorless world they dwelled on. But it offered Sam a subtle warmth, far different than Hugo or Mary's, but strangely just as alluring.

He found his eyes stuck to it and his eardrums pulled by the wisping crackle. *Who are you?*

The fire crawled closer, and Sam scooted back with every inch it shrank between them. It wanted something, but Sam couldn't tell what. He stood with an unbalanced wobble and limped to the side, but the fire changed direction . . . to him.

"Are you the voice in my head?"

Then, a white flame sprouted around it, as if it were a cute, little eye. The dark fire in its core rose and stared at Sam.

*I can help you; all you need to do is let me. . . . Touch me when you're ready to see beyond this dream.*

Like a kind lady, that was the voice, so soft, yet it stung his poor eardrums. Sam sighed with a glance around the seemingly barren planet. "You can help me out of here?"

After a moment of staring at each other, Sam sighed again. *Whatever. This is only a dream. And I guess you're my only hope. . . .* He leaned down and extended his right wing, allowing the tip of his longest feather to meet the fire. The white fire sucked into its dark core like a black hole; then the fire crawled up his wing, promptly curling a scent of smoke to Sam's nares.

His suddenly shaking wing almost put out the fire, but almost was not enough. The fire crawled and swelled along his wing, and it started to burn and boil his skin. "Wait. . . . Stop! What are you doing?" It started hurting so much, his beak gnashed enough to crack, and his toes gripped the ash.

The fire left nothing in its conquest but ash that twinkled down and blended perfectly with the ground. Sam tried to flap his wing and even bury it in the ash. But regardless, the fire grew in heat and size with the passing seconds. The fire crawled up his neck like a hundred wasps sawing off his head. "Stop!" he screamed.

*You are nothing, but together, I can be everything.*

The fire met the edge of his watery, worried eyes before all went dark.

Sam snapped awake and flung from the nylon passenger car seat onto the carpeted floor. His lungs stung with a burning pinch as he gulped for air like he was drowning, and his body trembled enough to wobble the car.

"What the!" George yelled with a firm twitch of the steering wheel, smacking Sam into the door.

Sam flopped onto the cupholders between them before he gagged and emptied his stomach onto the back seats.

"Oh great—Sam!" George yelled again and realigned the car to the correct side of the road.

By instinct, Sam patted his wing against George's thigh, looking for someone to hold him. He didn't care that it was George; he just wanted comfort, even if it was from the man who had turned him into a monster. George volunteered his arm before Sam grasped it tight within his trembling wings.

"Are you alright, Sam?"

Sam tried to breathe slower, so he could speak. But his weighty lungs proved too much to control. So George waited and simply listened to the heavy patter of rain against the windshield.

Sam took a while, not just to catch his breath, but to handle the sorrowful and worrisome images of Mary and Hugo. But the burning feeling of that fire stole his thoughts and echoed across his body as if it crawled beneath his feathers, ready to bite once again.

"I'm fine," Sam lied. He didn't trust George enough to share how he felt. *And I don't want to worry George already. He promised to make me stronger. . . . So I can't show weakness. I need to show him that I'm not a burden, that I can be like Hugo.*

"Would you like some water? . . . I even have some fancy bottled tea if it takes your interest."

"Where?" Sam asked before George pointed to the passenger cubby. "Which one's your favorite?" Sam opened the compartment with his foot.

"The tea, but–"

With many nervous clacks and tings, Sam scooped a glass bottle of green tea within his wings and cradled it before George. "Is this what you wanted, M-Mr. George?" he murmured, shyly looking at the floor.

George smirked.

With Hugo on his mind, Sam's heart stung at the fresh thought of leaving him on Somnium. *M-Maybe I can make up for my mistake by helping others, like how you helped me, Hugo.* The tea bottle suddenly felt heavier, and his wings sank with its weight. He still blamed himself for everything that had happened to Hugo.

George accepted the tea with a smile. "Thank you, Sam," George said before Sam's head bobbed and eyelids drooped.

Sam quickly saw George looking at him, so he turned and

grabbed a water bottle. But before he could hook the lid with his toes, his head numbed. *No . . . I can't go back there.* In that instant, a bolt of lightning shot a telephone pole alongside the road and boomed Sam awake with a flinch. But George kept driving like nothing had happened, almost like he had predicted it. To mend the awkward silence, Sam opened his beak. "Where'd this storm come from?" he yawned, feeling sleep yank down his eyelids once more.

George grabbed Sam's seatbelt and clicked it into place before patting Sam's chest, telling him he was safe. "From the west, near the mountains. . . . Here, let me tell you some things that always help my students fall asleep," he chuckled.

"No, please. . . . Help me stay here," Sam moaned. He tried desperately to keep his eyes open. But his body commanded him with the thoughtless pull of sleep, and he leaned back with his eyes closed and his beak wide open, nearly sinking back into the cozy night sea.

"The fun thing about lightning is that once it hits the ground, the energy doesn't disappear; it turns into ground lightning that can easily shoot back up if conditions are right." George looked at Sam, who almost snored. "And lightning normally occurs when the storms are most mature, not developing, nor at the final moments, but right in the middle."

George took a moment for himself with a sip of tea before reaching his hand to Sam's head. "This should stop those nightmares from happening." He pressed his thumb and pinky on Sam's temples. "A dream about your family, one where you're helping them with everything your brilliant mind can come up with."

"No . . ." Sam murmured, but then relaxed with a moan and released the water bottle with a sloshy thud against the carpet floor. *What did he do to me?*

"Oh, you're quite the fighter to survive my weather discussion." He smiled and looked onto the open, early-morning road. And just past the heavy, dark rainclouds rested the rising sun that just had time to paint the distant clouds with a rose pink under a carrot hue. And once the violent beating of raindrops ran dry, autumn leaves crunched under the wheels and brushed away with the air racing the car.

"You are growing fast, but I can only hope you're growing in the right direction." George sighed, then looked at Sam's wing, which rested gently over George's thigh. "You had such a horrid nightmare that you spoiled my backseat, then have the mindset to tell me you're alright?" He looked at Sam with a raised eyebrow. "Be very careful, Sam. Being helpful to others is splendid, but not at the expense of your health, especially when you try to hide it as such. . . ."

*How did he . . .*

"But don't worry. . . . I promise you will be helpful. We only need some time and the patience to fill it." George leaned forward with a squint at the college's spires peeking over the trees on the horizon. He turned onto a dirt road, shrouded by large oak trees, then cradled Sam's head as the potholes shook and bounced the car.

*Where is he taking me?*

Not long passed before they arrived at a sizable house made from old tree logs. To Sam's blurry sight, this house was a mansion. But to usual standards, it was a simple countryside lodge.

George parked the car beside the stairs that led to the front porch. "I hope this place can help you find the peace you need. It's not as fancy as my second house, the one I built with you slightly in mind . . . . But you're a different person than I anticipated. Someone with a soul ability as powerful as time . . . well, let's just say I thought you'd be a little more confident. But don't worry; Ai was the same, and she loved this abode."

"Wait. . . . Ai?" Sam moaned, losing a tug-of-war against sleep.

George seemed to laugh. "Oh, still awake, are we?" George cradled Sam within his right arm and winced. He took a few breaths, then grunted as he opened the car door.

*Is he . . . okay?*

George took his cane in his left hand, then limped through the front door and up creaky wooden stairs. All the while, he was grimacing. His face begged him to yell. But, eventually, he found the first room on the right just as the sun showed its face above the distant hills, and the morning fog blessed the plants with the natural twinkle of dew.

He laid Sam on a simple, rustic bed and tucked a pre-heated, electric quilt around him. And at that moment, George tapped the floor with his cane and nearly fell over with an exhaustive sigh.

The soft mattress and warm blankets were too tough of an opponent for Sam. And with his tense head sinking into the plush pillow, he lost and dropped into the deep ocean of sleep without a single ripple. But instead of feeling wet, he felt the echoing sting of fire.

*Chapter 2*
# DISTANT SHORE

The ocean was gentler than a warm bath. Few waves dared to challenge the sunset's sinking height, and fewer had the momentum to lick the sand in sizzling white foam. The thin knitting of clouds was splotched with colors of a fruitful breakfast, forcing all who saw to hear their stomachs growl instantly.

In the center of Hugo's sight rested the silhouette of a gondola before the sparkling infinity. The boat's oak boards whispered many creaks to the yearning call of water burbling at the bow. The natural pull of wind and sea inched the hull and cracked the creamy sail further from the sand and closer to freedom.

"Would you two idiots hurry up already?" Ventus complained with his leathery foot splashing the sand with every impatient tap. The boat cloaked him in shadow from the final, fruity beams of sunset, but even in shadow, Ventus' ink and snowy feathers shimmered like stars mixed perfectly with an azure sky. His shiny, gray beak pointed at Hugo with the annoyed pushes of breath through his nares, and his bony, dark-leathered legs supported all of him like a pair of crooked towers to the skies he embodied.

Every step Hugo took creaked his bones. Every breath he heaved ached his spine and chest. He was so sore that he'd still be in the cabin if it weren't for Bipp helping his every step.

"Why are you in such a rush?" Bipp adjusted the soup pot in his slipping grasp.

Ventus scoffed with a sharp squint at Hugo, who struggled to take his first steps from the Glowshroom Forest to the beachside's glimmering, golden sand. "I rush, because I have better things to do than sail across the ocean with–" Ventus' eyes narrowed further, and he scanned them from feet to ears, "you two." His face scrunched with the sour sting of how disgusted he was by them.

Bipp sighed, then after a moment or three, he finally reached the boat with Ventus already sitting comfortably at the bow. He set the pot and blankets against the left hull and cradled Hugo's underside with both hands. "Alright, easy does it," Bipp grunted as Hugo stepped into the cramped boat and wrapped his lengthy body along the circumference. Then, he collapsed and nearly tipped the boat upon his impact; Ventus just about squawked in panic.

"Sorry. . . . Thank you, Bipp." Hugo's mind thundered with . . . well . . . everything. His mom, dad, Sam, Earth, Somnium, all things that required his full attention, but he couldn't give it.

*What am I doing? I thought life was going to be simple. I'd go to college and study with Sam. Then maybe we'd buy our first home together once we graduated, if he wanted. . . . I hope he'd like that. . . .*

*Maybe he could fly in a plane with me, and we could search for dinosaur fossils with his new paleontology knowledge while our plane lights become one of the stars. . . . But now, I'm a weird dragon, trapped on a planet far away from my family. Do I want to be a dragon for the rest of my life? . . . Not really. . . .* He sighed once more and looked at his claws. *I guess all I want now is to see Sam again. And . . .* His hands trembled from his control. *I need to know if he's okay. . . . What if something terrible happened to him? What if George is Apotheosis and wants his soul? What if–* His thumping chest punched the boat's side and formed ripples in the water.

Ventus thoughtfully squinted at him. "Stop doing that." But Hugo didn't hear him.

*What is this feeling?* He tried to slow his breaths and smell the fresh sawdust that escaped the cinnamon boards in wisps of salty ocean air. *Why is my body doing this; it's not dark out yet?* He closed his eyes to calm down. *Okay, okay. Just think about Sam. Just think about Sam. He's okay. . . . He's right here beside me.* A sudden itch pinched his chest.

Bipp grabbed the stern and pushed forward. "Ventus, a little help?" he grunted.

A soft wind slithered along Bipp's back, then cracked the canvas sail with tremendous force. The boat yanked from Bipp before he stumbled into the sand. "Hey!" He dashed, then leapt to the fleeing boat and landed with a perfectly balanced thump.

The boat was sucked out to sea with the wind howling louder and blowing stronger. Bipp looked down at Ventus, who sat before him with a devilish smirk.

Bipp's eyelids sank, but he gave a smile. "Thank you for the help," he said sincerely, then turned to Hugo. Ventus was left alone with a confused squint.

Bipp sat beside Hugo's head, leaned back with his elbows over the edge, and sighed. He then grabbed his ears to prevent them from flapping around. "I don't know about this trip." He glanced at Hugo, who stared at the stars past the cotton clouds with a sorrowful twinkle in his eye.

*Where are you, Sam?*

"You've been awfully quiet. What's on your mind?" Bipp folded his ears back, tucked them through the neck-hole of his cloak, and began sorting through the pile of bowls and blankets until he found Hugo's scarf. He admired it for a second, then tucked it to the side, hidden from the wind.

*It's going to be his birthday fairly soon. . . . I'd love to give him something . . . but . . .* Hugo's head sank low; his eye was looking at his stubby yet fierce dragon hands. Then, with a sigh, his gaze slowly traveled up and across the gaps along the boards. "Yeah."

Ventus and Bipp looked at each other just before the splashing waves and burbling water hushed. Bipp, with a worried look on his face, slowly brought his hand to Hugo's shoulder. "Hey, are you alright?"

Hugo's ears pierced the sky. "Oh." He raised his head and looked at Bipp, poised even while seated. Hugo couldn't help but watch his silver fur shimmer like stars in the sparkly mist of the sea. "I'm sorry. I–" Hugo then looked back at his extensive body; he had ruby and honey scales like an organized pile of autumn leaves. He moved his hind toes, more than fifteen feet from his snout. "To be honest . . . I don't understand what I'm thinking." Hugo looked at Bipp's jade, attentive eyes. "I promise I'll tell you when I figure it out. But for now–"

"Idiot." Ventus stood, walked, and sat between Hugo and Bipp. "You're obviously thinking about Sam." He sighed. "I never liked your connection with him. Besides him being rude and selfish, he's on another planet, right? . . . If I were you, I'd let that daft bird go, save you the stress of trying to traverse worlds again, if all that nonsense is true about Earth and whatnot."

As Bipp growled and Hugo looked down, Ventus leaned back, allowing Bipp and Hugo to see each other. "But all in all, it's you two who baffle me." Bipp froze as Ventus looked right at him. "Like I would ignore what you said to him while he was comatose."

Hugo's ears twitched at the sound of Bipp's heart suddenly thumping against his ribs. Without delay, Bipp raised his hands with each finger flexed, ready to strangle.

Ventus looked at Hugo. "Bipp wants to know if—Mff!"

Bipp grasped Ventus' beak shut with a firm clack.

As Ventus flapped against him, Bipp shyly looked at Hugo, who looked at him as if an eyebrow was raised. "I'm sorry, Hugo. I guess we both have something to talk about later."

Bipp let go of Ventus, who instantly stood and glared at him. Then, he removed Bipp's tall ears from the cloak and promptly slapped them with his wing before walking to the opposite end of the boat.

Bipp's ears sprang back up.

Ventus scoffed, turned his beak away from their view, and sat with his wings crossed. And to Bipp and Hugo's surprise, a dense fog instantly rushed around them. Freshwater specks met Hugo's cheeks and formed dew-like droplets between his scales. Bipp squinted, but simply relaxed next to Hugo with a sigh; that is, until the fog passed, and they looked down. The ocean was long behind and below them. Only a dense forest packed with canopies of golden leaves rolled three-thousand feet under them.

"Ventus . . . what are we doing up here?"

"Anzu said to bring a boat; he never specified the method of *bringing it* or that we had to return it. So expect us to leave it there," Ventus snickered, but he still refused to show them his beak. "Flying west over the mainland is much faster than flying east to Dawn, and with this boat lugging us around, we need the extra speed. Besides, I'm not about to sail us over Archipelago's ocean in such a small boat. One blink from that monster, and the waves would topple us, especially with Hugo's weight nearly sinking us already." He sighed. "If only you weren't a flightless idiot."

"That's not true," Bipp whispered and sadly looked at Hugo, who stared at the floorboards with a spark igniting his imagination.

A few minutes passed, and they all grew comfortable with the view of their familiar land: Rafflesia's moat connected by two rivers and the grand field of King's Garden within the tight grasp of an infinite forest. Even the wind that flapped and cracked the sail's canvas calmed the sounds of their travel. Those minutes turned to hours, and only the occasional glance from Ventus broke their thoughts. He would sometimes reach his wing out as if he wanted to ask something, but he never did. As the sunlight sank at their backs, and the starlight began to conquer the western sky with an army of trillions, Hugo continued his search for Sam.

*I'll find you. I just have to spot one familiar constellation in all this* . . . his vision went blurry when he saw how tiny this needle was in such a giant, dense haystack, *mess.* His heart suddenly felt heavy. *And once I find you, I just have to get to you. . .* . He looked at his stumpy dragon fingers. *I may need some help building a spaceship. . . . Maybe I should've studied astronautical engineering while at college.* His forked tongue flicked out in thought. *But what if . . . I propelled the ship?* He tried to remember the science behind breathing fire. He promptly shook his head and just breathed out, allowing a faint kindle past his lips, only to be hushed out by the roaring wind. *If only I could fly . . . then I could at least close some distance between us.* He looked at Ventus. *But without wings, how is it even possible?*

"Ventus? Did you happen to bring any paper on this trip?" Bipp asked with a relaxed squint to the sky. Hugo snapped from his deep daydream and looked at him.

"Do I look like I carry anything?" Ventus rolled his eyes at the ridiculous question. His wings gestured over his blue, snowy white, and midnight body; he only wore tan harem pants with no apparent pockets.

Bipp stood and withdrew his ebony dagger. "Bummer." He walked to the sail and grabbed it by the edge. "Then, may I take a piece of this canvas? And maybe a splinter of wood? I've never been this far west before, and I'd like to add it to my maps if it's alright?"

There was a long pause that brought their attention to Ventus. "Sure, idiot. Just don't poke any holes with your stupid charting. We'll be back in the water soon, once I get tired." He glared at the floorboards with the knuckle of his toes skating along the hull's upward curve.

Bipp stared at Ventus for a second. Curious, he aimed the tip of the dagger against a board. "You sure?"

Ventus growled. "I said it's fine. . . . I was just thinking about something else." His voice was different, much less sarcastic than usual.

Bipp looked at Hugo, then shrugged. "O-Okay." With some hesitation, Bipp poked his dagger into a board and pried off a sizable splinter. Then he ripped off a tiny piece of canvas. With every movement, Ventus winced.

"Could you catch this on fire? Only a little though." Bipp

held the splinter to Hugo.

Hugo nodded, happy to get more practice, then blew fire like a whisper onto the stick. It caught flame, then, after a moment, Bipp snuffed it out. He didn't hesitate to begin mapping with the soot-stained pencil.

Hugo glanced between Bipp and the stars he tried to map. "Hey, why don't I tell you what I learned during college? I don't know everything, but if space interests you, I'd be happy to share what I know. And who knows, maybe we can find Earth together." He looked to the stars with a relaxed sigh, and a flood of his old stargazing memories filled his mind.

Bipp paused his drawing, then rested his hands over his lap. "I would love that. But before we begin to discuss the academic side of astronomy . . . I would really like to know why you find such an interest in it—I mean, besides finding Sam."

Instantly after Bipp said that, Ventus glanced at him with a curious look in his eyes. Bipp ignored him and smiled at Hugo. "I'm sorry if it's personal. It's just . . . ever since I met you, you've had an interest in the stars far greater than myself with even cartography."

Hugo scooted closer until his head was right next to Bipp. With a slow inhale of the cool, thin air, he looked back to the stars. "Well, it's a little hard to explain. . . . But ever since I was a kid, I've been addicted to watching the night sky. I don't know why, but when I look up, I calm down. Because even in the darkest, most life-barren place in the universe, there is still light no matter where you look. . . . Before I met Sam, I used to stare at the stars endlessly. I even filled my room with them," he chuckled. "They helped. The stars always showed me that no matter where I was, I was with lights who I could call friends, my mom, my dad, and eventually, Sam."

Hugo smiled without knowing. "He was—is the brightest light. I don't know why, but when I'm with Sam, even the darkest nights feel like day." Stinging tears and warm snot dripped from his face. *Sam....* He paused, about to fall apart. "I know, I'm weird for having these reasons for liking space. But even now, I can look at the stars and see his eyes, those shy, bright green eyes."

Hugo paused for what seemed like the entire night to Bipp's speedy heart. "And sometimes . . . when I'm with him, I don't need to look up the stars; I just need to look at him, and I feel it." In instinct, Hugo's giant hand covered his chest, as if he was searching for something.

"It?" Bipp's ears tilted before he watched Hugo droop.

"You're obsessed," Ventus snorted, then Bipp growled under his lips. "What? It's obvious he's obsessed. That bird is all he talks about! I don't know why anyone would want to be around someone so rude! Sam literally said he wanted to eat me! . . . Look, I get that he's your brother and all, but you're a complete idiot to want to be around someone who–" he pointed his wing to Hugo's face, particularly to the three scars from his horn to his cheek, "I'm assuming, cut out your eye, is too small to be of any use, and–"

"Shut up, you stupid pecker!" Bipp snapped and stood quickly with a beak-silencing glare. Even though Ventus and Bipp were similar in stature, Bipp suddenly appeared to be much taller and much more powerful. "You're just jealous because he loves someone! While you never loved anyone, nor has anyone loved you–" Bipp stopped instantly. Then, he growled again and looked away with the tight bend of his fingers nipping into his palm.

Those words froze Ventus. But after a few seconds, his eyelids drooped, and he turned his beak slowly away. "You don't know anything . . . idiot."

Bipp sighed and bowed his head to Ventus. "I'm sorry. I don't know where that came from . . . But you shouldn't say those things about Sam. I know you don't like him. But Hugo cares a lot about him. So please consider–" Bipp froze . . . and his hands met his throat.

He choked as his chest shrank until they could see his ribs under the cloak. Before Hugo could react, Bipp's knees thunked against the floorboards. Ventus' beak lowered with a sigh, and his eyes watered over like shiny pearls. But he had no interest in Bipp. Whatever sank his mind pulled his eyes to the clouds below, as if the infinite fall allured him. And just at that moment, the boat fell from Hugo's claws.

Before Hugo could look down, he fell from the clouds.

Bipp wheezed and choked with the feeble attempt to fill his lungs. He reached out to Ventus, who no longer seemed to care if Bipp perished.

Hugo shook his head to rid the fear of falling that sank his stomach, then angled his body to fly in front of Ventus. "Hey, stop," Hugo commanded and grabbed Ventus, but Ventus kept the air from Bipp's needy throat without any give.

Just as the veins in Bipp's eyes reddened, the boat splashed in the water, and Ventus cushioned their fall cozily into it with a quick gust of air. Hugo grabbed Ventus once more and slammed him against the floor with a mighty thump that nearly tipped the boat. Hugo veered back to Bipp, who coughed and gasped in the precious air with several gulps.

Ventus wheezed after that strike. "Idiot, I wasn't going to kill him. And besides," Ventus' red, watery eyes narrowed in a way that slithered worry into Hugo's head, "you couldn't stop me, even with all the fire in your chest."

Bipp took a second to fill his lungs and stop the dizziness. "That's it." He marched with steps that rocked the boat, then stood over Ventus with his large foot pressed against his chest. "You and I need to talk," he growled, then looked at Hugo. "I'm sorry, but could you cover your ears if you don't mind? This is going to be a conversation not meant for you . . . yet."

Hugo nodded, then turned toward the other end of the boat. At first, he looked at the bright moon, shining across the stretching clouds as they reached for the distant stars behind him. Then he saw a faint halo made from the ice crystals in the air, high enough to catch the moon's shining light in a magnificent ring. It looked like an eye with the moon as the pupil, but he'd seen those winter halos back on Earth many times while looking at the sky. So he stared at the water for something new to him, where the starlight bounced off every smooth ripple. It was hard to ignore what they were discussing with his large ears, but he tried and listened to the gentle waves burbling and occasionally thumping against the hull.

After a few moments, something far below the surface caught his attention. There were some fish. They didn't look much different from Earth's fish, but their scales were shiny and colorful enough to distract Hugo from the ocean's dark bottom. And to his comfort, his stomach was too full from Bipp's soup to be hungry for them. He smiled and relaxed his neck over his hands, simply watching the fish come to the steady boat and peck at it with a mindless curiosity. *I don't think I'm obsessed. Besides, if Sam ever thought I was too much, he could've just told me to go away. . . . Like . . . when he left me on this planet. . . .* He reached down and placed a claw in the icy water, careful not to disturb the fish. *Sam . . . was I too much? . .*

*. Are you happier without me?*

Bipp grabbed Ventus' beak with a grip that could crack steel. "I don't care what you do to me. But please try to be nice in front of him. He's not from this planet, and things may be scary already. I know for certain he misses his family. . . . I just . . . want him to like it here. . . ." His eyes welled. "And I don't want him to leave," Bipp whispered with his head low.

Ventus rolled his eyes at Bipp's hand.

Bipp let go, but didn't apologize.

"Idiot, that's your problem? If you want him to like this planet, do something or show him something he likes. I mean, a good start would be to stop being a coward and ask him to be your soul–"

Bipp clacked Ventus' beak shut once more. Ventus growled, about to rocket Bipp into space. After staring at each other with eyes that would frighten even death, Bipp let go once more.

"Why are you so shy about asking him?"

Bipp looked at Hugo. "Because I don't know how he feels about this planet or me. What if he doesn't like me and hates this planet so much that he would never agree to such a thing? What if he hates my cabin, and my soup? I'm much more comfortable with both of us living in ignorance."

Ventus gently slapped Bipp between the ears with his wing. "Stop being afraid of others rejecting you. Just be yourself, even if that means being stupid." Bipp gave a curious look at Ventus, who then sighed. "But if you are serious about those questions, I would at least look at him." Ventus turned Bipp's head to face Hugo, who stared at the spectacular aquatic life. His hand was ghost-quiet as he played with the water's surface. "You may be surprised by how he sees this planet. Idiot." Ventus paused.

"Just watch this." He excused himself from Bipp and walked to Hugo's head.

After a few seconds, a soft breeze goosebumped Hugo's neck, and he turned to Ventus.

"Hey. . . ." He shyly looked to the side and held his opposite wing. "I'm sorry for insulting Sam." He squinted at the water beside the boat.

"It's fine; I know Sam was rude to you when you first met. You don't have to like him. But are you and Bipp alright?"

Ventus glanced back at Bipp, who was obviously listening to their conversation with his ears high. "Yeah. . . . We're well." He paused for a moment and sat beside Hugo's snout. "I have a question for you. . . . Hypothetically speaking, if you were trapped on this planet forever, how would you feel?"

Hugo paused for a second. *Why would he ask such a thing?* He then looked at the stars with a sigh, continuing his search for Sam. "I don't know," he started with a low and soft tone, a sad one to Bipp's ears. "Hypothetically . . . I would miss my family more than my heart could handle. I would miss the simpleness of life and the tiny aspects of Earth that made it great. . . . I don't know, maybe I would miss being human as well."

Hugo looked at Ventus and Bipp, who both stared at him without distraction. "Even with all the great things this planet has to offer, I don't think I could enjoy it the way it deserves. But don't get me wrong, it's a beautiful place."

Hugo sighed again and looked at his cupped hand, slowly pouring water back into the sea.

"I-I just don't know if my mind is ready for *that* kind of news. . . . I'm holding onto a thread that I will see my family again, especially Sam . . . . I just want to know if he's okay." He then shyly looked at Bipp. "Though, I'm so fortunate to have my brother beside me. I couldn't do this *new planet thing* without you."

"There you go, cloudtail, you just needed to ask," Ventus murmured under his breath and turned away from Hugo. "Thank you for your thoughts, Hugo. Now, nobody bother me! I'm going to try and sleep through this pointless voyage. . . . I set us in the ocean's main central current, so no more wind from me." He sat at the furthest spot from Hugo and Bipp, then folded his feet over his thighs.

"Thank you, Ventus," Bipp murmured before Ventus flapped his wing at him, as if to say, 'forget it.'

Bipp cautiously sat next to Hugo with the nervous fiddle of his cloak. "Sorry for the interruption, Hugo. Please, tell me more about space." He picked up the splinter pencil from the floor, then resumed writing and drawing.

"Oh, yeah . . . certainly." Hugo nodded before they began a lengthy discussion from the simple idea of what space is, to astrophysics, and eventually, rocketry.

Bipp's eyes began to bulge wider and wider with every word Hugo spoke. "C-Can I see your planet from here?"

Hugo looked up, still unable to see anything that looked like the star patterns around Earth: The Big Dipper, Orion, anything. *This sky is so dense with stars and nebulae, I'm surprised I can see the moon in all that.* "I'd like to be hopeful and bet one of those stars is Earth's. But your space is unlike anything I've ever seen; even fantasy movies haven't touched this density."

"Yeah. . . ." Bipp scratched his head, for he had no idea what a *movie* was. "Well, is there a way we can find it? How about moving Somnium? Or building one of those rocket ships or telescopes?" Bipp asked with wonder pouring from every word.

Hugo smiled with a steamy exhale against the cooling night air. "That's a little complicated. It might require a little more time than we have to build a functional rocket ship, though I have been thinking of a spaceship that doesn't *really require* a rocket...." He breathed out a whisper of fire for practice. "And I know nothing about building a telescope, especially with these hands." Hugo raised his left hand, bringing notice to the sheer size and awkwardness of it. "As far as moving the planet . . . I don't think that's possible."

"Sure it is!" Bipp laughed. "Anzu can control the ground, Ella can control the water. . . . We can ask them to move the planet! I mean, it'll be difficult, but it can't hurt to ask if it's possible. We just need a map, and I think I can handle that part after we learn the direction. Then, we can see your family!" Bipp's excitement for his idea wiggled his toes. He grasped the suddenly creaking seat below him, trying to contain his anticipation.

"It's your family too," Hugo chuckled.

Bipp stood with an impressive posture and pointed to the sky. "This is my promise to you. I will find a way to bring Earth and Somnium together! This way, I can meet Mary and Andrew, and they can meet everyone on Somnium! Everyone will have a great time if your kin are as kind as you! And of course, you can see Sam again."

Bipp spent the next several minutes talking about his idea to bring the two planets together. Hugo chuckled from time to time at Bipp's excitement. Even Ventus peeked open his eye at some ridiculous things Bipp said.

"You also need to move the sun for warmth, idiot. And nobody on Somnium can control fire." Ventus' whisper twitched Bipp's ears.

Bipp looked at Hugo with a significant smile. "Then we find Hugo's soul ability, which will be something amazing. We will see if fire can be conquered. He's a dragon! His soul must be related to fire, right?"

Ventus snorted mockingly, then looked away. He tried to combat the sharp nip of dark ocean air by folding his wings around himself.

Bipp sat and looked at Hugo, whose eye was stuck on the stars. Bipp's eyes drooped with his nose, and he grabbed a quilt from the pile of things he had brought and wrapped it around him. "I'm getting tired. Thank you for indulging me, Hugo. Have a good night," Bipp said before a twinkle in Hugo's eye caught his sight. Not thinking much of it, he lay against the floorboards and closed his eyes.

In secret, Ventus grabbed the fluffy tip of Hugo's tail and laid it over him for an excellent source of warmth. As Hugo looked at him, Ventus looked the other way, telling Hugo to ignore him.

*I don't know.* Hugo looked at the stars once more and rested his neck on the boat's edge. *Sam . . . why can't I stop thinking about you?* He felt an emptiness within his hands. He hugged himself, but it didn't feel like he hoped it would. *What is this feeling?*

After a few minutes, Bipp felt a gentle tap on his shoulder. He peeked open his left eye to Hugo, who stared at him with tears flooding onto his cheek and tapping the floor. "Hugo?" Bipp whispered.

"M-May I . . . hold you?"

Bipp instantly became alert with the sharp rise of his ears. "Y-Yeah? You may–"

Hugo hugged him tight, but cozy enough to go back to

sleep. For a second, Bipp was confused. But as Hugo held him, he considered what Hugo must be going through. Being on a new planet, away from family and forced to start a new life, was something anyone would be scared of. "You're okay. . . . Just . . . put your head on my chest and breathe with me." Hugo glanced at Bipp's deep jade eyes over a nervous smile, then lowered his head onto his chest. And as Hugo's silent tears soaked into Bipp's soft fur, he just hugged Hugo's large head in return, hoping to bring him some comfort on this curious world.

## Chapter 3
## NEW DAWN

"What can I do?" Ventus' overly proper and dramatic voice twitched Hugo's tired ears out from Bipp's shadow and into the warm sunlight. "I refuse to go back there," Ventus growled and held his head within his wings. "Come on, stupid brain, think!"

Hugo peeked open his blurry eye and squinted at Ventus, looking out to sea while standing with one foot in the boat and one wrapped around the bow's curved tip. He raised his right wing and seemed to nudge a few clouds from the boat's path. "Maybe." He swiped his wing to the next thought, shoving another cloud to the side with it. "Wait . . . I stole the air from Bipp's lungs. Maybe I could– . . ." He sighed, then glared at some cute, puffy clouds. "I don't know much about lightning or the ground lightning that I've rarely seen him use. But if I created a vacuum like space is rumored to be, I would win, right?" He paused in deep thought for a second. "Maybe Hugo would know; he seemed somewhat knowledgeable with those things."

Hugo sluggishly stood from Bipp's hug, then walked to Ventus' side. But to his surprise, his body felt much lighter and springier. He was still sore in his chest and back, but the feeling was barely there, like a memory echoing over his body. He blinked as he looked back at himself. *How am I . . .* He then shook his head to get on to present matters. "What about me?" Hugo asked with a sudden deep yawn.

"Ah!" Ventus flinched with a quick glare at Hugo's gaping mouth. "Nothing, idiot. You and Bipp are so intrusive of my business that I wish those wings you call ears would fly away." He slapped Hugo across the ears before he stopped and looked down at his harem pants; the stitching and fabric were so dense that nothing could pierce it. "But at least you're not as bad as a *few* birds on Zenith. Living there only has the benefits of beauty. If you consider its creatures . . . it's hardly worth an apple seed," he said with a slight smirk, then he looked out to sea and pointed his wing. "But whatever, our little chore is almost halfway over anyway."

Hugo squinted ahead, below the freshly-bloomed sun and strawberry clouds that sweetened the air. A large span of land cut the difference between sea and sky. But as Hugo blinked the morning blur from his sight, his jaw began to fall.

"Looks like Bipp needs to update his maps. . . . Even I didn't know there was a mountain there." Ventus glanced back at Bipp, whose eyes were closed.

There was indeed a profoundly curious mountain, one that crowned the entire horizon. It had two white peaks that speared the sky and cupped the morning sun. And in its broad base sat a forest so dense, so colorful with the shades of autumn, that the entire mountain acted as a jeweled, golden crown: one to sit above the planet's head with the leaves like rustling fire in the sunlight.

"W-Wouldn't you have seen this from Zenith?" Hugo murmured with his mouth and eye gaped. He had never seen a mountain up close before, especially one so beautiful.

Ventus snorted. "I've only been off Zenith three times: One, I was learning how to fly for the first time." He sighed and looked at the clouds once more. "Two, I was captured by the queen. And three is this stupid trip." Ventus' voice croaked as he gave that list.

Hugo tilted his head.

Ventus glanced back at Hugo, then swiftly turned away once their eyes met. Ventus' eyes, in particular, were turning red. "Whatever." He brushed his wings along his sides to even his feathers. "I don't plan to spend more than an hour or two here. Apotheosis sacrificed many, and he scared the rest so much that they fled. So it should be deserted. . . . I'll just fly around, then come back to the boat after glancing over the area." Ventus looked at Bipp, still asleep with the quilt hung messily from his waist. "You can let him sleep in that awkward position. I won't be long." He sighed and squinted at the floorboards. "If I may . . . whatever you two do, don't get off this boat." He looked Hugo dead in the eye. "I mean it."

Ventus' concentration alone made Hugo shrink back. He didn't dare ask why, for rarely was Ventus so serious in tone. But Hugo squinted curiously, seeing a few drops well in Ventus' eyes. And without another word, Ventus spread his wings and took off like a rocket toward the island. Wind blasted past Hugo and nearly lifted him from the floorboards with Ventus' departure. *He's pretty good at that . . . maybe he'd be willing to help me get off this planet?*

Hugo looked once more at the mountain's twin peaks, then glanced back at the endless ocean. His chest felt hollow yet heavy enough to sink the boat. He sighed, then turned to Bipp. "Hey." He nudged Bipp's arm with his snout.

"It's fine; I'm awake." Bipp wiggled his large toes to signal he was attentive, but he was too sleepy to open his eyes to such a warm morning sun. "Ventus has been talking to himself for the past hour," he sighed and sat up. Half the fur on his face was messy from lying against the hard, misty planks. "I like that you try with him; it keeps him from getting too comfortable in his ways," he yawned, creaked open his eyes, and began to fold the blanket he used.

"Do you know why he's acting like that?" Hugo asked. "He seems . . . weirder than when we first met him . . . and a tad more rude."

Bipp sighed and looked at the blanket on his lap. "I don't know much. But what I do know is very personal to him, so I have no right to talk about it." He set the blanket to the side and leaned over the side of the boat. "Anzu knows much more about him than I do. He told me little, but there was a reason he told Ventus to bring the boat and not just fly here." He sighed, cupped the salty water in his hands, and splashed his face to even up his fur. "Without being insensitive, all I can say is Ventus is in some form of the word . . . drowning. He has a lot going on and–" Bipp's fingertips nipped his palms as he sat back in the boat. "I'm such an idiot. I shouldn't have said those things." He paused for a minute with the firm shift of his cloak and pants from their uneven position. "I guess what I'm trying to say is . . . be patient with him." He looked at himself with the flick of a frown, then he chuckled. "Honestly, just be yourself. You're better at befriending creatures than I ever was."

Hugo lowered his head and looked at the land growing closer by the second. The water beside the boat slowly turned mint green as the shallow beachside sand rose from the deep. "No, I just got lucky with you."

"Ah–" Bipp opened his mouth to reply, but when those words reached him, his eyes widened, and his cheeks ripened. "I–" He looked down; his toes subconsciously spiraled around a gap between floorboards. "That's not true. Literally everyone you met, except those you ate, became your friend. That's not luck. That's just you being you."

*Me . . . being me?*

Bipp watched Hugo's thoughtful eye move away. "I'm sorry. Forget I said anything." He twiddled his thumbs and looked at the many shells decorating the shore. "I-I was wondering, if you don't mind me asking, why were you sad last night? Is it because you're homesi–" Bipp stopped with the slap shut of his mouth upon looking back at Hugo, who stared right at him.

"It's that obvious, huh? . . ." Hugo sighed. "I am homesick, but that's not the reason. I guess you could say, I'm confused. It's about Sam, but–" Hugo looked down. *I don't know what's going on with me.*

"Hey, it's okay; forget I asked." Bipp gulped before the bottom of the boat began to scratch against the sandy bottom of the land. "Are you still sore?"

Hugo shrugged. "A little, but I think I can walk by myself."

"Good! That was fast." Bipp looked at the land, then hopped from the boat with a mighty splash. "Maybe you have a soul ability of healing?" Bipp joked.

Hugo snorted.

"You can stay there; I think I can handle this." Bipp waded through the waist-high water. He came on the stern and pushed, nearly stumbling Hugo from his stance. "Sorry. Shoulda given you a warning," Bipp said with a sigh, then looked at himself.

Hugo stared at the water. His jaw dropped at how the boat

pressed through the sand at such a fast rate. And within seconds, they struck the land. But Bipp continued to push; he grunted until most of the boat was on the shore. "How strong is he?" Hugo murmured in thought.

Bipp looked up at him with a smile. "Rabbits have strong legs. Not to brag, but you should see me run and especially jump," Bipp said before Hugo looked down, not knowing he spoke aloud. Bipp walked beside the boat and clapped his hands rid of salty sand with a smile. "I think that should be good. You up for a little exploration?" He grabbed Hugo's scarf and his charting materials from the boat.

Hugo looked at the skyscraper trees of the beachside, just like the scene he first saw when he came to this planet, only more colossal and more . . . creaky. Most leaves were shades of gold and ruby, but all shone twinkles of sunrise from fresh dew. A shivering wind spurred the forest and excited Hugo's fur; it occasionally blew massive leaves onto the beach with a gentle, dry crack. If he listened without breathing, he could hear a subtle trickle of water flow from the mountain. "What about what Ventus said?"

Bipp snorted and waved his hand to extinguish that question. "Don't worry; we'll be back before Ventus notices. And if he does, I'll take his complaints. Besides, there's nothing dangerous on this continent, and every creature is known to have left." Bipp held out his free hand to help Hugo from the boat.

Hugo hesitated, but he accepted Bipp's hand. "Thank you."

Bipp helped him out, and Hugo took a moment to feel the stiff, uncharted sand and the forest's . . . much cooler air. It all mixed in a salty, mossy scent that whispered into Hugo's snout.

"I'm glad I managed to get some writing material. I strangely didn't think about cartography when starting this trip. I only thought of–" Bipp shook his head and tucked the canvas and burnt splinter into his belt. "Uh, here's your scarf." He displayed it before Hugo, who eyed the scarf curiously. It was thick, and it glittered sunlight through every knitted hole.

"Thank you." Hugo bowed, allowing Bipp to put it on him, and once he did, Hugo heaved and huffed with the immediate sinking of his throat.

"Oh, sorry! . . . It's a little heavy with the oven-mitt material. I can make you another if it's too much," Bipp said with a worried glint in his eyes and his hands ready to help Hugo.

"No. I-It's perfect. Just surprising is all." Hugo took a moment to recover and get used to the aching weight.

Bipp retreated his hands into his cloak and looked at the sand with his ears drooping behind him. "If you say so. . . . Come on, we'd better get going if we want to see enough to tell stories of what happened to this place." He sighed quietly, then walked forward with Hugo close behind.

The forest they came upon had a reason for such cold air. The colossal leaves were bigger than the boat they sailed and blocked all sunlight that dared approach. The trees were slimy to the touch, and within the finite ripples and patternwork of bark, weaved the sparkle of salt. Hugo, of course, couldn't help but touch it and lick the tip of his claw to verify. *Do these trees absorb the water . . . and the salt?* He looked up, seeing the gentle twinkle of salt within the leaves as they rustled in the whispering wind.

As they walked deeper with the steep incline and rocky terrain along with the tree roots acting as individual mountains, Hugo's breathing and heart rate sped up. He paused and tried to take back his breath, but he found that he couldn't relax. The light fled further behind with every crunchy step upon dry leaves. And once he took that last step, and the final flicker of light vanished behind a tree, Hugo stopped dead.

"Hey, is something wrong?" Bipp asked.

Hugo gulped. His heart thumped at such a ferocious pace, he could barely gather the air needed to fuel it. He heaved and huffed with such force that anyone could hear it from a mile away. "No, everything's–" Hugo's pupil shrank once he stared ahead to the forest's deeper and darker incline. His mind went dizzy and numb until darkness was all he could see. In a snap, he yelled at the top of his lungs. His chest swelled with the buildup of fire, about to set the forest ablaze.

"Hey! What's wrong? What are you doing?" Bipp exclaimed.

Hugo unhinged his jaw and roared—Bipp slapped his mouth shut with an upward thrust. He then grabbed Hugo's snout and yanked it down, hugging his face to prevent his mouth from opening. Hugo smelt the scent of Bipp's stomach, and their ears met, instinctively twitching against each other.

"What's wrong, Hugo?" Bipp asked before tears began to well across Hugo's eye. He struggled to part his trembling lips even when Bipp loosened his grip.

"Can you . . . do *the thing*?" Hugo's chest sank. He didn't want Bipp to know about his fear, remembering how embarrassed he was when he told Sam this truth.

Curious what that meant, Bipp looked at Hugo's closed eye. "The . . . thing?"

"I feel your heartbeat against my head," Hugo began.

"Wait, what are you doing?"

"I feel the cold soil and sharp, fragile leaves beneath my feet and hands."

Bipp's ears stretched up as he heard Hugo's slowing heart

thumps.

"I smell you. . . . You smell wonderful, like well-cooked vegetables and herbs mixed with the salt from the sea. And I hear your breath fade with the cold wind."

Bipp's eyes were wide at Hugo, and his jaw bobbed with the effort to speak.

Hugo sucked in through his snout and made sure his eye kept closed. "Alright. Okay . . . thank you, Bipp." Hugo's chest grew and shrank with the calm breaths he now gave.

"Umm, Hugo . . . what was that?" Bipp whispered, dumbfounded by what happened.

Hugo sighed and pressed his head harder against Bipp's chest. "Can we . . . can we go back to the boat? Please," Hugo asked, his cheeks turning redder than his ruby scales had to offer.

"Sure?" Bipp said, then let go of Hugo.

Hugo grabbed his hand before he could finish a step. "Umm. Can you help me out of the woods? I don't want to open my eye," Hugo murmured with his head lowered in defeat.

Bipp rejected Hugo's handholding with a firm yank. "What's going on with you?" Bipp yelled. "You're scaring me!"

Hugo heard Bipp's feet crunch the leaves as he stepped away.

"Please, Hugo, just tell me what's wrong!"

Even though Hugo couldn't see it, he knew Bipp was crying by the way his words quavered up his throat. Hugo's ear flicked as the loud plops and taps of his own snot splatted onto the crunchy leaves; he was a mess, and he knew it. He was scaring Bipp because of his stupid fear. So, he opened his mouth at the gamble of losing his only family on this planet. "I'm afraid of the dark!" Hugo shouted. Even though it embarrassed him, Bipp needed to know.

"What?" Bipp whispered with his eyelids spread far apart.

"I'm sorry! I can't. I don't know what's wrong with me! I just can't handle the dark. Please, Bipp, help me out of here, and I'll tell you everything." At this point, Hugo's legs were floppy noodles, and his head bowed so low the scent of old leaves and icy stone invaded his snout. "Please don't leave me here," Hugo squeaked, not hearing a single sound from Bipp.

Then, after a few seconds, he felt the gentle touch of Bipp's hand against his cheek. His thumb wiped away some of the tears. "Okay," Bipp whispered. "Take my hand, and I'll lead you out."

Those words lifted Hugo's heart more than Bipp could ever fathom. Hugo raised his trembling hand and held Bipp's hand that was over his cheek.

Bipp calmly pulled Hugo toward the ocean. Neither of them spoke, making Hugo nervous about what Bipp thought of his childish fear. It wasn't long until the cold soil turned into warm sand. "Alright, we're here," Bipp sighed with his nose pointed to his feet.

Hugo peeked open his eye and saw the bright light of the sunny beachside. And once he heard waves ebb and sizzle against the sand, he collapsed.

Bipp sat beside him and sniffled with a longing stare out to sea. "I want to do well as a friend. . . . I-I want you to feel comfortable enough to tell me anything." He breathed for a moment to calm down, but began to weep. "I know we each have our secrets. And they're secrets for a reason. . . . But please, Hugo, tell me. What am I missing? Why can't you tell me how you feel? Why didn't you tell me you're afraid of the dark? I would have never pressured you to go in there if–" Those words struggled to escape his squeaking throat. He grabbed his ears and covered his eyes with them. "Please, Hugo, tell me what I'm doing wrong. I'm trying my best to make you happy! But it's just hard to know what you're thinking sometimes!" He collapsed on his stomach, and his eyes drooped in a way Hugo had never seen.

Hugo quickly brought his head next to Bipp. "No. . . . No, none of this is you. You're great at being my brother." Hugo scooted closer to him until they were shoulder to shoulder with their backs to the sky and eyes to the sea. "I'm the one who has issues telling people how I feel." In shame, he grasped his snout with both hands. "I haven't even told Sam I love him."

Bipp froze with his eyes wide at him. "Hugo. . . ."

"I know . . . I'm an idiot. It's just so hard to get those difficult words off my dumb tongue," he said, drooping his forked tongue out. "Don't get me wrong; I wish I could tell him. But it's–"

"Curious," Bipp sighed, his chin meeting the sand and eyes looking away from Hugo.

"Yeah."

Bipp took a moment, then rubbed his chest with a subtle frown. "Not to seem nosey, but could you be more specific on why you didn't tell me about your fear? . . . Is it . . . something I did?" He tugged his cloak tight over his chest.

It clicked. Hugo promptly looked at Bipp, whose eyes barely glanced at him. "No! Not at all! I'm just horrible at it! . . . A-Am I hurting you?"

Bipp's ears fwipped up, and he looked at Hugo, who looked dead at him with his head lowered to his level. "Oh, no, no, no! Forgive me; I was only being nosey! Heh." Bipp smiled with his hand over the back of his neck.

Hugo looked down, and his chest sloshed like a stinging bucket of heavy poison. *I really am stupid. . . . I can see why Sam left me. . . .* He grimaced and hid his face beneath his hands. "I need help," he said accidentally aloud.

With tears welling in his eyes, Bipp looked at the sand.

After a few moments, Hugo peeked past his fingers to the boat. But something peculiar caught his sight. A midnight and snow-white figure of immense length stood adjacent to the boat. Hugo squinted with his lone eye, struggling to make out much detail. It moved closer to the boat, then slithered into the hull; its lower half still stood in the sand. "Hey, there's someone there." Hugo pointed.

Bipp veered his head and pointed his ears. "What the?" He stood. "Who–" He took a hesitant step forward. "Nobody but Ventus should be here, and–" His eyes bulged from their sockets, and his ears pierced the clouds. "Impossible. . . . H-Hey!" Bipp shouted, and in a flash, he sprinted across the beach.

Hugo tried to catch up, but Bipp was far too fast for that dream. Before Hugo reached halfway across the sand, Bipp reached the boat and jumped in. It startled whoever was inside as the boat shook into noisy creaks and thumps.

"Hugo!" Bipp yelled before the midnight figure leapt from the boat, spun around, and vanished behind a sudden wall of white fire. Bipp jumped from the boat with his hands stretched far above his head. "It's okay; we don't wish to hurt you! Here!" Bipp removed both daggers from his belt and tossed them into the sand, having learned from his first experience with Hugo. "Come out, please. My name is Bipp Atlas, and this is–" Bipp looked behind him, expecting Hugo to be there. But right as he turned, Hugo walked past him and through the wall of fire.

Hugo froze upon the sight, and the dark dragon before him froze too. She was similar to Hugo, but slightly longer, bigger, and much shinier than Hugo ever was. Her ears, hands, snout, and feet were particularly larger, but they only seasoned her appearance with compliments. Each of her scales was the definition of a shimmering midnight, and her white fur was pure enough to combat any cloud. She was naked by Somnium standards, but being an ancient dragon and being alone on a continent were reasons enough not to understand such modern cultures.

They gawked at each other's eyes. Hers were just like freshly-bloomed azalea flowers. The calming ocean waves and crackling white fire were interrupted by Bipp's sand-sloshing footsteps as he ran around the fire behind Hugo. After Bipp turned the corner, he covered his mouth and stared at the two.

"Uh, hello," Hugo said kindly, giving a slight bow to attempt a formal introduction. "My name's Hugo; what's yours?"

But no response came. Hugo looked up from his bow and saw her pointing to the sky, the eastern night sky to be precise, with the moon fleeing the late-morning sunlight. She lowered her claw and formed four letters with her digits. The first was L, but the rest was foreign to Hugo and Bipp.

She tilted her head at their confusion, then pointed to her throat and pretended to slice it with her claws, bringing their attention to a faint trio of scars across her long neck. Then they got it. The dragon then pointed to the boat, patted her stomach, and opened her mouth.

"You want my soup?" Bipp asked.

She nodded mightily.

Bipp ran to the boat, grabbed the pot and bowls, and returned to her without delay. "Here, sorry if I scared you back there. I was just excited to see another dragon; I thought Hugo was the last one." He poured the soup into the biggest bowl and placed it before her. "It should be kinda warm; it's been sitting in the sun for a while. Tell me if it's too cold, and Hugo or I can warm it up for you."

She put her hand at the base of her lips, then tilted her fingers forward with a bow. She then ate the soup faster than Hugo ever did. And Hugo was indeed impressive when it came to eating.

She promptly eyed the pot with her pink, forked tongue cleaning her lips. "I-I don't know if I brought enough food for *two* dragons." Bipp then paused at her, seeing that her head was bigger than half his body. He looked back at Hugo with a nervous gulp.

"She can have my share. You filled me quite a bit before we went on this trip, so I'm still good."

Bipp chuckled through his nose. "Alright." He placed the entire pot before her. "Eat as much as you like. I'll take Ventus' complaints if he cares." The dragon smiled, leaned her head forward, and opened her mouth wide. Before they knew it, she bit the pot's steel rim and raised her head back to allow gravity to do the work of filling her throat. Some splashed against her broadening cheeks. "Oh, I like her." Bipp squinted with a smile, then leaned back to Hugo. "She reminds me too much of you," he whispered in a chuckle.

She finished the pot in a blink and lowered it gently to the sand; not one drop remained after she licked her cheeks. "Welp, there's that." Bipp placed the bowls and pot to the side. "By any chance, are there more dragons living here, or any other creatures for that matter?"

She froze for a moment while looking at the mountain's

dark forest. With a quick blink, she looked at Hugo and stood beside him with a shake of her head. Her claw poked his shoulder; then, she pointed to herself. After a few body and hand gestures later, Hugo and Bipp both understood that she and Hugo were the last dragons.

Bipp, however, gave a slight, nervous smile upon this news. "Heh."

# Chapter 4
# AWAKENED

Asleep, a moan of sheer bliss escaped Sam's beak. His feathers rubbed the silky sheets the sun gifted with heat. He pressed his head deeper into the plush pillow that surprisingly formed well around his hard beak. And for the first time in what seemed like forever, he smiled.

He found himself scooting farther down until the blankets weighed over his cheek like a gentle hand, and these blankets were heavy. It was as if they hugged him and told him he was okay in this unknown place. It all seemed like home as those blankets sank him deeper into the accepting mattress. He inhaled the fresh oak scent of the room before slowly opening the eye that wasn't buried in the pillow.

Before him was the room's lone window, and what a sight it was. The midday sun gifted Sam's eye with the multiple colors of autumn as the treetops rustled like ruby and honey gems calmly sparkling in the wind.

He hugged his pillow with all his strength. The hot sunlight felt so good against his feathers, almost as if– "Hugo . . ." he moaned, finally feeling the embrace of his dragon brother. He buried his face in the pillow before his eyes snapped open.

"Hugo!" he yelled and sat up with a glance of the room. His heart thumped with joy at the blurry sight of Hugo, who lay on the floor. But then, he blinked to a crimson desk in the corner and his small birchwood cane resting against the bed's base.

"Oh." Embarrassed, his shoulders and beak sank toward the floor. *Stupid dream, tricking me- . . . wait. . . . Did I just have a good dream?* Looking at his tingling wings, he felt pressure around his back, like Hugo's hands were still there. *Impossible. . . .* He wrapped his wings over his chest and back, trying to recreate his dream and prolong the feeling. "I miss you . . . so much." Part of him wanted to go back to sleep, hoping to see Hugo again, but another part couldn't help but notice how lively he felt.

He took a moment to come back into reality, reluctantly shaking his head to forget the near-hypnotizing pull of sleep. Then, he sighed. *I'm going to be thinking about you all day, aren't I?* He felt his chest sink when he looked at his body. Before he knew it, he had nearly drooped back against the bed. *No . . . I killed you . . . I don't deserve such thoughts. . . .* His back curled like a poison shriveled him. *I wonder if Mom or Dad are wondering where I am?*

*They're happy you're gone.*

Sam flinched, then tucked his wings tighter over his chest. "N-Not you. . . . Please . . . go away." After carefully scanning the room and listening to the rustling forest outside, he lay back against the mattress. *Where even am I?*

He reluctantly shoved the heavy covers off him with a grunt, then looked at his body with a sigh. For the first moment since college began, he had time, not much to worry about, nothing chasing him, nothing wrong was happening apart from the voice creeping around. This feeling alone weirded Sam out with a shiver. He held his head with a squint. *Didn't George say something about my mother?*

After a few moments of adjusting to the room's cooler air with the help of sunlight, he sat up, then looked at his cane. "Oh no. . . . Do I have to–" He looked at his left leg, and he hoped it was all a dream. But after many grunts and nudges with his wing, it didn't move. He shivered, and his body felt heavier and weaker with every second. *I have to be strong.* With the heavy weight of reality sinking him, he scooped his leg within his wings and dangled it over the bed, parallel to his right.

With a deep inhale, he plucked up his cane with the firm scoop of his wings. "Alright. I can do this. It's just my first time walking with a cane and a limp leg; no big deal," he said sarcastically before scooting from the bed and landing on the wooden floor with a clumsy thump and tap. He wobbled horribly as he arched his back straight. "I'm fine, I'm fine. Just don't fall or break the cane," he told his pumping heart as he relied entirely on the cane. Every nervous tap forward sounded like a woodpecker curiously pecking at the floor.

He reached far up on the tips of his toes to the door handle, then leaned forward with a twist. He wobbled as he pushed the creaky door open while trying to keep balanced. The fresh air of the hall wisped within his hot feathers, and a scent of something delightfully filling curled into his nares. It pulled him forward without any hope of friction.

"What is this place?" Sam examined the oak lodge, catching sight of the various oddities or artifacts that hung and sat around. To Sam, it was a beautiful museum, which was no small feat with such plain cinnamon wooden floors and pine-logged walls. But one of the perks of being a 'dinosaur nerd' is the great attentiveness to such historical treasures. He tapped forward with his sharp eyes jotting many notes, until he met a set of steep, dark oak stairs. "Oh no . . . I don't–"

"Sam?" the familiar fruity voice of George said, followed by the repeated sound of thumping footsteps and creaking wood.

Sam watched as George made his way up, but it looked harsh for George. He had his cane, which helped, but it didn't do much for George's old legs. He was wobbling, and his face looked older than Sam remembered as he winced with every step.

"Here, let me help you with this," George said right before Sam stuck out his wing.

"Are you okay?" he asked bluntly, seeming to freeze George.

George looked away for a moment. "I'm quite well, but we can talk about my aged health after getting you situated." He smiled at Sam with the accepting raise of his open hand.

"No. No. I-I think I got it. . . . Thank you, though," Sam said with a gulp. *Who am I kidding; I can barely stand. But I don't want to trouble George—I mean, look at him, he's leaning on his cane more than I am! . . . Okay, just gotta make it down.*

Sam took a wobbly step, then another. Each step looked awkward and showed obvious discomfort. But as he achieved crossing the halfway point, Sam saw a slight smile flicker across George's cheek.

George turned around and carefully led Sam to the bottom, where even more artifacts lay.

One that snagged Sam's eye was a sword, sharp enough to cut an atom, hanging parallel to the central doorway. The blade was darker than night and had no handguard over the long handle, bound by a woven strap of fur so white that it glittered and bounced the light better than a snowy mountain. It looked like it was made to swing through anything, fast. Sam shivered as he stared, but he was also intrigued to keep looking with a squint. *Why would George want that thing so close to the front door? And–* Even with his sharp eyes, he struggled to make out the tiny holes along the blade. *Is it . . . hollow?* Sam's mind spun with more questions as they tapped into the kitchen, where George had been preparing breakfast.

He reached bare-handed into a stone fire-oven and pulled out a single-serving loaf, which steamed when it met the cool kitchen air.

Sam gawked. *How is his hand not on fire?*

"Alright." George set the loaf on a lone, two-seater oak table. He then grabbed a spoon and spread crystalized honey over the bread. The honey melted instantly.

But Sam couldn't keep his eyes from the chair on the right. It was a perfectly normal wooden chair, but it was a mountain to him. There were at least a few pillows on the chair to help him sit higher . . . once he climbed up there.

"A bowl of chopped spinach, plenty of blueberries, various nuts . . . and the seeded bread for dessert, along with a simple glass of water," he said, pointing sequentially at the items on the table. He turned to Sam. "Does this all look good? I tried to make things you liked."

"Y-You made all this, for me?" Sam asked, surprised. *No. Wait.* Then he raised his wing, promptly interrupting George. Like an angry wolf, Sam's stomach growled at him for pausing. He wanted to stuff his beak with all of it, but questions weighed heavy on his mind, forbidding him to eat for the first time in nearly three days. He sighed, now feeling his sharp ribs bulge his skin with every breath.

"What do you want with me?" Sam was nervous about asking that. He didn't like the idea of George knowing he was suspicious, but he needed to get it off his chest, especially before he put anything more from George in his mouth. To Sam's surprise, George smiled a little, then gestured his hand to the table for Sam to relax. But Sam didn't budge as he stared at the floor.

"I don't want anything *from* you at the moment. I wish only to help you become who you want to be." George sat down on the opposite chair to Sam's. "When I saw you at the college, and what I see now in your eyes, is hope. Hope to help out all those around you, especially your brother."

Sam squinted at himself. *But I killed him. Even if he was alive, there's no way he'd forgive me for leaving him. . . . I would love to help him, but–* Sam lowered his beak deeper into his chest feathers as he thought of Hugo's horrified, bloody face when he left him on that planet, *he may have loved me once, but now it's impossible. . . . I doubt he'd even want to see me.*

George leaned forward, trying to help Sam look at him. "But that hope is buried deep under anxiety and more."

Sam felt a rush of heat flush his cheeks before he looked further away from George. *How can he tell that much just by looking at my eyes?* He peeked up at George's eyes, trying to understand. But he instantly retreated his sight, feeling his shoulders rise over his neck in discomfort. *I guess I'll never learn that.*

"My goals just so happen to go well with yours, because I too want to help people. But you must be brave, for even I cannot complete such goals without you."

Sam shyly raised his wing to pause George. "Second question: How do you know about me? How did you know I would need this cane? How do you know I am the right person to help you?"

George smiled. "Whoa, hold on–"

"How did you know what foods I liked? . . . And are you okay? No offense, but you used to be . . . springier before you brought me here . . . is it something I did?"

George's eyelids snapped apart. "No, no, no." After waving his hands, George smirked with a thoughtful look at Sam. "The watchful eyes of a bird . . ." he murmured, then gave a sincere smile with a fragile clap before rubbing his hands together. "A little more than one question, but alright. I suppose it's only fair I tell you about me." Again, he gestured a hand to the chair for Sam to sit.

Sam took a breath and stared at the chair. He tapped to it, the seat about eye level. In short, he climbed it with many grunts and pulled himself up with much struggle. In the end, it was surprisingly comfortable, especially with the pillows and the hole in the back allowing his tail feathers to escape.

"Where to begin? . . ." George thought for a moment, then raised his finger at an idea.

"As you can probably tell by my name, Dr. George, I am a doctor, a medical one at that."

Sam nearly froze. And he could feel his back press harder against the chair until it creaked.

"I became a doctor to help, and due to my blessed length in years, I've had time to study, well, everything, from my focus on animal and human anatomy to the more . . . psychological. But in all my time studying how to help, I still cannot help everyone. I spent decades working at hospitals, trying to help everyone and learn how to cure the next illness, but I was never enough. . . . There was always someone who would slip from my grasp, no matter how tight I held." He took a moment with a slouch.

"But one day, your college appeared nearly two miles away. I still have no idea how it got there and why it was a perfect replica of the royal library on Zenith. But it was filled with information about souls and Somnium. I learned about my soul ability, the door thing. Then, I went to Somnium, hoping maybe the creatures there would have the answers to cure everything. . . . Surprisingly, they were all rather feral, but immensely curious. There wasn't a single building like the college, or any house for that matter. But I was curious to learn more. During my first years of visiting every once in a while, they taught themselves everything and experimented just after watching me for a few seconds. And they eventually learned to speak, read, and build. But even with their wits, their medical knowledge was severely limited due to the vast difference of creatures, and they relied on whoever had the lucky soul ability for it. So then I knew they couldn't help in the way I hoped."

George sighed and looked out a window. "Once they built Dawn, I fell in love with a fellow doctor at my hospital. . . . But shortly after, something I didn't expect found me on Somnium, something I hope you will overcome. . . . But at this point, I had collected a *few* souls, trying to search for the key of helping everyone without fail. That is why I may be a bit strange to you, how I can predict certain things and see into your mind."

George raised his open hand to calm Sam's obvious worry. "Don't fret though. I can only tell how you're feeling—nothing like mind reading. Your thoughts are your own. . . . Just think about it like extreme empathy. . . . And the predictions are a bit flimsy. I'd say seventy percent are accurate, and don't get me started when important choices must be made." George chuckled. "I used to be very keen on what would happen next back in my day. But now, the accuracy fades. I don't know *exactly* why, and I can't tell everything except a few branches of probability here and there. So pardon me if I tend to avoid that soul ability."

George sighed, then looked right at Sam, who instantly veered his eyes to the food. "To summarize the end of my story, I had given up on searching for the ability to help. Until I saw you, cradled in your birth mother's arms, in my hospital wing after she gave birth to you."

Sam's eyelids snapped apart, and he actually looked at George's face.

"After studying souls for a bit, you learn to see a person's soul from their eyes." George pointed to his silver eyes.

"Like the old expression you may have heard: 'Eyes are the windows to the soul'. . . . And as I saw you, I saw your soul. That is to say, one way to remove a soul is to remove their eyes, because, without the windows, one has no more access to the light outside. But this weakness is only true if you are a creature of Somnium. Pure humans have their . . . particular resistances to this." He suddenly had a worried look about him. "So . . . just as a *friendly* precaution . . . be very careful with your and especially Hugo's eyes, given that he only has one left."

Those last words punched Sam in the chest.

*You ruined Hugo's life the moment you were adopted. He would have to be careful because you couldn't control yourself when you gouged out his eye. If he were alive, he'd be much better off if you were dead.*

*Please, stop.* Tears suddenly began with the horrible sting of his nares.

"Oh. . . . Sorry," George sighed and skated his finger around the organized silverware on his side, then pushed some napkins closer to Sam, who only stared down at his lap, beginning to shake. "B-But the strange thing I never understood, is giving a soul away. I've heard it be done, and it can form an unresisted connection to the body and strengthen it more than a hundred stolen souls, but why would anybody do it? It would kill you, and your soul would forever be part of someone else, at least until they die." George squinted at his reflection in the spoons.

Sam's head went numb from all this. *Can we please move on to something less . . . violent? Like how college is going, or what we like doing in our free time. I like playing with dinosaur figurines and pretending to help them find their fossilized ancestors. And no, I'm not too old to be playing with dinosaur figurines.* He mused, trying to distract himself.

"And holding hands only offers a mere fraction of a soul connection; the only way to amplify that is to hold somewhere closer to their soul. . . . I could barely take those arrows from your chest back in Sauria, though I had to dig a bit deeper than comfort. Don't even talk about how hard it would be to take you back more than a few seconds to become human again or even fix your leg. Time is . . . touchy, and if we tried to make you human, there's a chance . . . not everything would be reverted to normal, like you still only being three feet tall, or keeping any scars you've gathered as a bird. So if you attempt to use your soul, please let me be there, at least until you are confident enough to really focus your ability."

At this point, Sam was trembling, and his foot held the front of his chair with a creaking grip. *Eyes are the windows- . . . why would I need to remove- . . . Is he going to take my soul?* He looked down; his head suddenly felt lighter. *No, not now. . . . Please, just a little more info. I don't care about souls. I want him to talk about my mother.* He squinted shut his eyes to fight his body from passing out.

"You have the soul of time, and with time, you can fix everything. No more friends dying from accidents; no more worrying about that stupid cancer." George's fingers curled into a fist. "Sam . . . you have the ability to fix everything; you have the ability to start over."

And with that, George finished with a recline against his chair, observing Sam fervently.

He squinted open his eyes with a sigh. "Y-You knew my birth mother?" Sam murmured while looking down with his wings tucked between his thighs. He was nervous about the subject, but it brought him so much curiosity his throat nearly begged him to scream that question.

"Yes. Mrs. Ai . . . the most loving, selfless person you could meet. She and I had a . . . long history. But when she knew she was having a child, all her attention was on you. Trust me when I say, you were *everything* to her. I know it may sound cliché of me to say such a thing. But I really thought you should know."

"C-Can you tell me about her?" Sam stammered with his leg twitching to stand in anticipation.

"I'm sorry, Sam. My moments with her were . . . complicated. I reckon I'm not the best choice to tell you. . . . But, maybe later we can visit someone who knows all about her. . . . What I can tell you, however, is that she had green eyes and black hair, just like you."

"Before my hair became feathers," Sam grumbled under his breath and looked down at himself. Something he didn't think he needed, left his chest with a hollow, numb feeling, like a chain snapped. "T-Thank you, George, for telling me. Even though it was little, it meant much. . . . My family doesn't like to talk about what happened to my birth family, since it was kinda horrible with that home invasion and the dark figure Hugo's scared to talk of, so thank you."

He sighed as he looked again at the attractive food. *Whatever, I'm already a stupid bird. It can't get too much worse.*

"At least you're not a mouse. On Somnium, they're recorded to be one foot tall at the most, but you rarely see them anymore. Like with dragons, most died in the first waves of war– . . . sorry."

Sam's eye twitched at George. *I thought you said you couldn't read my mind.* He waited for George to respond.

But George chuckled at Sam's face. "Did I guess correctly? . . . I wouldn't sabotage your food, if that's what you thought. I could simply tell by the way you were hesitantly looking at the bread."

Sam didn't want to respond, or think anymore for that matter; all that conquered his mind was the scent of food. So he finally relaxed and ate, opening his beak and clamping down on the bread. It was so soft that he didn't need teeth to eat it. Each fibrous inch melted on his tongue, forcing him to recline with a deep moan in delight. The honey was like sticky, warm cream, yet it sank smoother than butter with every gulp.

"So, to summarize, mff, I have the soul of time, and you want me to help people with it?" He gulped once more. *Wow, this is good.*

"It isn't about what *I* want. You've wanted to help people for some time now. Though, if I'm mistaken, and you don't want to help people, all you must do is tell me, and I'll take you home. I'd hate to make you feel trapped."

Sam's mind raced at that offer. *I can go home?*

*Your family hates you, remember? You have nowhere to go.*

Sam's chest felt wrong. He wanted desperately to go home and get away from George. But those words were right.

*You are alone.*

George squinted in thought at Sam's drooping beak. "But . . . you're taking this differently than I thought you would. I don't recall you knowing anything about souls."

Sam exhaled through his nares and blinked away the tears starting to well. "I honestly don't know," he squeaked accidentally, about to cry. "I-If I could guess, it would be that Somnium affected me in some way, and I learned a thing or two. On Somnium, I was terrified, but like you said when you sent me there, 'I needed to learn how to be brave.' I suppose I already knew about souls by reading in that library and watching all the crazy magic stuff people were doing."

Sam took a moment to take another bite of that soft bread, trying to suppress his quavering voice under a pillow of food. He had forgotten entirely that George could have sabotaged it to turn him into something worse. "Mff, but I still feel afraid, as you can probably tell. . . . I guess I'm just better at handling it. Like when you said you were a medical doctor, I felt my head numb and my chest press harshly on my lungs, because I've always been afraid of doctors. But at least I didn't pass out, right?" His eyes reddened, and he could hardly see through the welling tears; he didn't know what to do. If his family didn't want him anymore, he was trapped with George.

George raised an eyebrow at that. "Wait–" He put his hand up to stop Sam. "Why are you afraid of doctors?"

"T-That doesn't matter." Sam shook his wing and head to vanquish that topic. He wouldn't dare talk about his fears in front of George. *He sent me to Somnium after discovering I was afraid of talking to people. I can't imagine what he'd do to me if he found out about this.*

"Is that why you always call me Mr. George and not Dr.–"

Sam blushed, hard enough to sting his cheeks. *I-I didn't even notice I was doing that. . . .* He looked at his lap, trying to hide his thoughts and carry on. "I still don't forgive you for taking me to that planet, but now that I look back . . . it seems like I've grown in some way. Although, I'm not sure what way that might be. And, of course, I still need some work." Sam looked up at George, and to his surprise, George was smiling, but his eyes were squinted thoughtfully at him. "So, heh, how do you think I should help people?" He glanced to the side, feeling dizzy from the amount of eye contact.

*You are the anchor to everyone around you. You drown all who are linked; don't even pretend that you will ever be helpful.*

George leaned to the side to help Sam to look at him. But once Sam saw him, he closed his eyes, like Hugo had taught him when afraid; then he continued eating. Yes, with his eyes still closed. His eyelids were his last hope of shielding his emotions from George as a few tears sneaked through their tight grasp.

George gave up, then leaned forward with a subtle smile. "I have a few things in mind that you could help with, one of which may cheer you up a little." George respectfully nudged a few more napkins toward Sam.

"Mff, a-and what's that?" Sam asked, eating some blueberries and spinach.

"You're going to help Mr. Hugo."

Sam's attention instantly burst with his watery eyes snapping open. He had to re-close his beak to prevent blueberries from rolling out. "Hugo!" He swallowed and gawked at George. "He's alive?" Sam shouted, slapping his wings against the table.

"Yes, but he's not in the most favorable condition. That is why I think your soul ability may help him." George watched Sam's chest swell and shrink with every hurricane breath.

"Take me to him!" Sam commanded, wiping his tears away with a napkin.

"Of course. But finish your breakfast, and make sure you're hydrated."

Sam promptly dug in, his wings like shovels and his beak like a bucket.

"Carefully," George murmured with a slight chuckle.

Within seconds, Sam claimed to be finished by hopping off the chair with his chest inflated like a balloon from the quickly eaten food and gargled water.

George smiled, then knocked on the table just before the familiar door to Somnium appeared beside him.

Sam clumsily grabbed his cane, stumbled forward, and nearly smacked against the door. After seconds of hastily trying to grasp the handle with his wing, George opened it for him.

Sam leaned forward against the door with all his might, and . . . there he was. An instant scent like pine sap, moss, and cooked vegetables grabbed Sam's nares along with the burning aroma of Bipp's fresh, windowsill candles. But he focused on what he saw, lying on a large span of hay beds, under an ugly-patterned quilt. Apparent ruby scales sparkled in the linear light from the window. The dirty map-filled room danced with papers cracking in the air with every deep, steamy heave Hugo released from his large snout.

"Hugo!" Sam dropped his cane and collapsed at the bedside. "I'm so sorry I left you! I was so stupid, I—Please, forgive me!" Sam bowed his head into the hay mattress, pleading with little hope that Hugo would forgive him.

But the only sound he could hear was Hugo's snout pushing hot air onto Sam's ruffling feathers. This close to him, the room began to feel like a relaxing sauna.

"H-Hugo?" Sam looked up at Hugo, whose eye was closed. "Are you . . . sleeping?" Sam looked out the window, seeing the beam of daylight warm the room further. "Hugo . . . please wake up." Sam nudged Hugo's hand, which then dangled off the bed.

"I'm afraid . . . he's not simply sleeping." George yanked Sam's worried attention with those words. "He's in a coma from his injuries."

Sam instantly felt tears find their weight on his cheeks.

*You did this.*

*I . . . what?* He stared at Hugo for a long while through a fresh blur of tears, watching his brother's hefty lungs raise the blankets over his chest with every gulp of air. "No . . . Please, don't do this. . . . You know how this will make me feel. Come on. You can stop kidding, Hugo . . ." Sam wept and shook his head, feeling the final strings of his heart snap. And at the corner of his eardrum, he thought he heard something crack. "Not my big brother. . . ."

Sam's chest felt cold and empty, yet heavier. *I didn't mean to—please, I know I messed up, and I know I can't be much help, but please know I was trying! It was such a horrible planet, and I'm so small, I–*

*You're such an idiot.*

Sam harshly grasped the loose hay mattress within his

wings. So many words raced through his head, and every one felt like a slow stab into his chest.

"As you can see, you are needed. For there are very few things that can help him; one of them is time."

Sam tried to look at Hugo, but such a sight was too heavy for his eyes to bear. "I promise, I will fix this . . . all of this." He extended his wing, wishing to feel his brother's warmth once more. But he paused just before he reached Hugo's snout.

*You don't deserve it, burden. He doesn't love you, especially after hurting him so.*

As Sam pulled back his wing, Hugo's snout sucked in.

"Saaam?" Hugo moaned, instinctively leaning closer to him. Sam froze and watched Hugo find his way inches from his beak. "A-Are you okay?" he breathed right before his exhaustion sank him deep into the hay mattress.

Sam didn't move, nor did he allow himself to breathe. He begged for silence, so he could hear if Hugo spoke again. And after a minute, Sam gasped a breath. "He . . . recognized my scent?" Sam asked himself, gawking at Hugo. "George . . . how is he feeling?"

"He feels sad and a little confused. But just for a second, when he leaned forward, he felt happy."

"So, he still likes me? And he wants to know if I'm okay?" Sam scoffed. *Hugo liking me after all I've done to him is as bizarre and impossible as me becoming a dinosaur. . . . I would hate me . . . if I were you.* He looked down at his chest, not liking the feeling of that last thought. But it was all that made sense to him now. "Hugo, you're crazier than I remember." He took a moment to hold Hugo's limp hand, and his eyes struggled to find the confidence to look at his cut eye. But in time, he did. "I promise, I'll try my best to help you. Please, just hold on a little longer." He turned around and limped away. "I'll force myself to become stronger for you, no matter the cost."

## Chapter 5
# CALM BEFORE THE STORM

The sun raced to its highest height as Hugo and Bipp talked with the dragon. Her sweet bubblegum eyes grabbed their attention and shrank their shadows before they knew it was near evening. Though they didn't understand her at first, the graceful way she moved her hand and how her eyes sparkled like moonlight made it impossible to look away. But after she tried using her hand to communicate, she gave up with a quick smile and started drawing in the sand. Hugo and Bipp stayed dead still and quiet as they watched.

She asked them with a bow if they wanted to follow her to where she lived and spend the day learning about Dawn. Then, to Hugo's discomfort, she drew an arrow that pointed to the forest.

Hugo hesitated with one glance at the wooden shadows that creaked cold, eerie winds to his cheeks, but Bipp agreed it would be fun. And Hugo was indeed curious.

As they approached the forest, Hugo stopped dead where the massive roots began. "I'm sorry, I-I can't go in there," he said with his head low, now seeing the darkness this close again.

Bipp looked back at Hugo with a comforting smile, then turned to the midnight dragon. "Hey, can you breathe fire well?"

She looked back and tilted her head to ask, 'why?'

"I'm sorry, Hugo," Bipp whispered to him before looking at the dragon. "Hugo's afraid of the dark. And he's probably not . . . *the best* with breathing fire, especially because he seemed about to . . . well, burn down the mountain last time we were in those woods." Bipp pointed at him.

As Hugo's head lowered deeper in embarrassment, a slight snort came from the dragon's snout. Hugo looked up and saw . . . she was laughing? Her eyes were closed, and her mouth was wide open. Even her snout muscles flared with every wheezing breath.

Hugo blushed and shyly looked away from her.

She took a moment to breathe before she turned toward the forest path ahead and blew a few white flames along the side; the fire lit the way just enough for Hugo to see where they were going.

"T-Thank you," Hugo said with his head down, beginning to walk behind her with Bipp.

As they went along, the white fire died before reaching Hugo's tail. He could feel the cold shiver of darkness finger its way to his neck. The cracks of the mighty leaves flinched him upon every step. His lungs begged for more air than his throat could provide, forcing his legs to keep close behind her. But Bipp quickly stood right beside his head to bring him comfort.

"Sorry about giving your secret away," Bipp whispered, even though the dragon's ears could obviously hear him as they twitched with his words. "Well, even if she did laugh at you a little, I think you two hit it off quite we–" The dragon thwacked the thicker base of her enormous tail against Bipp's stomach, knocking the wind out of him. She glanced back at his temporary suffering with a smile.

"I'll shut up," Bipp wheezed with his arms pressed over his stomach.

To Hugo, it seemed like an hour between every step and an eternity until they arrived at the forest's end. The cool breeze that once howled up the mountain now bit at this altitude, and any trees unfortunate to grow here were long dead. At least the lack of leaves brought light to Hugo's eye enough for him to spot the snowy mountain peaks and a few cave openings along the upward path. After that hike, it took him a moment to calm down, watching a big roll of steam exit his snout with every exhale. "Thank you for the fire; I think I'm good now." Hugo leaned against Bipp, who was shivering like a jackhammer with his silver fur frozen stiff with the sparkle of ice.

She promptly stopped and nodded to him, as if to say, 'you're welcome.'

*Wing against wing, eyes seeing eyes,*
*you brought me on a journey to the highest skies.*

The three of them froze. "What?" Bipp said with his ears pointed up, and he looked to the remainder of the forest on their right.

*The life I had, the years I hoped for,*
*would be nothing without you to adore.*

Bipp quickly faced Hugo. "Hey, why don't you see what that is while she and I go ahead," he said, but paused with his neck sinking back. He gulped at the sky-piercing height of the two mountain peaks, and his ears fell behind his head once the shivering howl curled ice crystals a few inches from them. "Actually. . . . I'll come with you."

The dragon looked down and back at them.

"You can come too. Just . . . let Hugo take the lead on this one."

> *I should have seen it. You were the dawn of my joy,*
> *the dusk of my doubt, and I . . . let you go.*

Hugo peeked toward the direction of the sound, past the trees. It was a little dark once the sun hid behind the mountain, allowing a great shadow to cover the land, but it was still light enough for Hugo to nod his head with a slight glance to Bipp. *Why is he acting like this?*

With a minute of hesitation, Hugo took a step toward the sound. Then after many steps, and to his dismay, Bipp and the dragon were long behind him, as if they were hiding. For the first time in a long while, Hugo felt alone. For a reason unknown to him, his heart sank with a thumping panic, and his breaths became deep and fast. "Okay, okay," he told himself and walked quickly toward the sound.

> *How foolish I was.*
> *How stupid I am . . .*
> *to have never witnessed your love.*

"Almost there." Hugo was now sprinting. Every second that passed felt like he was in the fight of his life. He flinched and jumped at the several near-silent groans of dry trees croaking into his ears.

> *What I would give to have you back . . .*
> *my life, my dreams, my hopes,*
> *just for one more second with you.*

The sound slowly turned into an intelligent voice that Hugo somehow recognized. But it was . . . singing? To Hugo, it almost sounded like someone was singing a lullaby.

Hugo brushed past a bush, then froze at an opening in the

forest. At the center was a tree's stump, chopped some time ago by the frosted mushrooms enveloping its entirety. And a beam of light shone from the top of the forest where the tree's canopy once covered. The light shone onto the stump where Ventus was sitting. His wings held his torso tight, and there was a light sparkle from the frozen tears that barely had time to fall from his cheeks.

*But now, I know, you're gone forever.*
*My only curse, my only blessing, is when I look up,*
*I see your smile in the clouds. . . . How I wish I could say,*
*I'm sorry.*

Hugo tip-toed out into the area, hidden by the tree shade. *Why did Bipp want me here?* he mused as he inched closer. His heavy hands crunched the thin sheet of leaf-packed snow, forcing him to slow down. He didn't like snooping in Ventus' private matters, but the words Ventus said and the sad tone he sang allured Hugo to know more.

By this point, Ventus' tears froze his harem pants stiff, and the steam that left his nares faded with his slowing breaths. Hugo was a few feet from him but didn't know how to alert Ventus to his presence without seeming like an absolute jerk for listening. So he bowed his head to the snow. "I'm sorry," he said, catching Ventus' instant attention.

Ventus' eyes went from watered and red to sharp and cold in less than a second. Hugo's back fur spun and whipped before the forest's canopy cracked and ripped from the branches. And just before he could blink, he was in the eye of a tornado with sparkles of snow dancing around the flickering sunlight. The tree's absence revealed Hugo clearly, with his head even lower to apologize a second time.

"I didn't mean to intrude. I was just wondering what the

singing was."

Ventus marched up to Hugo, grabbed him by the neck with his foot, and forced him to look him in the eyes. They were still red from the stinging tears, but they were full of hatred. "You're dead," Ventus decreed as he raised his right wing.

"Who did you lose?" Hugo pressed further. He knew it was none of his business, but it couldn't get worse than death, *right?*

Ventus opened his beak, about to respond before he clacked it shut and growled. "You don't get to know. This is the stupidest thing you could've done, lizard." The massive leaves and pine began to rip off the remaining trees and spiral around them in a golden, autumn tornado.

"Is there anything I can do to help you? I don't know much about losing someone close to me–" He paused and looked down with instant thoughts of Sam filling his head. *Maybe . . . I need someone to talk to about that. . . .* "B-But I can be there for you if you want to talk. . . . Please?" Hugo had to raise his voice over the howling wind for that sentence to reach Ventus. As Hugo's eye welled, Ventus' eye feathers furrowed at him for a second, but he continued.

With a single flip of Ventus' wing, the surrounding naked trunks ripped from the ground. At this point, Hugo couldn't hear his own words even if he shouted. He didn't know what else to do but step forward and wrap Ventus in his arm. It was gentle and affectionate. Yet, it was still enough to knock the wind from Ventus' lungs.

But then, something squinted Hugo's eye. As he held Ventus tight, he couldn't help but feel the similarities between his feathers and Sam's.

Ventus' eyes drooped with fresh tears, and he began to sob into Hugo's shoulder. "I hate you so much! Why can't you just go away?"

Hugo sniffled.

Ventus instantly froze and was rendered speechless before Hugo held him tighter, wanting to hug his brother more than anything. The winds then stopped altogether. And all that was left was a field of massive branches, trunks, and leaves thwacking and thumping against the soil upon landing.

"You stupid–" Ventus began but stopped. And after a few moments, he held Hugo with his wings. "Why are you like this? . . . Why didn't you listen to me and just stay in the boat?" he murmured, not wanting an answer.

"We can spend as long as you need here. No rush." Hugo's words confused him even more.

"Why?" Ventus murmured, thinking to himself. The two stood there for many moments until Ventus let go first and stepped away.

"Do you want to talk about it?" Hugo asked, looking up at the hole in the forest to hide his tears. . . . He doubted he could call this place a forest anymore.

With his eyes showing concern, Ventus reached out his wing to Hugo. "Do *you* want to talk about it? . . . You know what I mean, idiot." He wiped a tear from Hugo's cheek.

Hugo looked down as another tear dripped from the ridge of his snout. He wanted to spill all that he felt about Sam, but his heart punched his chest, and his tongue felt sweaty at the thought. "Well . . . maybe someplace warmer. . . . You're shivering." He gave a single laugh.

"Yeah, but–"

"Bipp and I found another creature; she's showing us around if you're interested." Hugo pointed to the side of the forest where he came from. "They should be–" He froze as he saw Bipp and the dragon staring in awe at them, neither daring to take another step past the forest's new border.

Ventus sighed and looked down with his eyes squinted in deep thought. "Wait. D-Don't tell Bipp about this. . . . I would like this to be just between us, if you don't mind."

Bipp's ears rose, and his eyes gaped open, searching for a place to hide. But the dragon stepped toward Ventus. Her feet crunched the snow, but Ventus thought Hugo made those sounds.

Hugo gawked at the dragon. *What is she doing? . . .* "I-I won't tell Bipp. . . . And if you ever want to talk, let me know. I'll be there for you." He rushed that.

Ventus sniffled in response and did nothing else but smile. "Stupid dragon."

Before Ventus could look up at Hugo, the midnight dragon stood before him, grabbed his wing, and placed it on her head. Ventus squinted up, then– "Ah! What the–" His beak gaped, and his eyes seemed to roll back for a moment. His body twitched and wobbled, nearly about to collapse. Then, after a few seconds, his eyes returned to her. "Get away!" His shout echoed up the mountain.

With his wing's swift movements, he pushed the dragon back with the wind. He gulped in the icy air with his back bent and wings over his thighs. "What did you just–" He looked at her with a new flow of tears welling in his eyes. "Don't ever do that again, you idi–ack!"

Before anyone could blink, Ventus was slammed into the icy leaves by the sharp talons of a massive owl, whose feathers were doused with ink splots like dark stars in a void of white. Its ebony feet had fluffy, knee-high golden socks with holes where its talons began, and its sword-sized, bony toes wrapped around Ventus' throat as he squirmed. He didn't have time to realize what just happened, only to panic at the results.

The midnight dragon stepped forth with her fangs showing toward the snowy owl. By instinct, Bipp removed his silver dagger, ready for blood.

Hugo just stood with his mouth and eye gaped. That owl was nearly ten feet tall and had a wingspan that was much, much greater. Even its hooked beak was large and sharp enough to gut Hugo in one slice.

"I demand to know the meaning of this!" Ventus shouted.

The owl looked down at Ventus with a smile that shivered Hugo. "Good morning, Prince Ventus. Lord Exos was deeply troubled upon your lengthy disappearance." The owl's head turned completely around, facing Bipp. "So, your plan of escaping to Anthophyta was successful?" The owl's grasp tightened around Ventus. "I saw the boat you stole. . . . Maybe we should report all this to him. He'd like to hear why you left in such a manner."

Ventus' gaped beak only wheezed, but his eyes showed the horror of what those words meant. The owl's head turned to Hugo; then, it gave a smile that once again shivered him.

Before Hugo could step back, his throat was smacked into the ground by the cold, bony hooks of a mighty eagle and the fluffy, silver socks it wore. Just by the way the toes wrapped around him, this eagle was bigger than the owl.

"Give Luna all the bread. A prince runs a high price, but a dragon's soul . . . if the bread stacked higher than the tower of memory, it wouldn't be enough," the owl spoke before the hefty thud of a bread sack twitched Hugo's ears.

A white glow shone behind her rising fangs as she stomped her claws into the ground. "Unsatisfied, are we? Don't worry, you will get infinitely more, but only if this dragon's soul is better than your stupid—"

Luna's chest swelled, about to evaporate the owl with her fire. But the owl simply held Ventus between them, so Luna closed her mouth and snarled.

Ventus looked at the owl. "Please, don't take me to him. I beg you. I'll be your servant; I'll pleasure you. Anything," he wept.

Then, in one downward swoop, the ground left Hugo and Ventus. The tawny eagle carrying Hugo grunted, but was still quickly successful. Luna roared fire at the eagle, but she stopped once they were out of sight. She turned back to Bipp . . . who was gone. Only a snow trail of his mighty footprints leading to the mountain peaks remained.

# Chapter 6
# EXOSPHERE

Hugo hung from the tawny eagle's sharp, leathery hooks gripped around his throat. Every breath felt sucked through a straw. He begged for that icy air, even though it stung with every tight gasp. The howling wind curled sharp, icy flakes from the mountain and stung Hugo's side. His vision darkened as he saw the mountain peaks up ahead.

"Hugo!" Hugo's ears flicked up.

"What the?" The giant eagle turned around, and Hugo saw Bipp, who sprinted up the mountain at an impressive rate. His silver dagger was firm in his left hand, while his large feet acted as perfect snowshoes; they barely broke the snow's surface.

The eagle spun around and flapped its wings harder; no land creature could keep up with such speed, especially on a mountain climb. The end of Hugo's tail slapped the very tip of the mountain . . . before they heard a grunt.

The eagle turned around again just as Bipp stepped on the mountain's peak and leapt at them. It had to be at least fifty feet. *No way. . . .* Hugo mused.

With a loud, barbaric yell, Bipp missed the eagle. But he didn't miss Hugo as he grabbed onto his hind foot. The eagle's grasp loosened around Hugo's throat as death climbed up Hugo's chest. The eagle lost his only chance at survival with a glance to the west as Bipp plunged his dagger deep into its chest before it finally let go.

But sadly, they were a long way up. Hugo looked down at the rocky snow and steep decline, then he quickly looked at Bipp, grabbed hold of him, and pressed him hard against his chest without permission. He then brought his tail behind Bipp as a shield before closing his eye.

*Please be okay. Please be okay,* Hugo mused.

Bipp looked up at his worried face, showing the fear Hugo was going through, but it wasn't the ground that worried him. "What the?" Bipp murmured with a thoughtful squint.

Hugo then furrowed his eye in thought. . . . *Wait . . . what if I practiced here?* He spun around with his snout pointed to the ground. At that moment, Hugo opened his mouth and roared a beam of fire straight down. The fire panned out from the sheer thrust he roared. It rose them slightly before Hugo's lungs shriveled and his head felt numb. But once he took that gulp of air, they struck the mountainside with a hard crack and thud.

They stumbled down the steep snowy rocks, but Hugo still held on to him. Then, it stopped with Hugo's back smacking against a leafless tree, forcing the snow on the branches to jolt off and slap them.

Hugo let go of Bipp with a deep wheeze.

Bipp rolled out of Hugo's arms and instantly stood. He ran around him and scanned for apparent wounds while patting away the snow.

Hugo's chest rose and shrank with the sudden gasps his lungs forced him to swallow. The steam from his mouth shot out like a geyser, then wisped up the mountain with every breath. "I did it. . . . I was the rocket!" He laughed, overjoyed by his progress, even though it was slight. He spread his arms to the fluffy snow and pressed them deep, still a bit spooked by the fall he luckily cushioned. *I'll have to tell Sam next time I see him! I know he was worried after he and I fell from Zenith. Now we can fall from any height! But if I could just learn to fly like a storybook dragon, like Bipp mentioned, then we wouldn't . . . even need a plane to accomplish our dreams. . . .* Hugo delved into deep thought.

The snowflakes were now massive on this side of the mountain. They bunched together upon their descent to form spheres; most were the size of a packed snowball back on Earth, and few were like a snowman's bottom. But they all teetered down at speeds slower than a feather. In an instant, Hugo was distracted. He held up his hands to catch one. And when its soft flakes entered his cupped fingers, it stayed in shape for a moment, but melted after a few seconds. Hugo smiled a little. He had forgotten he was so warm that snow struggled to exist. Even the snow on his backside melted as droplets now found their weight under him, and a wall of snow rose around him as he sank. *What if . . . I stayed a dragon?*

Bipp knelt over Hugo's chest and grabbed his face. "Are you alright?" he begged to know.

Hugo grunted as Bipp's weight pressed on his lungs. "Yeah, I'm fine. Though I kinda wish I went to flight school before this," he joked. "How are you? Did my fire cushion you enough?"

Bipp lay on and hugged Hugo's long neck. "I'm great. . . . And thank you, for breaking that fall. I'm so happy you're learning more about yourself."

Butterflies danced in Hugo's chest at such words. "And

thank *you* for rescuing me. . . . That was quite the jump."

Bipp opened his mouth to speak, but promptly closed off his thoughts to his tongue before Hugo's eye drifted to the snowballs floating around them. Bipp looked up at them, some finding their weight onto the naked tree beside them, filling it with oddly shaped lumps that sank its branches. "I've only read about these." Bipp held out his hand like Hugo, and one found his palms. It didn't start to melt for a while as Hugo and Bipp stared at it for its remaining life. "I believe they were called, snowbulbs? We don't get them on the mainland; the winter snow there isn't as packy due to the lack of a closely surrounding ocean." He set it on Hugo's chest and stood up before it melted. As he extended his arm, about to help Hugo up, a subtle crackle like a campfire rose their ears to the sky.

They both squinted up to a bright white light that shone on everything around them like the sun came crashing down. They squinted shut their eyes. Hugo heard several crunches within the snow and the crackle of fire snap so loudly, he couldn't hear his breath. But then, it all went silent with a sudden thump. Hugo and Bipp peeked open their eyes and saw the midnight dragon, Luna, who stood before them with a lumpy brown sack before her claws.

Hugo looked up at the snow-littered sky with a squint. *Did she just . . . fly here?*

"You!" Bipp exclaimed. "Get out of here! You manipulative–" She bowed with her eyes closed, then made a fist and rubbed her chest. "What?" Bipp paused.

"She's saying sorry, idiot." Luna, Bipp, and Hugo looked at Ventus, who flew down next to them. This took them all by surprise. The snow he landed in sank him waist-deep. "Eww." He kicked and brushed the snow away.

"What the! How did you escape? And you can understand her?"

"Ha, of course I understand body language. It's imperative to learn for every bird. How else are we supposed to communicate when flying? Not by screaming over those high winds, that's for certain. Besides, it would be a waste of our glorious sight to listen for words like some idiot with big ears."

Bipp was done.

"And of course I escaped; I control the wind, you fat-toed monster."

Bipp looked shyly at his toes and hid his left foot under his right.

Ventus thoughtfully squinted at Bipp.

Luna untied the sack and opened it to them. Hugo's snout yanked to it, and his eye met a pile of freshly baked bread. He could practically see the scent trails curl from it and hook his snout with a gentle tug to pull him forth. Luna slowly pushed it closer to them while keeping her bow.

"Why are you doing this? First, you pretend to be our friend and sell us off. Now you're giving us the food you earned?" Bipp asked, then watched Hugo take a loaf. "Hugo!"

Hugo raised his head from the sack and looked at Bipp with the loaf peeking from his lips.

Bipp couldn't help but smile at that ridiculous face. "Oh . . . never mind."

Luna raised her shaking hand, pointed to herself, then made a cup with her palm and gestured it down her neck.

Ventus lumbered through the snow, grabbed a loaf with his wing, and then cradled it before her. "You dolt, if you're starving, don't give all this away in an unnecessary apology. I, of course, don't forgive you. In fact, I hate you for putting me here."

She looked up at him.

"But don't be an idiot, alright?" As Luna stared at Ventus, he set the bread on the bridge of her snout and grabbed a loaf for himself. He put it in his beak, then turned his back to her with a pause. "Mff, why are you here? Surly a dragon would be able to escape *him*." He glanced at her with his right eye.

Among a few gestures, she pointed down the mountain, brought her open hand to her forehead, and seemed to withdraw something imaginary from her side. Then she opened her mouth and gave a few more gestures before eating the bread over her snout.

"Your father's sword is in that castle, huh? . . . And since you can't talk . . . you've found it quite fun to hold the sword in your mouth, so you can communicate while fighting?" Luna's mouth dawned an agreeing smile.

Ventus paused in thought for a minute. "I see. . . . It must be some sword to make you want to stay here." Before Luna could nod, he walked away and found another tree to sit under, one farther from them.

"Pardon me . . . but can't we just go back to the boat?"

Ventus sighed and peeked an eye at Bipp. "Look around you, and tell me what you see. . . . Might wanna take a few steps back, get these trees under your view."

Hugo and Bipp paused for a moment, took many steps up the mountain, then turned to the land before them. They saw the mountain's circular curve on either side, meeting an ocean bay to the western shore. But at the ends of the mountain, rested two skulls nearly more giant than the mountain they stood on, for their horns were the size of buildings, and their fangs alone were the length of Hugo. Their lengthy fur crowned much of the grassy mountain ridge that traveled with their spines.

The air in Hugo and Bipp's lungs escaped, seeing just how long their spines were. *This isn't a mountain range. . . .* Hugo looked back at the two peaks, seeing where he struck; the tannish color of bone peeked from the white snow. *Is that the tail?* His jaw actually dropped.

"What happened here?" Bipp asked.

"Apotheosis happened, in two attacks. But by the way your eyes are traveling, you're not even seeing the whole picture. Forget the two dragons buried under snow."

Bipp and Hugo both froze.

"Look at the center of them."

Hugo was curious enough to slowly look where Ventus said, but Bipp was stuck gawking at the dragon's claws, forming hills beside their skulls. "See Hugo, storybook dragons." He gulped. "Told you they were real."

*These dragons had wings. . . .* Hugo's eye traveled down the mountain ridges, along a connected slope of sizable, bone-shaped hills covered with autumn trees. Their lone wings met the center of the deep valley on either side. And this valley was so deep, it looked more like a crater to Hugo.

There was a tall black, castle-like tower that surprisingly didn't catch Hugo's attention at first. It stood firm, right at the center of everything. And to Hugo, it looked like a rocket ship with beams and window lining so sharp, it seemed made to pierce the hardest meteorites. *Maybe I could use that as a spaceship?* He whispered out a flame. *Though I may need to improve my rocketry a little to get a building* that *big to go anywhere.*

Everything about the area distracted and overwhelmed both Hugo and Bipp. They didn't even take note of the thousands of flowers dotting the land beneath the trees and the patchy clouds crackling with thunder above.

"Who were these two?" Bipp asked, returning the topic to the dragons.

"Dusk and Dawn, the previous king and queen of this continent, which was named after the queen for all her help in making this beautiful paradise. T-They were lovers. One had the power to control the moon, and the other, the sun. Together, they made day and night? . . ." Ventus looked at Luna, as if trying to understand what he was saying. With her kind nod, he continued. "At least, that's the legend for how day and night began. And there were even legends of two moons being present at that time, but that's a ridiculous notion." He waved his wing to excuse his comment. "Apotheosis killed the moon dragon first, then in a single attack that changed even the topography of Dawn, he used the moon dragon's soul to kill the other. . . . This all used to be flatland, holding a bustling city with all the creatures one could imagine. But alas, the value of a dragon's soul was too tempting to steal."

*What kind of abilities does controlling the sun entail? . . .* Hugo took a quick glance at the large, warm sun and thought of all the things he had learned about stars in his astronomy courses.

After a while of gawking, Bipp looked at Ventus. "How do you know so much about this place?"

Ventus sighed. "She told me . . . through her memories." He looked at Luna. "Which were rather traumatizing by the way . . . and I hope never to see them again."

"Her memories?"

Ventus rolled his eyes, obviously getting tired of explaining everything. "Ugh. She has a soul ability to experience memories," he spoke quickly, then stared toward the castle with his eyelids sinking. "And there goes my time. . . ." He looked at Hugo. "This . . . may be the last you'll see of me, at least for a long while." A few tears reddened his eyes. "Please, just know, I-I really don't like you guys."

And with that, a dozen pairs of wings flapped through the cool air. Ventus looked down at his leathery feet and rubbed his harem pants as his beak began to wobble.

At that moment, several colossal talons crunched in the snow. The birds that bore them were like kings of the sky. Their hooked beaks were deadlier than claws, and their eyes even sharper. But what caught Hugo's attention was their gold, silver, or copper, knee-high, fluffy socks, each fitting perfectly around their bird toes. They landed around Bipp and Ventus with such elegance, no snowbulb broke apart.

The largest of the five, and by far the most breathtaking, was again, the snowy owl, who stepped forth and opened its beak. "To the rabbit and Prince Ventus, you are summoned by Exos. The rabbit will partake in battle as warm-up entertainment for the dragon. While we will bring Prince Ventus directly to Exos."

Bipp instantly withdrew his silver dagger, but a prison of talons was around him before he could use it. "What's going on here? The creatures of Anthophyta and Zenith are at peace!"

"The two dragons are to wait for further commands at the tower's entrance."

Bipp and Hugo looked at each other while a blur of hot air weaved through Luna's bone-cracking fangs. "May I ask what's going to happen?" Bipp asked with a gulp.

"You're going to The Eye of the Storm, an arena," Ventus sighed with his head down.

The talons around Bipp tightened, and a few claws sliced his skin. "You meant for this to happen, didn't you! Why did you let the owl go? You can easily–" he yelled before Ventus looked up.

"I have no power here. . . . I got lucky escaping the owl." A flash of lightning boomed through the clouds above as he said that.

Bipp also looked up, but with a growl. "Do I have the honor of knowing who I'm going to fight among you?" By the sound of his voice and the firm grip he had on his silver dagger, he was not in the mood for this.

"Stupid rabbit, you dare have the courage to ask such a thing? If I were you, luckily I'm not, I would savor every second you have left."

Hugo stepped closer to Bipp. "And what if I refuse?" A few of his fangs showed.

The snowy owl simply raised his foot and unveiled each, sharper than death, talon sequentially. "Like you could stop us. Though, it would be a shame if you got injured before your turn in The Eye, but who knows, an injured dragon might make for a more . . . entertaining fight."

Bipp sighed. "I'll go." He looked at Hugo. "I'll tell you all about it when I get back."

The owl scoffed. "Confident, are we? You'll be lucky to survive the transport with flesh as soft as yours. And by the way, you never had a choice in this matter." Suddenly the prison of talons gripped his throat and waist, not caring about his soft flesh.

"Bipp!" Hugo yelled.

"Better hold still, so us simple messengers don't cut you in half." The owl smirked before two birds flapped their wings in one mighty swoop and rocketed Bipp, dangled between them, to the castle-like tower.

Hugo hardly had enough time to blink before they were above the trees, but right as he looked down, a giant barn owl scooped Ventus in its talons, then followed the birds to the tower.

The snowy owl and a giant gray falcon stood before Luna and Hugo, staring at them as if a war was about to break. Their wings were canopied over the land as they stood on one foot with their talons pointed at the two dragons like spears. But with Luna's rising fangs dripping with fire and Hugo's breaths growing faster and heavier with each second Bipp was carried from sight, they were right to be on edge. "Let me pass!" Hugo roared, staring at Bipp shrinking on the horizon before the snowy owl looked back at Bipp with a smile.

"Better hurry; he's not going last much longer," the owl chuckled before he and the falcon flew away.

# Chapter 7
## AT THE EDGE OF DUSK

The darkest trench in the deepest ocean of sleep was where Sam found peace. The water's heavy pressure pushed on his chest until his back squished against muck. He gave no resistance to the sea's breaths, for his body yearned for this. The past seven weeks made him wish this ocean was real and he had drowned long ago. All he wanted was to learn how to use his soul ability and help Hugo. But with all this effort, all this struggle, his best proved one thing, that he was a waste of flesh, an anchor.

The recent dreams he had always contained Hugo. They were so peaceful and so warm. He knew George was a reason for the dreams, but his heart didn't mind, especially once Mary or Andrew appeared. But there was always an itch on the back of his head, reminding him that he did not deserve it.

This morning, in particular, Sam rubbed his face against the warm pillow, dreaming about his family. The warmth from the sun baked his feathers in such a way that he thought Mary, Andrew, and Hugo were hugging him, and he was hugging them. His pillow-squeezing wings begged for this, but the second his mind caught up with him, he snapped awake.

"Nooo!" he shouted as he promptly flung himself from the bed and smacked onto the hard floor, gulping to feed his stinging lungs the air they begged for. "Why am I like this? I hurt him, and I'm having these dreams about him being happy with me!" He grabbed his head. "It's not real!"

*You killed him.*

"What?"

*He will never wake, and it's all your fault.*

"No! Stop! I can help him; just let me–" Sam quickly stared at his limp leg, trying to send it back in time. He still had no idea how to use a soul ability, but he needed to try, just once more with the last speck of hope. He stared at his leg until his head hurt and dizzied. "Please, let me do it! Let me help my brother!" he roared with such anger, his throat stung. After nothing happened, he yanked out many feathers along his leg, adding to the collection already around him. He wept and slammed his head against the floor, hard.

His head numbed, and at that moment, he felt his heartbeat thumping wildly in his thigh. Just as he squinted at the ceiling, a bullet of pain shot up his leg and to his head. "Ah! What the–" He sat up, looked at his leg, then froze in fear. His thigh was cut open to the bone, and green goop dripped from it and tapped the floor. His heart fell with a mighty anchor, and his eyes spread wide open. "No . . . not this, not again! I didn't mean to–" He instantly felt the pain ebb away with the arch's dull numbness. He screamed and wrapped his wings around his leg. "No! Don't make me do this again! Undo it! Undo it!" he begged his soul to return his leg to normal, but no amount of begging and tears could undo what he had done. *What's wrong with me?*

*Useless. You can't even help yourself. Why do you think you can help your brother? And why do you think he would ever love you, especially after you abandoned him?*

He gasped in as much as his lungs could find, trying not to pass out. "I-I didn't mean to. . . . I left him because he liked it there, and so he could be far away from me."

*Exactly. You knew deep inside that you were the worst thing to happen to him. And now, even from stars away, you can't stop hurting him.*

Sam sank until he fused with the hard floor. He could've sworn he was just stabbed in the chest, and in that instant, he felt all his energy melt from him. Even his eyelids drooped as a cold numbness conquered his body with a heavy weight. And sadly, he stopped caring about the arch thumping its way through his blood once more.

*You know what you need to do.*

Sam's eyes shot open to the dizzy world around him with his heart skipping a beat. All he did next was weep. "Please, don't make me. I can help Hugo. I can- . . . ." Sam drooped, cheek against the floor. Not a muscle remained that supported him.

*You see it now, don't you?*

Sam's eyes closed. He no longer felt his body, nor did he care. . . . And now, it was futile to try and block out the voice, for he accepted it as his own.

With a quick knock on the door, George came with the hasty taps of his cane echoing into Sam's head. "Are you alright?" George asked worriedly, then paused as he instantly saw Sam's leg. "Did your soul do that?"

Sam barely had the will to move, but he opened his beak. "I can't fix it, I sent it back, but I couldn't control when. . . ."

George knelt beside him and held his wing. "Can you think

of the future for me? I might be able to help fix it."

Sam sighed and looked at George, who wore a tannish long coat to combat the late autumn cold—a rather colorful choice compared to his typical gray. Sam wasn't much for thinking about the future, for his past was always so heavy on his mind. But he tried with the squint shut of his eyes. The only future that could come to mind was Hugo's dream to fly a plane with him while searching for dinosaur fossils. But after that thought concluded, Sam felt the subtle thump of his heart in his leg once more.

"There, back to normal."

Sam didn't want to open his eyes again. Even though he had woken nearly five minutes ago, something exhausted him

George took a moment in silence. "Are you okay, Sam? It's good news that you finally got results, right?"

"No . . . what if I can't control it when I try to help Hugo? He could end up bleeding out from his past injuries if I touch him. . . ." *I guess this means, I'll never be helpful.*

George stroked his beard with a lengthy pause, then held out his hand to Sam. "You're not alone, Sam; you don't have to keep struggling like this. Here, let's get you off the floor . . . why are you on the floor anyway?"

Sam took a deep, raspy gulp of air. "Yeah, sorry. I guess I got startled by another dream—fell out of bed again," he lied, not feeling comfortable enough with George to tell him such truths. Sam's chest still stung, and it was impossible to move. It felt like his feathers weighed more than iron bars. He quickly thought of happier times with his mother, Mary, to hide from George's 'feeling detector.'

But there was a long silence that rang in Sam's head.

"I made you breakfast."

Sam's chest felt heavier.

George sighed and looked away. "The fridge is starting to get full from the leftovers. . . . And I'd really like to see you–"

"I'm sorry." Sam grimaced. "Your food is delicious, but I . . ." He paused for a long moment.

*You don't deserve it.*

Before George could attempt to help Sam up, Sam tried to get up himself, not to be a burden to George. But he found he couldn't move a single feather to wipe the tears from his face. "The fall hurt a little," he said with a smile, hoping to change the subject.

As George picked him up with a grunt, Sam drooped, as if he were long dead. And as Sam's body met the bed, George coughed. Sam's eyes instantly met George's grimacing face.

"Alright. Glad you're feeling well. If you need anything, please ask me anytime."

Sam sighed. "Mr. George . . . i-is something hurting you?" he asked just before George could turn around.

But George froze, then looked down at the wobbling hand holding his cane.

"You told me . . . you could heal, similar to that owl doctor on Zenith. . . . Is your condition something that can't be healed, like my leg?"

George sighed. "Not—I mean. . . . It's hard to explain." George kept his eyes down.

*He doesn't want to talk about that. . . .* "Then, Mr. George, what am I doing wrong? I'm trying my best to learn this ability to help, but–"

"You are doing nothing wrong. It may appear more natural for some, but it took me longer than a month to learn mine. And mine's a stupid door thing. . . . Of course, it wasn't easy;

souls always react differently per person. Otherwise, I would have discovered my soul by knocking on my neighbor's door," he chuckled. "For you, we're talking about time, and that's probably the most complicated thing anyone could think of. So I'd say you're right on track."

Sam sank deeper into the bed.

"How about thinking about it from a tinier perspective?" George sat beside Sam. "You're thinking pretty big about helping Mr. Hugo. Maybe think about just seeing the past; you've done that before, right?"

Sam squinted. "There's just no keeping secrets from you, is there?" *What doesn't he know? . . .* "I get what you're saying, and I'll try thinking smaller. But, may I ask a question, since you know everything?"

"I don't, but go ahead."

"What is Hugo?" Sam peeked at George's face to read his expression.

George gave a smile with his eyes closed from the force of his rising cheeks. "He's caught your attention, eh?"

Sam only stared out the window, where autumn trees had begun to lose their leaves.

"What did he do to earn your thoughts?"

"He exists," Sam said.

George chuckled, then gestured for Sam to elaborate.

"He's not like a normal brother that you see on TV, or in real life for that matter. Most brothers I've seen usually, I don't know—compete against each other in sports, play a video game or two, fight a little, but they still like each other to a *normal* extent. . . . But the thing is . . . I can't remember one moment when Hugo fought with me, heck, let alone yell at me. Even after all I've done, he was happy to know I was next to him while in a coma I had caused. Apart from all that . . . the way he makes me feel . . . confuses me. I mean, he's insane even to like me. I'm such a horrible person, but he never ceases to . . . well, care about me so much that it seems I'm the only thing on his mind." Sam looked at George's chest, begging for an answer to his next question.

"He's not my brother, is he?"

"Would you look at him differently if I answered? Because you seem to have a high opinion of him."

Sam looked away. "You're right. Don't answer."

"Well, how does he make you feel? If you had to guess, what is Hugo?"

Sam froze in thought, suddenly feeling a warmth rush over his body and stir the hardened butterflies in his chest.

"He *is* your brother, and he loves you more than you or I can imagine. But since you ask, is he something unique *to you*, perhaps like a father figure, or a best friend?"

Sam closed his eyes with his head spinning. *Maybe . . . I know I thought this once, but now that I think about it . . . he's just plain bizarre. But why? He does give me similar feelings to Mom. . . . They're both warm, kind, yet fiery, and great huggers. He is her son after all . . . while I stick out like a sore thumb in family photos.* His mind went deeper into thought until he was dizzy, and his shy eyes drifted away from George. *But why is he . . . so . . . Hugo?* Before George could say anything more, Sam shook his head to avoid the questions. He didn't know the answers to explain Hugo; he was a complete mystery to him.

After a few seconds to recompose himself, he opened his eyes. But George was gone, probably went out the open door. He took a few more seconds to relax, but couldn't find the comfort to do so. How Hugo made him feel was burned into his nerves.

"Why am I like this?" He could almost feel raindrops tap and sink the feathers on his head. "If I can help you out of your coma, I'm going to ask why? Why do you care about me like that? I need to know." His feathers quickly warmed and became hotter with the passing seconds.

"What's going on? Did George turn up the heat?" He looked around the room; nothing seemed out of the ordinary. But the warm air forced his mind to Hugo and how his dragon warmth repelled any cold. Sam closed his eyes, quickly remembering everything about Hugo.

Then, the warm air became blistering hot. He winced from the sudden pinch of heat as it grabbed his feathers, but then he felt his toes leave the ground with Hugo's hard chest against his cheek and his surprisingly cold hands pressed around his back. He subconsciously reached out his wings to feel Hugo's warm, smooth scales against the tips of his feathers.

An instant scent like campfire and ash overcame Sam's nares, and the sound of crackling and shifting rubble met his eardrums, but he didn't care about those. This feeling of love conquered all other senses.

"It's okay, Sam. I can take this for a moment. Just close your eyes and allow yourself to sink against me," Hugo said calmly.

Sam's eyes shot open to smooth and shiny, honey-yellow scales. But Sam couldn't help but look around at the collapsed brick buildings and airborne dust wisping in the wind. He looked at the charcoal and gray clouds above before looking at Hugo's grimacing face. *Hu-go?* he mused with disbelief before Hugo's brilliant sapphire eye looked at him. Sam's beak and eyes gaped; his heart begged him to speak, but then, Hugo's scales turned black; some even melted. Before Sam's eyes, he watched saliva drip from Hugo's gnashing fangs as a dark fire ate his flesh.

Hugo looked like he was about to scream before all vanished in green smoke. Sam's heart pounded against the jail cell of his ribs, and his head felt numb. Then, he opened his eyes to the familiar wooden ceiling above.

He blinked several times to get a grip on where he was. The sinking bed against his back, the window streaming in sunlight to his left, he was back in the room with his beak and eyes still gaped more than ever before. He gulped all the air in the room. "Hugo. . . . What was that—a dream? No. . . . I didn't fall asleep. But–" He rubbed the soft blanket to ensure his mind wasn't playing tricks on him. *Probably just passed out again.* Sam rolled his eyes. "I need to get better at controlling that." *But why was Hugo in pain? Those dreams have been relatively happy until–*

"Sam!" George yelled, flinching Sam. George was staring at Sam with his hands wrapped around his feathery torso.

"Yes?" Sam blinked, very confused about what was happening.

"You just passed out and were unconscious for a minute or two." He let go. "Sorry, your temperature was all over the place. I was just making sure you were alright."

Sam chuckled slightly. "Hugo used to do the same thing; he'd always get so worried."

"He had a right to be! You went from normal to near-fire temps in less than a second!" George exclaimed, making Sam nervous, but curious.

*My body temperature changed? So, it wasn't an ordinary dream. . . .*

Sam looked up at George's worried face and blushed. He

didn't want to be such a bother as to worry someone. He was grateful that George was watching out for him, but now he felt his chest sink as he thought what a burden he was. "W-When did I pass out?" Sam asked before George reclined, back against the wall.

"After I said that Hugo loves you and wondered how you see him."

Sam remembered, and once more, his mind went dizzy from it. He thought about how Hugo made him feel, then stopped. *Maybe . . . passing out is part of it?* "I'm sorry. I guess it was too much for me to handle. . . . You see, Hugo has never once said that he loves me."

That surprised George with the rise of both eyebrows.

"I know he does though, because how else could I explain his actions? He's so caring and patient with me that it's weird to think it has any other reason."

*Hugo only does those things so you would shut up. Your needy self is a waste of time to him. He'd much rather lose his remaining eye than spend one second with you.*

Sam held his head and pretended to scratch it.

George chuckled a little. "Mr. Hugo is just as pondering as you are. I don't know why he hasn't told you such things. Maybe next time you see him, you can ask him if he still loves you. I know for certain he'll say yes, but if you have your doubts, it's crucial to ask."

Sam looked at his body, and his heart thumped louder as he worried about Hugo saying no.

*He doesn't love you. If he says yes, it's only to make you feel better and stop bugging him about it.*

Sam then looked at his body in disgust. Each dark feather made him sick. He then paused and shook his head to get rid of the thoughts. "May I see him?" he asked before George instantly knocked on the bedpost, summoning the door as if knowing Sam would ask that.

"May I ask why?" He gave Sam his tiny cane.

"Because I want to test something, and even if I'm wrong, I need to see him. I need to ask him a few things, even if he won't respond; I just need to get it off my chest."

George smiled. "Testing something, eh?"

Sam grabbed his cane and leaned on it with all his weight, finding it still difficult to move much. After George twisted the handle, Sam nudged open the door; his thumping heart begged to help Hugo. Even if his passing-out and dizziness weren't anything special, he needed to try . . . now.

When he opened the door all the way, he could feel the tubes to his heart shrivel and snap off. "What?" Sam promptly collapsed onto his knees. His sharp eyes scanned the room for any sign of Hugo. But there was only a row of empty hay beds and a quilt on the floor before him, and each bed trailed a chasm where Hugo once lay. He slowly crawled into Bipp's house, for standing wasn't an option anymore. His heart sank deeper and deeper against the floor with the gravity of his mistakes.

*Useless.*

"I-I was too late." Part of him was used to the feeling of being useless. But with the urge to help his brother more than anything and ask why he cared, this feeling hurt. "Is he still alive?" Sam said without emotion, demanding to know.

"Yes, he just recovered by. . . . what?" George squinted as if trying to figure it out; then a slight chuckle came muffled by his sealed lips. "The rabbit?" George gave a huge smile. "Oh my, he's going to be an interesting one." As George continued to talk to himself, Sam ignored him.

He was happy to hear that his brother was well. But he had so many questions, and not one could be answered.

*You can't even fix your own mistakes.*

Sam sank until his cheek pressed against the dirty floor.

*He definitely hates you now. You wasted two months of his life.*

Sam felt his heart become so heavy, no strength on the planet could push his body up. "Please, I can help. I can–"

*You will never be helpful, just a burden feathered rodent that would make everyone's life better if you were gone.*

Sam didn't want to cry, not now, not before George again. What little thread of hope he held desperately told him to toughen up and be helpful. But how?

"What's wrong, Sam? It's good news that Hugo's well, right?"

That question made Sam feel like an absolute jerk. Of course he wanted his brother well; he just wanted to be the one who made it so, to fix his mistake. Sam winced at himself, forgetting that George could tell what he felt. "Nothing, I'm happy, just a little tired," Sam tried before George sighed.

"You are a complicated one. . . ." George sat on a hay bed. "I like you because you are not arrogant—quite the opposite really. And you want to help people to your core. I just . . . don't know if it's the best combination with you."

"What are you saying?" Sam asked.

"I'm sorry; kind of talking to myself there." He stroked his beard in thought. "Look, I may have another way you can get your spirits up, but it may be difficult. . . . You came here wanting to test your soul ability, right?"

Sam sighed. *I'll never get used to his 'knowing everything'. . .*

. "I just wanted to see if my dreams weren't exactly dreams, but visions. . . . When I passed out just then, I saw Hugo and a dark fire, then collapsed buildings. And with my body temperature being strange, I figured it was worth the test."

George paused at that moment with a glance outside.

"But it's weird; it was almost like I was dreaming. So I'm not one-hundred percent sure if I just passed out like I normally do, or I went to the past. . . . Maybe future? I just so desperately wanted to see him well that I bet everything I had to help him. Though I wouldn't dare use my soul without your help. The last thing I want to do is hurt him."

George gave a confident smile. "Maybe they're one and the same. Maybe all those times you've passed out or had those strange dreams, was your soul trying to show itself."

Sam thought hard about those words.

"I know you've had visions without passing out, like seeing your future self in the mirror at home and viewing your roommate's interrogation while in the Zenith library. So maybe, it's a matter of *how* you use it. Are you simply 'seeing' time, or are you 'going to' time? . . . What happened in this instance?"

It was a bit much for Sam, but it all made some sense. He just didn't like that he had to pass out every time he used an ability. "I went to a moment when Hugo was hugging me, and we seemed to be in an area I don't recall seeing before."

"Was all your focus on what you felt and saw?" George asked, and Sam nodded with his cheek still against the hard, map-layered floor. "Do you think you can repeat it, but this time, focus on what you said and heard? It's just like *the thing* you and Mr. Hugo do, but less of it."

"Sounds simple enough, but what are you planning?" Sam wasn't much in the mood for doing anything else for the day;

he was perfectly content just to lie there. He even doubted his body had the strength to move ever again.

"I'd like to see my daughter. But I need your help to do so."

Sam's head rose after hearing that. "Your daughter? . . . Uh, how can I help with that? Can't you just call her or . . . wait." Sam instantly stopped as he saw George's face. His sinking eyes and slumped shoulders spoke it all.

"She's been dead for some time. . . . I didn't build this large house only for me, you know. . . . After a hundred years of being alone, I met an angel of a lady, whom I married. . . . We adopted a little girl from a distant country. . . . Her parents didn't see the wonders she held." A soft happiness rose George's cheeks. "Her mother, my wife, was dying from a mix of old age and cancer after we built this house, and I . . . didn't react too well, as you might've heard on Somnium." He paused with a glance at his wrinkled hands. "Then, amongst my horrible grievance, my daughter suffered a similar end. . . ."

*A hundred years? . . .* Sam now felt worse. He spent this much time with George, and he never bothered to ask about his history . . . his long, complicated history. Sam grabbed the top of his beak in shame. "I-I'm sorry. I didn't realize. . . . But, h-how can I help? Won't it be hard for me to hear *that* past? I mean, it's not even my own."

George stood and gave his hand to Sam. "Leave that to me." Sam hesitated but accepted it with a slow grip of his cane, and George pulled him up before wiping the dirt from him. Then, they stepped out from Bipp's cabin and shut the door. "Okay, just think about the past to an event where you just talked and listened if possible, and I'll tell us where to go, alright? We can share the burden."

Sam paused for a moment. *Share the burden?* He looked at

his wing wrapped around George's hand. Then with a hesitant nod, he closed his eyes with his cane wobbling in his grasp.

George closed his eyes with his knuckle raised, ready to knock.

*Is this even going to work?* Holding hands still seemed ridiculous to Sam, even after all that's happened. But he continued anyway. With much concentration, he thought of what he heard, tasted, and saw, but he couldn't help but think of how he felt. And to his surprise, he saw his mother, Mary. They floated in a dark abyss, but he did not care. She hugged him so tight that the air escaped his lungs, and his wings pinned against him. She always did have that protective strength, similar to Hugo but different in a good way. He missed everything about her: her scent like baked bread, smooth skin, and gentle yet fiery blue eyes. He finally focused on what he said, just so he could talk to her. Then her soft, plump body turned to hard, smooth scales. Sam peeked open his eyes to Hugo's yellow and ruby chest. *No . . . I hurt you. You need to leave . . . please, before I hurt you more.* He begged. Hugo let go and looked at Sam with a smile that spun his mind. "I promise to protect you and love you more than anything in the universe."

Then a firm knock broke his dizzied focus, and his eyes peeked open to see a door made of oak planks and bordered by scarlet brick. This was far different from George's other doors. So when he looked at George, he was expecting to see confusion, but all he saw was George's mouth and eyes agape at the sight. "I didn't– . . ." He looked at Sam's foot with each toe curled to the knuckle after knocking against the floor. Then he looked back at the door once they heard the many bullets of rain pat against the door's opposing side. "Could you wait here for a moment, please?"

Sam looked down at his foot, surprised to see his toes curled. *Was I the one who knocked?* He set his foot down with thoughts spinning in his head. *A promise to protect me and love me? . . . When did he say that?*

George opened the door to an ear-numbing rattle of rain. "On second thought, could you help me out of this coat?"

Sam nearly stumbled at how fast he turned to his back. He grabbed the coat with a heavy grunt, pulled back, and freed George. Then, without delay, he lugged it to the front of George, whose eyes were closed with a wince.

*How bad is it, if that hurt?*

"Thank you." George took the coat with a smile that warmed Sam's cheeks and lightened his chest. "H-Hello?" George's voice creaked with the door as he pushed.

"Who's there?" A sickly yet soothing voice nearly melted Sam on the spot.

George raised his finger to Sam, requesting that he wait. George's nervous legs struggled to keep him up as he fully opened the door to a young lady, who sat on a street bench dressed in a plaid dress. Her delicate face under her short ebony hair was ghost-pale, cold, and far too drained to keep her eyes open long. As George stepped forward, Sam caught a glimpse of her hair over her sinking head.

"It's me, Ai. George." He walked into the bruising rain.

"Ai?" Sam's eyes lit up.

"Dad!" she wheezed, instantly turning her head to him. She shivered as her green eyes popped from her head. She tried to flee, but nearly collapsed in the attempt.

*Dad?* Sam's stomach sank.

"Please, let me help." George approached her with the trench coat, then hung it gently around her shoulders. "I'm so sorry all this happened to you, and for my wrongdoings. I just wanted—need you to survive this."

Ai squinted at the soaked road that shimmered the black asphalt as a few frogs found peace there. "This night truly is one of a thousand horrors," she sighed. "I don't know how you knew I was here. But still, I will never forgive you for leaving Mom and I. . . . I don't care who you are or what your intentions were. And the only reason I'm sparing your life right now is because you apologized," she chuckled a little, then coughed, a lot. "Ugh, sorry. . . ." She took a moment and held her throat to catch her wheezing breath. "Why are you here? Let me guess, to try and convince me to do another surgery, or to torture me further by telling me about Saiai's time soul and how we should kill him for it."

George reached to her shoulder. "I would never wish–"

"Get away from me." She nudged his hand away.

Respecting her request to a certain extent, George took a step back. "Please, I never wished to harm our family. I love you and Mom so much that my only goal is keeping you well . . . to the point where I would've killed, and for that, I hopelessly apologize." George knelt before her in the wet grass and looked at Sam. "You see, I have a new light now, one that has the potential to shine brighter than me, even at my best. And I would never wish it snuffed out."

Sam froze in thought from *that* look.

George looked back at her. "I've studied your disease for several years, and with some help, you will be okay."

Ai sighed. "I can't keep doing this. . . . The endless attempts, the endless surgeries, and drugs . . . It's too much. I want to believe you, so much. But my body feels so heavy. And every time you mention that fantasy, Somnium, or your expensive hospital, I feel my strength draining further. The only reason I have the will to move at all is because of him." She looked down at a baby in a green blanket tucked against her stomach. "He gives me the strength to keep going, even if the odds seem impossible."

George sighed from his nostrils, then looked back at Sam. "About that." George raised his hand and curled his fingers at Sam to step forth. "I may have found someone who can help you."

Sam stepped into the bullet-like rain. His toes and cane squished into the muddy grass, and his bones shivered from the nipping, wet cold. But all his attention was on Ai. He lumbered forth until he was next to George, but she didn't see him, for his dark feathers camouflaged the midnight rain like he belonged there.

"Ai, I'd like you to meet, Saiai." George gestured his hand to Sam.

With a quick squint and turn of her head, Ai spotted Sam, and she flinched at his sight.

"Hey . . . Mom?" Sam said, so shy he wanted to close his eyes on the spot. His cheeks were so warm he could've sworn the rain was steaming off them. He was nervous about calling her Mom, but once the word left his tongue, he felt lighter, like something unlocked his chest.

Ai leaned forward with a hard squint at him. "Oh . . . my–" She turned to George with a glare. "What did you do to him? I thought I told you to keep away from him and out of your crazy–" She coughed again, then painfully wheezed in any air her brittle throat would allow in. "You mean to tell me, Somnium, creatures, they're real? . . . Don't you dare tell me you saw this with your prediction soul, assuming you didn't make souls up either."

"That's not important right now." George gestured once more to Sam. "He helped bring me here, and he can cure you, right now. . . . Your dream of having a big family can finally come true."

Ai looked back at Sam. He had his eyes shut and his wing folded across his chest. *She probably doesn't want a bird for a son. . . .*

*Even as a human, nobody would want you.*

"How old are you, sweetie?"

"Almost seventeen," Sam squeaked accidentally.

Ai smiled. "Almost seventeen, huh?"

Sam kept his eyes clamped shut, but then, he felt something wrap around him. It was cold and hard, yet it gifted him a strangely familiar warmth. "You've grown up faster than a blink; please forgive my initial response. Seeing my son past my years was quite the shock. . . . Can you look at me, please?"

Her voice and warmth nearly knocked Sam out. But he slowly unveiled his wing to wrap around her. She was bony and rigid to the touch, quite the opposite of Mary, but Sam loved her all the same. He peeked open his right eye to her eyes, whose emerald colors matched his to the atom. His poor supporting leg hardly had enough strength to keep him in her sight, but before he collapsed, George helped him onto the bench beside her.

"What's your favorite food? Mine is blueberries with a spoon of crystalized honey."

Fresh tears blurred Sam's eyes. "I've loved blueberries for as long as I can remember, but I've never tried them with honey."

"We're here to cure your cancer, and once that's done, you will be with each other much longer than this moment."

George ripped that bandage off to get going, assuming Sam couldn't keep them here forever.

"You have cancer?" The tears that escaped Sam barely had time to live before the rain drowned them.

"Yes? A similar kind that killed my . . . adoptive mother." She glanced at George with sorrow in her eyes, then she slowly looked back at Sam. . . . "How don't you know this? Did I never– . . . Oh."

She looked down in sorrow. "Have you found a good family, one that makes you happy? Am I right about signing you up for adoption?"

"Yes, I've lived a happy life . . . but it'd be much better with you in it."

"Aww." She hugged Sam with her left arm. But at that moment, a street lamp across the road vanished into green smoke. This caught Sam's instant attention, and at once, he tried to think of the past, to a time when she was alright.

"You're so precious. I don't think some stupid cancer will get in our way of being with each other, don't you think?" She smiled

"Wait, what are you saying?" Sam squinted hard, trying to focus.

"Hey." She hugged him tightly. "Don't place the world on your shoulders. Some things cannot be fixed."

*You will never be helpful.*

"No. . . . Please, let me cure you; I can—I have this ability you see–"

She leaned back and rested her gentle finger on Sam's beak. Then all the butterflies fluttered in Sam's chest and flew him into the sky. "Tell me about your family; did you meet them quickly?"

"Y-Yes. The day you died, a very kind family adopted me."

Ai then returned to their hug, but tighter. "Do you love them?"

Sam's nares stung from the pressure of sorrow stacking within. "I do, I really do." He squeezed her as tight as his strength could bear. "Please, Mom, don't go."

Ai smiled and leaned back to look at his precious eyes once more. "I will never leave you. I promise, when I die, I'll find my way right here." Her finger met his chest like a gentle kiss that warmed him like the sun. "I hope to see your magnificent eyes and cute beak once more. And I really hope to listen to your voice again. I think that's my favorite part about you."

*Cute beak?* "But . . . I–" Sam tried to think of any way to cure her. But as his scrambling mind battled against his soul, the buildings around them started to vanish into green smoke.

"Sam, keep your focus!" George commanded.

Sam sucked in and blew out. *Just calm down.* He begged his chest-punching heart and closed his eyes. Then, he grabbed George's hand and placed his opposing wing on her shoulder, hoping it would help. *Come on. . . .*

Ai's shoulder still felt bony, and her breath still sounded like sandpaper sheets rubbing together.

"Come on!" Sam roared before looking up at Ai, seeing her tired face and some trees vanishing in the green smoke. She placed a loving hand on his cheek, forcing his stomach to rot with the feeling of failing her.

*I-I can't cure her. . . . So what can I do?* He needed her to live, even if it meant losing everything. With a final gulp of that cold, wet air, he looked at Ai's beautiful green eyes and opened his beak.

"Give me her cancer."

Even Sam could feel the weight that sank George and Ai. They both sat still, unable to close their gaped expressions. "What!" George and Ai shouted.

"Please, give it to me . . . so that you may live. . . . I survived that arch stuff; maybe I can do it again." Once Sam snuck a sniffle, it was time to go. George held Sam's shoulder–

Sam nudged him away.

"I'm not an idiot. I know you took the arch's pain from me after the vets. . . . Because you don't have the power to heal, just to transfer. It's the only way to explain your constant grimacing," Sam growled a little.

George simply couldn't close his mouth.

"I know the horror of what I'm requesting. But I won't let you go. . . . I refuse to be a burden; I refuse to leave you to die. . . . I don't know how to send you back in time." He looked at George. "But I know you can give her sickness to me, and I can carry it for a while, at least until I learn my soul." Sam chuckled. "It'll be a good incentive for me to try faster."

George and Ai looked at each other with many worries written across their faces.

She looked back at Sam. "Saiai . . ."

"I love you, Mom, and I want you to be okay, at any expense. . . . Please, let me do this."

George sat in silence, simply staring at the remaining street lights' reflection in the glimmering rain. "Okay."

Ai took a massive gasp. "Don't you dare! Just leave and live! Besides, we don't know if this is some time paradox or–"

"Even if there's a small chance that you'll be okay . . . this option, to me, is better than all outcomes," Sam interrupted.

"I'm saying no! I'm not giving you this horrible death sentence! . . . And what about your adoptive family? Don't let them go for me."

Sam froze at those words and thought hard about them. "They'd . . . be happier without me."

She looked at Sam with a sudden expression of sorrow. "That can't be true. . . . You love them." Then, to her discomfort, George stood.

Sam began to cry. He didn't want to let the Atlas family go, but how else was he supposed to save her?

George didn't do much else but turn and look at her. But that's when her eyes went wide. "You . . ."

The rain ceased, and the remaining buildings vanished into green smoke. "Is it over? Did you give it to me?" Sam begged to know.

"Yes . . . it is done."

Sam smiled and hugged her, knowing he would see her in the better future he had created. "It's going to be okay, Mom."

To Sam's surprise, Ai looked down at him with a smile.

"I will love you forever, my precious Saiai."

She vanished in his wings. He reached out with more tears than rain soaking the wooden floor of his bedroom. Then the door disappeared, leaving him with nothing but a ghost feeling of her warm hug in his . . . empty wings.

He openly stared at the room around him. His cane, the feathers on the floor from when he ripped them out, "Did it work?" He squinted at his bird body. "But . . . nothing has changed."

George fell to his knees, and with that sudden thud, Sam felt like he was just shot.

"She didn't. . ." George began as Sam felt a pinching pain he wished not to describe.

*Please . . . don't tell me.*

"She didn't die from cancer."

Sam felt it. Whatever it was, it was the worst pain he'd ever experienced. His chest sank horribly deep, and his limbs refused to move as he smacked against the hardwood floor. "I . . . couldn't save her." For a reason unknown to him, he didn't care that he just gave himself late-stage cancer. But he needed to move, to make sure George was okay after losing his daughter like that. So he breathed for a moment to stop crying. However, it was futile. He forced his body to crawl to George and grab his tiny cane along the way. "Are you alright?" Sam knew it was a stupid question; he felt like someone hung a scratchy brick from his ribs just for asking it.

"I-I need some space for a moment. Please, leave me."

Sam hesitated, and with those words, his head sank with his eyes. "Is there anything I can do? I can get stronger . . . I can try again. . . . Please–"

"I beg you . . . leave," George commanded with a heavy breath.

Those words hit Sam like a punch to the chest. He instantly turned around, and with much struggle, he limped from the room with the taps of his wobbling cane. He didn't bother saying what he was doing. He just left with the pain slowly numbing. But his body never felt heavier. Now, it was more than the weight of an ocean that sank him.

*You failed Hugo. You failed George, and you killed Ai. . . . You deserve cancer.*

He almost threw up from the sickness of those words. He

stumbled down the steps with his heart pounding against his ribs. The anticipation for what he was about to do dominated his mind like a throbbing infection. Then, he swapped the dark sword on the door's side with his cane and lumbered outside.

*You should die.*

## Chapter 8
# MOMENTO

Luna tried to reach out and stop Hugo. But the second the birds left the ground, Hugo dashed after Bipp. He heaved and huffed his heavy body past a thousand scattered, colossal trees with white, paper bark and ruby leaves like his dragon scales. He didn't even care about how colorful they rustled along with the perfect blend of amber sunset light and the twinkling stars. He only stared at Bipp, shrinking in the distance by the second.

"Let me fly!" Hugo teared up as he jumped. "I want to keep them well! Why won't you let me fly?" he screamed at his body, jumped again, and as he did, the birds lowered Bipp.

He lost sight of them beyond the leafy canopy before he entered the tower's surrounding field, full of colorful flowers peeking over a thin layer of snow. And just as he passed the final tree of the forest, he saw Bipp looking back at him.

"Hugo!" Bipp yelled before a colossal pair of twin doors shut behind him.

"Bipp!" Hugo cried, sprinting to those main doors that were so large, that even from a field away, they occupied all his sight with their chocolate boards, bolted together with dark steel and decorated with burn marks.

Hugo rammed his horns straight into the crack with a heavy thud that shoved the dust and snow from the craftsmanship. But the gargantuan door hardly budged a centimeter. He clawed up it until he was standing on his hind legs before roaring fire so loud and so strong that the flames swept across the entire wall. But it hardly stained it with soot. "Just let me be stronger! I need to save Sam! I need to know if he's . . . okay."

The world around him numbed and blurred from the impact of his headbutt against the door. He collapsed with his chin meeting the ground and lost control of his lungs as the thought of losing Bipp and Sam squeezed his malleable brain. *If Bipp dies, I will be the last Atlas on the planet. . . .* That thought made him tremble with his snout stinging. He couldn't help but hold his chest, trying to combat the empty, numb pain that pulsed with his heart. "Come on, chest, stop feeling like this!" He gripped it tighter, nearly piercing his scales with his sharp claws. "Why is this happening?" he wept and heaved in and out, faster and faster as his head felt lighter, about to pass out. His eye opened wide to the fear of being unable to do anything to save those he loved.

*He's going to be okay. . . . He's a perfect assassin; he can survive an arena battle with birds four times his size, right?* he told himself. *Also, Sam is brilliant and good at knowing when things are getting rough. He would never be in danger . . . if he could help it.*

But as the minutes passed faster than a blink, his heart sank with the sun. But, before he closed his tear-blurred eye, he saw a flower peeking over the ridge of his snout, to him unlike any other. It was a simple red dahlia that looked like a galaxy to Hugo, especially with its yellow core. *You . . . look familiar?*

Then, he felt a gentle tap on his shoulder. With his tears finally able to dry before tapping the ground, he craned his long neck to see Luna, who stared at him with a curious expression on her tilted face.

But, he focused on Luna's eyes, able to lighten his chest with sheer bliss alone. She pointed at him, spread her digits apart, and moved her hand diagonally up her face.

"I'm sorry. I don't understand." Nor was Hugo up for conversation. He looked back at the flower, then gently plucked it from its base before cradling it with the utmost care.

Luna squinted at him for a moment, as if in deep thought. But just before Hugo looked back at the door, Luna's fur burst into pure white flames.

Hugo had to squint for a bit. But it had to be the most beautiful thing he'd seen in a while. Her white fire whispered and crackled new light onto each leaf and flower petal, as if he were next to the sun, surrounded by a million colorful stars and nebulae.

She flew off the ground, but only by an inch. Then she hovered close to Hugo and put her hand on his chest. His chest melted from such heat, like wearing a sweater after it's been in the dryer, but much, much better. His bones felt like cooked noodles as they nearly pooled onto the soil. But to his dismay, she let go and pointed to the sky.

Hugo looked at his chest and rubbed it with his hand. The warm feeling itched his mind, but he shook his head to get onto more important matters. "Y-You want me to fly?"

She nodded with a smile.

Hugo looked at the ground, where his large, stubby fingers and long body lay pressed onto the thin snow and crunchy, cold leaves. But he also saw the dahlia in his hand. So, he placed it behind his ear. It looked nice in his ash-colored fur and blended well with his ruby scales. "I don't know how. . . . I'm sorry. I don't even understand the physics of how you're–"

She grabbed Hugo's mouth with a finger over the ridge of his snout. A claw threatened to take out his other eye.

He looked at her with great concern as she shook her head. Her fire vanished before she gently landed on the now-melted snow with a slushy squish.

She took a step closer to Hugo and rested her hand between his ears, shaking her head at once.

Hugo squinted with his mind twisting. "You . . . don't want me to use my head?"

She nodded and moved her hand to his chest once again.

"You want me to use my heart?" Hugo sighed at how much of a cliché that was, but part of him wanted to stall, just to keep her hand there. Hugo's eyelid began to sink with the relaxed thump of his heart against her smooth yet firm, leathery hand.

Luna rolled her eyes, shook her head, and then pushed hard against Hugo's chest. It hurt a little and made Hugo wince. But to test Luna's patience further, he shrugged.

"I'm confused."

Luna snorted, then brought her snout so close to his that they could feel each other's breaths. She pointed to her eyes, then slammed her palm against Hugo's chest.

Hugo wheezed after that strike. His ribs snapped in half, or so he thought. But after a moment of grimacing, he looked her in the eyes and gave his best guess. "My soul?" he coughed.

Luna's eyes went wide, and she gave a great smile. She then tilted her head and shrugged her shoulders to ask, 'what is it?'

Hugo looked at his chest to ensure he was alright, for he still felt her handprint's harsh yet warm echo. "I'm sorry to disappoint you again. But I don't know anything about that; I'm still a bit new to this planet. . . . But can you teach me? If it helps me learn how to fly, I'll do anything." *This might be it, Sam. I'm coming home. . . . I can't wait to see you.* He paused his thoughts and looked back at the colossal door. *But . . . I need to know that Bipp is okay first.* He placed his hand on the door and pushed, but not even a creak stirred his excitement. *If only I were stronger.*

Luna squinted at Hugo with her head still tilted from the weight of her confusion and that she hated him for being so difficult. After a few minutes of simply gawking at him, she pointed to her chest, her eyes, and then to Hugo's head.

Having no idea what that meant, Hugo just assumed. "You want to see my head?" Without delay, he bowed to her. "Uhh, sure?"

Luna exhaled like a sigh, but shrugged. After a slight pause, she rested her hand between his ears.

Hugo's head quickly felt weightless, and his eyelid sank. His body made him gulp so much air as his heart punched him with a sudden panic. *What is she–* His eye forcefully closed, but instead of darkness, came a blinding, bright light, like a blooming moonflower.

***

"I promise to protect him and love him more than anything in the world," Hugo promised to Ai. He looked at the floor, then back up at her. He was barely over three feet tall.

"You'll be a great brother. And I promise, if you ever need any help, I'll always be close by." Ai slowly released Hugo and stumbled back before standing with one hand against the wall for support.

With the remainder of his energy, he glanced at Ai before

she left the room. She looked back at Sam and him with a smile. "Take care. I'll come back to check if everything's alright after dawn." As Hugo looked at Ai's eyes, he felt the galaxy's weight on his shoulders. The feeling was something like he had never felt before. His heart thumped with an unfamiliar beat before he collapsed onto his blanket. His eyelids sank, and his vision closed around Sam. Whatever this feeling was, he wanted to keep it forever.

A shadowed hand peeked around the door's frame, and a heat wave tingled Hugo's skin. The figure could not be seen. Like a silhouette, it was as if it absorbed all light into darkness. It wasn't until the door was completely open when Hugo glanced at the figure's other hand, clenching a sharp object.

Hugo fell short of breath before a strange tingling flowed through his body. His heart pumped so fast that he could feel it beat in his fingertips. At this moment, his body took control. He flung toward Sam and miraculously leapt onto the bed before placing his body between Sam and the figure. Hugo's eyes became wide.

*What just happened?*

He glanced down at Sam before an unbearable stinging pain pierced through his back.

"No!" Andrew cried, grimacing from the boiling burns across his face and body. "Mary! Call an ambulance! The police! Anyone! It got Hugo!"

"Did . . . you always have a green eye? I could've sworn both your eyes were blue, like mine. . . . Perhaps we can get that checked," Mary asked, pointing to Hugo's left eye.

"He's been diagnosed with heterochromia iridium, rainbow pigmentation. Probably caused by injuries in the event. If I were you, I would watch him to ensure there are no psychological injuries as well. It's very possible a small child who experienced that may show some fears toward something he connects to the event. If he shows signs of trauma, I recommend taking him to a therapist," the doctor told Mary just outside of earshot to little Hugo.

"My friends are saying your brother is 'sick.' He passed out at the science fair in front of everyone and swore he saw a dead dinosaur! I mean, if that's not sick in the head, I don't know what is. . . . And if you keep helping him every time he passes out and hugging him every time he cries, they will say you're sick too. So please, stop caring about him *like that*. Just let that weirdo go. People are already beginning to talk," a friend from school told Hugo. But he didn't listen, and every time Sam needed help, Hugo gave it without hesitation.

"Please, Mom and Dad, can I stay here? I want to be homeschooled. I-It's getting to be too much." Hugo knew Sam hated asking it, because, to Sam, it felt like he was raising the surrender flag, becoming more of a burden to his kind, adoptive family.

Hugo listened to this conversation in the other room. He felt like he failed Sam, but he knew this was the best call, mainly because of how the other kids treated him. To them, Sam was an unwanted disease. Mary and Andrew agreed without question.

"My parents said I should stay away from people like you. They said you might be . . . sick."

"W-What?" Hugo asked, surprised.

"Oh, please. Don't pretend it's not already common knowledge that you *dig it* with Sam. You're so weird, loving him *that* much. You're probably the sickest out of anyone."

Those words boiled Hugo, and his heart sank once it clicked

in his mind. "Wait! Is that why . . ." he growled. "How far has this rumor gone? Did you bully Sam?" Of course, after a moment of listening to that mess, Hugo straight-up punched that kid in the face. "He is my brother! I would never lay a finger on him like that!" He began to gag with a sickening feeling rising from his throat.

"You could've fooled me."

Hugo was left in the hallway, weeping on the floor. He wanted to forget that entire sickening conversation, but before he could wipe the tears away, he got in trouble for fighting. And, of course, this wasn't the only time someone teased him for loving Sam.

But in the end, it got to his head. *Am I too much? . . . I wanted the best for him. But it seems . . . like that only made things worse.* Hugo stared at the floor of the principal's office before Mary came and knelt before him. *Is it my fault they bullied him?*

"Hey . . . are you okay?"

Hugo's face was too soaked with emotions to provide a proper answer. "M-Mom." He grabbed her tight and wept.

Mary returned the hug. "Never stop being you. I know it's hard, but know, every time I come to this office for you, I am so proud that you stood up for him."

"I-I-I-I can't keep doing this! It's all my fault! I couldn't keep out this stupid, loving feeling for him, and he got bullied for it! I-I-I wish I could hate him, so he could live a normal life."

"I understand. And I know that you won't mean those words in a few moments. But none of this is your or Sam's fault. . . . And that loving feeling isn't stupid, nor something you should ever wish away. Feelings are a pleasant truth about who we are deep down. Even if everyone around you believes that you and Sam are secret lovers, it doesn't change that truth. For you, Andrew, me, and even Sam know that family love, though sometimes *loosely* comparable to romantic love, is how you see us and we see you. . . . So please, if I could share one request, it would be never to bury how you feel, but to show it until all those around you understand the truth of you."

The tears that dripped from Hugo's cheeks slowly dried at the feeling of his mother's warm embrace and the soothing lullaby of her gentle voice. But the feeling of being too much scarred his thoughts, unable to be healed for a long time.

Sam's problems didn't cease on his first day of homeschooling. Once a week or more, Sam would have a vision. But Hugo wasn't there. Every day he watched Hugo leave for school, and he felt terrible and so, so scared. He needed Hugo and wanted to ask him to stay, but he didn't want to be a bother.

Hugo knew about this just by looking at Sam's eyes. He wanted Sam to live a normal life so badly that he kept away from him as much as possible. But one day, just as he left out the door to go to school, he heard Sam sniffle. It was subtle, but once he heard it, his legs stopped. And no matter how hard he tried, he couldn't take another step. Hugo's chest felt horrible and heavy before he almost fell to his knees and began weeping. After a few seconds, he ran back to his little brother and held him, never to let go again.

Later that day, after Hugo skipped school and held Sam for several hours, an idea popped in their heads into help with their predicament. Hugo then asked their parents: "Hey, guys . . . could I be homeschooled as well?" The question should've shocked them.

But Mary smiled as Hugo shyly looked at Sam, reading a

book in the other room about dinosaurs while occasionally glancing at Hugo with excitement moving his feet. "I'm sorry, honey, but we can't afford to homeschool two kids. The public school you go to has free textbooks, food, and other school supplies. . . ." She paused as Hugo looked down in sorrow. "But I can make you a deal. I can get a job and teach you two a little. But it would be hard work, so I'll need you to help teach Sam."

Hugo was ecstatic about that offer, but sadly, he knew that Mary would be working to the bone to accomplish a job, teaching both her kids, and being the loving mother they learned to appreciate. And Sam needed someone around all the time to comfort him when having visions. . . . It was Hugo or Mary, and a decision he didn't want to make. He looked back at Sam, whose eyelids sank with the weight of potentially being more of a bother. So, to Hugo's sorrow, he kindly refused Mary's offer, making everyone in the house question his thoughts.

Mary especially thought his refusal odd. So she kept an eye on Hugo to find out why he would refuse to be with Sam. In the end, Hugo regretted it. Sam didn't want to bother Mom or Dad about his visions, so he tried above and beyond to keep them a secret. This made Sam feel much more of a burden to Hugo. Sometimes, Hugo would come home and need to do *the thing* immediately.

After a long while of juggling their lives, Hugo arrived at college for the first time. And as he waved goodbye to Andrew and Mary, he felt a soreness in his chest and a pinch in his nose. By the time he finished the sign-in paperwork and arrived at his room, he was in tears. He dropped his suitcase adjacent to the doorway and promptly sat in the corner. He didn't know why, but he felt safer with the walls holding his back. He wiped his face in an attempt to calm down, then he curled up and wept into his arms. He was alone. Even when his first roommate arrived, Hugo never really talked to him, nor noticed he was ever there half the time. All he could think about, and all his body itched for, was the simple hug from his brother Sam. "Why am I like this?"

Every once in a while, Hugo would freak out and hide as he wept in shame. He just felt so terrified, until one day, when he was hiding in a bathroom stall, somebody knocked after he sniffled louder than he intended.

"H-Hello?" Hugo tried to sound happier.

"Mr. Hugo? Is that you in there?" a fruity voice spoke.

Hugo looked down at the classy shoes of the figure outside, knowing it was Dr. George, his current history professor. He opened the door to the accepting face of the old man. They had a long discussion about Hugo wanting to drop out.

"I'd like you to stay. Not because you're a brilliant student, or that you help fund my profession, but because you're doing this for your brother's future. Soon, he will be at the age of making those life-altering choices to go to college, and by you being here, you inspire him to make such choices. He will need your help to become the person he wants to be. To be the person who will do great things in a distant future." George leaned forward with a wink and handed Hugo a tissue. "Just hold on for another year, for him. And if you ever need any help, all you must do is knock on my office door, and I'll guide you through your current trial." Hugo thought hard about the choice, but in the end, he agreed and waited to be with Sam.

Then they were kidnapped by George and turned into creatures. They barely survived after that, but Luna seemed to pause at a certain point.

Hugo trembled at the dark crevasse before him. "I feel your

soft wing on my face," Hugo began.

Surprised, Sam glanced up at Hugo. "What else?"

"I feel the cold wind pushing against me and the crunchy snow under my feet."

"Now, what do you hear?"

After listening for a moment, she brought this memory into the clearest view.

"So, Hugo, what do you see . . . now?" Sam's voice was disrupted by what he was witnessing. Hugo could feel it. *I've never felt so light. . . .*

"How are you doing that with your hair?" Sam asked.

Hugo's head tilted. "What do you mean? I'm not doing anything."

"You mean . . . you don't feel that? A bunch of embers are floating from your back."

\*\*\*

Luna raised her hand from his head as he gasped and trembled. Embers rose from his fur like a thousand mindless fireflies. They lit up the area and danced in perfect sync with the tiny snowbulbs. "What did you just–" He opened his eye and looked up at her.

Her large mouth was agape with her eyes, staring at the embers. She was dead still; even her hand barely left his head.

"Did you just . . . go into my head?" Hugo asked, shyly looking to the side with his breaths heavy and fast. But she gave no response. He bowed to her with his heart pounding from experiencing all that again. "I'm sorry you had to see that. If I knew you were going back there, I would've–"

Luna gently lowered her trembling hand and cradled the bottom of Hugo's cheek. Tears began to flow from her eyes as she felt his smooth scales. She raised his head to look at her, then apologetically bowed before him.

Hugo stepped back, getting a weird feeling from that. "Uhh, what are you doing?"

She grabbed Hugo's hand before he could take another step, then, within a blink, she raised her head and hugged him close. Hugo flinched in surprise as Luna sniffled. She hung around his neck as her legs wobbled too much to support her for long.

In response, Hugo awkwardly hugged her with his right arm. He didn't say anything as his vivid memory flooded his mind once more, making him forget why she had gone into his head in the first place. For once she grabbed his head, he could hear Sam's voice and see his shy green eyes. How could he possibly remember after all that?

And for several minutes, only Sam took his mind as they listened to the calm embers and snowbulbs sizzle and crunch the snow. Tears escaped the grasp of his eye. He couldn't help but weep and hold Luna tighter. "I miss him," he squeaked and dove deeper into a daydream of him and Sam. That is, until the heavy creaking and screeching of wood and steel stabbed his ears and robbed his mind of Sam.

To his surprise, Luna held onto him tighter. She didn't want to let go for anything. Whatever she was sorry for, her apology was hefty.

Bipp walked from the narrowly opened door with slow steps crunching the snow in an eerie pattern. His fur was more scarlet than a rose and dripped what didn't freeze onto the crimson path behind him. Shreds of his torn cloak wisped like a cape down to his feet. Once he reached the point where the thick snow remained from the parting doors, he stopped and looked at the stars now shining in the evening dusk. His poor ears sank as the door closed behind him with a loud screech. But he continued to stand, ever so still, staring at the sky past the mountain's twin peaks.

After the quiet hush of the sunset fell below the distant shore, Bipp looked to Hugo and Luna, who hugged each other, not four skips away with a beautiful gathering of embers. He smiled, thinking the hug was romantic, but then he looked away at a silver flower. Its cute, fat petals barely surfaced in the snow. Bipp walked, then knelt with it between his thighs. He felt terrible for the flower, struggling to hold firm as snowbulbs tried to bury it. After a moment of thought, he blew over the flower to clean it up, gently cupped his hands around it, and pushed the snow from its stem. "Come, you don't need to suffer here. I know a way to make you live happily forever." He felt down to its base, then plucked it from its roots.

He stood and brought the flower to his nose. It smelt like honey as the petals tickled his nose with a soft, icy inhale. "You've grown so much. Let's not waste your potential here," he murmured, then tucked the flower under his rope belt, ensuring there was no blood there first. He looked at his chest, decorated with many scars. Then he grabbed his cloak and tried to cover his front, but it was nearly impossible in such a shredded state. "Come on," he grunted, and after a moment, he tied the holes together with a sigh. And now, with a deep gulp of air, he walked to Hugo and Luna. "What a curious day this turned out to be."

## Chapter 9
# DOUBLE-EDGED DAGGER

"Hey, you two," Bipp mumbled with his nose pointed to the ground and his hands pulling his cloak tight over his chest.

Hugo released Luna and veered back to Bipp, who still had blood dripping from nearly every hair. "Bipp!"

"Oh, wait, Hugo!" Hugo accidentally tackled Bipp into the snow, then hastily checked every inch of Bipp and wiped snow on him to remove the blood.

"I–" Bipp shyly looked to the wall of white, paper-bark trees around the field. "Thank you, Hugo, for worrying about me."

"Are you injured? What happened in there?" Hugo asked, coming up empty on his search for wounds.

Bipp's eyes began to well, and his nose scrunched with the many sniffles he gave. "I killed them. I killed every last one. They just wouldn't stop. Their leader, Exos, didn't like that I was still alive, so he sent in two at a time, then five at a time, until they were so afraid of me that the ones who remained refused to fight. So Exos let me go." Bipp dug his hands deep into the snow and grabbed the stiff dirt beneath. "I hate it. I hoped once we found peace, I would be able to stop all this violence." He looked up at Hugo, whose snout and eye looked right at him, and his kind, ruby cheeks sank with the weight of looking down like that. "I'm so sorry, Hugo. I haven't changed at all. And I made them thirsty for blood. If you go in there, they *will* throw everything they have to kill you."

"So, you're okay?"

Bipp's eyelids spread apart before a slight snort came with a chuckle. "You're insane. I just said–"

"I know what you said, but that's in the future; this is now. Are you okay?"

Bipp froze as more tears escaped his eyes. He looked to the side once more, then opened his mouth with a hesitating breath. "No . . . I'm not okay. I-I need to talk to you about something. And after what happened in there just now . . . I don't think I deserve to."

Hugo cleaned off more blood from Bipp, then smiled at him. "What do you need to talk about?"

Bipp gawked at Hugo for a second, then closed his eyes with his teeth gnashing. "I've been in so much pain holding it in. I think, I think I need your help in telling you. Because . . . I-I don't know how to describe it." He grabbed the fur over his chest. "Why does my past keep coming back to haunt me?" he whispered to himself.

Hugo glanced back at Luna, then looked to Bipp. "She has a soul ability to show your memory. Would that help?"

Bipp glanced at Luna. "I know. . . . I'm just . . . terrified of what my memories contain." Luna nodded to comfort him, then stepped closer. Now both dragons were looking at him as he lay in the snow. He sighed. "Is it possible to show Hugo my memory?" Luna nodded once more. "Okay, okay. . . . Good." He took a deep breath. "I think this will help." He closed his eyes with a squint, bracing for impact.

Luna looked at Hugo, then patted Bipp on the head while bobbing her snout to him. Hugo hesitated but set his hand between Bipp's ears. Then, without delay, Luna rested her hand over Hugo's before a blinding white light vanquished the darkness within their eyelids, again like a precious blooming moonflower.

***

"I figured out how to defeat Apotheosis! He steals all those souls, so we just need to liberate them!" A hearty-toned gentleman cheered.

This memory was blurred a little, like Bipp had just awakened.

"In a few weeks, Apotheosis will run out of lizards and birds and go straight for Rafflesia. We have to act now before he brings them to extinction."

Bipp looked up at a pure charcoal rabbit, who had him nestled in her arms. Her right eye was ruby red, and her left was bright pink. She had clothes covering her entire body, up to the brim of her neck. But she did have a pretty crown above her lovely short hair, one made from silver flowers and vines. She adjusted Bipp in her gloved hands with a look of sorrow that made Bipp's heart sink. "Please, can we just run like everyone else?" Her voice was like the softest petal kissing Bipp's already long ears.

A snow-white rabbit knelt beside her. "I know you're scared, but you are the only creature who has a chance against him. I can forge a weapon that won't melt quickly like the Saurian's arsenal, and all I need is your soul."

The charcoal rabbit looked down at Bipp. "Please, I can't. Before, I would have agreed. But now that we have him, it shows that I can be good and not some murderer." She looked up at the snowy rabbit with tears in her eyes. "Please, we can all live."

"But for how long do we have to run? How many more of our lizard and bird friends should die before it's enough? Please, he will survive, and we can finally guarantee this with a simple act."

Bipp felt uneasy at the charcoal rabbit's expression.

"He won't understand. He will think we just left him. . . . How can we be certain his life will be a good one?"

"We can be certain he'll have a life at all. Do you really want him to grow up with Apotheosis still sacrificing all those creatures? If it were to find out about your amazing soul ability, it would certainly try to kill you and our son."

"It's not that amazing." She looked at Bipp, who was confused by the words. He was more of a face reader, but he was slowly getting the hang of verbal language. "I'm sorry that you were given such a life. You just came into this world at the wrong time. Or by the wrong creature." She sniffled. "I hope you can understand that I love you more than anything. That you are the symbol that life can thrive. I was born a murderer; you were born for something different, something great. I hope you find a family who sees your extraordinary potential. My precious little silver flower."

After she said that, everyone's ears fwipped up at the sound of screaming. "No! He's here already! Quick, give me your soul!" The snowy rabbit rummaged to an anvil next to the thrones, then hammered away at an ebony dagger.

"We don't know if attaching my soul to that will work, even with your smithing soul ability!"

"We have to try, please! Otherwise, there's no hope."

The charcoal rabbit quickly looked down at Bipp. "Please, forget about us. This isn't the life a kind rabbit like you should have, especially with this cursed Rafflesian crown being in our family. I would trade it all for a little, content life." She threw the crown off her head, then sighed. "But the most important step in life is when you find someone you love, just be there for them. Be their rock; be the one who shows integrity; then, if it's meant to be, they will become your rock, and together, you can start to build mountains." She petted his ears back. "Oh, and I believe the meaning of life is to do what you love with who you love, but alas, I wasn't so lucky to get that far. This stupid crown burdened me from ever experiencing that. I always wanted to be a gardener or a botanist. Plants were always the one thing I could touch without killing them. If I could grow vegetables with you, my life would be complete." She paused, hoping to find any last words to tell him. Then, she smiled. "Just be yourself, and you'll find what you're born to do and who you're meant to be with."

And at that moment, all went dead silent as Bipp watched the snowy rabbit stab his mother deep in the chest. Her blood splatted on Bipp's face before the snowy rabbit's gloved hands pulled out a ruby-red orb and a pink orb from her chest, both like shining pearls.

"What! Two?" the snowy rabbit yelled.

Everything confused Bipp, but most of all, it drowned him in sorrow as her face lay without a blink. He gently pushed at her stomach, trying to communicate. "M-Mom!" he cried his first word. Her now-sanguine fur soaked Bipp's hands. But to Bipp, she was still alive; he needed her to be alive, so much so, anything otherwise was impossible. He tried desperately to get her to move. "Mom!" he wept and pushed as hard as his little arms could against her stomach. Then something zapped his mind and told him that he would never see her again. His lungs sank, and his breaths became weighty; his endless flow of tears swirled with the blood found on his cheeks. Something broke in him, something that would take an eternity to mend.

"Okay! Okay! I'll just make another." The rabbit hammered away, quickly making a poorly made dagger from something dark and difficult to forge by its sturdy sound against the hammer. He pressed the ruby and pink pearls individually into the knives, then held them in separate hands. "Why'd she have two souls? Nobody can have two, right?" He talked to himself for a moment, thinking. "Okay, I'll just cut him with both. One of them will destroy his souls."

Bipp's memory was blurry from the tears soaking his eyes. But just at that moment, the room grew so hot the wooden floors began to smoke and burn the snowy rabbit's feet. Even Bipp's tears dried before they could form. Then, the front door vanished in flames. A dark figure hovered into the long wooden hall, burning everything it passed. To Bipp, it looked like an eye with the narrow silhouette and snowy outside at its back.

The rabbit shouted as he ran at the figure and threw the new, pink-pearled dagger right into the figure's chest. The dark figure screeched so loud, Bipp's ears and head went numb. Not a second passed until the figure exploded in a pulse of darkness, sending shrapnel everywhere. The snowy rabbit evaporated with much of the room from the immense heat, but along with shrapnel, the ruby-pearled dagger flung back and impaled the throne Bipp was in. A splinter of wood sliced through the edge of Bipp's left ear, forcing blood to sink over his face and drip off his nose.

Then, the figure caught its breath as a swirl of dark fire

swept into the sky. Bipp didn't recognize what species of creature it was; it only had fur on its face and head. "What did he just do?"

The figure held its face and felt the white beard that weaved like frost till the middle of its neck. "I'm human?" It touched its chest and winced. "Are you still there, Snow?" the figure spoke again, but it seemed to be talking to itself. "Only a fraction, huh?" it sighed, then leaned over and plucked the pink pearl from the melted dagger on the floor, but it shattered into fine dust in its gloved hand. "A soul to remove another's soul?" It tucked its hand under its front coat buttons and grimaced. Once it withdrew its hand, its fingers dripped with blood. It looked at Bipp's mom, sitting dead on the throne.

"Luckily, I had a few tricks up my sleeve." It winced with a smile, then tilted its hand and watched the dust flutter to the now-ashen and snowed floor. "Impressive that she hid it in plain sight for so long. I always wondered why she had on so many clothes before the creatures of Zenith invent them in a hundred years or so." It laughed a little. "The creatures of this planet surprise me every day."

Bipp was so scared he couldn't move. The figure must've thought him to be dead with the blood all over him.

"I'm sure he knew that you can't use a soul outside of a body more than once. . . . unless he meant for it to be used only once." It seemed to smile. "Thank you for releasing me, but you almost killed me with that."

Then, the figure squinted at Bipp, who couldn't keep his chest still from his panicked lungs. "Oh." It lumbered closer, then stopped instantly as it spotted the ebony dagger. "I'm sorry, little one, for causing your planet such harm. I never expect you to forgive me, so–" It yanked the dagger from the throne and placed it on Bipp's lap. "If I ever return, cut me with this. Hopefully, you will never have to use it." It looked around. "Welp, it looks like you're in charge around here." It looked dead into Bipp's eyes and rubbed his ears, forcing him to squeak in fear. But it only smiled. "Protect this place. . . . Something about this planet is worth more than my future by a long shot." Its shirt dripped with blood.

Bipp couldn't fathom what happened next. The figure was gone after a swift knock on the throne. Only a trace of death remained. Bipp looked around; his mom and dad were dead. After a few moments of Bipp slowly attempting to escape shock, he passed out.

His memories blurred for a moment before the next clear thing they saw was a well-rounded cabbage in Bipp's hands.

"This one looks nice and plump, well grown. Wouldn't you say so, Dad?" By the way Bipp spoke, he was still very young. Bipp turned around to a giant rabbit sitting in a rocking chair before a sizable, cobblestone cabin with a hay roof. His body was so profound, it was problematic to the creaking wooden chair beneath. Even its arms were significant, but they only seeped fear for those to be struck by such tree logs.

"Shut ap, kid. I ain't your dad. How often do I have to explain to ya just to cut them from the ground and throw them into that there pile?" he asked in a condescending tone with the firm point of his stumpy index finger.

Bipp looked at the pile of dirty cabbages stacked in a wheelbarrow, and his heart felt uncomfortable, rather itchy in Bipp's opinion. "But . . . they don't seem very happy like that. Can we just clean them and put them back home with their friends? I mean, look at it. It spent its whole life trying to grow. I think a simple cleaning will make them feel much bet–"

The giant rabbit punched Bipp, hard. Bipp collapsed on the garden's dirt and held his numb cheek. "Do you want to go another week without food again?"

Bipp's mouth wobbled, about to cry. So he shook his head and hid his face from the rabbit.

"Then I want to see that pile doubled by the time I come back, or you will wish you were *only* starving." He wobbled away, holding up his stomach from scraping the ground.

Bipp looked at the cabbages and ran his fingers over each chasm of his malnourished ribcage. He quickly and angrily grasped the cabbage to yank it out; then, tears began to flow down his cheeks. "I'm so sorry. I need to do this to you." He began to cut at the roots with his silver dagger. "Don't worry; your family will be right behind you . . . in the . . . dirty pile." Bipp was sobbing.

After a moment, he slowly let go, then tried to fix the leaves he crunched within his grasp. "I'm so sorry. . . . I don't care if I starve again; I don't care if he beats me again. If it means you'll grow happy with your friends, then I won't lay a finger on you."

"What is wrong with you?"

The rabbit's voice sank Bipp's ears in fear. In an instant, Bipp's body tensed up with his shoulders higher than his neck, and he turned his head to the rabbit standing over him.

"It's a freaking cabbage. Did I get unlucky and find a snowflake coward in that there castle next to all that silver?" He sighed and revealed a whip made from a braid of sword grass that bloomed along its length with many cactus needles. "Stand up and face me," he commanded with a sigh.

Bipp's eyes stared at the familiar whip, and he knew what to do to prevent further lashings. He obeyed everything the rabbit told him. He stood firmly, faced him, then took off the potato sack he used for armor. Bipp instinctively placed his arms over his naked chest, but as the rabbit glared at him and grasped the whip tighter, Bipp knew he had to submit and expose his whole front. His body was one of immense sorrow and pain. Scars and dried blood decorated his chest and stomach more than his once-beautiful silver and white fur.

The rabbit began to count the cabbages in the pile. "For every one you didn't mirror, I will add a whip. I left with twenty-six in the barrow. . . . And there are still that many." He adjusted his wrist to get comfortable before taking a few paces back. "And if you wish to stop this at any point, cut just one from its roots," he scoffed, as if knowing Bipp would never do such a thing.

Bipp stood dead still and looked the rabbit in the eyes, just like he was told to do the other times. He was told it was to make him tougher. And oh boy, did it make Bipp tougher, just not in the way anyone would hope.

The rabbit pulled back and whipped Bipp diagonally across his sternum. "One," the rabbit said before pulling back again.

How slowly the rabbit whipped him was on purpose. Because, to Bipp, the wait was more painful.

He whipped again, against his lower ribs. "Two."

Bipp rarely gave him a blink.

"Three."

He listened to his fresh blood drip and tap the dirt. He stood consciously away from the cabbages, not to dirty them with his blood.

"Ten."

"I just want to know what it feels like to have a friend. Can't I pretend with the cabbages?" Bipp asked, knowing he would get punished. But his throbbing chest begged him to scream how he felt.

The rabbit scoffed at that. "That flowery comment just added another ten."

At this point in his life, Bipp stopped caring about pain. He experienced it so often that he forgot what pain was supposed to feel like to the average creature. However, the emotional pain was still somewhat fresh . . . but after every whip, his emotions felt colder. Like they no longer needed to exist.

"Fifteen."

Bipp looked at his tiny pile of belongings on an outside table where the rabbit allowed him to store his items. There were a few scratchy potato sacks for his pretend armor, the holster for his silver dagger that the rabbit gave him to cut the roots off the cabbage heads, and his ebony dagger with the ruby pearl handle. By this point, he'd forgotten how that dagger came to be. But he loved it. It was the only thing that he could say was truly his.

"Thirty."

Bipp's legs wobbled. His body couldn't take much more. Thirty-six was a lot for Bipp. He breathed carefully to keep conscious. If he passed out, the rabbit would start over like the other times. Then, he looked at the silver dagger in his hand, and tiny ideas became deep thoughts.

"Thirty-six."

Bipp gasped for breath and collapsed to the ground. *You want me to cut roots from cabbage heads, huh? Well, how about I cut the roots from* your *head and throw your skull in the-* . . . *No.* He sobbed as he feared what he was becoming. So much torment, so much hunger, it was eating him alive. He closed his eyes and held the cabbage beside him for comfort. "Anyone, please . . . like me." As the cabbage's moisture softened his hands and brought him the only friendship he had ever known, he passed out.

His memory struggled after that point. A few emotional things sparked, like the rabbit dumping him in the woods to fend for himself, and him completing the building of his little cabin. He was particularly proud of the time he made his first map in his planetary search for his family.

But the next vivid memory was when he knelt before the queen in the grand castle of Rafflesia. Soot marks still stained the floors from Apotheosis' end, but now, blood was a more apparent decoration. There were even splats of it on the ceiling. His only clothes were a burlap potato sack, a pair of brown, dirty carpenter pants, and a twine belt to support his knives. "I wish to serve under you. I hear you are searching for the souls of Apotheosis, and I can grant you ease in your search."

The white fox queen laughed at that. "Oh, a bold one. Tell me, what can a mere . . . peasant rabbit do to empower me further?"

Bipp stood and withdrew his silver dagger. The antlered knights charged at him with spears firmly aimed at his chest. He quickly threw the dagger at the queen from half the great hall away. The dagger stuck into her throne, a centimeter above her head, between her ears.

The queen glanced up; the dagger was so firmly stuck into the wooden throne, it didn't even wobble. She looked back down at Bipp, who stood over her knights with their spears through their throats, kebab style.

"Kill anyone you wish," Bipp said with a shrug and removed the blue cloak from one of the knights, then quickly wrapped it around himself after removing the potato sack.

The queen smiled. "And what shall you wish in return? I'm

certain one with your abilities wants more than to be a servant of mine."

Bipp stood firmly over her knights; his posture was divine. "What I wish is for your aid in finding my family. Please."

## Chapter 10
# DYING LIGHT

The early night was cold; the colorful leaves only hid more shadows in the edging forest. The rusty nails that loosely held the steps in place scratched the base of Sam's feet as he lumbered forth. But he felt nothing, and he heard nothing. The only thing that yanked his focus was the deadly tip of the black sword.

His good knee gave to his weight, and with it, his face and body smacked the sharp rocks of the gravel path. But yet, he still felt nothing. Because, simply put, he did not care. George could stab him in the throat, yet he would not blink.

For a reason unknown to him, his body was trembling, and his every breath came heavier and faster. He crawled to a shed with the sword carried by his clenched toes, and he collapsed behind it. And at that moment, all that had happened to him raced through his mind. *It's my fault Hugo was comatose. It's my fault he has so many scars and missing an eye. . . . It's my fault Ai is dead, and George is hurting. . . .*

With his wings hardly able to find the strength to move, he pushed himself off the gravel and pressed his back against the shed's spine-chilling wooden wall.

As the moonlight cowered behind a cloud, and the loose leaves rustled through the brisk wind, he grasped the sword's hilt with his wobbling foot and pointed the tip at his throat.

His body was trembling so much, he could hardly keep his grasp tight. And with his heart pounding like a war drum, every instinct he had was screaming at him to put the sword down. *I can be strong; I can be brave, just like you, Hugo. . . .*

Do it.

Sam wept. "Come on," he begged the sword as its tip wobbled through his neck feathers. The back of his head smacked the splintery wall as his body begged to retreat. He tried with all his will to pull the sword a little closer. But his heart pounded ferociously against his mind, pleading for him to stop. "Please. Stupid body, just let me–" Those words were all he could say as his tears tapped against the black blade and slipped down to his toes. In defense, his body began to numb his head, nearly forcing him to pass out.

*Nobody will miss you. Everyone will be happier when you're gone. And they will finally be able to breathe without you, the constant anchor, drowning them.*

Those words were familiar to him, for they were his own. The words he learned to grow up with, and the words that sank him until his final breath. . . . *Mom, Dad, Hugo,* George, *and Ai, let me help you find happiness. . . .* He closed his eyes, re-aimed the sword to make sure it'll do the job, then, at full strength, he yanked it to his throat.

The passing clouds allowed moonlight to peek onto the landscape. But this light changed the wind, warmed the frozen shadows, and hushed the leaves with a gentle embrace.

. . . . *Am I dead?* He felt the soft fabric of the sword's handle beneath his struggling bird toes and the nipping air. He peeked through his eyelids, shooting apart at what he saw.

"Please, Sam . . . don't," Hugo said, holding a claw between the sword's tip and Sam's neck.

"Mom!" Sam squawked. *What the?* He blushed at his miswording, then blinked several times in confusion before looking at the ground in sorrow. "No, you're not real. If you were, you'd want me dead if I'm not already. . . . I'm just crazy."

Hugo smiled. "I want to talk with you . . . and if you're going to kill yourself because you think it would make me happy . . . can I at least have one conversation with you before you make such a decision, please?" He relieved his claw from the sword and cradled Sam's cheek. Hugo's face was compassionate, his gentle hand, affectionate. Everything about the Hugo before him allowed his grip to loosen against the sword.

"You're part of my imagination. The real Hugo couldn't possibly know what I'm going through," he murmured in shame. *I've kept Hugo in the dark for as long as I remember. How could I tell him? My family's done so much for me, and telling them I want to end it all would change everything. But . . . would telling them be so bad? These secrets . . . they're too heavy to bear much longer.*

"Then tell me. When you find the time to go back to Somnium, find me and tell me how you feel . . . truly. And I promise I will be there for you." Suddenly, the peaceful night air took Hugo in a swirl of ruby and honey leaves that disappeared in the distant moonlight.

"Wait! Hugo!" Sam reached out and leaned forward, feeling something nudge his throat. He looked down at the sword, still grasped within his trembling toes.

"I see. So that's how you feel," a fruity voice exhaled beside him.

Sam creaked his head to George, who was now completely bald, kneeling beside him with a finger between the sword and Sam's neck. His beak opened and closed, trying to speak as new tears dripped off his cheeks.

"How long have you felt like this, Sam?" Now, George knew. Sam could no longer keep it a secret, and strangely, it almost felt liberating.

"I'm sorry."

"Don't apologize," George demanded, surprising Sam.

"I-I'm fine, really. I just needed some air, and I was curious about this sword–"

George leaned in close with his silver eyes shining in the moonlight and a sigh steaming in the cold. "Now that's out of the way, could you tell me the truth?" he asked with kind patience. And all Sam could do was water the grass with his fresh tears.

"I-I need a lot of help. . . . I can't go on like this anymore," he murmured, wishing George would take his thoughts away. George, however, took the sword away, then removed his gray coat and laid it over Sam to block the late-autumn cold. Sam looked at the night stars shining wonderfully across the countryside. "I just wish I could . . . I don't know." Sam's eyes drooped away from George, and his shivering toes gripped the grass. The urge to end his life was extinguished, but something tickled his mind: *But for how long? How long until I feel this way again? This isn't the only time. . . . I wish . . . I could . . . fix it forever.*

"Would you like me to call an ambulance or a help center?"

*You would be proving that you are weak and a burden if you ask for help.*

"No . . . I'm not worth getting help for, especially with how busy those heroes are with more important issues. And besides, I wouldn't know what to say to anyone even if I got help. Wouldn't they all just look at me as some selfish, ugly-feathered bird?"

George looked at Sam's toes, gripping the grass and dirt. "You are truly special, Sam. It pains me to see you like this. You departing from this world would shatter many hearts. And with the many lives you've touched and will soon touch, your absence would mean much loneliness and sadness for others. Your brother would've been alone his entire life if it weren't for you. And we would've never seen Ai again. . . . Please, I beg you, seek how much people value you, and I promise, not even the planet's weight in diamonds will amount to what they think of you." George pressed his head against Sam's shoulder, and for the first time to Sam's eyes, he began to weep. "Please, forgive me. I never took you as seriously as I should have." Sam looked directly at George. "Whatever's wrong, allow me to help. I can't do much in my current state, but please, above all else, never think you're a burden, because it's the furthest thing from the truth."

"But, we lost Ai because of me." *I hurt my brother . . . and you, Mr. George. Even when my mom looked at me and didn't recognize me when I was stuffed in that cage made me feel . . . like . . . she didn't want me. . . . I know she didn't mean it, but it still . . . hurt. . . . She too would be better off if I were dead. . . .* He looked at the sword.

George sniffled. "That was my fault alone. My ambitions got the better of me, and I dragged you into it. And for that, I desperately apologize, hoping you'll forgive me."

"Of course I forgive you. Even as a monster, I still have some humanity left."

George didn't like that last comment as his eyebrows drooped. Sam still blamed himself. And he wasn't seeing how much others valued him. No matter how hard he tried, only his failures, awkwardness, and how much people hated him occupied his mind. There was something about Hugo though. Despite all his flaws, Hugo looked at him with more love than anyone could ever dream of giving. And at this time, Sam needed to know why more than anything. *Why does he care about me?*

As Sam drifted away into thought, George looked at his intelligent eyes. "Come here." George carefully brought his hands around Sam and hugged him close. "Please, Sam, can you tell me how long you've felt this way?" George asked with a gentle and slow tone.

Sam took many moments before he felt comfortable talking about himself. Luckily for him, George was patient and simply kept him warm in his bony arms. He rubbed his wings against George's tweed vest and sighed. "It's a long story. . . . Why are you bald?" Sam tried to change the subject.

"We each have a way to remember and keep our loved ones close. . . ." He sighed with his fingers meeting the smooth skin on his head. "About you now, we have all the time in the world for a long story."

Sam chuckled a little to hide how serious this was for him. He took a long moment, hoping George would talk first and change the course of the conversation. But with no progress, he sighed. "Alright. . . . I-I guess it all started in elementary school. I was normal and was trying to be more like Hugo. I helped my friends with homework, carrying their books to class. It was fun."

"But, one day, at the school's science fair . . . I passed out after having a vision of a dead velociraptor. It was so lifelike, and there was blood everywhere." Sam closed his eyes and shook his head in a shiver. "And the more I think about it, the more it reminds me of Anzu, that dinosaur with the white shirt I met. . . . But I like him, and I hate thinking about it and those black, lifeless eyes I saw. So I'm going to shut up." He took a moment to breathe with his wings over his eyes, doing *the thing.*

*It's not real. I don't see those black eyes or the blood soaking my shoes. Just close your eyes and know it will be okay. . . .* He took a deep gulp of air, then continued.

"In the end, the doctors wrote it off as stage fright, but I doubt it was the case, especially with the new info on my soul being connected to passing out in some way. . . . Anyway, I-I didn't get better. Once the feeling of passing out stuck, it was over. And I would pass out during school several times a week. I got to be so anxious about it, that it was all I thought about. And eventually, when my old friends tried talking to me, it would be too much, and I'd pass out. Hugo would frequently leave his class and visit me in the nurse's office. I always gave him a bad grade because he wasn't in class . . . he was taking care of me." Sam looked down. The feelings he had back then were coming back fresh as he spoke.

"My mom came as well, but after the hundredth time or whatever, Hugo told her that he would take care of me by himself, because she was busy with errands, and spending that much money on fuel kinda made me feel like a burden. So, he took care of me. Then the bullying began. My old friends wouldn't come near me or drink from the same fountain because they said I had some contagious disease. And if anyone spoke to me or interacted with me at all, they would 'get it.' The teachers ended up in the mix of all of it, and they believed the other children because I was too socially anxious to say anything in defense." He took a moment to think.

"Eventually, I begged my parents to homeschool me. They agreed, but I know Hugo felt that he failed me. He and I had such fun on the bus rides to school, and I know he didn't mind seeing me in the nurse's office. But I just couldn't take it anymore. No matter what I did, I was a burden. I hated it, all of it. Going to school was a nightmare, and I felt like an anchor to everyone around me. I even heard teachers talk about putting me in special classes, so I wouldn't bring the other students down with me . . . especially with the team projects." Sam covered his eyes again, trying to calm his breaths. "E-Even the homeschooling didn't help much, because I felt I was wasting my mom's time as she tried to teach me."

He paused with his wobbling beak about to burst, remembering Mary's kind face. His cheeks became warm before he shook his head. "B-But I decided to be homeschooled, and from then on, I was alone for most of the day. Hugo still had to go to school. He asked to be homeschooled with me, but we couldn't afford it. Since I was adopted, I might have gotten free school supplies or something, but that doesn't matter. . . . I always thought they told me that so I wouldn't feel bad. . . ."

"Anyway, Hugo would leave, and I would be alone with my books, trying to control my stupid visions and blacking out every time I got a little anxious. I needed him. But he wasn't there until the afternoon and summers, and," Sam's eyelids fell as he looked at the grass, "it was a lot for me. I started seeing myself as more of a pest my family needed to take care of, rather than an actual member of the family. . . . I guess that about sums it up, apart from what happened at college and after. . . . Sorry to go on for so long. I did say it was a long story."

"Do you still think of yourself as a pest or an anchor?" George asked.

Sam looked at the tall grass filling the vast space between his leathery toes. "No–" Sam paused for a second. *Don't lie; I need the help. And I think I can trust him now. He wouldn't have saved me just then if he wanted me dead. . . . Okay, okay.* He took many deep breaths and shyly looked at George's leathery shoes. "Yes. . . . I try hard to be helpful, so people don't look at me like a pest. But it's so odd, like I'm cursed to always need help."

"You said earlier that you needed help, but do you want help? Know there is a big difference."

Sam squinted at the grass again, his beak half open. "I–" but he closed it and looked away from George. He exhaled through his nares with a stinging sorrow rising in his throat.

"Hey . . . you're not a burden."

Sam's eyes welled with tears that he couldn't suppress.

"Can you say it for me?"

Sam opened his beak, but not a sound left his tongue. Even with his greatest effort, that was one lie he couldn't tell.

"Can you look at me?"

Sam closed his watery eyes and hid most of his face under his wings.

George sighed. "Alright then, a topic for later. . . . But is this why you fear doctors, because you're afraid of receiving help and being a burden in the process?"

His stomach squirmed at how close George was to figuring him out, but his heart felt lighter, as if George knowing was actually a good thing. "Y-Yes," he forced out his beak in a murmur, unsure if George would hear. He left it up to fate whether he deserved help.

George smirked. "Well, needing help is what makes people human." George leaned close to Sam with a peculiar smile. "And even changing into a bird won't help that." With a mighty grunt, George stood and carried Sam back to the house in his arms. He limped without his cane. "I think it's important to let others help you. As a doctor, I never looked at my patients and thought, 'oh, this person's a horrible, no-good, burden, and they're wasting my time with their problems.'"

Sam almost laughed at that. But as his beak snorted, his blurry eyes caught a white flake of snow dancing in the moonlight. It fell onto the garden of ruby autumn leaves with such a gentle touch.

"No!" George chuckled, and Sam flinched as his mind returned to the conversation. "I never once felt that with them; I was happy to help! So, why do you think they feel that way toward you?"

"I don't know. . . . I guess I developed that way of thinking over time." Sam watched the sky for more, and to his surprise, many snowflakes followed. *Is it winter already?*

George smiled. "Don't worry. If you ever think of the reason, I'll be here. But just think, when you help Hugo with his fear of the dark, do you feel like he's a burden?"

That question jump-started Sam's head like a punch to the cheek, and his eyes began to water with the regret of how stupid he was. He loves Hugo and would never think of such a thing. And if Hugo loves him more than he could imagine, as George says, *then it's impossible for Hugo to look at me as a burden.* He looked up at George, particularly his frosty beard right before his beak. He felt his cold hands holding his backside and his beating, human chest right against his wing. Then, butterflies fluttered about Sam's chest as he thought about one thing.

"M-Mr. George? M-May I become a doctor, like you?"

George froze in place.

Sam instantly regretted asking that. "I-I know. How can I be a doctor if I'm afraid of them. . . . But if you–" He blushed hard as George looked at him with a thoughtful squint and slowly resumed the walk. He tugged George's coat over his beak. "Well, I was wondering if you'd be willing to teach me to help people?" He hid completely, tucking the coat over his head, feeling safe from *that* conversation. *I'm such an idiot. . . . How could a useless bird, who can't even help his own family, ever dream of helping people to the extent of a doctor. . . . Just laugh at me and get it over with.*

"First step. Don't worry about people thinking of you as a pest or an anchor, because it's not about you. To help someone, sometimes you need to care, really care about them like they are the only person in the universe. If you worry about what they think of you, you'll only sink deeper into that ocean of yours. And above all, place their needs before your own, but not instead of your own. . . . Do you understand? That last part is crucial."

Sam slowly peeked from the coat to George smiling at him.

"I think you can be a great doctor, especially if you keep that lesson close to you. But there is a reason I am not a professor for med students, so I'm sorry to say, if you want to change your program from paleontology with a history emphasis, to medicine, you'll have to find a new teacher."

"Thank you . . . Dr. George." Sam hated saying his name like that. He felt the unconscious ocean try to suck him in with a dizzying head, and he threw the coat over him again.

*No matter what you try, you will never amount to anything. No matter how hard you weep, you will always be the monster in the mirror.*

Sam nearly threw up from the venomous sound of that voice.

"Pardon me for changing the topic, but this has been on my mind for a moment. . . . Those *ugly feathers* you see, are critical differences that made you, the person your family fell in love with. So please, if I could ask a favor, don't change who you are, especially the good parts." He winked, gesturing to all of him as he peeked from the coat. "I like that you'd consider changing who you want to be. But if that's not who you want to be, rather what you think you're supposed to be, be careful. You are going to fail many times along the path of being who you are *supposed* to be, especially if meeting unhealthy expectations is what defines success."

"But the best way to succeed is by simply being you and being really good at it. If who you are is a potential doctor, who wants to help a million life forms, then go for it. If who you are is a bird, who wants to ride dinosaurs toward the sunset on top of Hugo's spaceship, then absolutely go for it." He winked at him with a smile and a nasal chuckle. "You are already enough; you were enough the moment Ai saw you for the first time. . . . And if you need help in any phase of life, please ask, no matter how difficult it may seem with that social anxiety of yours. Fight through and ask, because hardly anyone can tell how you feel, but almost everyone around you is glad to help." George took a moment for Sam to settle after that. "So, are you ready for your next step?"

*Please, stop reading my mind. . . . Though, thank you for that speech.* Sam didn't want to talk for a long while. He felt too vulnerable after George dissected his brain and told him all that. He trusted George, but he simply needed time. And after a moment or ten of deep thought, Sam looked up at George's face. "What's my next step?"

George scaled the porch steps with his face grimacing; then, he knocked on the main door's frame. "To finally understand who you want to be. . . . I'm sorry the other two steps of helping Hugo and Ai fell through. I originally assigned those as exams and this final one as an early 'final exam or graduation present.' Pardon me for my college professor ways, but I'd say you've passed well enough."

George opened the door to his college office with the familiar bookshelves and desk that refreshed Sam's memory. Then, George turned around and shut the door behind him.

"What are we doing here?" Sam looked around at where it all began.

"Just a slight detour for reasons that may or may not come. I simply like to prepare, just in case." George slid off his old shoes and knocked on the empty wall beside the bookshelves. The entire time, Sam stared at him quizzically. The familiar wooden door to Somnium appeared with the flowers and spheres that resembled the planet. George opened the door to the stone room, where he turned Hugo and Sam into creatures.

Sam instantly recognized the altars and two burbling vials under the glowing blue hue of the wall torch's flickering flame. Even Hugo and Sam's old clothes remained on the floor.

George braced the door with his shoe, then walked to another wall and knocked on it.

Sam looked down at George's legs, and . . . he wasn't using a cane! "Wait! How are you carrying me?"

George opened the door to a forest with trees broader and taller than most skyscrapers. Many glowing mushrooms dotted the roots with a multi-colored glow. He slid off his other shoe against the door to hold it open before looking at Sam with a smile. "We're almost there, just one more door. You ready?"

"No! How are you walking? Doesn't this hurt you? And why are you taking off your shoes? How are you breathing on this planet? You lied to me! You said humans can't survive on this planet!"

George knocked on a tree, and on that knock came a wooden door. But there was a look of sadness across his eyes. "You're worth every pinch of pain. . . . And I didn't lie to you. Pure humans indeed cannot breathe on this planet. It's just, I'm not . . . all human. You see, I once was an Anthophytan before I lost the soul that made me such. Luckily, it wasn't my own." George winked, then opened the door to a freezing wind of shooting white sparkles.

Sam flinched from that brisk wake-up. "You mean, if I get rid of my soul, I'll become human again?" He tucked George's coat tight around himself.

But George simply stared out with his frosty beard whipping in the wind, as if he were unaffected by the cold. "You'll see what I mean, maybe one day." George squinted in thought for a long moment. "But, please . . . don't try to change this way. . . . *You* only have one soul, one chance. . . . The potion you drank sticks to that soul and part of your mind. . . . If you somehow acquired another soul and removed yours, there's no telling what could happen. Sure, you might become human again. . . . But you might not be you anymore, and if that soul isn't given to you by its owner, you will feel pain unlike any other. . . . Trust me, when I was a cat, I was in so much pain, I could hardly think. . . . Souls make up a *huge* part of who we are. So, since you only had one soul when you drank my potion, I'm sorry to say–"

"The only way is to use my time ability."

George looked away with a thoughtful nod. "Though be very careful when trying. If you go back in time, you will become a pure human. So make sure you're on Earth when this happens. Otherwise . . . well . . . you know why." George paused his walk. "That being said . . . I wish to give you a final chance, for what lies ahead may be too much. We can go back, and together, we can try to turn you into a human again. You can go home. . . . Just let me know."

Sam didn't even have time to open his beak.

*Considering giving up already? All this effort, all this time, wasted? You should've killed yourself before all this happened to spare everyone you've touched the burden of knowing you.*

Sam felt a cumbersome weight on his chest and his body instantly weaken. Even after all the kind things George said, just those few sentences were enough to make him want to have never existed.

And after a moment of uncomfortable thoughts, he shook his head to what he saw, watching the frail, old man continue to shift through the knee-high snow while carrying him. He then knew frail was the opposite word to describe him. Sam accepted it, but didn't like it. He thought he was being helpful to George, helping him walk, make breakfast on occasion, but–

*He doesn't need your help.*

With a sudden weight sinking his eyelids, Sam lowered his beak beneath the coat's collar to hide his feelings from George. Then, a stench like iron and fish teased his cold, snot-filled nares. "What?" Sam murmured, looking to his right before he saw it: the massive glacier wall from when he and Hugo were lost in this infinite winter. "Why are we here?" Sam asked, mildly afraid. Just as he saw the same crevasse he entered once with

Hugo, a wisp of black fire retreated into the dark. His heart dropped before George carried him closer.

"This is where my journey as your professor ends, Sam. This is where you become the greatest person to ever live and gain the ability to help everyone."

The stench forced Sam to grimace. "W-Why can't you do it? You're more than capable! You can walk for goodness' sake!" Sam halfway joked, refusing to accept such a compliment.

George looked away from Sam with a world of thought dragging him down. "I shouldn't. . . . When my wife was losing the battle against cancer, this power convinced me to try anything to help her. . . . And I hurt creatures, stealing their souls. . . . Then, Ai died. . . . I lost myself and attempted to steal your time soul to save her and undo my horrible actions; I was blind to see the damage I was doing, even when I stabbed Hugo."

Sam froze.

"I thought once I had the power, I could save people from death. . . ." He looked Sam in the eyes. "I shouldn't have this power, for I still want more than anything to bring Ai and your grandma back. And I fear it may tempt me to kill once more."

*So it was him that came that night. . . . He is the reason Hugo had those scars and is afraid of the dark. . . . But if it weren't for me needing to be protected, Hugo would be fine.* Sam looked at his leathery toes. "Is that why you didn't adopt me, Grandpa? Because you were afraid of hurting me?"

For the first time in Sam's eyes, George froze stiff. "Don't call me that, please. . . . I'm not worthy of such a title." He sighed, shyly looking away from Sam once more. "But you're right; I didn't trust myself after I attempted to take your soul. And I deeply regret hurting your family, especially the damage

I caused Hugo that night. . . . I have no excuse and nothing to say other than . . . I'm sorry. . . . Though I should really be apologizing to Hugo."

Sam held George's hand with his wing and looked right at him. "It's okay, Grandpa. We can apologize to him together."

Tears dripped from George's eyes. In fear, he liberated his hand from Sam's gentle grasp. But he couldn't help but look at him. "Ai never trusted me with you for many good reasons. . . . But when she died, I went to your hospital room because I was the only living relative. And boy was I nervous that I might hurt you. But when Hugo came in demanding to be your brother, even after all the damage I did, I saw hope for you to live a normal life, and I put you up for adoption the second they got the papers ready." George chuckled, but only for a moment. "Everyone thought I was some lawyer by the way I was dressed. Such a bizarre family you've stumbled upon."

The sadness within George's face turned more joyful. "I'm glad who you grew into, wanting to help people not out of a desire to be with them, but your generous heart hoping for them to be happy." George poked Sam's chest. "Right?" He asked just as they reached the crevasse. He set Sam down into the waist-high, fluffy snow.

The blood river flowing from the glacier soaked the snow crimson and warm where George stood. Sam looked at the darkness before them. "What if I'm not what you think I am?" Sam's throat begged him to ask that with a gulp.

"Don't worry. So as long as you hold firm to who you are and wish to help others, truly. Then, it should give you the power to do so without question. Just don't think of anything else with this power, or it will change just as easily as your thoughts and seep through your uncertainty. It's very . . .

tricky."

Sam growled at that dodged answer. "I know I'm not strong enough for this, and I'm not what you say. I mean, I *desperately* want Ai back. And to be honest, part of me still wants to . . ." He grunted. "You know. . . . Will it just finish the job? . . . And also . . . can it cure the cancer I just received? That's going to be hard to get off my mind." Just as he finished that sentence, the sound of fire crackled from the dark.

*You've finally come to me.*

He froze, not wanting to move a millimeter.

George sighed. "You're right; it will see that you wanted to kill yourself . . . but don't worry. It shouldn't be able to finish the job, only try to convince you of doing such to obtain your soul. But you'll know when that time comes if it does, because it will start by forcing its voice in your head."

Sam didn't blink as his wide eyes crept to George, who glanced at him with a hint of worry that made Sam's stomach sink.

"The second I started hearing it . . . I discovered I couldn't even control how I breathed." George looked at the snow. "And when it didn't see me as a good co-pilot, I noticed I couldn't control the fire, my body, or even my soul ability in the worst case, as if I was sharing a body and soul with someone far more assertive."

Sam's chest and throat began to itch with a familiar tickle, like the throbbing memory of something sliding up his gullet.

George chuckled and excused his previous words with a wave of his hand. "This is why you must be strong and show your body that you are worthy of it when the time comes. . . . Anyway, cancer cannot be cured by this power as it is now. . . . But with *your* soul ability, once it teaches you about your new abilities, you can take your body back a few hours or years if needed." He paused with a hopeful smile at Sam. "You'll probably be more than twice as strong as me when I used it and finally eradicate cancer from everyone. . . . It is risky, but I'm sure you'll be okay," he finished with a nervous chuckle.

All Sam could do was stand frozen before the crackling flame that crawled from the abyss. Even though his heart was thumping and his leg was shaking at the long list of dangers and risks associated with this flame, he couldn't help but feel his wing twitch at the thought of touching it.

"I-I can finally be helpful?"

# Chapter 11
## TALL EARS, SHARP CLAWS, AND BIG HEARTS

Bipp's eyes slowly peeked open to Hugo and Luna's snouts. They looked at him with great concern.

Bipp instantly held his head as tears ran down his face. "Did you two see that?" he asked before they both nodded. With a shy squint, Bipp looked at Hugo. "Good. . . . C-Can we go over there in private?" He wiped his eyes and pointed to a distant, lonely, paper-bark tree. "I just need to talk with you." He looked at Luna. "I'm sorry, but could you wait a moment, please?"

Luna bowed, respecting Bipp's wishes.

Hugo simply nodded, for his mind scrambled with what he saw in Bipp's memory. *That figure . . . was the same one from when I was a kid. . . . So, Apotheosis . . .*

Bipp excused himself from their immediate presence and walked with his head down in thought.

"So, that's it then . . . George is Apotheosis, the same figure I saw *that* night." Hugo turned to Luna, who then gave a concerned nod, but it was confident enough for Hugo to accept. *So George came into my house and stabbed me when I was a kid. . . . But why? Was it to obtain Sam's soul? If all that is true . . . then why didn't he finish it? Why did he show Sam and me so much kindness when we were at college? We roomed right across the hall from his office; he could've easily killed us! There has to be something more to this that I'm not seeing!*

He shivered, looked away to think of something less stressful, and then turned back to her. "S-Since Bipp and I saw Apotheosis when we were kids . . . how long is a year on this planet? Because Bipp says Apotheosis disappeared about two-hundred years ago, and it's hard to believe Bipp is two-hundred. . . . George . . . maybe."

Luna raised her right hand with all four fingers extended, then made a zero.

"I understand . . . thank you." He bowed to her as a secondary thank you, then turned to follow Bipp. He looked near the sun, *much* more significant in the sky than Earth's sun and slightly more amber in color. *To have that few days in a solar orbit. . . . I would guess a dwarf star of some kind if it had lower luminosity. But since it's quite bright, maybe an orange supergiant then, and we're just orbiting super fast? If so, I wonder if its mass affects time here, or how far it is from collapsing into a supernova. . . . If time is involved, then how long have I been away from Sam in his perspective?* He shook his head as his eye stung with the welling of tears. *I need to stop being such a space nut.* He paused and looked at the grass between his fingers. *But a forty-day year . . . that makes Bipp about my age. . . . I'd like to know more about the creatures here, like life expectancy, different species and attributes, seasons, and especially all this soul stuff. . . .*

He followed Bipp until he sat near the base of a white tree, whose creaking branches bore no leaves to block the night sky. Large clusters of snowbulbs gently kissed Bipp's head and melted in his fur, making him wipe his eyes even more.

"They died to protect my future," he murmured to himself as Hugo took a few steps and lay next to him. "I'm glad we met Luna. I would still be searching for my family in the back of my mind." He patted his side, then withdrew the ebony dagger with the rose-red pearl. "I-I'm so lucky I never used this to harm someone. I knew it was special, but–" he rubbed the pearl, "I never would've thought my mother was with me this whole time.... Sorry for using you to cut vegetables, Mom, but I'm glad you were there to help me with the gardening," Bipp chuckled. He couldn't contain his rising cheeks from the joy of speaking to his mother for the first time. "Thank you, Mom, for everything you've done for me, and for the advice you gave before you passed.... To do what you love with who you love..."

After almost a minute of staring at the distance in thought, Bipp carefully put the dagger back in the sheath and looked at the stars and nebulae past the tree branches. The view sparkled around the tower's silhouette like a shimmering coat. "I am the luckiest rabbit in the universe to have found you on that beach. It could've been anyone, or a different time... and our stories would've been... *really* different." He gulped, then reclined back against the tree. He felt the cold paper-like bark shift and crack under his weight. "Because of you, I see this world differently. I look at the stars and see what you mean when you say 'curious.' Before I met you, I was so focused on finding someone to accept me.... Heck, it hurt trying to find a creature who would even smile at me, because nobody ever did."

He paused again for a long while to look at the scene around him and feel how lucky he was. "Thank you so, so much for accepting this rabbit and for helping me escape," his throat subtly squeaked before he turned to admire Hugo. "S-Since you know a lot about me, do you have any questions, something I forgot to explain about this planet?"

Hugo shifted his body until his eye and snout were a foot beyond Bipp's eyes. "I have a thousand questions, but you're more important right now. Are you alright? Your memories were . . . traumatizing."

Bipp blushed as he looked away from Hugo. "Yeah, my past isn't great. But every challenging thing in my life has made me the creature I am today. And because of who I am, you accepted me. I think that's the best life anyone could wish for. Sure, it makes me angry that there are creatures like that farmer. But I wish not to harm them, only for a way to throw back what they do to creatures. . . . I just feel like . . . if they felt the pain they give and understood the creatures they hurt, they would stop, right? . . . I think I hate that feeling above all others, that you're hopeless and just have to take it."

Bipp's fur sparkled like someone just threw glitter all over him. Hugo blinked, assuming his eye and the moonlight sparkling through the branches were playing tricks on him.

"A-Am I evil for thinking this? I don't like bad things happening to creatures; I just want a way to show them who they are and what they've done, you know?"

Hugo smiled. "I have never once thought of you as evil, Bipp."

Bipp chuckled with a nervous grasp behind his neck. "I'm glad . . . because I experienced the worst with that farmer, and I feared to become like him. . . . I guess I still fear it. . . ." He gulped. "I just want to save creatures before they get to that point, where they have no other choice but to . . . well . . . decapitate their bullies."

Bipp waved his hand to forget it. "That's why I'm so glad I met you. You corrected me and showed me a little light. You show so much care for others, it makes my wish to help the hopeless seem possible." He shyly looked down at his lap, and his breaths steamed farther from his nose. "With all the things you do and say . . . you make me want to be a better rabbit. . . ." He withdrew his silver dagger and stared at it in his wobbling hands. "It's time. . . . I need to get rid of this. . . . Can you, help me?"

Bipp tried to drop it, but his instinct refused. Even looking at it forced him to grip it tight, ready to kill. "I haven't been able to do it on my own."

"Here," Hugo spoke and wrangled his body until they were shoulder to shoulder.

Bipp looked at Hugo's eye, how calm it was, and how he was willing to help him without hesitation. Hugo rested a hand beneath the dagger, and for the first time in a lifetime, Bipp's arms relaxed and lowered until his empty hands curled in the snow.

Hugo took the small dagger and observed how clean it was considering its history of blood. He then looked at Bipp once more before Bipp nodded.

Then before Bipp could blink, Hugo wound up his arm and threw it deep into the woods, near the trickling sound of a river, hoping it would be swept away and rusted into nothing.

Bipp then felt relief he had never experienced in his life as his shoulders relaxed and his breathing slowed. "The silver flash is gone. . . . It's you and me, and whoever else wants to join our family." As Hugo lay there with the snowy wind waving his fur in the moonlight, Bipp couldn't help but stare. Hugo's heat raised the snowbulbs around them like hot air balloons, forming a grand canopy of ice-twinkling spheres upon their renewed descent. His large, stumpy fingers and strong arms were willing to hold, or his sharp claws ready to protect. And his single eye and big ears were always listening to every word, like he genuinely cared. "Remember, when you said that telling Sam you love him was . . . difficult?"

Hugo's ears rose; then he looked at Bipp, who looked at his lap with a shy grimace built by his scrunched cheeks. Hugo wrangled his body again until he was all in front of Bipp. "Yeah, it is difficult, but yet . . . oddly curious. . . . I want to tell him how I feel. But how I feel is just so hard to say. . . . I hear people say 'I love you' to describe their feelings in many instances. But when I listen to them use it, I don't feel it. I don't see the value of that word. I mean, it means something nice, but not what I–" he grunted and thought for a second. "I try never to use that word unless I really mean it, so it doesn't get dulled by my overuse. But just listening to others use it so much might have dulled it into being cliché. It's rather sad not having the words to say. But when I think about telling him, all I can think are those words."

Bipp chuckled with his nervous smile. "You are the most bizarre creature I have ever met." He sat up and consciously breathed deep and slow breaths. "There are more ways to tell someone you love them than just words."

Hugo's ears rose at that, and he wanted to slap himself in the face at how obvious that was. But then, Bipp grabbed his attention when he withdrew the fat, silver flower from his rope belt.

"I see creatures doing this sometimes." Bipp shyly looked to the side with his eyes begging to shut. "I . . . like this method. .

. . Giving creatures things to show how much they mean to me . . . I guess I'm more of a gift-giver." Bipp held onto the flower near his lap, looking at it as he continued. "But there are other ways, of course. You just need to do what feels right, and I'm sure Sam will understand. . . . Show him in your way, the special *Hugo* way."

*The Hugo way?* Hugo looked back at his scarf, then observed Bipp holding the back of his neck again and closing his eyes over a grin. He was incredibly nervous about eye contact. *A gift-giver, huh?*

"I–" Bipp paused and scooted a little further from Hugo. The words that tried to escape him were so heavy that his face drooped to his chest, and his eyes closed.

"Hey, it's okay." Hugo lowered his head to meet Bipp's sinking expression. "Just take your time. I don't plan on going anywhere."

"Heh," Bipp peeked open an eye and raised the flower to Hugo, but he kept his head down. "I-I have been meaning to ask you a question. I guess it's why I've been a bit . . . awkward lately. . . . May I ask?" The flower began to wobble with his hands.

"Sure, what is it?"

Bipp took a moment to prepare by fingering his hair and drooping ears away from his sight. But once he looked Hugo in the eye, he scrunched his eyes closed and opened his heavy mouth. "Now that you know all about me, flaws and all . . . w-would you like to be my soul companion?" He tensed up, shoulders above neck, as if he was expecting Hugo to punch him in the face for asking that. His arms were fully extended, presenting the flower to Hugo, whose head tilted in confusion.

"Umm, what's a soul companion?"

Bipp slowly yet deeply breathed in and out until his heartbeat slowed, then he shyly looked at Hugo. "Heh, sorry, I sometimes forget you're not from this planet. . . . Well, a soul companion is a sort of promise to a pair of creatures that they will always be together. And after death, their souls will be together in the afterlife." Bipp was blushing with his head low. "It is a bit awkward since it's an old tradition, but I always liked the idea of having a soul companion. I just never got to know any creatures that well, until I met you. . . . You are the first creature in my life who was kind to me and thought I was good enough to call family." Bipp's mouth wobbled, and his eyes welled. "And you never stopped. . . . I-I . . . really like you, and I . . . love being with you. S-So, do you want to be soul companions with me?" Bipp asked again but with river-flowing eyes soaking his warm cheeks.

But Hugo was still confused as to what it meant. "May I ask for a little more detail?" Hugo asked with his head low, trying to seem gentle about the question.

Bipp's hands began to shake, and he retreated the flower back to his chest. "Uh. That's really all it is. Just a promise to be together. I-Is there something you want me to change? Because I can change! Whatever you want! Cut my fur, make you more soup, anything!"

Hugo quickly put his hand over Bipp's mouth. "Please, don't change anything about you. I . . . really like you too. . . . Heh." He relieved his hand from Bipp. "Just explain this promise to me. I'm very confused, and I don't know what most stuff means quite yet. Because, to me, it sounds like you want to marry me."

Bipp froze, then once it clicked, a subtle snort twitched his nose, and he smiled. "I see. . . . No, no, no. Marriage is much more . . . intense than this. They are similar, just without the . . . you know . . . kissing." Bipp looked away from Hugo and waved his hand to relieve himself from *that* topic. "Marriage usually involves a bracelet, made from something that represents the asker and asked. If you're asked, one goes on your left arm, right if you're the asker. Plus, there's a tradition-type rule in Anthophyta that states you can only marry if both creatures have seen two shooting stars, wishing upon the first, to help you give love, and the second, to help you find love."

He looked back at the flower. "However, soul companionship can be done anytime and is represented by a flower wrapped somewhere on the arm of your choosing, leg if you're a bird. . . . I swear, *this* is only a promise. I'll be with you, and you'll be with me. Protecting each other, going on more adventures together . . . and maybe, if you're comfortable with it . . . living together in our cabin. Basically, what we've been doing this whole time but more official, and with a little hope for the myth about souls being together to come with it. So, you want to?" he asked a third time with a shy smile, looking at Hugo.

Hugo couldn't help but smile back at him. The culture of this planet intrigued him so much that something sparked his mind. *Maybe Sam was right. . . . I think I like it here. . . .* "Yes, I'll gladly be your soul companion," Hugo said, quite excited about the whole thing.

Bipp gave a huge grin, and his foot thumped the ground with many instinctive twitches. "Thank you!" Bipp squeaked and bowed to Hugo before gesturing that he'd see either arm. Hugo curiously gave his left hand to Bipp, who then tied the flower around his lower arm with a fancy knot. "There, now it is official."

Hugo looked at the silver flower. "So, is this like a friendship bracelet?"

Bipp snorted. "No . . . well, kind of. Each flower is grown from a soul, the orb things you may have seen. . . . Souls second as seeds. It's a little nerve-wracking to see flowers, because it means someone died, but it also shows something beautiful: that life can continue even after death. Flowers are the only plants that bloom year-round, because there's a hint of a creature's memory-magic in each one, or so I've read. . . . And the evilest act someone can do is destroy a soul, because it robs creatures of their forever happiness and the beautiful flowers their afterlife memories create. . . ." He paused for a second and looked at the ruby pearl at the pommel of his dagger with sorrow sinking his eyes.

"Also, out of respect for each memory, it's best not to step on any flowers. I know it's hard, given there are so many, and our feet are big. But trust me; I learned that the hard way." He looked at the flower wrapped around Hugo's wrist. "The flower we pluck for soul companionship is a way to honor the dead by keeping them in our lives. And, when you pluck a flower from the dirt, it will last forever; this is why it is the symbol of a soul companionship." Bipp smiled a little. "In addition to all that, few still believe that the flowers and souls who still want to be part of our lives, can hear us. . . . That's why I've been talking to my mom's soul here, hoping she can hear me. . . . But now that I know this is a soul . . . I feel like a proper burial is needed soon; I'd hate to postpone her wondrous afterlife." He nuzzled the soul against his cheek, hoping to receive the feeling of his mother's embrace.

"Flowers are the result of souls that have been buried?" Hugo asked, a little frightened, especially once he thought of

King's Garden and where they currently were with how many flowers he saw. He removed the ruby dahlia flower from his hair and admired it. *Flowers last forever, huh?*

"Yup, but don't worry. One will grow back once you pick it, because the creature's memory will remain with the soul's *seed* per se. Just think of them as perennial plants. I chose that flower because it looks like me, and I saw it once I knew for certain I wanted to ask you."

Hugo took a moment in a thoughtful squint. "What happened at King's Garden?"

Bipp's eyes widened. "Oh, you didn't– . . . I'm sorry. It's such a common thing that creatures know; I guess I might've skipped it. . . . Then, I'm assuming the flower thing is not the same on your planet?"

Hugo hesitated, then shook his head.

"Oh." Bipp paused with a blink. "Well, King's Garden is a sad story, and it has the name 'garden' for a reason. . . . The king, Apotheosis, did a lot of 'harvesting' when it came to souls. Then on the last day of his rule, he wiped out an entire city, Rafflesia. But before he could take the souls from the bodies, he vanished and left a valley full of souls to be sunken into the mud from the occasional rain before they all bloomed into flowers."

Bipp looked away for a second. "I guess I was there when it happened . . . when my dad removed Apotheosis' souls." He scoffed. "I need to do more research on the previous rulers of Rafflesia. I never thought they'd be the king and queen. . . ." He shook his head. "But, in the end, it was such a place for memory, they rebuilt a smaller Rafflesia to honor the loved ones who passed on that day and remember why the flowery garden was there. But it was defiled when Ella's mom tried to mine any deeply buried souls that hadn't yet turned to flowers." Bipp chuckled. "But that's nearly impossible. Once the soul is buried, it turns into a flower, and we can't touch them. I always liked that factor, as it shows with certainty which creatures have made it to the afterlife. . . . I believe that is all. Did I miss anything?" Bipp gently asked, trying to soften the culture shock Hugo showed through his attentive eye and tall ears that listened to every word.

To their discomfort, the great doors to the arena screeched open with a horrible sound that rumbled of Hugo's impending doom.

Bipp slapped himself above his eyes. "I'm such an idiot! I should've coached you instead of being selfish and asking you all that." He instantly grabbed Hugo by the face. "You need to come back! Forget about me if you have to!"

Hugo looked back at Bipp and snorted warm steam from his snout onto him. Bipp blinked it away and looked at Hugo's eye. "I'm glad you told me about yourself and this planet. Don't regret a moment of it. It might have been long, but every second was worth it. And I promise, nothing would ever make me forget you."

As three owls swooped down onto Hugo, more tears escaped Bipp's eyes. He held out his hand, and to his heart's demise, he was speechless.

Before Hugo could speak, the talons of the snowy owl wrapped around his snout and mouth. And before he could blink, he left the ground as the other owls grabbed him. He watched Bipp run after them as they carried him through the closing door. Bipp reached out to him, but didn't make it. Then, the battle began with the ear-popping thud of the door's close.

# Chapter 12
# BLOOD AND FEATHERS

The slow, heavy drum thumps beat so loud, they pumped Hugo's blood for him. The sea of crimson-stained sand rumbled with a snake's hiss upon every thump. He couldn't see much with the owl's talon wrapped over his snout, but he could see red, lots and lots of red splashed upon the dark, brick walls he flew past. He felt his head numbing with the idea of his body adding to such decor, so he closed his eyes and thought of Sam to calm down.

"Oh . . . what have we here?" A voice so proper, so soothing to his large ears, allured Hugo's eye to search for it as it crept into his mind like an addicting song and quickly echoed to all in the tower.

"Welcome to The Eye of the Storm! A different voice echoed like a sports announcer back on Earth, and a crowd thundered into a great cheer. *I was never much for sports, but I didn't mind watching them on TV back home.* As he finished that thought, the owls let him go. Hugo fell, but only for a second until he landed with a slight bend to his knees.

"We have a dragon fighter today! Around twenty-eight feet long and weighing over . . . two-thousand five-hundred pounds! My, my, he's going to be a tough one!"

The audience cheered, nearly deafening Hugo's poor ears with a loud ring. This tower's walls might as well have been made from microphones and speakers, for Hugo doubted even a whisper could hide in such an arena.

"I didn't think Bipp gave me *that* much soup," Hugo joked. He was in such a good mood from his previous conversation with Bipp, he could make light of anything in this scary place. He tried to glance around, but the cheers and roars of the arena shook the ground so much, Hugo thought he was about to blast off in a rocket ship. Loose sand layered the great arena he stood in, sloshing his hands and feet with every clumsy step as each grain shifted with each voice from the crowd. As his eye eventually traveled around, he saw crimson and feathers splattered on the sand from Bipp's turn here.

Before long, the audience hushed. Hugo hardly heard a chirp, and such a ghost quiet crept goosebumps along his spine, but soothed his ringing ears better than a compliment. He looked up, then his mouth gaped. He was indeed at the base of a colossal tower, but every inch his eye climbed saw only birds and the near-cylindrical nest they dwelled in. And this nest was more extensive than anything he could imagine. Each fiber and twig typically found in a nest was replaced by the colossal, paper-bark tree logs from the nearby forest. There were thousands of birds, and each had an overhanging log to perch on as they stared down at him. And at the very apex was a hole for a roof, where Hugo could spot the starlight in the rather dark arena. *It's very similar to Anzu's tower of memory.*

"You remind me of something, dragon," the pure and soothing voice echoed around the arena. Even with Hugo's ears, it was impossible to discern who just spoke in the echoing tower.

"To the west," the voice said with a hint of impatience.

*Okay, we traveled west to get here, so . . .* He looked at the great door, then slowly turned his head to the arena's opposite side.

"There you go," sighed a great white heron, who sat upon a great throne above colossal stone steps, stained by a river of dried blood. But that heron was far more elegant than any throne could hope to dream. Unlike the other birds Hugo saw on this continent, this snow-feathered bird had no socks over his long, ebony-leathered legs. He would be considered naked by Somnium standards if it weren't for the shimmering white robe that draped from the throne and drooped loosely over his shoulders. He simply lowered his wing, and it was breathtaking. As every beak in the nest dropped in a bow, this heron stood. A hint of cool wind came through the roof and brushed against Hugo's fur as if it were playing with him. But it did make a lovely humming sound on the way down, like a woodwind instrument.

"I must first welcome you to my arena. Here, you will fight for our amusement." As he leaned forward, clouds moved over the tower and blocked the stars. "Tell me, dragon, before we begin, who are you? Where are you from?"

Hugo lowered his head. He didn't mind public speaking, and he wasn't worse than Sam, but when those clouds passed over the starlight he clung to, his knees wobbled, and everything else braced for impact. "Hi . . . I-I am H-Hugo Atlas, and I'm from a different planet named Earth." Hugo had to squint to see the heron across the grand arena. But as he squinted harder, he thought he could see Ventus' blue colors under the throne's right side.

"A planet, you say?" Exos smiled and stepped forward with the sharp clack of his talons against the stone, trembling the arena in fear. "By any chance, does this planet have humans–"

"Is that Ventus?" Hugo interrupted, then froze. "Wait! Humans! You know about humans?" His ears found a sharp discomfort when many in the audience gasped at his interruption.

The great heron scoffed, then glared to his right at Ventus, who stared beak-agape at Hugo. "Is Hugo a friend of yours?"

Ventus trembled and gulped. His legs dripped with blood and wobbled as the heron eyed him. "N-N-No. . . . He's just s-some stupid snake I met in Anthophyta," he said with his throat quavering every word. He wrapped his wings around his body to stop trembling, but it helped little.

"I'm so sorry for interrupting you! Please, continue what you were saying about Earth!" Hugo begged.

The great heron glared back at Hugo with eyes gifted by the heavens. But his long neck seemed to creak as he turned his head to face him.

Even from such a distance, *those* eyes forced Hugo to step back.

"Ruby and honey scales like autumn leaves. . . ." The heron brought his wing behind Ventus. Each feather was smooth, like cream and flower petals. It would bring great comfort for a normal creature, but for Ventus, it shivered his bones. "Fight him."

Ventus froze and creaked his head to the heron's stare. His irises were more pure than gold as they even shone in the shadowed light of the stars, like this creature was a god from heaven. "Pardon me, Exos?" His voice softened, and his shoulders covered his neck.

"Go down there and kill him. You saw what that rabbit did

to all our contestants before you belatedly informed me that he was the legendary silver flash." He leaned atoms from Ventus and pointed his sharp, golden beak at Hugo as if he was giving a romantic whisper. "Kill him, my prince. I beg you." A few feathers at the tip of Exos' wing caressed the bottom of Ventus' beak. "If you win and fetch his soul for me, I'll grant you what you most desire. For this dragon seems to have what I've been searching for." Then he gently pushed Ventus forward until his toes gripped the colossal stairway's edge.

Ventus hesitated in thought, then looked back at Exos. "Y-Yes, my lord." Ventus spread his wings and leaned off the edge before gliding down.

"Today, I offer you, birds of the Exosphere, a glorious fight between the Prince of the Sky, and the dragon, Hugo." Exos spread his wings apart like a beautiful blank canvas as Ventus landed before Hugo. "Begin!" Exos clapped his wings together as the sound of thunder rumbled the arena. Thankfully, the clouds had left, and warm starlight shone again onto Hugo's back.

However, there wasn't much fighting as Hugo and Ventus simply stared at each other. "You idiot," Ventus began with his beak down, then he scoffed. "Why do you have to get in the way of everything?" He hesitantly raised his wing to Hugo.

Hugo could smell iron and hear the thick crimson drip onto the sand from Ventus' pants. "What happened?" Hugo stepped forward, wanting to help. But Ventus pushed him back in a sand-prickling gust.

"I beg you not to help me. But to either run out those doors or kill me now. I will give you no other choice." Ventus spread his wings, ready to fight.

Hugo growled. "What happened to you?" he asked again,

stepping forward with his fangs showing, but his eye showed more compassion than a concerned mother.

Ventus stepped back as *that* face neared. "Stop looking at me like that!" Upon his command, the wind blew Hugo off the ground and slammed him against the arena's stone wall.

It dizzied and hurt him, but not as much as it should've. Hugo shook his long body free from the pain and then walked to Ventus once more. From such a dizzying distance, Ventus almost looked like Sam, making Hugo's heart skip a beat. He instinctively sprinted at Ventus to embrace him before his mind caught up to his heart and slowed him down in disappointment. *Even here, I can't stop thinking about him.* "D-Did that heron do this to you? Because if so–"

"What! What can you do? He is a god! Even I can't beat him, and I have dominion over the air! You think you can fix everything by being kind and loving?" A sniffle escaped Ventus' nares. "You're a complete fool! You can barely hide the fact that you're a complete mess about Sam leaving you! And yet you try to help me? You barely know me! Why! Why do you keep looking at me like that when you are the one suffering?" At the end of that, Ventus paused, finding his wing practically in Hugo's snout from his aggressive pointing.

Hugo was frozen. He didn't know Ventus was on top of his thoughts like that. "You . . ." He stepped back from Ventus' wing and shyly looked him in the eyes. "You remind me of Sam."

Ventus froze too.

Hugo gave a fake chuckle, but tears welled and snot quickly flowed from his snout onto his lips. "It's not much, because you're a completely different creature. It might just be your feathers, your beak, or the way you weirdly yell at me, but whatever it is, it's enough for me to start thinking about him. . . . I'm sorry," he said in a nasal-clogged voice.

Ventus looked away in thought, scoffed, then brushed his wing at Hugo. "Whatever." He paused for a moment. "I'll ask you again . . . do *you* want to talk about Sam leaving? If you say yes, don't hide any of it. I'm sick of you, constantly thinking to yourself, keeping all of it inside. I'm a bird with great attentiveness, and I sometimes see what you try to hide through your stupid eye. It's annoying. . . . Idiot, you're such a messy crier." Ventus wiped a few tears from Hugo's cheek with his wing. "But you're not alone on this planet . . . especially with that idiot, Bipp, as your soul companion. . . . Congratulations, by the way." Ventus glanced at the silver flower wrapped around Hugo's wrist. "Even if you don't talk about it with me, at least open up to him about it. . . . He cares about you much more than I ever will."

"Thank you?" Hugo shyly looked down at Ventus' wing and snorted deep through his snout to vanquish the snotty clog. "Please, pardon me, but I-I'd like to move onto a different topic . . . one that's been on my mind for some time now."

"What is it?" Ventus rolled his eyes at Hugo, but while doing so, he saw Exos, seated on his throne with an entertained yet impatient squint.

"I-I was thinking . . . since I don't have wings, and you don't use your wings to fly . . . well, could you teach me how to get a feel for flying without wings? So, once I learn to fly like Luna, I'll be so good at it that I can instantly blast off so high that the stars will think they're looking in a mirror." *And then, maybe, just maybe, I'll see Sam again.*

Ventus just about had enough of Hugo's nerdy quirks.

"Luna and I were talking about it earlier, but we got . . . distracted by something." Hugo paused for a moment. "At least, if I learn to fly, you won't have to call me a flightless idiot anymore, heh."

Ventus looked at his wings and sighed. "I'll consider it later . . . for we don't have time for such things right now." After glancing at Exos once more, he saw the weight of his toes spread out, about to take a stance in annoyance. Ventus promptly fell to his knees and stared at the ground. "Before Exos gets bored, you need to kill me or leave out those doors. They won't like it, but they'll accept a surrender, especially since Bipp killed the other contestants. Exos can't possibly offer what I most desire anyway."

"Oh . . . you can't leave with me, right?"

Ventus sniffled as his body trembled once more. "No. Exos has me now. I escaped once. Now, he'll never take his many-thousand eyes off me; even if I win this, I lose." He looked at the audience of birds, watching him and listening to their rather awkward conversation. "But hopefully, someday I'll be free . . . and I can teach you all about flying."

Hugo watched Ventus drip blood and tears onto the sand. His feathery body sank as he suppressed his cries. And just for a second, as Ventus shyly looked away from him to hide his tears, Hugo again saw his little brother in that bird. *I promised to protect you and love you more than anything in the world. . . .*

At that moment, Hugo gulped and looked up at Exos. "I challenge you!"

Not a single gasp shook the stands, for fear of what was to come froze every bird who heard him. Even Ventus had his eyelids stretched apart with his beak dead closed. He didn't dare look at him, for all he could see now was Hugo's future as a skeleton. "Now *that* was stupid."

Exos gave a smile that rotted Hugo's stomach. "Very well, dragon. . . . I accept your challenge with one regard: if I win, I get your soul."

"And if I win, you will tell me everything you know about Earth and Humans, and let Ventus go!"

"Ventus . . ." Exos' voice slithered into Ventus' eardrums.

Ventus crept his eyes to Exos with a cold shiver, as did every other bird in The Eye. "Yes, Exos?" He gulped.

"Guide this, Hugo, to the basement while I prepare his duel." With his wing's rise, the tower's great door moaned, and Bipp instantly fell through the opening crack. "And invite his friends; there's something I'd like them to see." Exos looked to the sky, where dark clouds slowly inched over the castle's roof again. Then, he gave a grin that he couldn't suppress. "Oh, and after he dies, you and I will have a long . . . *discussion*."

There was silence throughout the arena, but everyone's heart raced and thumped into their heads. Hugo could hear Ventus' heart pounding and breaths growing heavier. "Y-Yes, my lord." He bowed with the tip of his beak piercing the sand, and Exos simply brushed up his wing in response.

As other birds flew to Exos and offered him trinkets and drinks, Ventus turned around with a horrified stare meant to disturb Hugo. And without a word, Ventus brought up his wobbling wing and brought forth the wind to rise Hugo and him from The Eye of the Storm and toward the basement steps.

# Chapter 13
# IGNITE

"I'm such an idiot," Anzu grumbled as he trudged through the nipping blizzard. "I can't believe I let Hugo convince me to search for this *glacier*."

Whenever the cold numbed his hind feet, he shifted the ground into hot rock, melting the snow for a while to warm himself. His once-heavy, chest-puffing breaths now barely left his mouth in steam before the sharp wind yanked it away. His cinnamon eyes slowly shut without permission, and his usually strong legs yearned to collapse.

"But I need to do this; I need to make sure the creatures of this world are safe," he growled and gripped his shirt tight around him. The wind was the most painful, it once stung, but now it numbed him dead.

"Maybe I should've brought Ventus. . . . Was I too hard on them to send them out like that? I was just so nervous. Everything was happening so fast; I didn't want to make a mistake on my first day as king of the entire eastern continent! But sending three of the planet's strongest creatures to Dawn while the rest prepare for war?" He rolled his eyes. "Maybe I'm not fit to wear this crown. Hugo was second on the king vote; maybe I should give it to him? I don't care for it anyway. Ella's the better one at ruling; she could practically do it by herself. But I wouldn't want to put that much stress on her."

His hands froze faster than before. He looked back to see his progress, but he could only see a few footprints beyond the flat, windswept snow. "Maybe after all this is over, I could ask her if she would like to marry me." He tried to make the ground hot, but it only warmed him enough to revive his nerves into feeling the painful cold anew. "Stupid Zenith, taking up most my energy. . . ." He looked at Zenith, just orbiting around the horizon. Then, he growled and pointed at it. "Once I know Apotheosis is dead and this whole war thing was just in my head, I'm dropping you!"

He gave a heavy sigh that barely steamed past his chattering teeth. "I don't know though; I'm not the most attractive creature, and I still have a *few* anger issues. But I'm trying to get better at it. Plus, I feel so happy with her, like anger can't possibly exist. Every time I look at her, I nearly cry because of how lucky I am to have someone like that in my life. . . . And maybe, someday, we could build a sandcastle or something; she'd be great at it." He sighed again. "I just want one peaceful day with her."

He stopped to catch his breath. But the cold took advantage of this and stung him more than he could bear. With what remained of his energy, he raised his hands to create a stone wall to block the wind, and he collapsed. He tried rubbing his legs to help warm them. "I could've used Hugo for this." He packed the snow to create a dome without a roof, then tucked his legs as close as possible to his body. "But Hugo needs to be with Ventus. That bird is way stronger than me, but he'll never be able to use his strength in his current mental state." Anzu smiled a little. "I wonder if he's smart enough to see that I requested to bring a boat . . . to prolong their time together. . . . Hugo has an odd connection to Ventus. If I just let him fly there, the healing that bird needs would've been rushed."

After a long wait, Anzu dug his hand deep into the snow and pulled up a layer of hot rock. He almost fell asleep from how cozy it felt against his leathery skin. "Maybe I should've brought a coat; talking to myself isn't as comforting as it used to be." He laughed at his stupidity, then grimaced at the idea of plunging deeper into the heart of Sauria. "Just a little more until I know Somnium is safe. . . . Just a little more until I can run back to see her and ask if she would like to be my soulmate." Once he thought his shirt was on fire, he stood and marched on.

Then, before his heat nearly faded, he spotted the glacier in the distance. He ran toward it with such light footing that the snow didn't break; it was him versus the wind. But that haste stopped once he saw Sam, who stared into the dark crevasse. "What's Sam doing here?" Anzu squinted and wondered who the shoulder-strapped, gray-clothed figure was. But the second he saw the black fire crawl from the darkness and toward Sam, he sprinted and tried to hide his noise under the wind.

Sam stepped back from the fire and grabbed his wing before it touched the fire without his permission. "I thought you were just a voice in my head," he grunted, trying to fight the sudden movements his body begged for.

George's eyes instantly popped open, and his face turned grim. "Wait. Stop. You've heard the voices already?" His words were hasty.

"Uhh, yeah." Sam's shoulders rose over his scrunched neck. "Why?"

"What do they sound like? And what are they saying?"

"Like a lady, a gentle one. But her words are harsh. . . . She told me to kill myself. But those words were already in my head, so she didn't really influence me. I just thought she was my self-conscious–"

George stared at Sam in a way that boiled Sam's stomach with bleach and stung his chest with a heavy needle. "It was a mistake to bring you here." He grabbed Sam's wing. "Come, we need to leave, now!" George yelled. It was creaky, yet sour to Sam's eardrums.

"Why! What did I do wrong?"

"Nothing. I was just foolish not to see the signs. . . . I didn't think those thoughts were hers," he murmured out of earshot.

"Am I not good enough?" Sam began to wilt. He didn't need to ask that; he knew he wasn't good enough.

George stopped with a growl. "It's not about you!" he roared with his arm slashing through the conversation.

Sam wanted to die.

"It's about all those creatures who need you! And if that *thing* is already seeping into you before you even touch it, there is no way you can help them. It's not about you being weak; it's about the requirements being too treacherous right now."

George then sighed and knelt to Sam, who was shivering in fear, hating himself more and more. George had never yelled like that before. "Sorry." He smiled at Sam and patted his head feathers to help him feel better, but it only pumped a stinging venom into his chest. "You are the strongest person I know. To persevere through all you have and not touch this fire even when it's inches from you, it's impossible not to see your strength. If you can't do this, nobody can. . . . You just need something to fight for and to get you on your toes, not just to persevere, but to thrive and repair that leak. Like the motivation of helping Hugo, or turning back into a human. . . . That voice you've been hearing is something bad . . . horrifically bad."

*Just say the word, and I'll kill you. It will be quicker than blinking and quieter than a breath. Your soul will finally know genuine warmth and comfort, belonging to me.*

Sam looked at the snow where he buried his feet. He didn't want to talk, but to get better, he needed to. "I-I care about my family so much that I almost died to make them happy." He turned his back to George. "I've been fighting that voice every day since I heard it. And every time it tells me that I'm useless and that I should die, I think of my family. I just get so confused, because the voice tells me things right as I think them." Sam wanted to collapse into the snow. "Just know . . . my family is the only reason I can stand at all. Without them, I would've- . . ." Sam paused and glanced back at George. "Please, don't think for one second that I don't fight. . . . I try . . . I really try."

"We've run out of options. . . ." George winced and scratched his chest. "With that cancer, you don't have much time left. And that voice you've been hearing means you have a crack that it recently found. And if you've been hearing it a lot, it means that crack is more like a break or a hole, and all your precious water is pouring from it, especially if you've been listening to it. . . . I wish you would've told me this sooner, then I could've seen the future more clearly and mended this a little. I was hoping to have your leg fixed by now . . . but even that fell to the bottom of our to-do list." George looked at Sam's drooped eyelids and lifeless eyes.

*You are a burden. You should've killed yourself sooner, so you wouldn't have wasted George's time.*

George hugged Sam. "I'm sorry for telling you this grim news." Even Sam froze at this. George looked to the fire with a sigh, and he coughed a little. "My opinion still stands. That fire is stronger than I anticipated. And you won't be ready for it until you deal with whatever's eating you. . . . I thought this planet would've made you harder to break. . . . But it seems I was wrong. And for that, I apologize."

*I'm going to die from this cancer . . .* he mused with his head and eyes sinking at the thought of disappointing George. Sam winced at himself for forgetting. *It's not about me. . . .*

George simply sighed, but to Sam, it sounded worried. With George's arms still wrapped around him, Sam could feel George shaking.

*You desire me; you understand yourself more than anyone. . . . Ignore the old man and touch me. Once you and I become one, we will never be an anchor again.*

*Please, shut up. . . . Just give me a moment to think.* Little did Sam know, the fire was surrounding him. Wisps of black fire reached out to him like swords ready to claim their victim.

George's right arm lifted from Sam.

"Stop! Don't touch it!" Anzu roared, stunning Sam.

But George sighed with the sinking of his chin. "I was hoping you wouldn't come." George let go, and both Sam and he turned toward Anzu.

"You. . . ." Sam blinked.

"I'm sorry, Sam. . . . I have failed you."

Sam looked up at George, and to his surprise, tears were flowing through his wrinkled cheeks like a river delta. "H-How–"

"The cancer cannot be cured quickly enough without you

and this power. . . . And with Anzu here, we've run out of time and options. Now, very few futures remain with a positive outcome. . . . I'm terribly sorry for what you are about to see."

Sam could only stare at George. *What is he going to do?*

George's shoulders drooped as he kept a keen eye on Anzu. "What do you want, Anzu?"

Anzu glared at George. "Are you Apotheosis?" he yelled.

George removed his right glove. "I was an age ago, but it seems time is not on anyone's side."

Sam looked at George with concern, and Anzu growled at him. "What are you doing here?"

"Hoping to bring help to all lifeforms. But it has been put on hold." George looked into Anzu's fiery, cinnamon eyes. "Don't worry; we were just about to be on our way."

Anzu walked closer. "It's on hold. . . . So that means you intend to be back."

George tilted his hand toward the black fire.

"Wait, Mr. George," Sam said nervously.

"I can't have you come back. You started a war that lasted two-hundred years! You killed countless! How can I possibly let you be on your way?"

"I'm going to protect you, Sam," George whispered. "Our choices have caught up to us. . . . Now, we are left with one."

Sam turned to Anzu. "Anzu! Run! Please, just live your life," Sam begged, and George smiled. It was worth a shot.

Anzu stepped forward, unable to control the anger swelling inside. "You made life on this planet agony. You made the peaceful creatures of Dawn separate. It was all you. . . ." Anzu tried to consider what Sam said to him, but he was drowning in instinct and anger. He couldn't help it. He roared, then sprinted at George, barely able to launch a few stone spears from the ground.

George sighed.

"Wait, George! Don't!" Sam tried to grab George just before he lowered his hand into the black flames.

The stone spears impaled George throughout his torso. His breath wheezed out in a gasp before his body went cold and limp, only staying on his knees because the spears supported him.

Sam could no longer hear or see George's raspy breath. But as he watched the black fire crawl up George's arm, steam curled from between his lips. Anzu sprinted to George and stopped once he saw the fire over his neck.

"No!" Anzu roared, then grabbed Sam. "Quick, before he gets back up, what are his weaknesses? Tell me!" Anzu sprinted away from George with Sam held against his chest.

"I-I don't know! The way he described it made it seem invincible."

Anzu growled at that. "Then what does he care about?" he asked in haste, glancing back to see the fire wrapping around George's eyes.

"His family, a-and maybe me? I mean, probably not me, because I was the one who put him through all this." Sam drooped. *Why do I think like this? Why do I always blame myself?*

"Don't blame yourself. He is a monster. No matter what you do, he will never change."

Sam looked at Anzu's large head. "I don't think he's a monster. *I've* always been the monster. . . . Maybe he's just misunderstood. His default *is* confusing; even I still don't get him. But . . . after all this time . . . he doesn't peg me as bad. Like me, he just wants to help," Sam murmured under his breath, not confident enough to tell that to Anzu's face. *But at least Anzu talks to me like a person, not in code like George always does.* Just as Sam finished thinking that, the air became stiff; only Anzu's panting breath stirred it. Without hesitation, Anzu collapsed into the snow before an ear-ringing boom shattered the world around them.

"No, no, no!" The dinosaur's panicking heart patted against Sam's cheek. "What do I do? What do I do?" Anzu asked himself on repeat.

"Come here, Sam." The fruity voice of George spidered into Sam's head. He could feel it crawl on his brain with each tickling step. It was no longer raspy or slow, but smooth and calm.

"Don't listen to it, Sam. There's no telling what it could do to y–" The air suddenly became so hot that Anzu grimaced. But it was sadder than that. Anzu had tears running down his long nose, and his hands shook enough to rattle Sam.

*Okay, here we go. It's not about me. . . .* "H-Hey, you're going to be alright. Mr. George wouldn't hurt us." Sam tried to help, but that was the best he could do, given his breaths were heavier than Anzu's. He was confused by his body's reaction. It *was* only George. But something in the air begged his body to shiver with the feeling of a spidering death crawling up his spine.

Then, without notice, Anzu was lifted from the ground by an unknown force. He was so scared that he couldn't move, and with Sam trapped in his stiff arms, he couldn't move either. But once Anzu saw what George had become, any hope of living was vanquished. George's entire body whispered in the black flames; not an inch of skin peeked out. The only things that weren't sheer darkness were his flaming eyes, which were brighter and whiter than the snow.

Sam was brave enough to look at him and watch the air around George warp, as if the fire was stealing the light from the world. *An event horizon, Hugo would call it,* Sam mused as his eyes dried the second they met George. "M-Mr. George? I know I messed up. But please, there must be another way."

The fiery figure before them seemed to droop. And before they knew it, the fire vanished with a loud push of wind. It was simply George, wrinkles, shoulder straps, and gray clothes. "I'm sorry, Sam, but those ways are shut."

Sam promptly shook his head and tried to consider what George felt. "You're right. I'm sorry. It's impossible, right? So, why don't we talk about it? We have all the time in the world," Sam said, humorously gesturing to himself.

George's eyes popped open, and he reached up to Sam. His fingers twitched at the temptation to grab the soul straight from Sam's chest. But then a sharp growl clenched George's teeth. "Run, Sam," George begged with a worried voice. "I can't keep it out of my head. . . . Please, I want you to be safe."

But Sam only sighed in defense. "Take it. It's not like I can do much with it anyway." This comment flinched both Anzu and George. "If it will help, then please ta–"

Anzu grabbed Sam's beak shut with a clack and looked at George, who seemed to be at war with his thoughts as his molten fingers pressed against Sam's chest. "Don't say another word. If you tempt him too much, he may actually take it. . . . Good acting by the way," Anzu whispered.

Sam shyly looked away before George retreated his hand.

"There is only one other way," George gulped with many exhausted breaths. "My mind is starting to falter already. Please, if you ever feel like I'm going to hurt you, run as fast as you can. . . ." Then, George's eyes burst into white flames, and the dark fire surrounded him everywhere else.

"He . . . cares about you." Anzu blinked. He was utterly shocked that such a monster cared about something. Anzu looked at Sam, observing every feather. "You're his weakness," he murmured just out of earshot.

Without knocking, George's wooden door appeared beside them.

Anzu growled at that. "What are you planning?" he shouted before George opened the door to a gust of wind and a calm blue sky.

Sam peeked through it and saw the ground, many-thousand feet below them. "Wait a secon–" George pulled Anzu and him through the door behind him. Sam's stomach sank as only air separated his dangling feet from the ground.

"I don't need you," George said. Suddenly, gravity grabbed Anzu and yanked him down. He held onto Sam for dear life with his tiny arms.

"Don't stop trying. You are his weakness. You can control him."

Sam felt sick in his chest. *I'm a weakness?* Before Sam knew it, Anzu's weak hands gave, and he fell, yelling in panic as he disappeared through the clouds.

Sam squeaked and covered his beak in fear. George lowered Sam until his toes spread under his weight. His mind numbed for a second, questioning how he was able to stand without a palpable floor. The cold air weaved through his toes, making his heart sink with the worry of falling.

"Don't worry about the velociraptor; he'll be fine. In fact, once I'm done here, he will have the energy and anger to face me."

"Once you're done here?" Just as Sam finished that sentence, beyond the windswept clouds, he saw the capital city of Rafflesia bustling with life and the attempt to rebuild the city from its previous ruler.

"I need the power to save everyone. . . . I need a power equivalent to yours. To achieve such, I just need the right combination of souls."

If Sam didn't hate himself before, he certainly did now. George was talking about killing others, *while he could just kill me and receive all the power he needed.* "I don't know what you're thinking, but please, don't value other lives over mine. Just kill me and get it over with. Nobody has to suffer." *At least, this way, I could say I helped people.*

"To me, you are the most valuable person to ever live. I would never harm you for such a reason." A sigh sounded from the crackling fire. "Just because this power isn't yours, doesn't mean your journey ends here. You will still be helpful. I must keep my promises one way or another." He gave a wink with that white fire.

"Yeah, but–" Sam didn't know what else to say. Only for a second did he give up on trying to counter George.

But in that second, George stepped forward as if walking down some stairs. He looked at the planet below and the city of Rafflesia. "Today, history shall repeat itself." He raised his hand, then simply lowered it.

The planet shook like a meteor had just punched it in half. Then, within a flash and an ear-popping boom, the valley of King's Garden and the city of Rafflesia exploded with the upward eruption of debris and smoke. Sam fell backward from the shockwave that rattled the sky like a crackling earthquake. The few clouds above the epicenter became gray in a blink, and ashen flakes fluttered down to the now-white valley.

And all Sam's face could do was gawk at the endless white landscape before them with his eardrums ringing enough to dizzy him. *A-Are you a monster?*

Suddenly, the dark flames around George vanished, and a few specks of moisture tapped Sam's cheek. He looked up at George's face and saw the faint sparkle of teardrops flying off in the windswept sunlight.

George turned to Sam, who then froze at George's welling eyes. "I'm going to drop you. Don't worry; you'll be safe. I want you to run and hide until . . . someone you trust finds you. . . . For this is only the start."

Before Sam could open his beak, the invisible floor he lay upon gave. He reached up to George until the clouds consumed his sight.

*This is all your fault. If you were successful in killing yourself, those creatures would be happy.*

# Chapter 14
## PAPER, HONEY, AND PUMPKINS

As they flew toward the arena's edge, they spotted a wide, stone stairway, sprinkled with sand. Ventus' neck sank into his shoulders, and Hugo couldn't help but notice Ventus' eyes constantly looking to the sky above the tower.

"Ventus, please tell me what's going on. I promise I only mean to help you."

"I told you to walk away or kill me! Not this!"

Ventus didn't even grace him with a glance. He even flew Hugo slower, so he wouldn't see that worried eye of his.

"Is this worse?" Hugo didn't need to ask that. The still eyes of the audience told him he was doomed.

After an annoyed scoff from Ventus, they landed in the loose sand and spotted the dark shadows that crept just past the first few steps. There were two armored birds with spears and a chicken standing guard, a rather short one and quite fun to look at, especially as a distraction for Hugo. Then the sound of footsteps thumping through the sand roused Hugo's ears.

"Hugo!"

Hugo turned around to see Bipp running at him, and Luna, who flew with her fiery light shining throughout the entire tower. "These your friends Exos mentioned?" the chicken asked with a cute voice as Bipp ran to Hugo and promptly hugged him. And with that, the chicken needed no answer. "Alright, when Exos is ready, I'll call for you." The chicken gestured his wing down the stairs.

But as Hugo peeked over Ventus' shoulder, he saw only darkness. Not even the light from Luna's fur offered Hugo much mercy. By instinct, he stepped back.

*So, the brave dragon returns.*

A familiar voice, loud enough for anyone to notice, numbed Hugo's mind and froze his legs. "Please tell me you heard that."

Bipp's ears sprang up and rotated around. "Heard what?" Bipp watched Hugo tense up.

Ventus turned around and tilted his head with the roll of his eyes. "What's the problem now?"

Luna landed beside Hugo, pressed her shoulder against his, and signed a few things with her hands.

Her words seemed to hurt Ventus as his face scrunched at Hugo. "You're afraid of the–" Hugo shyly bowed his head in shame. "How? You're a dragon! Just breathe fire, you idiot!" Ventus was clearly done as he breathed for a second, then rolled his eyes. "Whatever. You three will just need to stick together like paper and honey, alright?"

"Like paper and honey?" Bipp blinked.

Ventus flapped his wings, getting impatient considering they weren't even a single step down yet. "I'm not explaining it! Just breathe fire, and you'll be fine!" Ventus marched forth, down into the depths. This entire time, the chicken stared awkwardly away from them as the other two armored birds just looked at each other.

Hugo watched Ventus' blue feathers vanish under the hasty teeth of a dark fog.

Bipp leaned against Hugo with a smile. "Like paper and honey then. . . . We'll be right beside you." He pointed his hand to the dark entrance. "Whenever you're ready."

Hugo looked at Bipp to his right, then Luna to his left before stepping forth.

*Where is your precious bird? Where is your brother?*

Hugo's ears flicked as the sound of eerie laughter crept into him with a chilling shiver. He looked at everyone sequentially, but they didn't react. "It's all in my head. It's all in my head," Hugo told himself. He shivered so much, Bipp struggled to hold onto him. That voice was too familiar for Hugo. His mind raced, trying to think of where he heard it.

Once his lungs worked faster than an engine, and they took their hundredth step, his hand finally met the stone floor of the basement. It was slick and icy to the touch. And the hollow gaps between each brick shivered him into imagining what could be slithering between them. Hugo instantly looked back, hoping to see the light from upstairs, but he saw nothing. He couldn't tell the difference between opening his eye and shutting it. Luna quickly blew a bit of white fire onto the dark brick floor. Hugo veered to it and stared like it was the last thing keeping him alive, even though the dark haze barely snuffed it.

"Calm down, you idiot! It's just dark!" Ventus yelled at Hugo.

Bipp glared at Ventus before looking at Hugo's eye. "Ignore him," Bipp said and walked in front of his face. "Hey. . . ." After staring at Luna's light, Hugo looked up at Bipp, who nervously spun his toes on the smooth floor. "Could we try that *thing* Anzu showed us with Ella to remember her soul ability? You know, kinda like *the thing* you showed me in the forest just a bit ago. I wanted to try it out with you when Anzu first did it." He chuckled. "I guess we got so busy, we didn't have time or reason until now. And if you're scared, maybe it could help."

Ventus scoffed and looked deeper into the castle. "I don't have time to listen to this. . . . Luna, do you know where your father's sword might be? Maybe we can get it while we're here. . . . I just need a reason to get these two off my back."

Luna looked at Hugo, then shook her head at Ventus.

Bipp watched Ventus' eyes narrow at the three of them. "Here. Don't worry about Hugo; I'll take care of him." He grabbed an already-torn strip of his cloak and ripped it off. He wrapped it around his ebony dagger, then held it before Luna. "This should keep the light for a while. Go get that sword."

Luna looked at Hugo, who still heaved every breath. She hesitated, but nodded and blew light onto the dagger torch. It burned pure and white, but shrank quickly.

"Go now; we got this," Bipp spoke with a nervous haste.

Ventus sighed as he and Luna ran from the room.

"Come, let's find a cozier spot to wait, rather than the middle of this cold room. I'll do *the thing* there." Bipp wrapped his arm under Hugo's chin, his shoulder on one cheek and his hand on the other. He guided Hugo through a few doors until they met a room so expansive the light struggled to reach the walls. "Heh, sorry, maybe this is–"

Hugo's ears rang and popped.

*Come deeper into the darkness, brave dragon. Come closer to your brother.*

Hugo collapsed against the hard, cold floor as fire dripped from his panicked lips.

"Hugo!" Bipp knelt beside him and held the light close to his face. But Hugo couldn't see Bipp nor the light he carried.

*He is ours now. You're too late.*

Hugo's body scrunched as if he was bracing to be hit. "Get me out of here," he commanded with a whisper. He closed his eye and began to shiver tremendously.

"Uh, here, let's do the thing right now." Bipp tried to sound calm. "Alright, close your eye." Bipp smacked himself on the face when he saw Hugo's already closed eye. "O-Okay, feel . . . the damp, smooth brick against your warm stomach."

Hugo did so, but it didn't help much. The bricks were cold and shivered Hugo even more.

"Oh, I uhh. . . . ." Bipp leaned onto Hugo's shoulder and wrapped his arm over him. "Feel my chest as I breathe; feel your air raise your chest. Let these feelings settle you, and breathe with me."

Hugo's heart slowed as Bipp's soft warmth comforted him, and he breathed with him. "I'm sorry, Bipp," he murmured before Bipp smiled.

"You have nothing to be sorry for." Bipp held Hugo's left hand and looked at the flower around his wrist. "You're trying something outside your comfort zone. Nobody expects perfection. . . . Now, smell the individual bricks in this room. Smell that fresh, rocky air from the mountain." Bipp gave Hugo a minute to focus on those. "Listen to the life around you: our deep and repetitious breaths, melted snow calmly flowing through the cracks in the sand upstairs and tapping the brick floor beside us, the ceiling's support beams creaking under the sand's weight, and the gentlest actions of wind that excites and weaves through your grass-like fur."

Hugo's ears never felt so good. Though he expected nothing

less from someone with the most enormous ears he'd ever seen.

"So, Hugo, what do you see now?" Bipp asked.

Hugo tried; he really did. But he couldn't see much other than the times he did this with Sam and how he felt back then. Just for a second, as he peeked open his eye, he thought he could see a light and Sam's shy, green eyes. Then, he felt his body warm up in an instant.

"Oh . . . my–" Bipp murmured.

*Sam?*

Hugo squinted in the darkness. "Could you please put that light over there?" He bobbed his snout to the deeper part of the room.

But Bipp didn't respond.

"Bipp?" Hugo turned to look at Bipp, whose mouth gapped wider than his eyes as he watched Hugo. To Hugo's instant discomfort, he saw Bipp's knife torch wisping with smoke; but he paused as light still filled the room.

"You're . . . making those embers again," Bipp said, unable to avert his gaze.

Then a ruby ember landed on Hugo's snout with a sizzle. He blinked, then looked up at the countless honey and ruby embers floating around them, like this room contained a galaxy. Hugo looked back to where he saw Sam, then paused with a squint.

Two things caught his attention instantly: a green image painted brightly on the gray block wall, and a pile of glowing, colored orbs that sat directly beneath it.

"What the?" His stomach dropped as he gawked at the wall.

Bipp forced his eyes away from Hugo with much struggle, seeing what Hugo did. "Oh . . . no."

The block wall had a mural of many flowers and two blue

circles that sank below. Hugo's eye gaped wide as he looked at the center flower. "S-Sam?" He stepped forward. The flower had long, pointy black petals, and the core was a stunning emerald, matching the color of Sam's feathers and eyes to the atom. Hugo's limbs became wet grass, and his throat stung with a rising poison he had to gulp down. After learning about flowers and death, this was harsh on his mind. *Why is Sam on the wall?* His vision blurred as he continued to stare.

Bipp, however, just stared at the pile below. It was near twice their height, and to Bipp's ears, he thought he heard whispers creep from it.

*His body will burn in darkness, and you . . . will be . . . alone forever.*

Now, the voice poisoned Hugo, and dizziness crept into his head. But he needed to know more, so he quickly glanced at the other flowers, trying to understand it all. The one on the top right was ice blue and, to Hugo, it was beautiful, but strangely familiar. It could've represented Ventus, but he doubted it. *Who is that?* He shook his head to move on to the next.

The left flower had a deep jade center with silver petals; it was Hugo's favorite, especially with the white dots within the grayish parts to make it look like space and stars. Hugo instantly looked at the flower on his wrist. It too had silver petals, but luckily for Hugo's heart, it had a blue core and no dots. He refused to look at the other flower as just a glance of the autumn colors numbed his mind. So he stared back at Sam's flower, then at the circles below. Those looked like Earth and Somnium, each with their moons.

The embers began to fade, and Hugo's worry for Sam rose. *Is this just a coincidence? No, not on this planet. . . .* Sudden fear blinded him from thoughts, and his body forced a step back.

*There is nothing you can do to save him now. The eye of the galaxy will shut, and the darkness you fear will be all you see.*

"Bipp, help me," Hugo begged.

Bipp looked at Hugo, whose eye rolled back. "Hugo!" Bipp yelled as Hugo collapsed and gasped for air like it was the most important thing to him. "That's it! We're getting out of this place!" Bipp commanded, quickly trying to think of how to help Hugo. But after a few seconds of panicked thinking and searching where they came from in the fading light, Bipp began to cry. "I don't know how to help you! I might be able to carry you, but. . . ." He paused as he looked at Hugo's long, heavy body. "What do you need?" Bipp watched Hugo extend a hand to him. Bipp promptly took it and held it tight.

"Please, Hugo, tell me why you're afraid," Bipp asked with his eyes closed. "I really want to help you with this, and if you tell me, maybe I can." Bipp nervously looked at the few remaining embers sizzle against the floor.

Hugo gave up what little pride he had left and sank with his chin meeting the floor. He struggled to speak as various grunts escaped his fangs. But he knew he had to do it. He wanted to get over his fears, and with Bipp listening with his ears at the ready, it was time.

"I'll try."

Bipp scooted closer with his ears taller than ever before. Hugo took a moment, trying to mix his thoughts and feelings into words. "Okay. . . . Okay. I discovered my fear of the dark after a person, maybe George, came into my home, killed Sam's mom, then tried to kill us. The whole experience gave me a feeling I never wanted to feel. And every time darkness surrounds me, I feel it. It's like my stomach and mind are pulling away from each other, and sometimes, I can feel that knife pierce my back. I have no control of my lungs or my heart; I just lose it. All things went wrong that night. My nightlight was out of battery. George had the light behind him, so he looked like a demon from the night. I don't know why, but when I saw him, I felt in my chest that he was going to take Sam away. I panicked and threw my body over Sam to protect him. The only friend I had. I was ready, even then, to die for him, because the feeling of his absence, to me, was far worse than death."

Bipp watched a few tears form within Hugo's eyelid.

"I guess you could say I have post-traumatic stress, which is what a few therapists have said. . . . But I think it's a little different, because every time I see darkness, I am reminded of how someone so wonderful could disappear right before me. So I guess it's not necessarily a fear of the dark. It's–"

"You're afraid of being alone," Bipp finished with his head tilted and his jade eyes showing sorrow and compassion.

Hugo's hands hid his face in shame. Bipp nailed it right on the mark.

"Is that why you wanted me to stay with you in that dark forest and a reason you didn't go to flight school? And . . . actually, wait; this explains a lot of things." Bipp looked away in thought.

Hugo gave a nervous nod and expected the sound of Bipp laughing to meet his ears, but instead, Bipp's gentle hand cradled his chin.

Bipp raised Hugo's face. "Hey . . . I'm here, and as your soul companion, I hope we will always be together. . . . As for Sam . . . well, he has a few things to work on. He just doesn't understand who you are quite yet. Because if he thought what I do, leaving you would be the last thing he would ever want to do." There was silence for a moment. "Not to seem selfish, but I love that you have this fear, because it means you understand the value of having a friend. More than some." Bipp smiled with a gulp. "But could you maybe tell me why you close your eye? It doesn't make sense to me, you closing your eye to do *the thing* if darkness sparks your fear response."

Hugo's chest rose and sank with his attempt at calm breaths. "Yes. It makes it worse, much worse. But it's what I taught Sam to do when he's scared, so it makes me feel like I'm with him if I also do it. The first time I did *the thing* was near that glacier with Sam. I didn't think it would work on me, but . . . that was the first time I felt . . . lighter. Like, light enough to float . . . because I was with him. I don't close my eyes to defeat darkness. I close my eyes to remember the feeling that Sam is beside me, helping me through the dark. I don't do the thing forever, because I get too scared of the darkness under my eyelids. But the feeling of Sam next to me kind of counters it. The feeling is short, but that's usually all I need to feel better."

"Awww." Bipp couldn't help it with a smile that made Hugo blush. "Wo-would you like to know what my fear is, apart from my obvious fear of . . . heh," Bipp slouched and looked away, "well, we can talk about that later . . ." he chuckled, trying to lighten the impact of this topic.

Hugo nodded.

"Pumpkins," Bipp chuckled some more, knowing it was silly.

Hugo's eyes scrunched.

"Yup. The very first pumpkin I ate had a nest of spiders in it. . . . Nobody ever taught me how to eat a pumpkin, but I knew they were edible; because why else would they sell them? So, just like any other fruit, I took a bite from its side. And before I knew it, hundreds of spiders were crawling from the hole, some around my mouth." Bipp gave a nervous chuckle with his eyes closed, remembering *that*.

"That's literally a nightmare," Hugo spoke, still with his eye closed.

"Yeah. After that . . . event, I didn't touch a pumpkin for several years. But, I spent a lot of time reading about them. Then, once I thought I knew enough about them, I ate one by chopping it up . . . violently, then putting the good stuff in a soup."

"And?" Hugo peeked open his eye.

"Meh, it was alright. Not really my thing. I'm more of a leafy greens type of creature. Maybe with a few drops of squeezed lemon or honey for flavor. . . . Heck, maybe I'll make a cookbook with all the things I've experimented with and the many combinations of things I can mix into an adventure pot. . . . Anyway, I still get a bit nervous around pumpkins, because I'm still reminded of that terrifying event. But at least now, I know they don't taste too bad, and they're fun to look at—all big and round like they are. . . . I learned more about them, and I occasionally call them plumpkins to keep them silly. Now, they don't bother me too much. . . . Maybe you could do something similar. Learn about the dark or loneliness in some way that makes them seem less scary," Bipp said, ending his story.

"Thank you, Bipp."

Bipp snorted. "You're so strange. Always saying thank you and sorry for the most bizarre things. You know I'm glad to help, right?"

"I mean it. Thank you, for everything. For calming me down, for being with me through all this. . . . I'm so glad you're here." Hugo then looked at Bipp's eyes. "May I . . . hold you?"

Bipp smiled. "Since we're soul companions now, you don't need to ask me every time you want a hug you know. . . ." He chuckled a little, then looked at Hugo's eye, staring right at him. "But, please do."

With his gentle yet strong arm, Hugo held Bipp tight to his chest.

Bipp hugged him back with another chuckle through his nose. He finally understood and took the time to appreciate him. He looked around them at all the new, beautiful embers Hugo gifted the room. "Hugo's way," he whispered, feeling butterflies lift his chest.

## Chapter 15
# RAIN CLOUD

"Ugh, idiot, I can't believe we did all that for nothing," Ventus complained as he walked through a door with Luna. He froze as he spotted Hugo and Bipp, who hugged each other with many embers floating from Hugo's back. "What the–" He then looked specifically at Hugo, whose back fur swayed like wind-stirred grass. "Oh no. . . . Luna . . . is he–" he didn't want to say it, but as he looked at Luna for a response, his eyes drooped with her sorrowful nod, "an emberlight?" He finished with a heavy sigh and slouch of his shoulders, as if those words cursed him. "How long have you known?"

Luna pointed to her cheek, then to the back of her head with a glance to Hugo.

"After seeing his memories, huh?" He squinted at her. "Did you tell him?"

Luna pointed to Hugo, shook her head, then flicked a finger to the ceiling.

Ventus sighed. "That idiot . . . making me explain everything to him." He spiraled a talon around a brick in thought. "Okay. . . . Those two aren't going to like this." He took a deep inhale and walked within earshot. "Oh great, you two were *ro-*

*mancing it up* while she and I were off on some useless errand."

Bipp rolled his eyes and let go of Hugo. "I assume you found what you were looking for then?" he asked with a sarcastic glance at him.

"No! Idiot! There was nothing in that contraband chest apart from clothes consumed by moths!" Luna walked with him through the door and blew a wisp of white fire to aid the embers' light. Her head was low, as if in deep thought. "She swore it was in there, but nooo. . . . What a hideous place; the only thing left in that part of the castle were cells, each with at least one skeleton without a soul." When Ventus finished his rant, he paused as he saw the pile of glowing orbs. "Oh . . . well that explains that."

Luna then walked into the room and froze as she spotted the pile.

"I see. . . . He's trying to become the next Apotheosis." He scoffed. "Makes sense why someone like him would be in such a messy place."

Bipp and Hugo raised their ears at Ventus, who glanced at them, then shyly looked away.

"This castle is where Apotheosis sacrificed many creatures back in the golden age of Dawn. That's why you see blood stains everywhere. . . . But Exos turned it into an arena, so he wouldn't dirty himself by killing anyone; they'd just kill each other, and he'd keep their souls."

Bipp looked down, thinking about the number of creatures he added to that pile. "Is there anything we can do?"

"No. . . . I know for certain we aren't alone here. If we so much as touch that pile, we'd be added to it. There is nothing we can do. Even surviving that fight is impossible."

"Why do you assume Hugo can't win? He ate the queen's

head; maybe he can do it again?"

Ventus scoffed. "Have you seen the size and lethality of Exos' beak? That thing has claimed many lives already, so putting your mouth next to it is a great idea." Ventus squinted at Bipp with a smile.

"So, how can we win?"

He sighed. "The time has passed for *winning* once Hugo decided to spare me and challenge Exos. Honestly, I would enjoy what little time you have left on this world. . . . But, alas, there is something I feel obligated to tell you, and do pardon me for being blunt. . . . I've never been subtle when it comes to these things." He looked at Hugo.

Hugo tilted his head.

"You will never fly."

Hugo froze a moment, but once he understood what that meant, those words crushed him. Every part of his body felt ten times heavier, and a sudden, harsh pain pinched his heart. *Sam. . . .*

But even more so, those words destroyed Bipp, who instantly collapsed onto his knees with a surprised gawk opening his mouth. "W-What?" Bipp whispered, nearly dazed from confusion.

Ventus looked at Luna as she described the scenario. "You see, those embers from Hugo's back mean that Hugo's an emberlight, and emberlights are . . . well . . . disabled. It's a dragon's worst nightmare, an unwanted and incurable curse per se. You can't create enough heat to fly. So you are forever bound to the dirt with no hope to go up and join your fellow dragons, adding numbers to the stars above. . . . You see, dragons use their souls to fly—Luna thinks of a memory to fly. But . . . with you . . . I fear your soul . . . just . . . isn't strong enough." Ventus looked down at his toes, scrunching up. "I'm sorry for calling you flightless several times before. I didn't know you were an emberlight; I just thought you were stupid or something. But, at least I was correct on both accounts," he murmured that last part, then shyly looked away. "Sorry."

Hugo didn't know what to say or do. He just . . . lay there. He wanted more than anything to fly to Sam, and after his many practice attempts, this . . . this hurt. *So long as I can still accomplish my dream of being one with the stars with Sam, I'll be okay. . . . It's just going to be a bit harder now.* He closed his eye. *Sam, don't worry. I'll find a way to get to you and help you search for dinosaur fossils. Maybe, we just need a bigger plane for me to fit in . . . once I find you.* He breathed out a whisper of fire, but tears started to well in his eye. *Maybe I can still propel myself like a rocket instead? But is that even possible on such a large scale?*

Bipp watched as tears welled and quickly broke from Hugo's eye. *I can't give up . . . There has to be something on this planet to help me.* More and more fluids poured from Hugo's face as his mind spun deeper and deeper. *N-No . . . I don't want to give up. . . . Please don't make me . . . I just want to see Sam again.*

"I refuse to believe that!" Bipp stood, fingers gnashing against palms. "Hugo is perfect the way he is! His soul is stronger than anyone's! Sure, we don't know what it is, but we're so close! The embers have to mean something, especially if his soul is connected to them! I can feel . . . it?" Bipp stopped as he saw a few tears escape Ventus' sky-blue eyes. And Hugo stopped daydreaming once he caught a whiff of Ventus' drying blood within the stitching of his harem pants.

"You idiot. . . ." Ventus looked away. "It's not like I wanted this to happen. I'm trying my best here. But this is just how Somnium works. . . . One disappointment after another until we either die or get over it and move on. . . . I'm sorry to say, Hugo," he glanced at the silver flower on Hugo's wrist, then to Bipp with a sigh, "that I think it's time you focused on things other than Sam, at least for a while."

Bipp froze at that.

To everyone's surprise, Hugo stood. It took a few sniffling breaths, but he got there. "Would it help if you told me what Exos does to you? I can smell the blood even in this cold, strangely wet room. And I want to help you. That's the reason I challenged Exos in the first place."

Ventus and Bipp froze. Even Luna seemed a bit thrown off by Hugo's change of topic.

Ventus growled at himself, then looked away from Hugo. "You daft lizard. Helping someone you hardly know is a way to shorten your lifespan. . . . Like I said, you can't even fly, you're rubbish at fighting, and you're going against someone who's undefeatable."

"Stop trying to hide it. I'd like to know what he does to you. And if I hardly know you, then who are you?"

Ventus growled, about to lose it with this dragon. But after he breathed for a few moments and circled his wings like Anzu, he wrapped his wing around Luna's hand, then placed it on his head. "I will show you everything if you just promise me one simple thing."

Hugo's head tilted.

"No more hiding your thoughts from me. I'm opening up to you with this, so you better respect that and open up when I ask. . . . Okay?"

"I promise, but—" Hugo hesitated as Ventus began to tremble, "are you sure? I don't want to if–"

"Just do it, you cave-snout idiot." A few tears formed in his eyes. "Besides, I feel like I owe you something for trying to help me out of this mess, even if it is a foolish attempt." He tried to scoff, wanting to hide his statement as invaluable, but he meant it, and even with his greatest efforts, he couldn't scoff.

"Oh, and Luna," Ventus looked at her, "don't show me when I'm–" He blushed and looked away from her. ". . . well, you'll see."

Hugo looked to Luna, who nodded at him. He hesitated with a glance to Ventus before carefully raising his hand and sliding it gently under Luna's; then, the familiar white light came forth.

\*\*\*

"Hey, Ventus! School starts in ten minutes! Have you finished?" A shy and gentle voice, one like the flowery lullaby of a tiny bird, sang from the bottom of the stairs.

"Coming! Just writing the last words!" Ventus stacked books with his wings and wrote an essay with an inked quill grasped within his right foot. Even though he spent every waking moment trying to learn and improve, each feather was adequately brushed and cleaned to perfection.

He stacked the last book on his desk before a tiny, barely knee-tall, spherical wren with eyes like rosemary plums, hopped up the final step and looked at Ventus' stack of papers beside his leg. Her wings were tiny like the rest of her walnut body compared to the other wrens in school, but she knew everyone gets their time to grow; some just took a bit longer. "You'll definitely get accepted into the Saurian program with that large of an essay! You realize we only had to write about a hero or role model we favored, right? . . . Did you accidentally write about yourself again?" the wren giggled with a glance at her lone page tucked beneath her left wing.

"Ha, ha," Ventus mocked, then laughed shortly after. "I'm sorry, Nimba, I really want to do well with this . . . my one shot of becoming someone important." Ventus quickly set the quill down and slapped the final page on top.

"You're important to me . . ." Nimba whispered and spun her foot around the carpet while her beak sank into her breast feathers. Ventus ignored her, grabbed his thick stack of papers, and tucked them under his left wing. "Ventus . . . if you don't mind me asking, who's your role model?" Nimba murmured with her head still down.

Ventus lifted Nimba in his free wing, and he carried her down the stairs to the front door with a skip in every step. "Lord Anzu," Ventus said simply, holding out Nimba. She opened the door with much struggle into a feather-fluffing chill of snow.

"Why him?" She shut the door behind them with a squint to block the fluffy snowflakes that nearly blinded them with their army from the sky.

"He's someone I aspire to be like, wise enough to rule a kingdom, strong and kind enough to create Zenith for us to live in peace from the war while he fights it. . . . He has lost hundreds of his kin, including all his family in this pointless war, and he fights every day to not lose anyone else of any species. He may be slightly . . . agitated by it all, but he still tries to help. . . . That velociraptor is my definition of a hero," Ventus explained and carried Nimba toward a large stone academy with banners cracking in the wind. Each bragged about the main subjects of Zenith education: science, art, music, and language.

Ventus quickly scaled the great quartz steps and heaved

with relief when he reached the top. "Wow." He took a moment and set Nimba down. "I think you've gotten bigger over the weekend. How tall are you now?"

"Almost a foot and a half," Nimba said with a great smile. She was perfectly content with her tiny height, especially because it meant Ventus would carry her everywhere. "Is that why you want to study with the Saurians? Because of Lord Anzu?" They began to walk toward the massive stone doors of the academy; each was carved with the history of the school and the many birds who did extraordinary things after graduation. But all of them were bigger birds.

"Mostly . . . But a lot of it is what they have in the tower of memory. I wish to learn as much as possible. And I feel like staying here for my future education limits me." Ventus glanced at the many, much larger birds, who walked or flew into the building.

"Why learn all that? I feel like with who you are now, you can accomplish more than most birds on this island."

"I want to become wise enough to help as many creatures as Anzu. And since I'm a smaller bird, and was born rather poor, I'll have to work on smarts more than anything. I don't think I can accomplish all that with our current academics. No offense to this academy, but I feel like I'm wasting my time with some of these class assignments. In Sauria, they give you unlimited access to their library tower, and you learn at your pace, without instruction. So you can learn whatever you want, how fast you want, at any difficulty. Then, when you think you're wise enough, you may challenge the current librarian to a battle of wits, and if you win, you become the new librarian. I think that's how education should be, free to discover what you want in your own way, but with a touch of healthy competition."

"Ah, so you wish to learn from the Saurians?" A voice, smoother and more proper than any voice, flowed like a soothing river from the doorway.

Ventus and Nimba looked up at a great white heron, who walked toward them with such grace, his head stayed perfectly level, and his leather toes never made a sound against the snow-buried quartz. Ventus knew who this was. It was Exos, one of the few birds on Zenith that one would consider royalty. He was in a few of Ventus' more challenging classes, being slightly older, but he had a servant fill his seat most of the time.

"Y-Yeah," Ventus said, at a complete loss for words as he gawked up at the creature, whose feathers couldn't be discerned from the pure snow.

"So, I assume *that* is your entrance essay?" Exos asked, tipping his beak to Ventus' wing.

"Yeah, I spent the past year on it."

Exos revealed his wing, requesting to view it.

Ventus hesitated, then bowed, for the honor of such a bird wishing to see his writing was a dream come true. Ventus then gave Exos his stack of paper.

"Hmm." Exos scoffed and held up the papers before reading the first few pages in a blink. "Ugh, how trivial." He threw the stack of papers to the side, into the winter wind.

"Noooo!" Ventus' eyes burst open, and his chest sank into his feet, quickly trying to reach for them. But to no avail, every page was yanked by the curling wind and consumed by the distant haze of snow. Ventus fell to his knees with his beak gapped wider than the academy door.

"You jerk! Why did you do that? Do you realize how hard he worked for that?" Nimba yelled furiously.

Exos barely glanced at Nimba before walking to Ventus. "I

do admire your efforts to gain that silly reptile's attention. But writing about him in such a worshipful manner will never do." He extended his wing and caressed Ventus' back, begging him to stand.

Ventus stood with his legs wobbling. "That was my only chance," he murmured.

"No, for with me, you have a *guaranteed* chance." Exos' longest wing feather tilted Ventus' beak to face him. "I've been watching you for a while, and since you didn't chase after those papers, and upon other factors, you can't fly. Just like a poor emberlight dragon, beautiful, but useless. So why would Anzu accept you only for an asinine list of words? With me, I can give you a great word with the professors here, and if I'm in the mood, I may teach you and your little . . . pinecone how to fly."

"Why are you doing this? That essay was great! And you just . . ." Nimba froze. Only did Exos look at her with his gold eyes, and her tiny body nearly fell over.

Exos looked back at Ventus, who was weeping. "Oh dear, someone as beautiful as you shouldn't shed tears." He gently cradled Ventus' cheek within his massive wing. "If you want to be someone important, like Lord Anzu, meet me in the paint room after school. There, we will discuss your future in . . . deeper detail. And don't you worry, from now on, I will treat you like royalty, my little Prince Ventus," Exos whispered, then spread apart his great wings and flapped away like a rocket into the bright, snow-twinkling clouds.

Ventus fell to his knees and stared at his empty wings. "My essay . . ." At this point, his face was soaked in tears that quickly froze the feathers on his cheek like a hundred icicles hanging from a leafy tree.

Nimba tried to comfort him by placing her wings over Ventus, but she was too short for such a reach. "Hey, don't worry about it."

Ventus' beak wobbled. "T-That was my only chance to be accepted in Sauria . . . and he just threw it away like it meant nothing."

Nimba untucked her essay from her wing and instantly placed it in Ventus' open wings. "Here." Nimba raised her wings, revealing her essay in Ventus' feeble grasp. "I'm not anything special compared to you. I'm surprised Exos even looked at me. . . . Please, take it."

Words escaped Ventus as he gawked at Nimba, making her blush slightly. "Thank you . . . Thank you so much. I'll find a way to repay you. I promise," Ventus said, cradling Nimba's essay with great care.

"You don't owe me anything. Just remember to erase my name and put yours down."

Ventus hugged Nimba so tight that the paper crunched between them. "I'll find something . . . I may owe you my life."

Nimba chuckled. "Dramatic much?"

At this moment, the academy bell dinged, signaling the start of the first class. Ventus' eyes popped open. He didn't even blink before he lifted, grunted, and carried Nimba through the decorated hallway and into their classroom. It was full of many species of smaller birds, who sat attentively at their seats with lengthy quills in their wings. The cockatiel teacher glared at Ventus with sinister intent. "Sorry!" Ventus bowed slightly, darted to the nearest open seat, and rested Nimba on the desk.

"Alright, class, turn in your Saurian application essay to the bird on your left," the teacher commanded.

Ventus quickly dipped a feather in a cup of white paint

and covered Nimba's name from the essay. He then took up a quill and wrote his name before sliding it to the bird on his left. Nimba and Ventus smiled at each other as the teacher collected the papers and began class.

"Now, I was informed that the reason the selection process of Sauria's school is tough, is not due to the sheer number of applicants. Lord Anzu is happy to receive many applicants, and he likes to see so many creatures wanting to learn more about the world. But the reason for learning must be selfless. Anzu selects the students by seeing who they strive to be through their role models: someone who cares only for their self-gain, or someone who wants to improve the world. This can show much of who you are as a bird and if you are worthy of the title, librarian. Honestly, if your role model is Anzu, you'll get in for sure," she murmured that last part.

Ventus felt his chest sink. His vision blurred, and he thought he was going to be sick.

A few birds in the class muffled their cheers.

Nimba rested her wing on his shoulder and smiled at him before he nervously smiled back with a gulp.

The rest of the class was relatively simple for Ventus, but Nimba squinted hard at the board and struggled to write notes with the teacher's speed. "Don't worry about taking notes; we can share mine when we get home. Just focus on understanding the content, no rush," Ventus whispered before Nimba set her quill down and gave an exhausted sigh.

"Thank you."

The class lasted until the giant academy bell rang at the top of the hour. Ventus tucked his notes under his wing before helping Nimba from the room with a hundred birds scattering about to their next class.

All the remaining classes went similarly. Nimba squinted at the board so intensely it hurt, and Ventus took notes. But something bothered Ventus. In the back of his mind, he thought of the words Exos told him. He couldn't shake the feeling that something was horribly wrong. But it was Exos, one of the elites. Nothing could be wrong with him at the helm. "Right?" Ventus whispered.

Nimba looked at him as he mouthed a conversation to himself.

After the end of their last class, Ventus carried Nimba into the hall and glanced around for Exos. "He said paint room, correct?" Ventus murmured. Nimba took the stack of notes to relieve Ventus.

"I'm not so sure about this. I mean, what does he have to gain by helping you get into the Saurian program?" Nimba chuckled a little. "And what if my essay was good, and you don't need him?"

Ventus looked down, thinking about those questions. "It can't hurt to have a backup plan. . . . And maybe Exos will get extra credit or a place on the academy door for helping me. Who knows?" Once the school was almost empty, Exos flew from the entrance and landed without a single whisper next to Ventus. "Excellent; I'm glad you considered my offer to this degree. Shall your little pinecone wait here, or is it going home? I'd like to discuss your future in a . . . private setting."

Nimba glared at Exos. There was something odd with how he spoke. It was still calm and very regal. But there was a little haste to it that made Nimba even more suspicious. "I'll stay here. I'm not the best at walking in the snow, since it's taller than me." Nimba turned to Ventus as he lowered her to the floor. "Are you sure about this?"

Ventus looked up at Exos, who was smiling in a comforting way. "Not really, but what could possibly happen?" Ventus smirked. "But if anything goes wrong, I know you'll be right here. I'll call for you if needed."

"I must say, your suspicion goes unwarranted. All I wish is to discuss a future that will benefit both parties. If you want out, just say so."

"No! I want your help."

Nimba eyed Exos with all her suspicions before she sat against the wall and began to glance at the class notes. "Oh, and Ventus..."

Ventus looked back at her as Exos delicately cradled his wing behind him and aided him to the paint room.

"I... lo–" she grunted, "I mean, I wish you luck."

Ventus exhaled through his nares and smirked. "You too. Study hard, then let me know if you have any questions." The door shut behind him with a haunting creak.

The memory went blurry instantly, and it seemed not to be real. Like this was just a guess of what Ventus thought happened or a simple blurry daydream.

"Throwing away his hard work, then making it seem like he's his only hope. It's practically manipulation!" Nimba told herself. Almost an hour passed as Nimba sat, diligently waiting by studying and observing the pretty murals the art students painted that autumn. Nothing suspicious caught her attention during that period, except a few strange noises that she assumed to be the winter wind flapping the school banners.

The memory cleared, and they could see Nimba sitting in the hall.

But it was at this moment when all things peaceful ceased to exist. The door to the paint room creaked open to Ventus, who wheezed every subtle breath. He was hardly able to stand, for his legs wobbled like cooked noodles, and he had eye-widening cuts from the knees to his waist, bleeding and forming a line of puddles beneath him. His shallow eyes showed no signs of life as they drooped with his body. His front feathers were still perfect, but his back feathers were in chaos; some areas were missing many.

"Ventus!" Nimba screamed as Ventus limped to the nearest window curtain and ripped it off the pole. In Ventus' eyes, Nimba could tell what once held life and wonder, now poured despair and regret. Nimba instantly darted toward him as fast as she could. Ventus wrapped the curtain around his shivering body and collapsed on his face. "What did he do to you?" Nimba yelled and knelt beside him. Ventus didn't move, let alone acknowledge Nimba's presence. When she gently rested her wing on Ventus' shoulder, Ventus twitched and quickly tucked the curtain to his neck.

"What a great performance. I daresay that for a smaller bird, you were perfection." Exos left the paint room without a single feather ruffled.

Nimba growled and charged at Exos. But being no taller than his ankle, Exos brushed her to the side with ease. "You pecker! What did you do to him?" She quickly ran next to Ventus.

Ventus blinked at Nimba, now standing between him and Exos with her tiny wings spread out.

Exos' eye twitched, then glared at Nimba. "I simply discussed his future, and based on how it went, I'd say he's earned *some* of my recommendation for his Saurian dream."

"Some! Some! You promised to–" Exos leaned down and pressed his sharp beak against Nimba's fluffy body.

"Are you insinuating that I am not true to my word? I only said *some* because I believe there is one flaw he needs to work on before the professors here will even consider his presence. . . . He needs to learn how to fly. Then I promise I'll give him a recommendation more precious than a thousand essays. But he still has to be a good little prince . . . or my recommendation will mean nothing." He eyed Ventus.

Nimba's face scrunched with her fragile wings ready to fight. She cared about Ventus, and nothing was worth seeing him in such a state. Even though she was a speck compared to Exos, she stood as tall as she could, tiptoeing the carpet. "What did you do?" she growled, wobbled in the unbalanced stance, then clenched her tiny talons through the carpet.

Exos scoffed. "Come, my prince; we have a little more to do." He shoved Nimba forward. "You're joining for this part, you asinine pecker." Exos walked and guided Nimba along, and Ventus wobbled until he stood.

"I can do it. . . . Just one more step until I become somebody. . . . Just one more step until a smaller bird gets on those doors." He then limped after them and glared at the academy doors as he passed.

The sun now shone onto their heads and sparkled the snow across the ground and castle tops. It wasn't long before they arrived at Zenith's edge, where it's mandatory to jump for birds first learning to fly. The cold wind crept through Nimba's feathers as she looked down at the thick sheet of clouds below with many moisture lumps hiding shadows from the sun.

"Now jump." Those words froze the wind and hollowed their chests.

"What! You're not going to show us first? Ventus doesn't know the first thing about flying! He spent all his time studying academics. And besides, flying is not a prerequisite to the Saurian program! You just have to be kind and ambitious for learning!" Nimba said.

Exos laughed. "Of course it's not a prerequisite; it's an obvious and simple skill they didn't even bother to mention. I mean, how will he even get down to Sauria if he can't fly?"

Nimba stopped and looked at Ventus, who stared at the planet far, far below. "Ventus . . . let's just go home." She turned to Exos. "We can plan for a future without this PECKER'S help."

Exos' feet clenched the snow, and his eye twitched at Nimba, who devilishly smiled at him.

Ventus said nothing. It was obvious he was thinking something as he stared at the clouds below, but what, was a mystery.

"Ventus?" Nimba reached out to him, but he twitched away once more. And with that, she sighed with a long pause. "I'll jump." This instantly caught Ventus' and Exos' attention, and surprisingly, it seemed to wake Ventus up.

"What?" Ventus yelled.

"I can learn how to fly, then carry Ventus down to Sauria. This way, he can focus on his studies for when you hold your end of the deal." Nimba glared at Exos, who struggled to suppress a deep smile begging to curve his beak.

"No! I won't let you do this! Your wings aren't even grown in yet!"

Nimba gripped her toes around the edge.

"I want to help you, Ventus. You're special. You have a chance at a life far greater than mine. The least I can do is learn to fly. And if one of us doesn't jump now–" She glared at Exos. "I think he'll push us both."

Ventus crept his eyes back at Exos and felt the painful truth to those words, lowering his wings over his bloody thighs.

Exos shrugged. "I'm certain the professors will allow this flight exception if the pinecone thing learns for you. But do make it quick; I have other matters to attend to."

Nimba turned to Ventus. "You won't live your dream if I don't jump. Because I doubt my essay will be any good." She froze as she turned to the planet below. "But I'm terrified. I can't do it by myself. . . . Sorry, but you're going to have to push me. Heh."

Ventus froze and dared not breathe, for his greatest friend stood at the dawn of death. This moment was so important, so fragile, that a blink could ruin it all. He glanced up at Exos, who glared at him. His eyes spoke of something he dared not describe. Ventus raised his trembling wings and pressed them against Nimba's back. His heart ached as if she had already died. Thinking about a future without her was the worst future he could imagine. He was growling at the raw hatred for his decisions up to this point. He found himself hating nearly everything around him. But the one thing he loved stood before him within his fragile grasp. He could feel Nimba's scared little heartbeat in the tips of his wings and the friendship that fueled him all this time. "Please, don't make me," Ventus begged.

Nimba smiled with a nervous glance back at Ventus. "I . . . love–"

Exos nudged Ventus' back with his foot. Ventus gasped as he accidentally shoved Nimba off the ledge. He instantly covered his beak with his wings, watching her fall into the clouds.

"Well done, my precious little Prince of the Sky. Once she returns, I will hold my promise dear and set up a meeting with the ones who will make your future." He leaned forward. "And maybe, after you're done here, you can pleasure me with your company once more. I found you immensely satisfying to be with." He caressed the bottom of Ventus' beak with his longest feather before turning around. "Hope to see you soon, Prince Ventus."

Ventus stared at the sea of sunlit snow clouds below with Nimba's warmth fading from his wingtips, hoping, praying that she would fly back. But as the many cycles of the sun and moon curved over him, and his open wings felt the cursed sting of winter cold, his body sank with the fading joy of life. He didn't care about Sauria anymore. He didn't care about school or himself. He just wanted to know if Nimba was okay. The curtain he held froze around him like a shell as a deep hole caved his chest, never to be filled again.

He loved that bird. And he hated himself for not seeing it until now. And as the third sun reached the apex of his lifelong regret, he felt his heart numbing to the last icy seconds of life. He stopped breathing and leaned forward, submitting to the alluring call of death.

The wind stole the curtain away as he plummeted toward the ground. He still felt nothing but the subtle memory of Nimba in his grasp. How warm she was, how she smiled at him every day. Her unyielding kindness and patience for someone as stupid as him. Just as Ventus was a few hundred feet from the ground, he felt the familiar warmth of Nimba in his chest.

"What?" He peeked open his eyes as his frozen wings instinctively cracked apart. And suddenly, a gale from nothing roared beneath him and stopped his descent, hovering him just a few feet from the snowy ground. "Noo! Nooooo!" Ventus squirmed against the wind.

He folded his wings against his chest, but the wind still took him. He flapped and cursed the wind until he felt the cold snow of Zenith beneath his toes. In a final attempt, he tried once more to jump, but the wind now refused his toes even the grace of liftoff. He collapsed with his face frozen by the tears, for even the mercy of death had escaped him.

"Don't make me live without her!"

Suddenly, heavy footsteps crunched the snow behind him. "I've been watching you for a while now. . . . I saw what happened with your friend." The giant figure stood in front of Ventus. She was a great horned owl, cloaked in umber down to the large bumps of her toes. "Those gnashes on your thighs and the missing feathers on your lower back, I can aid you. I'm a doctor, and if you ever need help, just come in. I'll treat you for free. I hate those larger birds, always taking advantage of the little ones."

Ventus looked down at his thighs. "No. . . . Thank you, but I want to remember this." He rubbed his leg feathers. "Is there anything I can do to hide it though? Like wrapping a blanket around the injuries. I don't want creatures asking *those* types of questions."

The doctor nodded and helped him to her castle. She showed him a pair of pecan-brown harem pants primarily used for holding casts and gauze in place. Ventus didn't mind the look and slipped them on; and thus, the discovery of recreational clothing on Somnium.

"What time is–" Ventus paused when he finally registered the many clocks around the room. "Oh . . . Well, thank you for your help. But I should get going to school."

The doctor looked at him quizzically. "I think you should take a few days off, but if you really want to go back so soon. Here." She handed him a note to excuse his many-day absence.

"How did you–" Ventus glanced at it, then shook his head,

ignoring the strange doctor's ways. He waved goodbye and left the castle before slowly lumbering back to the academy. In his mind, it was pointless to mend his wounds; he wanted to carry his pain forever. To remember Nimba with every painful step he took.

He arrived in his classroom and gave the doctor's note to the teacher before sitting down. "Alright, class, your essays for your Saurian admissions have been graded, and all the ones that passed were copied and sent to Lord Anzu." She walked around the rows and handed the students their papers, glaring at Ventus as she handed him his.

He looked down at it and nearly froze. "Fail. Narcissist. Get checked for dissociative identity disorder," he read with a confused squint, thinking as he looked down at the words below. A few students chuckled at him as they peeked at his essay. It was rather short.

*The creature I deem my hero is Ventus Libertas, the stubborn, arrogant, yet secretly kind-hearted and fragile blue jay. After our parents left for Sauria, he found me and accepted me into his castle. Since then, even though he's my age, he's shown me true courage, treated me like family, and helped me when I struggled to walk up those stairs.*

*I've never been good at much, so having him by my side has made my life much better. One day I hope to make it up to him and tell him he means the world to me and that I . . . love him. Hopefully, I'll build the strength to tell him all these heavy things. He makes every morning a joy to wake up to, and for the future, I hope we can spend it together.*

*P.S. If Anzu is really reading this . . . could I . . . go to Sauria with Ventus?*

Ventus' tears tapped the paper. "That stupid wren. . . ."

As the students around him snickered at the word 'narcissist,' the air around him spun and whipped many papers around the room. Lighter students suddenly were sucked out the door while the teacher and others screamed as they ran away. The stone walls cracked and broke apart. Suddenly, it all spun into a tornado as Ventus only stared at the essay through a blur of tears. The ceiling snapped off the walls and flung into the sky. And at the storm's end, the academy was nothing more than a pile of rubble and paper.

## Chapter 16
# RISING TIDES

"No, no, no!" Anzu quickly moved his arms as the wind watered his eyes and the flowery ground of King's Garden rushed toward him.

The valley rumbled and quaked, then erupted out a tall spire with a curved bottom. Once the spire's tip met Anzu's altitude, he dug his claws into it. He barely slowed his fall before he met the curve at the bottom.

He felt the slant against the pads of his feet before he lost his grip, smacked on his back, then tumbled down the rest of the way. It hurt everything. And when he slid along the flowers at the bottom, he moaned in pain and struggled to imagine getting up after that. Even his aching body told him to stay down.

"No. I need to warn them." He slowly looked up at Rafflesia and reached his hand to the castle on the grassy hill. "Ella." His vision blurred, and his head bobbed. "I need to–" Anzu coughed, then placed the tip of a claw on a stone. "Take me to the city," he commanded with his eyes closed.

The stone melted into a puddle, then hardened into a disk that slid beneath Anzu and picked him up. He pointed to the castle with his remaining strength, and the stone did all he begged and flew him toward it.

He peeked back toward the clouds with George and Sam. "He's so brave. He seemed like the shyest creature when I first met him." He looked at his trembling hands. "To face that monster and tell me everything's going to be okay . . . he's changed. . . ."

Just before he arrived at the bordering moat around Rafflesia, he roared and cried as he forced his legs with the burden of standing. With his position trembling more than an earthquake, he pointed his hand to the city and began to raise his arm. The valley started to shake as a wall of diamonds peeked at the water's surface. But then Anzu vomited and collapsed with his wheezing throat swallowing the little air he could grasp.

"I . . . need to." He tried to raise his arm again, but such a small task now seemed impossible. "If only I could drop Zenith." He gulped. "But who knows where it would crash land once I exhaust my ability on building a wall. . . . Let's just hope he doesn't intend to destroy everything. Maybe he's here for a diplomatic solution." His eyes sank, and his cheek pressed against the stone. He wanted to believe such blissful things were possible. But he knew that was only a fantasy. He looked at the castle before the stone flew him closer.

As he spotted the guardsmen at the castle's entrance, the stone gave up with the last of his energy. "King Anzu!" A moose guard said as Anzu fell. Luckily, the antlered guards banded together and caught him, stumbling them into a collapsed pile from the impact.

"Take me to her . . ." Anzu whispered before he passed out.

The guards looked at each other and carried him through the doorway. They bumped into a sizable, round bird in their haste. But the bird only smiled and bowed, letting them pass.

The great hall was no longer a place that reminded creatures of bloodshed and war. The pillars were sanded and painted over with a mural of many flowers and leaves. The architects roamed about, removing large parts of the walls to be replaced with windows. Even some botanists found enjoyment in decorating the corners with various plants. Ella chose to make the castle seem more open and friendly for those who wished to enter. In fact, she had the front doors removed. Now a cool, early-winter air freshened the halls slowly back to life.

Ella stood at the center of everything in a lovely ocean-blue dress that moved like gentle waves as she walked. She helped the creatures around her while making the future for the kingdom. It was peace, and with it, hope. But that all stopped when Ella turned around and saw the guards carry Anzu through the doorway. Her face went from kind and smiling to terrified and eye-widening with the rise of her sharp ears. "Anzu!" she yelled and dashed to him. "Set him down, please."

Her heart weighed heavier than granite as they lowered his dirty, icy body to the floor. She knelt beside him, raised her hand, then sucked all the water from the plant pots around them, angering a few botanists. "Anzu!" She hoped he would respond, but not a whisper came. "What happened?" She opened his mouth and flowed the floating water down his throat. Her gentle hand guided the water into his stomach and throughout the rest of his body, trying to spot any injuries.

"He was floating on a rock, then he fell at the doorstep, asking to see you," the big moose guard spoke.

Ella placed her ear next to Anzu's nose to feel or hear any breaths. After a few moments, she sighed and concluded he would be alright. But at that moment, his breaths began to hasten. "Anzu?"

He smiled at the blissful song of her voice. "Good. You're alright."

"I'm alright? What do you mean? You're the one who–" She stopped as Anzu slowly moved his hand to her.

His eyelids were too heavy to open, so he searched the ground. Ella grabbed his hand, but right as she did that, the ground shook, and a massive slab of the hardest rock Anzu could find pierced the wooden floor of the castle. It covered them at an angle, like one side of a pyramid.

"What are you doing?" Ella asked. Her eye twitched from seeing everyone's hard work being impaled through the heart.

"Everyone, get under here," Anzu begged with a gulp before two more walls erupted from the ground and stabbed into both sides of the slab. And that was when the air became stiff, so much so, it was hard to discern if there was any air at all. "Now!"

Everyone within earshot ran beneath the angled barrier, confused about what was happening. Even Ella's head tilted. "What's going on, Anzu?" Just as she asked that, his grip squeezed her, not enough to hurt, but enough that begged her not to let go.

"Apotheosis. It's here–"

BOOM!

The castle walls instantly evaporated. The floorboards outside Anzu's now-cracked diamond barrier disappeared in a blinding flash of white. By the time everyone's eyes adjusted, there was nothing left apart from their little group of a dozen or so with Anzu holding them up in his little fortress.

He opened his mouth to pop his ringing eardrums. "I tried. . . . I tried to save as many as I could." Anzu then opened an eye to the results, seeing only the gray sky and the terrified creatures around him.

Ella peeked from their nook, and her stomach rotted with the poison of what her eyes consumed. The giant hill that once supported the castle was replaced by a canyon that howled far below the planet's surface. Then, Ella found herself gripping Anzu's hand harder than he was. She wanted to ask him what happened, but her trembling heart was in such shock, she couldn't feel it beat, let alone think about using her gaping mouth.

"Is everyone alright?" Anzu asked, but no response came from any of them. They all just stared at what once was their growing city. Some creatures began crying, but all sank to their knees or passed out, for the weight of so many memories was impossible to carry. The lives of their families and friends would forever be nothing more than that, a memory. Some slowly clenched their hands into fists at the revenge they wished to erupt.

Only a few houses remained at the sides of the canyon, but most of their walls or hay roofs were gone. Anzu lowered them onto the eastern side of the canyon. "E-Everyone who is able . . . go to Petal." Anzu choked up, for many of his Saurian friends were starting their lives here.

And now, with the only ones left in such a big city, his cheek hit the floor. He couldn't protect them, and he blamed himself for it. Even if he spared their souls, their lives were over. Their children, family, and friends were all dead. There was no point in searching for survivors, for what lay before them howled death and death alone. No screams of pain raised their ears, no rubble shifting. The only life was that of hot wind rising from the canyon, blowing flakes of ash to tap Anzu's walls like specks of sand. "Could you help me up?" Anzu requested with a sniffle.

Ella looked at Anzu with sadness in her eyes. "I know what you're thinking, and no, I won't let you go out there. If Apotheosis is capable of this on its first attack. . . . I'm sorry, but your ability, even if you dropped Zenith, isn't remotely comparable, especially as you are now."

Anzu looked at the sky. White flakes began to fall from the now-charcoal clouds above, and the scent of ash finally met his snotty nares. "It was all burned away." He looked at the canyon walls, layered in a black, soot-like substance. Most of it was turned into a glassy rock from heat fusing with the dirt. There was also the familiar stench of soot that the queen once mined. But the rivers that once formed the moat around the city, now poured into the canyon, extinguishing the stench with a steaming sizzle.

"My mother tried to mine all this," Ella said, thinking exactly what Anzu was. Her teeth showed from her scowling lips. "I'm coming with you," she growled.

"Together then?" Anzu peeked down at his leathery hand wrapped around her soft yet firm hand.

Ella looked at Anzu fervently. "You take care of me, and I'll take care of you. But you shouldn't have to worry about me." Ella stood and helped Anzu up. "For I'm going to remove every drop of life from the creature responsible for this."

Anzu blinked with a nervous smile. He was getting a little scared of Ella. But he cradled her face and led her eyes to him. She paused as she saw his cinnamon eyes. "Let's make sure these creatures are safe first. Then I can help you by forcing it to eat rocks and removing them from its stomach."

Ella's ears flicked, hearing Anzu's heart pounding fast enough to fuel his rage. But he kept a calm appearance for the creatures watching them. Ella turned to them and smiled. "Alright. Head over to Petal; an elk should be stationed there to get you situated. Tell him what happened. And if he's too stupid to understand, or he is rude in any way–" she looked at the creatures, and among the group of frightened or enraged Anthophytans and Saurians, stood the profound bird. Its body was nearly spherical, about eight feet tall, and covered with tawny feathers. It seemed to stare at the ruins with a thoughtful squint. "You will be the new general."

Anzu smiled at the bird, who looked at Ella with a confused tilt of the head . . . and body. "That's the librarian."

Ella froze, and her jaw fell with disbelief.

The enormous bird walked toward Ella, with each step quieter than a romantic whisper. "I am sorry to reject your general offer for this time. . . . You see, in addition to collecting more food for the creatures sent back to the tower of memory, I've come to Rafflesia specifically in search of a friend of mine. But once I've found him and have brought food to those creatures, I would be happy to offer my services."

Ella bowed to the bird. "Thank you; it's an honor to finally meet you. And I hope you find your friend with ease."

The bird raised Ella's head with the gentle raise of her wing. "Don't worry. I'll show these creatures where they need to go, then resume my search. Only the general thing may have to wait."

Ella blinked at the bird and took note of her large, round glasses and lengthy amethyst knitted scarf. After a nervous nod, Ella turned to Anzu, who bore a warming smile from seeing the librarian well.

"Where is Apotheosis?" Ella asked, recomposing herself.

"North. At the beginning of the canyon, I would assume.

But I–"

Ella looked in that direction, then instantly ran toward it.

"Wait!" Anzu reached out his arm, then nearly chuckled as she ran away. He looked back to the bird with a nod. Then the bird turned to the creatures and began to help them.

Anzu held his arm out and opened his hand to the ground. Within a blink, a jewel of every color and type rose from the ground and fused into a rainbow bracelet. His body felt light as a bubble with a final glance at Ella. "I hope she says yes." He held the bracelet gently in his hands, then, with a heavy limp, he ran north with the help of his newfound energy.

But little did they see, Sam limping toward the ruins of Rafflesia to hide from what was coming.

## Chapter 17
## EYES OF THE STORM

They opened their eyes and relieved their hands from Ventus' head. His tears tapped against the hard floor, and his face was scrunched in frustration. "I know you're stupid and new to this planet. . . . But please, understand that I can't lose another creature. . . . Just walk out of here. I'm not worth it." Ventus looked up at Hugo.

"Alright, it's time to fight." The chicken's voice echoed around them.

Ventus stood with a sigh, placing his wing over Hugo's mouth to block further stupidity. "I reckon this will be the last moment we have together." He shuffled toward the chicken's voice and the sound of rain rushing down and pecking the sand like a barrage of bullets. Hugo, Bipp, and Luna simply followed him until his talon hit the stairs, and he stopped. "I was thinking . . . if Exos never found me, and I became a hero like Anzu . . . I bet you and I would've been great friends." He glanced back at the three of them. "I'm sorry for all of this." With a sniffle, he looked forward and climbed the steps with the scent of rain finding their nares.

At the top, the chicken stood before them. Like the rest of

the now-muddy arena, the raincloud's shadow cloaked and drenched the chicken.

"You and you will attend the stands wherever there's an opening." The chicken pointed his wing at Luna and Bipp; then, he pointed at Ventus. "You will go to Exos' throne. And you–" he pointed at Hugo and stepped aside with his wing pointed to the muddy field before them. "Please, win," he spoke louder than before, trying to be heard over the rain.

Even Ventus froze for a moment after hearing that. He looked to Hugo and mouthed: 'please go.' It was hard to tell with his beak, but Hugo wouldn't have listened anyway as he nodded to the chicken with his heart racing from the worrying anticipation of the fight. Luna, Bipp, and Ventus walked and flew to their spots. Ventus sighed and drooped in defeat as he left.

Hugo tip-toed through the mud until he met the center of the arena. His heart was beating faster than the war drums that thumped in his head. He never passed out like Sam when in front of people, but he sure felt lightheaded enough to do so. He was alone in a dark room, hardly able to spot the walls with rain this dense. He only had his noodle limbs to carry his suddenly heavy, soaked body. The atmosphere was different from the last visit. Instead of a bustling crowd, the audience was ghost quiet. Few even acknowledged Hugo's presence, for most had their beaks down and eyes closed.

Then, the drums hushed.

Upon Hugo's final step, he turned to look nervously at Exos, who petted Ventus while eyeing Hugo. Then, to Hugo's surprise, a single bird opened its beak and began to sing. It was calm and subtle, barely heard over the rain. And after his ears adjusted to listen, many other birds battled the rain in song for who was superior. To Hugo's ears, their voices were perfect with the sudden mix of stringed instruments and vocal cords. But it all shivered him, for he knew they were setting the scene for what was coming.

"Welcome back, my dear prince." Exos' voice cursed Ventus. His great white wings spread apart and robbed Ventus' feet from the ground's security with a soft hug. "How was your basement adventure?" His voice spidered into Ventus, shivering every part of him. There was a canopy over them, so the rain wouldn't soak them, but Ventus would've preferred drowning over this.

"I-It w-was good," he said without much thought, hoping Exos would let go.

But Exos squeezed him tighter. "While you were gone, my scouts retrieved the gondola you stole from me."

Ventus' stomach boiled and weighed like a sack of bricks. He wanted to die right then to avoid the horrors of his future.

"You dare leave Zenith without my permission; you dare steal from me, then damage the boat."

"Damage, my lord?" Ventus said, hoping to play stupid.

Exos scoffed. "Why was there a ripped sail and splintered wood?" he growled and squeezed the breath from Ventus. "Why was there a sail at all? Do you hate me that much to leave my property in such a state?"

Ventus only responded with his trembling legs and toes curling up to protect himself.

"Such stupid actions will warrant some costly favors. . . . But we can *talk about* that later." Then, luckily, Exos let go and set him beside his throne. "Now tell me, Ventus, who is this dragon? And don't you dare lie to me again. A scout told me what happened down there." He glared at Ventus. "You two seemed to have an odd connection. Plus, it has a particular fear of the dark, and it's an emberlight?"

As Ventus saw his forthcoming death in *those* eyes, his mind went dizzy. "He's nobody, I swear. . . . But I must warn you, my lord . . . he bites." Ventus smiled a little with his last hope to mock Exos. If Exos knew what he said in the basement, he was a walking corpse. But to his discomfort, Exos smiled and ignored the latter.

"Pity, I was hoping his soul would be worth all this effort, but since he's just an emberlight, I might as well entertain the crowd with his entrails," he sighed, but his golden eyes looked at Hugo in a way that shivered Ventus. "Now then, witness, my prince, the reason I became ruler of Dawn." Exos ceased his wing over Ventus, stepped out from under the canopy, and raised both wings swiftly like an angelic statue. The music intensified with a thousand birds starting to sing as they raised their beaks to the sky.

Hugo couldn't tell what they were singing, but it forced his stomach to boil bleach and his tongue to excrete a venomous salt into his mouth. Then, the great wings of Exos flapped once upon his exit with a mighty thrust that pushed Ventus to the floor. And upon his landing, his right foot, with many dagger-like hooks, kissed the mud without a single splash. And at this moment, as he raised his head to Hugo, the music dawned upon its apex.

Hugo took a step back, now seeing how massive Exos was, for Hugo's height barely passed his knees. If Hugo had to guess, he was twenty feet tall and had a wingspan greater than his sight could bear from this close. The Eye of the Storm closed with black clouds and crackling thunder. Exos curled back his long neck, aimed his needle-like beak at Hugo, and then stepped closer and closer.

"Please, entertain me with a response, dragon. Why did you dare to challenge me?"

Hugo gulped. "Well, I wanted to help my friend, The Lord of the Sky."

Exos glanced back at Ventus with a subtle twitch in his eye. Ventus froze at that, but Hugo's words forced a smile from his beak. "Lord of the sky, huh? . . . That idiot."

Exos' eye sharpened at Ventus along with the crackle of thunder. But Ventus' attention was no longer on him; it was the dark clouds that robbed his attention with a sudden, nervous grin.

Exos scoffed and turned back to Hugo, who gaped their distance while he was distracted. "Ah—This is a fight! Cease your fruitless attempts at flirting and get on with it!" he yelled to reach Hugo, then walked closer to him with a sigh.

"He's in for a big surprise if he thought *that* was Hugo flirting," Bipp murmured with a chuckle. Luna looked at Bipp with a tilt to her head. He blushed as he saw her look, then resumed watching the fight.

"But one final question before you die: what did you think of the prophecy on the wall? It seemed to disturb you more than my scouts could fathom to describe." The thunderclouds thickened and shadowed the once-starlit ground in a dark envelope.

Hugo responded with a sludgy step back with every firm step Exos gave, but Hugo's legs were much shorter. "A prophecy? W-What do you know about that wall?"

Exos hastened his steps as Hugo's fur stood. It zapped and popped with static near his scarf, as if the lightning took aim. "You wish to know more? How far are you willing to go, for this information comes at a dire price?"

Particles of sunlight struggled to pass the clouds. The darkness forced Hugo to squint just to spot Exos' white feathers. "Just tell me about Sam! Did you paint that?"

"No. For this castle belonged to the great Apotheosis before I took over. But seeing your scales like those flower petals begs me to ask, who are you? Why would the great Apotheosis have you prophesied on the wall beneath his throne? And by any chance, was your left eye green?"

"I don't know! I just want to know why I saw Sam up there!"

"Sam. . . . Is it one of the flowers in the prophecy?"

"Yes! The big one in the center!"

Exos froze, and with him, the thunder crackle hushed for a second. Hugo's fur sank into his back, but he still felt spiders crawling along his neck. "What the?" he whispered and grabbed the scarf, relieving it from his neck. It slapped against the mud with a messy splash. And to his discomfort, he thought he heard the floor creak under the scarf's weight.

"You know the center flower?" A subtle grin crept over Exos' long beak as the thunder resumed.

"Yeah, it looked like my brother, Sam. Or at least, the raven version of him. . . . I think he's human now, so the whole thing confuses me." Hugo squinted at the scarf as it shimmered and popped in flashes of static.

Exos' eyes lit up.

Hugo touched the scarf before it zapped and numbed his finger. "What did Bipp put in this? Metal?" he whispered and picked it from the mud. His fur stood and zapped once more. He craned his head to the sky above and saw lightning bolts dancing around clouds.

"Thank you for indulging me, dragon. It's been decades since someone mentioned humans in such a manner. But it makes sense if Apotheosis is involved with Sam. . . . And since humans can't survive on Somnium, it's only logical that he is indeed a bird, probably on Zenith."

"What?" Hugo looked up at Exos' beak, inches before his snout.

"Goodbye."

Hugo's eye widened as a flash of light stole his eyes and ears. It boomed and shook the arena, pausing many hearts with its sudden impact. The music ceased as many in the audience cheered after seeing the bolt zap down the tower's hollow center. Ventus, Bipp, and Luna leaned forward with their mouths agape while their eyes adjusted to the dark anew.

"Why do you care about Sam! What do you know about humans? How come me and him are in a prophecy? Are all prophecies like that?" Hugo gulped, freezing Exos in place. As the clouds gave way to some light, Hugo stood with his scarf wrapped around the end of his tail, which craned over him like a scorpion. With its immense length, it dropped down to the mud. The fabrics smoked and sizzled from the heat and rain battling each other.

"Be-cause . . . he is . . ." Exos stopped, simply observing Hugo's odd position. His beak struggled to find the words to continue. "What did you just do?"

"I knew I wasn't over two-thousand five-hundred pounds!" Hugo smiled a little with his legs wobbling, numb from rogue electricity; he even felt his heart thump differently than before, but he still eyed Exos. "Tell me what's going on!"

Exos shook his head with a growl to cease his shock. "Enough!"

Another lightning bolt boomed Hugo's scarf and scorched any knitting Bipp had done over the metal. All the birds in the audience had their beaks gaping at the sight. "Is Sam okay?" Hugo roared, and his hind legs nearly collapsed. He couldn't feel the lower half of his body, and his chest began to hurt with a numbing tingle as he stepped forward and struggled immensely.

Exos growled, then slapped his wings together. Suddenly, the clouds became so dark that it was worse than a moonless midnight. Hugo couldn't even spot the end of his snout. "I hear you're afraid of certain things." A sharp, freezing wind stung Hugo's flesh and howled into his snout and ears, rendering his other senses blind.

"I see your companion flower. That old doctrine is nothing more than a childish bane of hope. . . . But in case that belief is true, once I kill you, I will keep your soul companion rabbit prisoner. So even in death, you will be alone."

Hugo's heart thumped in his head like someone was punching him. As the cold wind came, so did specks of ice nipping his scales. They bit harder until the hail felt like fangs racing from the sky to eat him.

Hugo tried to speak, but his throat swelled as he choked on something hot rising from his chest. *Don't you dare lay a feather on Bipp.*

"Let's see you take this," Exos said.

Hugo unhinged his jaw and roared out a wave of orange fire.

But before it reached Exos, a planetary rumble shook the clouds and tower like an earthquake. And within a blink, a golden beam of electricity zapped from the heavens and crushed the muddy floor. But the bolt didn't stop, even as the floor buckled and gave under the weight of constant rain. Exos unhinged his beak and roared out everything he had before the arena floor fell beneath them.

Ventus ran to the edge where the stairs collapsed and looked down, worried.

The audience gawked at the continuous discharge until it vanished into the shadows. The moonlight and starlight beamed on the floor through the now-patchy ceiling of silver, cotton clouds. Hugo was gone; at least, it took the audience a while to find him. The arena's muddy floor had collapsed into the dark haze of the basement.

Hugo couldn't feel much of his numb body. And to his best efforts, he couldn't see much through the dark haze as his heart stung with every heavy thump. The only thing he could manage with his zapping body was to listen and wheeze. He held a hand over his fluttering chest and shoved down, trying to help his breaths and heart to keep going through the numbness, but it seemed to help little. He heard the heaving of someone trying to suppress their gulping breath. He recognized it as Exos', who struggled to stand after that all-out attack.

"Is it over? Do I finally have a dragon's soul that's not some asinine memory thing?"

Luna's fangs cracked under the sheer pressure of her anger.

As the rain settled down and the dark shroud dispersed evenly through the tower, Exos peeked up at Hugo, who lay on the muddy ground, obviously not getting up as he gulped for air and held his hurting chest. He wanted to scream for help, but his cries only left his lips in a dry breath.

A small flash of lightning shot from the clouds in a blink and hit the ground beside Exos. And in an elegant swoop, Exos dug his foot through the mud, then yanked out a glass sword. It was beautiful; with finite spiderweb-like etchings formed with the electric current, the tip was sharper than a static bolt. With his beak low, he swung his sword-held foot to the side and stood at a perfect angle on one leg. He was so still, one could mistake him for a statue. But he still struggled to control his breathing. "Time to finish this."

"I challenge Exos, the pecker."

Even Hugo paused as those words met his ears. Exos' eyes squinted, but there was some concern as he turned his head to Ventus, who glided over the open pit.

"What did you just call me?" Exos growled. There was a quick crackle of thunder from the remaining clouds.

"Pecker. Must I define it for you? I probably should to recover your gawking beak."

Exos closed his beak with a growl. "During a storm? Are you sure about that, my prince?"

Ventus smiled with a scoff, then landed between Exos and Hugo. "Certainly. I wouldn't want to challenge you at your weakest; then, you'd give me some pitiful excuse. You see, I've learned a lot about you as your . . . prince, if that's what you call it. But you've manipulated me since before I knew you, and because of such, you've never seen me for what I truly am." He almost laughed. "With your daft manipulation, you assume creatures worship you and actually want to fight in your disgusting arena."

"Manipula– I've helped these creatures find a place to stay. What do you think happened to their homes on Zenith after many years in that Anthophytan mine? Plus, your hero, Anzu, had no room in Rafflesia after they were set free; he didn't even have enough space for all his kin. He had to send some back to the tower of memory and to that tiny village, Petal. So like you once did, these birds asked me for a new home after being so poorly treated by the chances of the world. I'm not the evil one here, Ventus. But I would consider you at fault for these accusations. You were the one who pushed that pinecone from Zenith; you were the one who destroyed the academy and all the tools of knowledge our kin held there in your tantrum. I was the only one left who saw your worth. I was even the reason you learned your soul ability in the first place. You would've certainly been arrested for all your crimes if I didn't help. But now, I can say my eyes deceived me for the first time in my life. You are nothing, less valuable than the muck we dawdle on, even with your petty wind."

He looked at Hugo, now speaking to him. "I'm surprised you can tolerate being with such a monster."

At the corner of Hugo's eye, he saw Ventus' spine curl with his knees about to buckle. Ventus' heartbeat was like a punching bag being abused. He closed his eyes, gulped, then looked at Hugo with a smile that rumpled his fur with goosebumps. "Thank you for holding my spot for me. . . . But now I think you should keep your eye shut, for Exos is right . . . I am a monster, and it's about time I committed an appalling monstrosity."

Before Hugo could attempt to move, Exos raised his sword. "Alright, then I accept your challenge. You and Hugo better–"

Ventus scoffed. "Idiot." He pointed to the mural of flowers, specifically to the pile of souls. Mud from the upper floor had splattered over each orb.

Exos looked to where Ventus was pointing, then his eyes gaped. "Noooooo!" He flapped his wings, instantly taking flight toward the pile of souls.

Ventus sighed, then looked up at the sky and simply moved his wing to the side, and with his wing, the clouds blew away.

"No more of that mess." He quickly spread apart his wings and summoned a constant gust of air against Exos.

"Noooo! That's years of work!"

"I'm just returning the favor you brought me. . . ." Ventus smirked. "You should have turned those in before the wind stole your chances."

Exos flapped harder and even lowered himself to dig his talons into the ground. "Enough of your insolence, Prince! I gave you life; I gave you hope. You should bow and be grateful that I–"

"You still call me prince, huh? As if it were a compliment? You should learn your manners; like Hugo said, I am a lord. You should be the one bowing and begging for mercy!"

Exos grunted, obviously trying to summon lightning, but with no clouds on the continent, it was hopeless for what Ventus was about to do to him.

"Continental vacuum." Ventus raised his head with a smirk. But to all the creatures in the arena, fear broke loose. Hundreds began to choke and beg for air, and some even passed out on the spot. Exos dropped the sword with his eyes gaped wide. "Is this why you came into my life? Because you fear me? Did you ruin my life because I was the only threat to your status? You knew if I went to Sauria, I would be more than you could ever be!"

Exos gagged, still trying to force his way to the pile of souls. But then, his beak and eyes gaped wider once a precious green bud formed on the surface of the muddy layer. "Let me go, you insolent peasant!" he choked.

But then a gust of wind came and raised Exos from the floor and smacked him against the wall prophecy. All he could do was gasp in the air Ventus used. Ventus growled, and with the swing of his wing and a gust of wind, the air returned to the creatures of the Exosphere.

"You monster...."

"Why did you do it?" Ventus stomped his foot into the mud with a boom of air that splashed mud at Exos and stained his white feathers. He opened his wings again. "The monster you see before you had a life! It had dreams! But you crushed them all!"

"Ventus..." Hugo moaned.

Ventus closed his eyes and lowered his wing violently. And with it, Exos was slapped into the mud. Ventus walked to Exos before stomping on his face with a firm grip, then taunting his left eye with each sharp, muddy talon. Everyone still in the audience froze, including Hugo. Ventus' talons teased the eye flesh before them like needles against an egg yolk. And every drip of mud from Ventus' foot flinched Exos in fear. "The crimes of Apotheosis, the one you worship, are what my talons beg to do. How about I take your soul?"

"Aren't you forgetting something?"

Exos gave a smile that instantly gapped Ventus' eyes. Ventus struggled to escape the apparent shock of what Exos had just said. And before he did anything else, he turned around to look at Hugo. "I'm sorry," he spoke just before a bolt of lightning shot from the ground and up through Ventus.

"It seems like you are the idiot here, my prince."

As Ventus fell back and splatted on the mud, Exos stood and wiped the mud from himself. Ventus twitched on the ground as tiny sparks of electricity zapped between his feathers. Ventus tried to look at Hugo, but his body refused to move. He grunted and tried to scream as his lungs shoved out all their air, but barely a whisper came. "Run."

Exos walked to the pile of souls and simply wiped the mud from them before plucking one from the top and shoving it into his beak and down his long throat.

Hugo heeded Ventus' advice and pushed his body from the ground. Every inch he heaved was a struggle, for his limbs felt asleep, and his heart still thumped with a frequent, numbing skip. He looked at Exos to see how much time he had to grab Ventus and run, but the pile was already half gone, and tiny wisps, like darkening fire, weaved between Exos' feathers.

And before Hugo could take a step toward Ventus, Exos turned to them with eyes more silver than gold and feathers still white, but they seeped out a dark flame from their shadows. Only a few souls remained from the pile as they had already grown into flowers, but Exos didn't seem to care as he peeked back at Ventus with a smirk. "There. Now, my prince. *Bow.*"

Right as he said bow, his voice changed from smooth and regal to deep and powerful. Even Hugo, Bipp, and Luna found themselves forced to rise up, get on their hands and knees, and press their faces against the ground. In fact, everyone who heard that voice obeyed, for every creature in the crowd found themselves in the same position.

Each step Exos took closer to Ventus, zapped the mud into sparkling glass. Hugo tried to look up to see what was happening, but he could only see Exos' feet gracefully step around Ventus' trembling body.

Exos caressed Ventus' neck with his warm wing and slowly brushed it down his spine. Then, to the twitch of Hugo's ears, he heard Ventus weeping. "Please, don't. . . . Not in front of–"

"Aww, my dear prince shouldn't be weeping. . . . *Stop.*" In that instant, not even a squawk nor sniffle escaped Ventus.

"That's better." He took one step behind Ventus and stopped just as his wing reached the edge of the blue jay's tail feathers. "You dare leave me and hoard such beauty for yourself." His wing caressed downward behind him as he raised his foot and hooked his toes around Ventus' thigh with a harsh, flesh-ripping descent. He sank his long neck right beside Ventus' head. "I should kill you for such selfishness," he whispered with a sigh. "Though it would be such a waste of *that* body. . . . So I'll let you borrow it as I search for Sam; consider it a gift from your lord. . . . And as for the dragon," he let Ventus go and walked to Hugo, "let's see what type of soul a pathetic emberlight has."

*"Rise for me*, and accept my grace of freedom." In that instant, Hugo, Ventus, Bipp, and Luna rose partially from their bow, along with all else who heard him. Exos lowered his beak before Hugo's snout and stared into his eye.

He paused for a long while, but then he began to laugh. "What! That's it? What's with the dragons these days? I've found more powerful souls in mice!" He scoffed. "How disappointing, even for an emberlight. But at least today wasn't a total waste." He looked to the audience. "My dear birds, take flight and search the planet for your new god, the raven by the name of Sam! And once he is found, bring him to me!"

Most birds cheered, spread their wings, and flew out the ceiling in a massive swarm. Exos looked at Hugo with a final scoff and annoyed flap of his wing before flying up and out in a flash of lightning.

Hugo watched in awe at the sheer number of colorful birds flying out, until Ventus snagged his ears with his weeping. Ventus resumed the bow with his beak shoved into the mud, but the thing that made Hugo worry was the fresh blood dripping from his torn harem pants.

With his body still tingling, Hugo wobbly stepped forth to him.

"Don't."

Hugo paused.

"We're done. I'll take you back to the mainland, and once we report to Anzu, I'm leaving."

"I-Is there anything I can do to help?"

"You . . . need to stop being around me." Then, not one of them spoke as Ventus just wept in horror for his future. Ventus stopped his bow and sat in the mud, looking at himself. Hugo wanted to talk with him, but, to his surprise, Ventus sucked in a deep sniffle, then sighed and looked down at the blood weaving through the leathery texture of his leg and toes. "The thing is . . . I, unfortunately, am starting to like you."

He waved his wings to block Hugo's sudden look. "Shut up; just know I didn't want you to get hurt is all. Because if I hadn't stepped in–" He scoffed and looked away with a long silence. "Whatever. . . . And about that prophecy and human stuff Exos was talking about . . . he only knew about them because he studied Apotheosis, who was said to be a species called *human* before he became an Anthophytan creature. I know the book he read if you're interested." Ventus folded his wings over his body. "And *that* prophecy is depicted many times throughout different branches of theory by philosophers, but nobody knows for certain what it means. Exos believes Sam will become the next Apotheosis, and the three flowers on top are the three signs before that moment comes. . . . He always thought I was the blue flower . . . and he must've gotten excited to see you and Bipp or that silver flower on your wrist, especially when you told him about Sam." He removed a few fabric patches from a hidden, interior pocket and began mending his shredded pants with sewing needles made from air, but he did nothing to stop the bleeding.

Hugo squinted at Ventus. "Wait . . . George was an Anthophytan–"

"Hugo!"

Hugo turned around to Bipp, who instantly tackled him to the ground with a big hug.

"Sorry! Are you two alright?" He searched Hugo's body for any injuries.

Even Luna, who flew Bipp down with her, kissed Hugo on the cheek, telling him in her way that he did well. Hugo's ruby cheeks reddened into the ripest strawberries. It was easy to discern; even Bipp could tell he was blushing under his suppressed smile and shy glance at the mud. Bipp had to turn away before he ruined their moment with cheers. "He's alright." Bipp then looked at Ventus and instantly saw the blood and how much he struggled to sew on the patches. "Here, let me help with that–"

"No." Ventus blocked him instantly. "But if you don't mind, keep your eyes open for a cloak with a hood. I'm suddenly in the market for one," he said before he looked back at Hugo and the silver flower wrapped around his left arm.

Bipp reached out to help Ventus through what had happened, but Ventus slapped his hand away. Then, Ventus looked at Luna, who talked with Hugo about the fight and how he could've done better with his dragon body. "This family is going to be the end of me," he whispered, followed by a sigh.

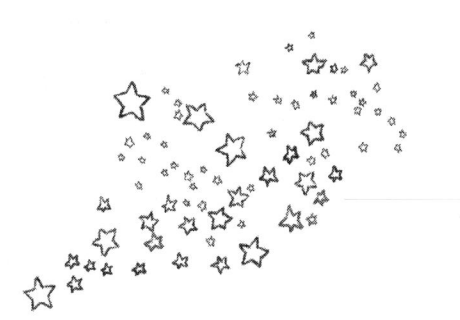

# Chapter 18
# EMBERLIGHT

Bipp's ears rose with his cheeks molding over a smile. He suddenly couldn't keep his sight from Hugo, who occasionally glanced at the many colorful birds filling the sky as they departed on their search for Sam. They all flew way up toward Zenith, expecting a fellow bird such as Sam to be there. Bipp looked at Luna, now seeing how wonderful she was as she tried to talk to Hugo using everything she had. She even gave an occasional whistle if Hugo ever fell into a daydream. It was funny to see Hugo squint at her in the hope of understanding. But as Hugo's cheeks dawned a smile, Bipp couldn't help but smile with him.

"He's starting to like this planet. . . . Hopefully, when we go back, there will be no war, no Apotheosis. Just us living comfortably in our cabin, eating soups and vegetables until our stomachs sink from their weight. Maybe he'll invite Luna from time to time. . . ." He looked down at his tightly folded hands. "Maybe then, with the three of us together . . . he won't need to fear being alone. . . ." He looked to the sky with a sigh as the final bird silhouette flew from sight. "If only that dream could come true, and I could finally snuff out those candles. . . . First, let's just hope Sam is still on Earth, and Exos never gets his wings on him."

After a moment of discussion, Hugo craned his tail to his foreclaws, then plucked the scorched scarf from it with a sigh. He brought it to Bipp with his head low. "I'm sorry, Bipp, I burnt your scarf."

Bipp shook his open hands with his eyes closed. "Heh, you're fine. I'm just glad it served you well." He took the scarf in his hands and bounced it around to test its weight. It was literally a chainmail sleeve. "I'll make you another one when I get the chance . . . maybe not from oven mitt material."

"You mean metal?" Hugo smiled.

Bipp nervously laughed with his hand behind his neck. "I'll make you a normal scarf. It's okay if you burn it again. I quite like making stuff for you, so go ahead and burn them, because one day after such practice, I'll get good enough to make you the perfect scarf, one that will never burn." Bipp dropped the chainmail strap to the mud, then looked at Luna with a point of his finger. He couldn't hold it in. "So . . . are we gonna talk about Luna kissing–"

"No." Hugo ended *that* topic with his shy face pointed to the mud, hiding it from Bipp. Because if Bipp saw his still-blushing face, he wouldn't hear the end of it.

Bipp, however, smiled at him. "Weirdo."

Ventus turned to the three of them. "So, this is all we can muster on this continent, huh? They looked at Ventus, making him uncomfortable. "Whatever. It'll do for such a stupid errand."

"Wait!"

Everyone looked up at the chicken, who flapped vigorously until he landed beside them with his heaving breaths. "Can you take me with you? I just need a lift to somewhere with creatures ... preferably not birds."

Ventus sighed with a heavy roll of his eyes. "Whatever." He raised his wings and summoned a gust that swept under them. Luna shook her head, and her fur burst into a white flame before flying on her own.

As they started their journey west by flying up and out of the tower, Hugo couldn't help but stare at the beautiful land once more. The sunrise gifted the continent of Dawn with a glorious amber light, and the returned puffy clouds were all shades of strawberry and lemon. *I can see why they named it that.* He looked at the two dragon skulls that formed a gateway to the day's opening, glowing with a similar, beautiful color.

Bipp frantically wrote and drew on the canvas he had tucked in his belt. It was challenging to hold it steady in the wind as he attempted to get every last detail from trees to hills. He paused and smiled as he looked at the two mountain peaks. "I know exactly what to name those two," he whispered and shyly looked at Hugo. Then, to his timely displeasure, Dawn fled under the horizon as they departed to the mainland. But it was at this time that a loud rumble pushed the clouds and trembled the sea below.

"Probably just Archipelago doing something dumb," Ventus scoffed.

Hugo spread his arms and leaned, so the wind could take him to Ventus. "Hey ... what was the name of that book about humans and Apotheosis you mentioned?"

Ventus squinted. "Yeah. . . . It's something like 'Apotheosis: A Written History of the Divine.' It had an odd cover, mostly a white canvas with a little splashed ink on the front. . . . But my certainty escapes me, so I'll just pick it up for you when I have the time, and Exos is still busy looking for Sam of course."

Hugo looked ahead with his shoulders drooped. *Why do I get the feeling that I'll never see that book?* He paused and allowed the smooth flow of air to bounce his hand up and down, feeling it weave through his expanded fingers. Then he slithered his body along with the windswept grace along his scales. "Hmm. . . . Hey . . . Ventus?"

"What?" Ventus spat.

"Since I'll never be able to fly on my own, I-Is it possible for you to send me into space? Like way, way up so the planet's gravity does not affect me?"

Ventus squinted in confusion at the horizon, then stared at Hugo. "W-What?"

"It's about going back to Sam."

Ventus blinked and looked back at Bipp, who was listening to their conversation, now with a look of sorrow across his face as he fiddled with his thumbs. "I . . ." he looked back at Hugo, "cannot. The air is so thin up there, even a creature as light as me can't ascend past a certain point. The most I can do is launch you as fast as I can, hoping you can break past the planet's pull," he sighed and glanced at Bipp once more, who was completely turned around with his back to them. "But . . . if you want my opinion. I think you should stay on this planet. Maybe . . . study space travel with Bipp in that pitiful cabin of his. It would be foolish to go into the dark of space alone, especially with your stupid fears."

Bipp squinted in deep thought at the sea. "What will it take for you to stay? I know you love Sam. And I wish you all the happiness in the world. . . . But . . . just once, say that you want me along with you, no matter the adventure," he whispered under the wind.

Hugo also looked down at the ocean. "Thank you." *Sam . . . it seems we will have to wait a bit longer to see each other again. . . . I . . . hate that I went to college. And I'm sorry if I pressured you to come with me. I should've just stayed home with you.* Tears welled in his eye and promptly blew back across his head. *I didn't know any of this would happen, but please, when I see you again, forgive me. . . . I'm a terrible brother.* He felt a harsh discomfort in his chest before a tiny thought popped into his head. *But . . .* he looked back at Bipp, *since I went to college, I met you. . . . And I wouldn't change that for the world.* He stared in a daydream before Bipp glanced at him. They smiled at each other, then looked away with an anchor of thoughts sinking them.

After a few moments of flying and conversing over Archipelago's sea, the mainland peeked from the horizon's edge, and an odd blend of smells like iron, campfire, and rotten eggs curled in the air. "What could they be doing over there?" Bipp held his nose.

"Thank you; I'd like to be dropped off here, please," the chicken requested.

Ventus looked at the chicken and the Glowshroom Forest below. "Good luck to you." And with that, the wind relieved the chicken before he awkwardly glided down.

Hugo glanced at a blanket of dark clouds forming from deeper inland and slowly creeping over them. But he could smell something other than that horrible, rotten-egg concoction. He inhaled deep through his snout, trying to determine the scent.

Bipp squinted ahead as the green forests below quickly became a valley of white. "What the? How is it snowing here? It isn't winter already . . . is it?" Bipp asked in great confusion.

"No . . . it's the middle of autumn. . . . And . . . we should be near Rafflesia." Ventus slowed the wind and sank them to a valley with a colossal canyon split down the middle. Flakes of white softly teetered from the sky and stuck to the ground.

Ventus gave a surprised gasp when his talons met the warm ground. His feet fell through until the snow was just below his knees. Everyone else hit the ground with a disturbed look about them.

"This can't be snow." Bipp wiggled his large toes through the plants beneath the white, almost-sandy powder. He scooped some in his hand and dipped his tongue into it before shaking his head and grimacing. "That's definitely not snow." He spat, then looked at where he picked up the powder. The soft, crimson petals of a poppy flower peeked from the white. "What?" Bipp wiggled his foot across the ground before several other flowers sprung from underneath. "Is this King's Garden?" Bipp squinted and looked around the valley with no obvious sign of Rafflesia. Hugo took his tail and swept the ground around him, revealing countless flowers.

"It can't be . . ." Ventus walked to the giant canyon that split the valley and looked down. He struggled to spot the bottom as dark rock covered the walls and basin. "But nowhere else on Somnium has flowers this dense," he covered his beak with a grimace, "and that horrible mine smell. . . . Did we accidentally discover a new landmass?" he asked himself in a nasal-clogged voice and looked to both sides of the canyon. The southern end held a waterfall that hastily tried to fill the infinite canyon. "No." He paused. "Everyone on Zenith would've seen a landmass this large . . . But there isn't any existence of a canyon this large recorded on any maps I've seen." Ventus thought for a second and looked at Bipp. "What about your maps?"

Bipp walked beside Ventus. "No . . . this place shouldn't exis–"

The ground quaked before part of the canyon wall split and fell to the basin with a splash. The violence suddenly stopped as Bipp and Ventus took a few steps away from the cliffside. Bipp tilted his head. "Quakes? Where on Somnium do we get those?"

Luna flew up a few feet to get a better view, then she pointed to the other end of the canyon and gestured a few things to Ventus. "She says some old ruins are at the end of this canyon. But everything seems to be covered in these flakes." Everyone looked to the right at the ruined buildings under rubble and ash.

Hugo paused as a hint of something familiar teased his snout once more. It almost smelt like his bedroom back on Earth. He had gotten used to the smell over the years, but he knew it vividly. If something could compare, it almost smelt of blueberries and sawdust, but there was a familiar hint of burnt chicken in this whiff that widened his eye. He sniffed deeper, trying to smell beyond the overwhelming scent of iron and rotten eggs. "Can't hurt to look," Hugo said, walking south with a hasty skip in his step. *Blueberries and burnt chicken. . . .* Everyone followed him.

Once they crossed the shallow river above the waterfall, it didn't take much time to reach the ruins, if that's what they could be called. There was little to identify apart from a few houses and what seemed like a stone wall just inside the surrounding rivers. Large mounds of dirt and rubble lay everywhere with the canyon in its center.

"What idiots built a city around a canyon?" Ventus mumbled as they walked above the rubble.

Bipp paused and squinted at the ground after each step he

took. He slid his foot over the snow to reveal loose straw, still hard and slightly yellow. "This is fresh. . . ."

Hugo instantly froze and stared at the ground.

"What's wrong?" Bipp asked after nearly bumping into him.

Hugo sucked in the air through his gaping snout. He slowly turned his head before looking at a group of crumbled cobblestone walls. "That scent . . ." His heart thumped faster as he quickly walked toward the labyrinth of rubble.

"Hugo?" Bipp questioned as he followed.

Hugo followed his snout between the walls. But then he froze as a subtle sniffle twitched his large ears. He gulped in all the air his snout could take and instantly stared at a split house with one half being a pile of rubble. Hugo's legs wobbled as he peeked over a rock pile. He froze completely still and stared at the shadowed corner. There was someone there, shivering in the corner, above some straw. "S-Sam?" Hugo spoke with his fingertips numb and chest thumping to the hopeful anticipation.

The creature opened its emerald eyes and looked at Hugo. Its eyelids then slowly stretched apart. "H-Hugo!" it whispered.

Hugo's heart couldn't keep up with his legs as he stared into those familiar eyes. He dashed at Sam and spread out his right arm, about to embrace him. But his hand froze just as it reached a centimeter from Sam's feathers. He then promptly retreated and sat just beyond Sam. "M-May I . . . hold you?"

Sam just gawked at Hugo with his wings open and regrettably empty. "What?"

Hugo's eye welled with tears. "I've been thinking about us, and if I've been a good brother to you." Hugo shyly looked down. "I'm sorry if I've been too much and made you want to leave me on this planet–"

Sam quickly grabbed him and hugged him tight around his stomach. It was so sudden and strong, Hugo's entire body budged. "You were never too much." *I can't believe he would think of such a thing.*

Tears flowed from Hugo's eye as he felt Sam's heartbeat against his. He wanted to speak, but couldn't as he was so overwhelmed with joy, he couldn't help but cry as he wrapped his arms around Sam. *I missed you so, so much.*

Sam held Hugo tighter and paid extra attention to the finer details of his smooth, bumpy scales to ensure this wasn't a dream. But Sam began to cry as he felt Hugo's warmth and gentle heartbeat. He then held Hugo so tight, no air could dare enter. "It's really you . . . You're alright," Sam murmured.

The tips of his toes went numb from the overwhelming senses. He had so much to tell Hugo that his chest tingled and mind spun. He wept and watched embers shoot from Hugo's back in a colorful blur of tears. His eardrums numbed at the thought of hearing Hugo's warm voice even more, but they were filled with sounds of sniffling and his feathers ruffling under the firm grip of Hugo's hands.

"I'm glad to see you too," Sam whispered with a smile.

Neither of them said anything for a long while, just holding each other. They missed each other so much that letting go wasn't even a spark in their minds. Sam took a moment to simply feel Hugo's massive arms around him and his dragon hands that cradled nearly half his body. *He's so much bigger and stronger than me, but he's gentler than I could ever be.*

Bipp walked on top of the rubble, spotted Sam, and gasped before covering his mouth. "How is he here?" Bipp whispered to himself with confusion and joy for Hugo swimming in his mind.

Hugo's hands slipped as he loosely tried to hold him tighter. Sam could feel the snot and tears soaking his back feathers as Hugo sniffled through that big snout of his. It was kinda gross, but it brought a certain comfort to Sam's mind. "Hugo . . . I have a question. Sorry if it's obvious, and please don't be weird about it. . . . But I just need to hear it from you. . . . Do you still . . . love me?" *And if so . . . please, tell me why.*

Hugo's movements froze. But he still wept, even more so by the sound of it. *He . . . doesn't know?* He slowly leaned back to look Sam in the eyes. A waterfall of bubbling snot and tears over his wobbling smile spoke it all. "I've never stopped loving you," he wept.

Sam's heartbeat increased at the look of his messy face, but for a reason unknown to him, his heart felt lighter with every thump. Sam had never seen Hugo soaked to that extent, and it almost made him laugh. Then to Sam's dismay, Hugo misread Sam's increased heartbeat and let go.

"I-I'm sorry. . . . I've never been the best at words, and I can be confusing. . . . It's just–" He looked back at Bipp, who smiled for him and gestured for him to continue. Hugo deeply inhaled. *Okay. Okay . . . I can do this.* "I'm sorry if this makes you feel weird. I just need to get it off my chest. Please, stop me if it makes you uncomfortable." Hugo stopped for a moment and breathed to calm down. The embers on his back lit everything around him like a night full of a million stars.

He looked at Sam's eyes—those shy, brilliant-emerald gems—and began. "Sam . . . you make me feel so warm and so light. I've never told you that I love you . . . b-because it's so . . . so–" he looked back at Bipp for a second, "curious."

Hugo's feet and hands slowly left the ground as a galaxy of embers shot from his back fur. Sam's beak gaped as

Hugo looked back at him. Bipp's jaw dropped, and his eyelids stretched around his bulging eyes. Hugo rose a few feet until his fur softly cushioned him against a wooden beam. But he didn't feel the ceiling cradle his back or the absence of ground beneath his feet, for all his attention was on his little brother and how his precious eyes sparkled the embers' light.

"I'm sorry . . . I've spent my whole life trying to find the words to describe how I feel. But none exist. I don't–"

"Hugo's way!" Bipp exclaimed with his hands circling his mouth.

Both Sam and Hugo looked back at Bipp, who then awkwardly looked away and hid behind a piece of wall. He was obviously still listening with his tall ears out in the open.

Hugo's eyes opened wide at that. After a few seconds, he cradled Sam's wing and pressed it against his scaly chest.

"What are you do–" Sam froze as the blissful and heavy thumps of Hugo's heart pounded against his wing, like a calming yet mighty drummer's song.

"Every time I look at your eyes, my body does this. Every time I see you smile, my heart begs me to smile with you. And when you laugh, I feel like I'm listening to my favorite music. I love everything about you: your addiction to blueberries, your kind heart, and your shy voice; I absolutely love listening to you. In fact, I've loved you since before you could talk. I want to be there for you and help you accomplish every dream. I don't care if you're a bird or human; I care about how you feel, happy or sad; I want to know all about it. And if it helps you feel any better, I even love your cute beak, especially when you squawk accidentally."

At this point, Sam's beak and eyes were wide open. *You . . . think my beak is cute too?* His mind relaxed as he felt Hugo's heart. Just the simple thumps against his wing brought him comfort beyond measure.

"And this whole time, ever since we were kids, I've held it in. I'm sorry; some of it was certainly me unable to describe it and understand what I felt. But most, I think, was me worrying how *you'd* feel. . . . And I'm sure mom or dad told you I was bullied for loving you like I do, and because of such, I recently became worried that I've gone too far, especially after you left this planet. . . . I've always thought it was my fault you were bullied all those years ago, so I stayed away from you as much as I could bear, but that didn't last long, did it?"

*You were . . . bullied?* Sam held Hugo's hand. "Hugo . . ." *Why didn't you tell me?*

"I know I'm just your brother, and it's . . ." his eye gaped wide at the floor, "*very* weird for me to be saying these things to you." He began to cry. "A-And I can see why people think that I'm your 'secret lover' . . . and I'm so sorry for all of it." He was shaking, worried Sam might be furious with him. "I've tried for years to stop this feeling, this need to give you everything I am. . . . And I know it's no excuse, but that feeling is something so deep down, I can't get a grasp on it." He took a moment to calm down. "I hope, one day, I can be a proper brother to you. And we can just sit on the couch, playing video games, punching each other, or whatever normal brothers do."

Sam almost laughed.

Hugo watched that smile dawn on Sam's face, and in that instant, Hugo's heart calmed. He sniffled and smiled as he removed the red dahlia from his head fur. "All in all, and after such a wait . . . you still deserve to know that you're *everything* to me." Hugo gulped in the air around him, trying to give his sniffling snout some air. He then looked at Sam's precious eyes and reached out the flower to him. "November seventeenth. I don't know if I'm late or early with days being different on this planet. . . . but if my math is close with the strong gravity of that orange supergiant star . . . then happy birthday, Sam." He paused as he looked at Sam's gawking face, and a slight nervousness thumped his chest. "I love you, because you are my best friend. . . . I love you because you are you, my shy, anxious, and amazingly strong little brother. . . . And I hope we will never grow apart." He carefully extended the flower closer to him. "And not even the great divide of space can change that."

"There he is," Bipp murmured happily with an awkward chuckle.

Sam watched Hugo's chest rise and sink as he listened to his heavy breaths push from his soaked snout. Even Sam's feathers brushed back from such warm exhaust pipes.

Hugo's heart pounded hard against his ribs with the silence Sam was giving. "I-I'm sorry for not telling you all that before. If you need space to think, I can leave," Hugo said. *I might've gone too far.* He let go of Sam's wing–

"No!" Sam shouted and grabbed Hugo's hand, flinching Hugo in surprise. Sam was dead still as tears dripped from his beak. Never had someone talked to him like that. And it was Hugo who did? *Actually, wait, I shouldn't be so surprised. But no normal brother would care* that *much about me, especially after all I've done.* "Hugo . . ." He paused for a long while. "Thank you . . . I needed that." Sam breathed to calm down a little. And he shyly looked away from him. "I've always loved you, Mom–"

Sam froze, and his cheeks instantly warmed into an apple-red blush. Even his dark feathers couldn't hide it. His heart sank from the gravity of that word. *Why do I keep calling him that?* He shyly looked at Hugo, who smiled at him and kindly waited for him to continue. Sam waved his wing between them to excuse his miswording. "Sorry, I don't know where that came from. . . . But, all in all, I'm happy—no, overjoyed that you feel the same." Sam thought for a moment and rubbed his cheeks to vanquish the blush. "Even as family, I've struggled to find the words to describe you as well. You're so kind and much weirder than anyone I know." He pulled his hand down from the air like a balloon string, into a great, big hug. "But I wouldn't dare wish for anyone else to be my big brother. . . . I love you just the way you are, even with your weird tendencies." Sam pressed his head against Hugo's chest and felt the warming heartbeat he had spent months dreaming about. But this dream was one of few he didn't want to wake from.

This entire time, Bipp stood with his toes digging into the ash, holding in the happiness and cheers with the struggling floodgate of his cheeks and teeth. Ventus and Luna walked from behind and watched with him. They froze as they saw Hugo's body still hovering off the ground. "I-Is that possible?" Ventus asked with a gawking beak.

Luna tilted her head with her mouth gaping. Then, to respond to Ventus' question, she slowly shook her head.

After many moments of holding each other, Sam leaned back and opened his beak. "Thank you, for remembering that. . . . You're actually right on time." Sam happily accepted the flower and placed it within his head feathers before returning to the hug. *I can't believe he remembered after all this; even I forgot about it.*

During that hug, Hugo couldn't help but notice how much Sam's spine poked against his fingertips and how his ribcage dug into his chest scales. *He . . . hasn't been eating again. . . . Where has he been this whole time?* "Uh, Sam . . . Why are you back on Somnium? And why are you still a bird? Didn't Mom and Dad–"

"They . . ." he sighed, "called animal control," Sam said with a sorrowful croak in his throat.

Hugo's eye gaped with his mouth, and he sank back onto the ground. "No . . ." His hind claws gripped the ash. He looked at Sam's talons up to his beak, but he didn't see a bird; he saw his younger brother, especially the second he spotted those green eyes. *He probably thinks himself more animal than human now . . .* "I'm so sorry. I thought–" He paused, thinking of what torment Sam endured in a pound. "I–"

"It's okay, Hugo; it's nobody's fault. Just a little accident." Sam's heart felt heavy as he murmured that. "George rescued me and brought me back here, to Somnium." Those words left Sam's throat with much thought. *Is George even okay? Did he kill Anzu and that fox? He still hasn't told me what's wrong. . . . Maybe I can ask him after all this chaos dies out.*

Everything Sam spoke overwhelmed Hugo to the point where his lungs sucked in so much to support his heart, but he didn't want to frighten Sam, so he tried his best to calm himself. "Are you alright, Sam?" Hugo forced out his mouth in a whisper.

Sam breathed with Hugo, not on purpose. Hugo's breaths were so powerful, deep, and yet, calming. "Honestly . . . no, I'm not alright. For the past couple of months, I've been . . . struggling with something." He sighed with a heavy glance away from Hugo. "But now that you're here, maybe it'll be better." His chest tickled to tell Hugo about how he almost killed himself. But after Hugo said all those words to him, he was unsure and uncomfortable about saying anything about the matter. How could he? Hugo just poured his heart out to him, *and I tried to die in return.* His heart sank from his chest, forcing him to feel sick.

Hugo gently yet firmly grabbed Sam by the shoulders, seeing the subtle sorrow in his eyes. "What do you need?" Hugo asked simply, but to Sam, it was not a simple question, not with Hugo looking at him like that. The question did not make Sam feel needy; no, it felt so refreshing in a way. Hugo just gave him permission to drop all his weight. He really had no concern for *what* worried Sam, for no matter what it was, he wanted to help. And this feeling made Sam cry. He was unsure if it was happiness or sadness, but he loved it. That question alone broke him. He wept against Hugo's chest, unable to grasp the words worthy enough to describe how he felt. His lungs forced him to gulp, and his body shook, begging him to speak his mind. "I'm here." Hugo held Sam's back.

Sam's chest felt lighter than before, and Hugo was all ears. Above all, there was one thing Sam couldn't hold in any longer. "I don't know if I can say this enough times . . . but I'm so sorry, Hugo. . . . I left you on this planet, and you were comatose and hurt, all because of me. I don't expect you to forgive me. I just want you to know that I regret doing it more than you can imagine." He couldn't help but look at the claw marks over Hugo's eye. And just like that, he felt horrible enough to die.

Hugo turned his face, so Sam wouldn't see his bad eye. "There is nothing to forgive, Sam."

Stinging tears forced their way from Sam's eyes and snot from his nares. *Why? Why are you like this?*

"You left because you thought you were a burden to me, right?" Sam nodded with his cheek pressed against Hugo.

"So, you were just trying to protect me. I understand. And I love you all the more for thinking about me. But you should know that you are not a burden to me or anyone." Hugo gently brought his hand beneath Sam's beak and tilted it to face him, eye to eyes. "You are the reason I get up at dawn. You are more precious to me than all the jewels in the ground and stars in the sky. And I would be the happiest and luckiest person in the universe to help you get through this. You are the greatest blessing I have ever known to bear, not a burden. . . . And if it helps you feel any better, this planet's actually pretty fun once you get the hang of things, especially with Bipp to help me through it. Though I missed you."

Bipp quietly cheered in the background.

Hugo paused with a glance to the side. "And please, if I am ever too much, and you feel like a burden, let me know." His mouth began to wobble with a few fresh tears curving around his cheeks. "Please, let me know."

Sam was weeping. He never imagined those words would come from anyone, especially Hugo. It gave him something he thought he had lost forever, the feeling that he was beloved. He knew he didn't deserve it. But Hugo was here, giving him all of it. Even with the world growing darker by the second, this one person gave him some light. *I want to tell you so, so much. . . . Maybe if you just asked me if I was alright . . . just one more time. . . . I think I'm ready to–*

*Be quiet. You need to die.*

Sam smiled shortly before sinking into Hugo's arms. Those words defeated him outright; no hope of recovery, no hope of help, just death and the happiness others would feel if he were gone. After many minutes, what seemed like only a few seconds, Bipp came closer. "Pardon me for interrupting, but where are we?"

Sam took a moment to build the strength and put on his facade, sniffled, then looked up at Bipp. "Oh . . . right. . . ." He looked down and tried to calm himself. "Before I tell you, I need to apologize. I called you Hugo's pet before and was very rude. I realize I was stupid. . . . I didn't see the value in creatures yet, and I might have been a bit jealous that you were a better friend to him than I ever was."

"Oh." With a shy glance to the side, Bipp placed his hand on the back of his head. "Heh . . . you're perfect. I completely forgot about that stuff you called me. I know you were scared of the arch eating you up, so I totally forgive you, and I would like to start over. Who knows, we might have a lot in common."

Sam smiled, now looking at the ground.

*He's saying that out of pity. Nobody will ever forgive you.*

Sam held Hugo tighter, now with all his strength. "Why does it still haunt me with you here?" Sam barely said that, less than a murmur. But Hugo caught instant attention to it and scanned Sam, beak to eyes.

"Is something wrong, Sam?"

Sam tried to think of anything to distract him from the voice.

*If you tell him something's wrong, he'll think you're weak, unable to do anything by yourself, and he'll have another reason to believe you are a burden.*

"N-No. I'm fine. . . . We're in Rafflesia, Bipp," Sam said, changing the subject. He felt horrible keeping the secret from Hugo. *He's right here! Just let me tell him–*

*You are a burden.*

*No!*

*You are an anchor.*

*I–*

Hugo watched Sam's body as he said that. His body was trembling apart from his left leg; also, his eyes drooped every time someone looked at him, even Hugo.

Bipp's eyes snapped open wide. Even Ventus seemed frozen at Sam's words. "R-Rafflesia?" Bipp's eyes crept around him, observing only rubble and the blanket of white. "Impossible." His hand trembled as he held it out to catch the falling flakes. "Then is this . . . ash?"

Hugo stood still and scanned every one of Sam's feathers. "Before I ask what happened here . . . Sam, please don't hide your feelings from me. No matter what the matter is, I won't think of you as lesser. I actually think you'd be the bravest person alive if you told me. Even I struggled to tell you my feelings until now. And I'm sorry if you ever felt like you need to keep secrets from me, but just know . . . I would love to help you no matter what." Hugo got it off his chest and breathed. "Alright, what happened here?"

Sam looked down with fresh tears welling; he had forgotten how smart Hugo was. He saw right through Sam's shell. Even though Hugo's words brought him comfort, he felt queasy about discussing himself after that voice destroyed him. "It was Mr. George. He did something. And before I could even blink, everything was gone."

*It's all your fault, remember? Don't cast the blame on George.*

He grabbed Hugo's arm. "Please, Hugo, don't go out there. Stay here with me, and I may be able to convince him to spare you. It's the only hope you have of surviving. I-I can't lose you again."

Hugo cradled Sam's cheek with the soft part of his hand. "I

will never leave you. But we need to know what's happening. Where is George, and what does he want?" Hugo asked calmly.

"He's just northeast of the city, battling Anzu and that arctic fox. But he's only playing with them. Nobody can win against Mr. George. He's become something even my imagination can't create." He grabbed Hugo and held him close. "Please, Hugo, just leave Anzu and the fox to this. They seem strong."

Ventus walked up when he heard that. "Anzu? He's out there? Why didn't you say anything before!"

Hugo felt Sam's heart pound faster, and he turned to Ventus and gestured that he slow down. But Ventus marched right to Sam and grabbed his head with his talons, forcing him to look at him. "I'm losing my patience with you. Tell me what's going on!" Ventus commanded.

Before Hugo could growl, Sam placed his wing over Hugo's snout. "Anzu and that fox will die if they haven't already. I hid here to wait it out." Sam stood on his one leg and glared at Ventus. "In fact, how about you go out there and try to save them? I won't stop *you*."

A sudden gust of strong wind rushed through the house and snapped the support beam and remaining straw from the roof. "I wasn't asking for permission," Ventus growled, flew up, and rocketed toward the city's edge.

"Sam?" Hugo said.

Sam sighed, then collapsed back down. "I'm sorry. . . ." He reclined and gulped for air.

Bipp and Luna inched closer. "I'd love to stay here. But . . . those are my friends out there. If they're in trouble . . . then I'm sorry, I must go, even if it's Apotheosis we're talking about. If you and Sam are safe here, then I can go out there accepting the risk."

Hugo looked down with his eyelid drooping. "Please, Bipp, be careful."

Bipp shrugged with a smile. "I haven't died yet from my decisions. I must be doing something right," he chuckled. "I'll see you in a bit. . . . Take care of him." Before he left, he looked back at Hugo and Sam. New tears met his fluffy cheeks, and his strong legs struggled to step from the sight of them. "Please, stay well," he whispered as he left. And with that, he sprinted in the direction of Ventus.

Sam grasped Hugo's arm with his wing. "I know what you're thinking. But please, trust me. Going to Mr. George is fine for a normal person. But you won't be able to handle it. I've gotten to know you better over the past year, so I know how you get with the dark . . . please, stay."

Hugo looked down at Sam. *Does he think I'll leave him just like that?*

Luna tapped Hugo on the shoulder. He turned around as she bowed her head, and he saw in her eyes that she wanted to go as well. But something about her expression seemed worried about Hugo. "I'll be fine. Go," Hugo said, trying to help Sam.

Sam hugged Hugo tighter than ever before. "Please, don't go! You don't understand! You can't win! I've thought about everything that could stop him, and the only thing is . . . time." Sam froze as both Luna and Hugo's ears rose from their fur.

"Then it sounds like we need your help, Sam." Hugo smiled. "Have you learned how to use your soul ability?" he asked.

Sam released Hugo and shook his head. "No! I can't! I don't know what will happen! Every time I try to use it, something goes wrong! And–" He paused. *How did he know about my soul ability?*

Hugo quickly held Sam's cheeks once more to look at him. "Hey, it's okay. We don't have to use it." Hugo tried to comfort Sam, but he didn't want to abandon his friends. He looked at Luna. "Will you be alright without me?"

Luna promptly shook her head to say no, knowing full well the power of Apotheosis from the remains of this city alone.

Sam then looked down. He accepted that Hugo knew about his soul, for it wasn't the weirdest thing that had happened today. And now, he had heavier things sinking in his mind. *I'm just a burden again. Everyone's going to perish because I am too much of a coward.*

*And all you had to do was die.*

Luna walked to Sam and raised his head proudly with the tip of her snout, as if she knew what he was thinking. She brought her hand to Sam's chest. Her touch caught Sam's attention; it was somehow gentler than Hugo's, like each leathery cell of her hand was a puff of cloud. Sam looked at her bubblegum eyes and large snout before them. His heart became calm, and his breaths, calmer. Her warmth nearly matched Hugo's, but it was different in a way; he just couldn't put his mind to why. She bowed before turning around with a final worrisome glance, specifically at Sam.

"Who . . ." Sam spoke, finding that he couldn't look away from her eyes. To him, they were more beautiful than any flower or sunset. Tears blurred his vision as she walked away. His heart felt like fresh mint, and his limbs were loose yet heavy. *Is that what I've been missing by looking away from people?*

Hugo smiled and looked at his wide eyes. "That was Luna."

Sam stared at where Luna was, then looked at Hugo's sizeable snout before him carrying a few new tears. *He . . . cares about them. But I'm in his way. . . .* Sam promptly shook his head to get back at more essential matters. "Hugo, would you like to run away with me, so we could both be safe? George isn't far from here."

Hugo's heart tugged him to his friends, but he knew, deep down, Sam wasn't well. And whatever the worry, Hugo wanted to help and be by his side. "Sure, get on and tell me the way." Hugo lowered his head.

Sam took a while to crawl onto Hugo's neck with one leg, but once he was on, he caught his breath with many heaves and huffs.

Hugo squinted at that. *Is he injured?*

"Okay, if you go this way, we should be safe. Just follow my wing." Sam pointed his wing to the northeast, and Hugo began to follow. *It's not about me. . . .*

## Chapter 19
# THE TRUTH

"Come on.... I just need a little luck," George said with his eyes scrunched shut and resting his fiery palms over the ashen ground. "Any souls with the ability to go back or teach Sam how to use his.... Come on, time, work with me here," he growled with his teeth about to crack in frustration.

"Hey! You!" Anzu roared as he and Ella ran from the remains of Rafflesia.

George's fingers pierced the dirt. "Please, anything.... Don't make the death of that city in vain. Just one soul to save countless...."

Anzu raised his arm, then a spear of diamond burst from the ground and rocketed for George's head.

George sighed and tilted his neck, allowing the smooth diamond rim to flow over his cheek, slicing off a few swaths of his frosty beard. Then, he opened his eyes with his annoyed eyebrows furrowed. "If I were you two, I would go back to Petal with the other Anthophytans."

Anzu and Ella did not care for his words, as they both began their assault. Ella first removed George's hands from the ground by swinging a sword made of plant moisture at his neck. In retort, he punched her right in the stomach. Her back bent from the initial impact, and the air around her burst as she rocketed into a distant gathering of trees from the Glowshroom Forest.

"Nooo!" Anzu stopped and stared at where Ella had gone. He felt his cheeks gush hot in anger before he instinctively ran toward her to ensure she was alive after that. But once he saw her hobble from the forest, he sprinted.

Ella held her stomach tight with a sharp grimace masking her typical, calm expression. Anzu promptly reached her and allowed her to rest by leaning on his shoulder. She slowly recovered, but still showed pain through her gnashing fangs as they reluctantly walked back to the fight.

Many moments passed, and the battle did not let up since it began. George never gave them an inch to work with. Anzu was beyond exhausted with cuts and bruises draining him further. Ella stood beside him with a few open cuts and a firm grasp on her left, limp arm. Her stomach was throbbing and was bruised horribly from that initial punch. She breathed slowly as she squinted at George with her swimming mind trying to invent a new strategy. But in the back of their heads, there was no hope.

"I . . . can't–" Anzu wheezed at the ground to catch his breath. He looked at his splattered blood across the ashen ground, then at George, who resumed his search with his palms firmly pressed on the ground.

"We can do this, Anzu. . . . Don't give up! Everything has a weakness."

Anzu wanted to believe that, but in the back of his mind, he couldn't, not since Sam was nowhere to be seen. "That bird is the only weakness this creature has!" He looked up at the monster, almost a hundred feet away. "Why are you here! What do you want with this planet? Why not just kill us and get this over with?" Anzu begged to know and threw a spear of stone at George.

Within a blink, George teleported an inch from his snout. His presence roasted and boiled Anzu's leathery skin, and his white eyes showed no compassion or love. Only death existed in those flaming white eyes. "Please, I need time. Your planet will burn if I don't get it."

Ella quickly stole the morning dew from the grass and doused Apotheosis with a whip of water. But it simply evaporated before it met him.

George sighed. "I suppose it can't be helped. . . . You're brave to fight me, Anzu, Ella." He bowed slightly to each of them, and they stepped back, terrified by how he knew their names. "Your sorrow will come. . . . But since I like you two, how about a final wish?"

"I wish you were dead!" Anzu raised his hand, about to summon a spike from the ground.

"Fair enough." Apotheosis raised his finger to Anzu's snout and flicked him.

The force of just his finger smacked Anzu backward like an insect. He rolled onto the ground until his back slammed against a mound of dirt and ash. Dazed, he stood. He tried to sniffle in the liquids forming over his lips and trespassing into his mouth, but his nose didn't work. He held his hand against his snout and tried to suck in. His numb, clogged nose squished like a wet sponge under any pressure. Then, he retreated his hand, soaked in blood. Suddenly, his vision blurred, and his stance teetered as his limbs went cold.

"Anzu!" Ventus yelled and landed swiftly next to Anzu.

"Ventus! Yes!" Anzu cheered with a nasal-clogged voice.

"Did you find anyone to help from Dawn?" he asked quickly before his legs buckled under his weight, and he collapsed. Ventus gasped and gave Anzu his wings to help him. But Anzu now struggled to blink away the blur, let alone stand.

"Well, we did find someone." Ventus gestured his wing to Luna, who landed behind him.

"Only one?" Anzu yelled, disregarding that she was a dragon and bigger than Hugo. Ventus observed Anzu's wounds, and an odd pain forced his wing to rub across his chest. Anzu waved his hand. "Never mind. Thank you. I'm glad you're here."

"What should I do, Anzu? Should I help you escape, fight?" Ventus leaned closer, hoping to help the velociraptor in any way he could, but before he could blink, Ella gently held Anzu's nose and dried the blood.

"Fight. We can't flee, or it will destroy everything. . . . Even though my hope for victory is shrinking."

Ventus growled and looked at George, who only stared at the ground. He raised his wings, summoning two massive tornadoes to sweep the land and intersect on George. Ella blocked such ferocious winds by enveloping Anzu and herself in a bubble made from grass moisture. George simply stood there; the black fire around his body seemed to grow from the tempest. Ventus took a step back, then looked at Anzu. "Have you or Ella hit him yet?" he asked with nervous haste.

"No. . . . We've been here almost an hour but haven't laid a claw on him," Ella said, mending Anzu's nose further.

Ventus scoffed and glared at George. "Fine." Ventus unleashed a gale of wind that threw him forward, reaching George within a second. He spun with the wind and forged a million air swords along the tips of each feather before sending them straight at George.

The fire consumed every atom of air; none of Ventus' swords even made George flinch. Ventus growled, then threw his wings to the sky. A burst of wind rushed beneath George and launched him into the atmosphere. Ventus smirked before pushing him down with a gale toward the ground, trying to smash him through the planet.

But George landed lighter than a feather and resumed searching King's Garden and Rafflesia for souls, almost like he was mocking Ventus. "Y-You . . ." Ventus stepped back again with his wide eyes and wings trembling. "How about a vacuum then?" He clapped his wings together, then spread them apart, sucking all air from around George. Suddenly the black fire was gone. Ventus stared awkwardly and amazed at the figure before him. It was George with his typical gray suit and profoundly wrinkled skin. "Oh. . . . That's . . . not what I was expecting." His beak gaped with the twitch of an eye.

George smirked before looking at Ventus. "You're a clever one to take my fire away like that," he said with a little humor in his voice. He raised his hand, then, as if he had increased the planet's gravity, Ventus grunted and instantly smacked against the ground. Ventus wheezed in agony as the air returned and refueled the dark fire around George.

Bipp ran toward the exploding, planet-quaking sounds of battle and to the top of an ashen hill, then froze once he saw George. "It's him. . . . It's really him," he murmured. Then, after a moment of gawking, his ears twitched to the soft crunch of Hugo's hands and feet through the ash.

"Bipp, what are you doing here?" Hugo ran beside him and stopped once he saw the valley and *who* it contained. He instantly felt smaller, remembering that dark figure opening his bedroom door with a heartstopping creak. He felt weaker and more vulnerable than a four-year-old as he collapsed in fear. "No, no, no, no!" he panted heavily and veered his head to Sam on his back, about to grab him and hold him tight.

Sam felt sick as he saw Hugo's horrified eye, and he suddenly hated himself for guiding Hugo toward his nightmare. "I'm sorry, Hugo. I didn't want you to choose between your friends and me." Sam's beak sank, and his body felt heavy before he nearly collapsed into Hugo's fur. *Why did I lie to him? I could've just told him I wanted to help, then warned him better. He loves me and would've come here if I had asked, even with George.* He held his head tight, thinking about killing himself. *What's wrong with me? Why can't I tell you how much this hurts? I want to tell you!* His eyes instantly soaked with tears. *Someone... please, help me.*

Hugo saw Sam's tears, but his numb head and punching heart forced his mind back to George.

"You okay?" Bipp asked.

"I should be. . . . Just give me a moment." But to his discomfort, his heart sped, and his empty hands trembled. He even struggled to give his body the air he needed for that sentence. "Please, may I hold you?" Hugo gulped.

Sam and Bipp looked at each other, confused as to who Hugo meant, but they both reached down and held Hugo's hand.

*I'm sorry I brought you here. . . .* Sam thought about the scars over Hugo's eye and chest. *I just can't stop hurting you, can I?*

Bipp looked at George, who approached Ventus with slow, spine-chilling steps. Bipp then let go and stepped forward with a glance back at Hugo.

Hugo couldn't tell what Bipp was thinking through those eyes, but once he saw Bipp's cheeks fluff up with a smile, it was too late. Bipp's only response was his thumping footsteps sprinting down the hill to Ventus. Hugo crept lower behind the hill and peeked through the ash lumps to ensure his eye wasn't deceiving him. Then only after a second, he cowered and ducked beneath the hill. His head sank, and he couldn't seem to get enough air. *Okay, okay, Hugo, don't pass out. . . . Sam is with me . . . I can do this. . . .* "Sam, did he harm you in any way? Does he want to harm you?"

Sam relieved his wing from Hugo's hand and quickly cleaned off his teary face. "N-No. . . . George doesn't wish to harm me. He . . . lost someone close to him, and this all started out just wanting to bring them back, but now . . . I have no idea what his intentions are. I think he wants the power to cure me, but . . . he's gone a bit overboard, even for him."

*Cure you?* Hugo took a long pause to breathe. "Thank you. . . . Sorry for not handling this well. . . . It's going to take a while to get over *him*. But I'm surprised you're so calm, because if he's who I think, he killed your mother, didn't he?"

Sam sighed, thinking he knew everything. But then he paused with a thoughtful squint to the empty white valley. "She . . . didn't die from cancer. . . ." He looked at George. "Then . . . how did she die, Mr. George?"

Hugo stood. Don't get him wrong; he was so scared that all his bones were floppier than spaghetti noodles. But this was it, the moment he faced his fears and ended them. "I need to help Sam. I need to get rid of this monster!" he growled with heavy breaths and shuffled down the hill, unable to feel anything but his heart thumping into his brain.

"He's not a monster," Sam murmured shyly, uncertain of

his words. He wanted to believe George was still in there. But after he blew up Rafflesia, it was hard to know precisely who they were dealing with.

Bipp ran to Ventus and easily picked him up, but Ventus still felt the moon's weight crushing him. "Ah, the friend of Mr. Hugo's, you're a *curious* one, aren't you?" George surprisingly smiled at Bipp.

"Run!" Bipp threw Ventus back near Luna and stood his ground against George. "You caused a lot of harm to Hugo, Sam, and even my birth family!" Bipp growled, ignored how George knew about him, and withdrew the ebony dagger from his belt.

"Idiot, you don't have a soul ability! You can't be here!" Ventus yelled.

Bipp glared back at Ventus, who promptly clacked shut his beak at *those* eyes.

George leaned closer to Bipp. "I believe that bird is the idiot here. For everyone has a soul ability.... Would you like help finding yours? Since you took great care of Mr. Hugo while he was in that coma, I feel I owe you one."

The pleasantries of George tilted Bipp's ears sideways.

"What the?" Bipp lowered his dagger with his eyes squinted. "Well, in that case ... if you tell me Hugo's soul ability and how he was able to fly just then, we'll be even." He pointed back to the ruins. "And why do you call him *Mr.* Hugo? That's unnecessarily specific."

"Stop negotiating with the monster!" Ventus yelled again.

George chuckled through his nose. "How noble of you, wishing to help your friends more than yourself. You really are a great fit for the Atlas family. But fret not. Like you, Hugo has his time. He only needs to wait and simply ... see." These words spun Bipp's brain, but before anyone could think, Bipp pressed his ebony dagger against George's fiery throat like it was instinctive. "Enough of your riddles! I know who you are! And I know what you've done!" Bipp grimaced from the heat of the fire against his knuckles.

George scoffed and calmly tilted the dagger away with a finger. "Don't bother using that dagger on silly old me. Such a precious family heirloom should be spent on something worth your . . . time." George squinted at the ground once more.

Bipp relaxed his arms to the side with a tight squint at George. "You are much more confusing than I thought you'd be."

"H-Hey! Y-You!" Hugo yelled, shaking horribly as he lumbered closer.

George peeked at him and smiled. "Wonderful. Mr. Hu–"

"Shut up!" Hugo interrupted. "I know you have some kind of hold on Sam! So, let him go, and leave Earth and Somnium alone!" Hugo nearly squeaked all of that. He couldn't even look at George while talking to him. He was trying not to succumb to fear, but his heart still pounded his skull, and his limbs still wobbled horribly.

"I don't have a hold on Sam. The decisions he makes are his, and he is free to do as he wishes. Just like each one of us here. Though I wish you'd all give me a moment of peace, then I might be able to save you from a few futures."

Hugo shook his head, refusing to believe that. But then, Sam hopped off Hugo and limped to George. Hugo paused, hyper-aware of Sam's left leg dragging behind him. *What did he do to you?*

Sam stopped a few feet from George before his feathers smoked from the heat. "George . . . if my mother didn't die from cancer, what did she die from? . . . Did you kill her?"

George smiled and nearly broke into laughter at that question. "Oh dear no, my boy. She was dead before I came to your house, and her body was just outside Mr. Hugo's room, on the floor."

This response froze Hugo, Sam, and even Bipp, who watched Hugo's mouth try to speak amongst his trembling jaw.

Sam's face scrunched in anger. "Don't you pity me with a lie!"

Suddenly the black fire around George vaporized into thin air. It was only the old man in his classy clothes.

Hugo instantly squinted at him. *Why . . . is he bald?*

"I apologize if this may be confusing for you. But, if you don't believe me, we can have Luna see my memory for you." Luna took a step back, almost too scared of George to follow such a request. But George's confidence about the matter forced Sam to pause and think.

Sam looked at Luna; he felt better the moment he saw her pink eyes again. *See your memory?* He thought for a moment before looking back at George. "T-Then . . . how did she die?"

George glanced at Sam's eyes with a slight frown. "That–" he sighed, "is the one thing I cannot teach you as your history professor, for I do not know for certain. . . ." George's eyes crossed over Hugo before he paused with a quick squint and gave a subtle smile. "But I do have my theories." He extended his hand, palm up to Hugo. "Could you please come here?"

Hugo froze dead still before his mouth opened with a hesitant, lung-shriveling exhale.

"Don't worry; I won't harm you. Just have a few questions."

Hugo raised his forehand with a pause. "Okay, but don't turn on that fire." George nodded before Hugo took a slow step forward, and his other limbs followed.

George rested his hands over Hugo's cheeks and furrowed his eyes at Hugo's scarred left eye. "Have you ever noticed anything odd about yourself, like you behave a certain way or move without knowing why? Heard any voices? Had a particular appetite for blueberries and crystalized honey mixed together?" George stretched down Hugo's cheeks to better look at his eyes.

"Well, not particularly. I like blueberries and honey, but I've never had them togeth–"

He paused once George leaned closer to him, and Bipp wrote that down.

"What's your favorite thing about Sam?"

Sam curiously stared at George.

Hugo looked at Sam in deep thought. "His voice . . . definitely his voice."

Sam froze and George smiled. "I know why you became a dragon. And do pardon me for misunderstanding initially. I must admit, you've surprised me."

Hugo could feel his confused mind numb as his heart punched him too loud to hear anything else. "W-What?"

George let go and looked at Sam with a great smile. "Ask Hugo what he thinks about Ai."

Sam slowly looked at Hugo. "You know what happened to her?"

Hugo looked down and scrunched shut his eye, trying to think straight. "I don't know! I was only four at that time!"

George chuckled a little through his nose. "I see. . . . Let's give Hugo some patience to think about that night. He's probably tried all these years to forget about it." George gave a kind smile to Sam and leaned in close. "But if you want my only advice about Ai, maybe dig a little deeper into that memory of his. Who knows, maybe you'll find something that even I don't see."

Sam didn't know what to think before he looked at Hugo and felt sorry for him. Hugo was even struggling to keep from passing out. "It's okay, Hugo. Take your time. Just tell me if you remember anything," he said, trying to be considerate to Hugo, for it was a heavy matter, and Hugo wasn't handling it well.

Amongst their discussion, Anzu slowly stood, wobbled a lot, and raised a claw. But, within a blink, George became engulfed in black flames, took up his arm, and smacked Anzu to the ground as if he had an invisible twenty-foot ligament to do so.

Hugo fled next to Bipp, who nervously smiled at him.

"Why are you playing with us? If you're so powerful, just end it already!" Ventus yelled before George laughed and lifted the heavy gravity from him.

"I have more patience than that. I've waited two-hundred Somnium years for this moment; I can spare a few more moments to entertain you. . . . Though not too much longer, for we're crunching the clock a bit." He looked at Sam, then back at the ground.

They all heard that and felt their bodies droop, especially Sam. But Ventus growled. "Anzu! Throw everything you got at him now!" Ventus raised his wings to suck the oxygen from the fire.

George sighed as the fire went away. Anzu launched a thousand needles of stone at George. But he simply raised his hand and reversed their direction. Anzu reacted quickly enough to slow many, but few stabbed into his blocking arms.

Ella ran to him to make sure he was alright. But he just about passed out before she got to him. She cried and tried her best to clean his wounds and dry his cuts with her soul ability, but she wanted to do more. She scanned Anzu's remaining injuries and begged her mind to think of something more she could do.

Ventus fell to his knees, and a few tears escaped his grasp. Hope just snapped like a twig, and even worse, he hurt Anzu in his quick plan to vanquish George. His clenched toes gave up and sank into the soft dirt, unable to find the will to combat George again. "I can't lose another creature . . . especially you, Anzu." Hugo watched Ventus' eyes droop. "I'm sorry." Ventus looked away from everyone.

To their surprise, the fire didn't return. "Sorry about that distraction, Sam. Where were we?" He looked at Sam, whose beak trembled at the sight of Anzu's dried blood.

*This isn't the George I knew. . . .* "Y-You stabbed Hugo and gave him nightmares for the rest of his life. You're the reason he's terrified of the dark! I honestly don't care if you killed my mother or not! You hurt my big brother and scarred him for life!"

George smiled. "Oh, Sam. . . . Hugo's fear of the dark is more complicated than you believe. But of course, I'm not the *only* reason for this fear. I would tell you the main reason, but I'm an educator. And I believe that Hugo needs to discover himself by looking at a mirror." He glanced at Bipp, only for a split second, but it seemed to catch Bipp's attention. "If he hasn't done so already."

"What's that supposed to mean?" Bipp exclaimed and threw his arms in the air as if he had given up.

"You still hurt him," Sam grumbled and looked away from

George.

*You hurt Hugo far more than that old man. Stop hiding behind him. You are the evil bane of your brother's life.*

Sam instantly felt sick. His chest pumped a stinging venom up his throat before he gulped.

"I know nothing about Ai. The investigators said she was murdered," Hugo said, beyond dizzy.

"Sure, I might have left burn marks on her when I–" he looked at the ground with a thoughtful squint, "*walked around* her body. I guess that's enough for an autopsy." This left Hugo with his awestruck jaw unable to find the following words. George cleared up some confusion from their past, but he shoved much more on top of it all. George looked around at the creatures, all standing in dismay or confusion. Then, he sighed and looked at the distant ruins of Rafflesia. "I think it's time we began the next phase of my assault." George looked at Sam. "Could you come here, please?"

*George . . . are you okay? You used to be someone who wanted to help everyone; never hurt them like this. . . . So what aren't you telling me? Is that fire controlling you? Do you hear its voice as well?* Sam reluctantly limped to George while his beak pointed down at his talons. *How can I help you fight it?* Among his thoughts, he subconsciously returned to his socially anxious ways and avoided eye contact. He looked at Hugo with great worry and sadness speaking from those emerald eyes. Hugo saw them instantly.

"I think it's time your adventure . . . went elsewhere, Hugo," George said. Hugo and Bipp's ears rose at that.

Hugo didn't know what George was planning, but if his words were valid, he only had a few moments to spare. "Sam, can you please tell me what's going on? I see that limp, and .

.. sorry to put you on the spot, but you haven't been eating again." With his head low to Sam's level, Hugo stepped closer and tried to sound gentle with his following words. "I've never felt your ribs that harsh . . . even with your feathers to cushion them. . . . You can tell me if George is bullying you, because, if he is–" He found a sudden confidence to glare at George.

*Protect him.*

Hugo's eye furrowed and ears twitched at that lady-like voice. It was oddly familiar to him. He turned his head back, but nobody was there. "Who . . ."

Before Sam could open his beak, George began to chuckle. "Oh, pardon me, I thought he told you. It was one of the more probable futures." George whispered that last part and gestured to Sam. "You see, Sam tried to kill himself for you."

Hugo's ears instantly stretched up from his skull, and his pupil shrank smaller than a pea within his gaping eye. Then his face slowly turned back to them.

Sam's heart struck him, forcing him to droop lower, embarrassed and ashamed as he watched tears well from Hugo's eye. He wanted Hugo to find out, but not like this.

"He blames himself for all your misery. Your eye, the large scar on your chest, the time you spent in a coma, and even you turning into a dragon and being trapped on this planet are constant reminders that he is a burden to you. So, naturally, he tried to remove himself from your life, thinking you'd be better. He didn't even deem himself worthy of food until you got better, which you never did in his eyes."

Hugo struggled to see from the stinging blur of tears, but he stepped closer to Sam.

"You are going to get hurt if you stay. So with Sam's permission, I'm taking you home to be as far away from him as possible and to continue your life in the best way possible." George looked at Sam, who knew what that look meant.

*I-I can finally help him.*

"And maybe I can get a few extra seconds to search for that soul before time runs out," George continued, then suddenly looked at the ground in thought. He paused, then something in his eyes changed before he slowly looked at Anzu. "Maybe . . . *you* could help this underground search with that soul of yours."

Ella glared at George once her ears scooped those words.

George saw Ella's glare and stepped back from her. He slowly knocked on the ground, careful not to spark the coals in Ella's deep ocean eyes, but his eyes still aimed at Anzu.

Hugo stepped a foot from Sam and stared right at him. Tears flowed faster than they ever have before. "Sam . . . is this true?" Hugo begged for the answer with his snout down to Sam's chest, hoping to see his gorgeous, emerald, drooping eyes. But Sam didn't give him a word. He just lowered his head further with his eyes about to shut.

"Please . . . don't use *the thing* against me." Hugo inched closer and completely ignored George. All his focus was on Sam's eyes drooping further with every second Hugo looked at him. "I can be there for you. I don't know much. But what I do know is that I don't want you to feel like that. . . . I want you to be happy with who you are," Hugo squeaked, "because I love who you are. . . ." He gulped, hoping Sam was listening. "We can do *the thing* like old times to help you feel better? But together . . . please don't leave me in the dark, alone."

The familiar wooden door appeared before them, decorated with spheres and flowers relating to Earth. George grasped the silver handle and pulled the door open to their living room with the recognizable burlap sofa. When Hugo took one step closer, about to hug him, Sam raised his wing and pushed against his snout to keep him away. *It's not about me....* With tears shining over his beak, Sam tried to look up at Hugo, but to his best efforts, he couldn't. Then he closed his eyes. "Go away."

Those words made Hugo wish to be stabbed in the chest, because what he felt was far worse. He could feel his heart slowly rip in half and his throat sting as he held back the cries to talk to him. "Can't I stay with you for one second more? You're not someone I need to deal with; you're someone I want to spend time with.... I-I would be devastated if you were gone.... Please, talk to me; yell at me if you must. I just want to know how to help you."

"You need to take my hand for this one." George lowered his gloved hand to Sam.

From Sam's throat to his stomach stung more than he ever could've imagined, but he wanted Hugo to be safe and happy from now on. He held George's hand, kept his opposite wing on Hugo's snout, and thought about Hugo's past: what he looked like, smelled like, and sounded like; then Hugo instantly felt it. Every new breath he gulped felt heavier as his skin shivered with a feeling of ice.

"Hugo!" Bipp stared at Hugo, whose tail shrank into his back and scales shedded off to soft, pale skin. His white fur blushed into copper hair, and he watched the ground come closer. He looked down at his claw—fingernails!

"Wha-" Hugo vomited instantly with the shriveling sting of his lungs. He coughed and gagged; his lungs and throat felt like they were on fire. His delicate human skin goosebumped all over as he sank to the ash. But he didn't care about his sore heart and scorching lungs; he only looked up at Sam, wishing to spend every drop of time left seeing those eyes and listening to his precious voice if he were to speak.

Sam stared at Hugo with a worried squint. *He still has those scars....*

Before Sam could notice much else he got wrong, George fell to his knees and coughed up an alarming volume of blood onto the ground.

"George!" Sam panicked before George raised his wobbling hand, and the door moved up and over Hugo.

With tears and snot drenching Hugo's face, Sam appeared blurrier by the second. "I'm so sorry, Sam," he wept while grasping his burning throat and throbbing chest. He needed to apologize, for it was apparent that this was the last time he would see him.

George let go of Sam's wing and held his shoulder for support before standing with a vicious wobble to his knees. "See how complicated it is to use your soul?" he whispered to Sam, who stared worriedly at him.

Before George set the door down, he smiled at Hugo. "I know this may be hard for you. And if you want to discover where you belong in life, I recommend retracing your steps. Perhaps, even take a visit to the college." He wiped his sleeve across his bloody mouth.

Hugo was too distraught to pay attention to these words. But they reached him, and without a doubt, they confused him like all George's words did. They especially reached Bipp with his ears high and ready for the softest whisper.

Ventus raised his wing, then quickly blasted Bipp under the door with a gust of air.

"Wait!" Bipp yelled and outreached his hand to Ventus.

Then he saw tears well from the blue jay's eyes.

"Don't waste this, idiot," Ventus murmured and pointed his wing to the silver flower wrapped loosely around Hugo's smaller, human arm.

Bipp froze at that before the door fell over them and vanished in a puff of silver smoke.

Sam looked down. "Please, Hugo. Don't try to come back to me." His heart sank as he said those words. *But give it time, Hugo, I know this will hurt, but you'll quickly learn life is better without me.*

George smiled at Ventus and engulfed back into flames. "Clever bird."

# Chapter 20
## THE WARMTH OF HOME

Hugo collapsed against the scratchy carpet of his living room, completely naked. His delicate skin goosebumped, and his entire body shivered even in the warm room's familiar air. But there was a distracting scent like baked sourdough bread that instantly pulled his imagination to the kitchen before Bipp stepped in front of him.

"Is that really you, Hugo?" Bipp asked with his head tilted, observing the scars and Hugo's eye. He rested his soft hand on Hugo's shoulder and felt the shivering goosebumps. "You're freezing!" Bipp glanced around in the hope of a blanket or a fire source. He paused as he looked down at his cloak; then he closed his eyes and grunted before grabbing it, about to yank it off. But his arms seemed to stiffen, and his breath heaved with his gnashing teeth. "What's going on?" His eyes welled as he opened them and released the cloak. But then the world around him caught his instant attention. "Uh, what is this place?" he asked as he stared at the furniture and television through a blur of tears.

As the creatures moved within the television, Bipp suddenly squinted at it, but he instantly shook his head to get back to

Hugo. He wrapped his arms around Hugo and lifted him from the ground before he rubbed him enough to create heat.

All the while, Hugo's heart struggled to keep up with his sorrowful and panicked mind. "Sam . . . what happened?" he whispered through the chattering of teeth. Bipp was indeed warm, and his soft fur felt like the world's most welcoming blanket. But Hugo's body refused to warm up. Even the goosebumps refused to soften.

"Andrew, where'd you put the peanut butter for those mice catchers?" Hugo's ears twitched in instinct from the sound of that voice. But it was subtle. The twitch and sound barely snagged his mind compared to his dragon ears.

"Who's there!" Bipp definitely heard it as he instantly glanced around.

"Andrew?" Mary turned the corner from the kitchen and gasped as she saw Bipp, whose torn cloak was stained with dry blood, and Hugo, who was still . . . completely naked. Her mouth opened and closed, trying to speak. "A-A-Andrew! There's another monster!" she screamed and ran back to the kitchen.

"Monster?" Bipp scoffed. "Who even was that creature?" Hugo's knees gave, unable to fight gravity. Bipp pulled up his weight by arching back and supporting Hugo entirely. "What did they do to you?" Bipp rubbed harder as he tried desperately to make Hugo warm.

"That lady . . . she's my mom, Mary. Call her back."

Bipp's eyes widened. "You mean–" he paused as he thought of all the stories Hugo told him, "this is the real you?" Hugo could barely nod before his eye rolled back, and he passed out. "Mary! Hugo needs you!" Bipp yelled.

"Hugo!"

Bipp's ears twitched with the sound of thumping from the kitchen. Mary veered around the corner and caught Bipp's sight. She wore an oversized orange sweater with pumpkins knitted on the front. Bipp couldn't help but notice her long, wild copper hair that matched Hugo's current hair color.

Bipp pointed at Mary. "That horrible sweater, give it to me! Hugo needs it!"

Mary froze as she now stared between Hugo's naked, unconscious body and Bipp, staring at her with his finger pointed. "What's going on here?" she thundered.

"Hugo was turned into this thing, and now he's freezing! I need some help! Maybe get some food and all the blankets you have."

Mary ran to Hugo and held his forehead for a temperature, then she observed him, seeing the many scars across his skin, especially the one across his left eye. "What did you do to him?"

Bipp's ears sank from how loud she was. "I'm trying to help! Is there anything warm you can get him?"

Mary paused for a while to get used to the talking rabbit. She looked down at his toes, then her eyes traveled up to his tall ears. "T-Take him to the room on the right." She pointed down the hall. "I'll be right behind you," she said in a suddenly calm tone that surprised Bipp.

She ran back to the kitchen as Bipp quickly carried Hugo into his old bedroom. He stopped and looked at the space and dinosaur décor that made him squint with curiosity. "I'm guessing this side is yours. . . . It's like the past and future in this room," Bipp murmured and walked to the side with stars and rocket ships.

Mary ran into the room, holding a box with the power chord clacking the walls behind her. She grabbed Bipp's upper arm to feel how warm he was. "Alright, lie next to him on the bed," she commanded. Bipp immediately did so after laying Hugo down, and as he did, Mary plugged in the electric heater and placed it across the room on Sam's nightstand before throwing many blankets over them. "If he starts to shiver, I want you to grab him tight. You're definitely soft, and you're probably a faster and safer heat source than that heater. But I'll leave it here since this room has gotten cold with nobody in it," she sighed and pulled a desk chair to the side of the bed. "First off, why is he naked?" Mary asked, thinking that would be the simplest question to start with.

Bipp snorted at that. "Oh . . . heh . . . Well, he normally has a scarf. But that got burned off . . . again. But don't worry; he's normally not naked. . . . But, do you mayhaps have any knitting or sewing materials? So, I can make him another scarf?"

Mary's right eye twitched as all formalities smashed out the window. She stood over Bipp and glared at him. "You're going to tell me what's going on, or you and I will have a serious problem!" she demanded with her clenched fists trembling.

Bipp's eyes drooped. "I don't know much . . . This is all new to me as well. I'll try my best to describe it for you. But to get started, I'd like you to know that I'm not an enemy, and I want to help Hugo with all my ability . . . I feel like that's something we can relate to, if you're his mom and whatnot."

Mary was now more confused than before. She had many questions, but not enough time in the year to ask them all. "What's your name, strange rabbit?" Mary sighed and sat back in the chair.

"I'm Bipp Atlas," he said simply.

Mary regretted asking that; every word Bipp spoke made her mind spin. "Bipp . . . Atlas?" She slouched and held the sides of her dizzy head.

Bipp nodded. "Yeah . . . Hugo said I could be part of the family. . . . I took his last name since I don't have one of my own. Sorry," Bipp spoke nervously, thinking of how Mary would feel to suddenly have a new family member.

Mary almost chuckled. "Hugo . . . you crazy boy." She carefully pulled down the blankets and observed the scars, but she stopped at the big one on his chest. Tears quickly formed and flowed down her round cheeks. "Please, Bipp, try your best . . . what happened?" She sniffled.

Bipp's eyes drooped as he looked at Hugo, who still shivered in his arms. "Where to begin? . . ." He sighed.

Hugo slowly woke, but he regretted doing so instantly. He was still shivering so much that one would think a jackhammer was beneath his blankets. For a second, he was hoping it was all just a long dream, until he felt the familiar, profoundly soft arms of Bipp wrap around him. He grasped the pillow beneath his ear in pain. His heart hurt so much, he wanted to scream. *Sam tried to kill himself.* That thought forced his nose to sting and tears to wrap around his face and soak into the pillow. He couldn't bear the thought of failing Sam like that. He tried desperately to find what he could have done better. "What did I do wrong?" he wept quietly. Everything hurt like a soreness that wouldn't go away. How Sam looked away from him when George told him of Sam's suicidal actions was burned in his mind.

Every time he blinked, Sam's disappointed eyes stole the darkness. He grasped the blanket over him harder, not even noticing his fingernails cutting through the fabric. *He hates himself because of me. But he knows I love him more than any-*

*thing. What can I do? Should I just leave him alone?* Hugo's weeping became audible as teeth-clenching squeaks forced their way out his throat. "Sam," he wept.

Bipp's arms held Hugo tighter; this brought Hugo's attention to Bipp. He could quickly feel Bipp's warm chest through the cloak and his soft fur soothing his tense skin. "I'm sorry, Bipp," Hugo said before a sniffle woke his ears.

"I don't want you to apologize ever again," Bipp said simply before a long silence of thought. But that's all that was spoken for much longer than they expected. Bipp was kind and gave Hugo time. Then, to Hugo's comfort, even though white light filled the room from beyond a thin curtain covering the window, Bipp reached over him and turned on his starry nightlight. When it shone stars at all shadows the room dared to hide, Bipp returned to Hugo and held him. "Mary told me everything about you that I didn't already know. So now I know who and what you are entirely. . . . She and Andrew were searching for you and Sam for almost three months. They went around the whole town, nailing up copies of your family photo. To them, you two disappeared off the face of the world. Should I get Mary? She has many questions for you. Some of which are from an investigation team they hired."

*Three months. . . .* Hugo struggled to speak. His nose was so stuffed with sorrowful snot, his face felt like a brick. "I . . . I want your opinion." Hugo paused with a deep sniffle, then rolled around to face Bipp. His eyelid stretched awake at the sight of Bipp. He was taller than he remembered, especially with his ears adding a few feet and catching some of the nightlight's stars. His arms easily wrapped around Hugo and fed him the warmth he needed. The top of Bipp's large, soft feet and toes like plump, yet supple grapefruits cushioned the bottom of Hugo's feet, gifting him the feeling like standing on a pile of warm pillows. "Have I failed Sam? Should I try to help him with this? He tried to– . . . and I don't know what I should do about it. I'm starting to feel like I was a bit obsessed, and now I should just leave him alone." He closed his eye and pretended to smile. "I guess he meant it on Zenith when he told me to kill him. . . ."

Bipp wiped his thumb across Hugo's cheek to temporarily dry his tears. "Sam cares about you very much, and you got hurt trying to protect him. That would make anyone feel bad about themselves. He sent you home to protect you. For now, you are safe, free to live your life without Sam needing to worry about you. . . . But after knowing you two for a while, I've learned that you two separating is the most difficult thing you could do. I know he misses you, and you miss him more than he could imagine."

Bipp paused with his eyes sinking to the sheets. "But, if you want my opinion, we should stay here, on Earth." Before Hugo could speak, Bipp just looked at him, and this alone closed Hugo's mouth. "Trust me; when you and Sam were in that destroyed house, there was a spark. Just a tiny one to your eyes, but to me, it felt like a supernova times a billion. And just that spark was enough to give Sam the caring love he needed. But . . . I've been thinking about you and Sam. . . . He's . . . complicated and doesn't want to be a burden to you; he wants to help you, and he definitely knows now how much you care about him and that you will do anything to help him, even if that means hurting yourself. . . . I think Sam has given you a chance to live your life not the way you want, but need. And I think, at the very least, you should focus on yourself and give it some time. It's not selfish to do what you need to do. So maybe do the things you've told me about, flight school, college, or simply look at the stars. Whatever it may be, I'm in, because I . . . like you, Hugo. And I hope to see your life blossom into your greatest potential."

Hugo hugged Bipp tightly, and his chest hurt more than it ever had. "Thank you, Bipp," Hugo murmured into the rabbit's chest with fresh tears and snot dribbling from his face.

Bipp let Hugo take a moment to accept his current condition and warm up a bit. "Are you going to be okay? Please let me know right away if you need anything," Bipp whispered, but Hugo just squeezed him tighter and wept. "Hey, it's going to be alright. . . . Here, I'll get Mary. She said to get her the moment you woke anyway, and I've been milking it." Bipp gave a subtle chuckle, trying to lighten the mood.

Hugo didn't want to let go of him, but after a few moments, he did. *Sam . . . what did I do wrong? Someone as beautiful and bright as you wanting to extinguish your light . . . It can't be your fault.*

"Alright, I'll be back as fast as I can. You've been getting cold quickly these past couple days." Bipp excused himself from the blankets, quickly turned his back to Hugo, and exchanged his near-shredded, cleaned cloak for a thick, green-knitted sweater. This sweater was large on Bipp, so large the sleeves hung from his arms, and the waist sank over his thighs. But it looked more comfortable than any clothing Hugo had ever seen. Hugo could quickly tell he loved it by how he looked at it. Bipp glanced back at Hugo with a subtle smile before leaving the room.

"Days?" Hugo murmured, then took time to look around the room, specifically Sam's bed. He instantly felt how empty his arms were without Bipp there; then, he blinked to rid the blur of tears and to look at a tower of his college textbooks on the floor. Rocketry, astrophysics, aviation, almost every subject he learned while at college, plus a few books of Sam's lay in a pile directly adjacent to his bed. *Has Bipp been reading?* he mused before Bipp lunged into the room and ran to Hugo.

"Are you alright?" Bipp asked quickly with his hands ready to fix anything.

Hugo hadn't even begun to shiver. So, he gave a fake smile to calm him. "I'm fine, thanks, Bipp," he said before Bipp sat on his bed with a sigh.

"Sorry for being jumpy. Even just this morning, you shivered the second I left the bed." He tapped his foot on top of the book pile. "I read some of these while resting beside you to get an understanding of what this world is like. . . . And Mary gave me a fancy pencil with an eraser attached!" His toes wiggled from his suppressed excitement. "I really needed to organize our adventure these past couple days. The burnt stick wasn't working that well," Bipp chuckled quietly. "You left out a lot of information about this planet. . . . Though, I guess we never had much time to discuss such things in detail." Bipp rested his hand on Hugo's forehead to check if he was okay. "I am sorry to say this, but part of me is glad we came to this planet. . . . I got to meet Mary and Andrew. They are exceedingly kind creatures, just like you. Andrew is at work right now and will be back pretty soon with a sign language book I hope to read for understanding Luna . . . if we can go back. . . . Mary let me borrow her sweater because she thought it was sad that I only had a torn . . . *poncho?* I think she called it. Right now, Mary is gathering some soup I helped make." Bipp shyly twiddled his thumbs and looked away in thought. "I talked with Mary quite a lot." Hugo watched Bipp's tongue bulge out his cheek. "She gave me something called mint chocolate."

He looked dead at Hugo with the point of a finger. "You've been keeping secrets from me, for that was the single greatest thing I have ever tasted!" He grabbed his own cheeks, squishing and stretching them. "It was the perfect blend of mint leaves and sweet, sweet cocoa." His eyes rolled back at the sheer bliss of the ghost taste left in his mouth.

Then he shook his head with a chuckle. "Anyway, Mary also thought it was funny that I'm part of the family. On this planet, usually the parents are the ones who decide that.... Luckily for me, she's getting the paperwork." Bipp smiled. "Now, it is going official on both planets! I will be Bipp Atlas...." He paused, looked at the pile of books, then shyly looked away. "Though, I'm just happy to be with you, family or not," he whispered with his eyes drooping in deep thought.

Hugo lay with a storm scrambling his mind. He wanted to return to Somnium; no, something deep down begged him to. *Is it even possible to return?* Hugo knocked on the bedframe, but no door decided to show.... *Well, that limits my options.* ... He paused in thought, searching for anything he could've missed. "What was George saying about retracing my steps?" he whispered accidentally.

Bipp looked at the pile of books with a nervous feeling stealing his thoughts.

Then, a knock thumped from the room's door before it creaked open. Bipp promptly stood next to Hugo and carefully helped him sit up against the wall, fluffing the pillow against his back. Hugo struggled to keep this position; he was far weaker than with his dragon body, and his brain wasn't yet used to being human again. Mary walked in with a bowl of steaming soup over her cupped hands and a towel. Her plump, rosy cheeks weighing down her strong smile brought Hugo comfort. It had been too long since he'd seen her. His hurting heart warmed a little, just enough for him to subconsciously smile at her.

Mary smiled back a bit more and handed him the bowl supported by a towel, in case of spilling. "How are you feeling, sweetie?" she asked, obviously trying not to burst into emotions like her fiery self begged her to.

"Good," he said simply, trying to avoid bursting into tears by describing how he really felt. He looked at the soup and smiled. It was almost how Bipp made it back on Somnium.

"This planet surprisingly has the same plants I used to make it, so it should taste quite similar. Except maybe a bit cooler, now that you're not a dragon. Also, I decided to add a pinch of rosemary for," he glanced at Mary with a shy smile, "unspecific reasons."

"Thank you," Hugo said before eating. The cold air outside his blanket conquered his arms in goosebumps, but as the warm soup filled his throat, his chest felt a fresh warmth. He couldn't help but close his eye and recline.

Mary tilted her head as she looked at the soaked pillow behind him. She looked at Hugo's face; tears dried against his cheeks. "Hugo . . . what's wrong; what happened to you? Bipp told me as much as he could, but . . . I know there's more going on here." She asked the thing Hugo feared.

His eye drooped at the soup. "What did he tell you?" he asked, still trying to avoid talking about how he felt.

"He said you went to a different planet, were turned into a dragon, did a bunch of crazy adventure stuff, made friends, went to war, and a bunch of nonsense about souls or whatnot."

"I left Sam out of my explanations. I think it's better if you explained him," Bipp whispered to Hugo.

Mary's eyes shot at Bipp. "You know about Sam?" she yelled with the fiery burst of her eyes.

Bipp backed away from Mary and shook his hands and head. "No, no, no. I-I don't. I mean, a little, but not enough compared to what Hugo could tell you!" Bipp bowed slightly, begging Mary to forgive him.

Mary scoffed and looked back at Hugo. But Hugo just stared at them. *What kind of relationship do they have?* After a moment, he looked down with his lips starting to wobble. But he knew Mary needed to know what had happened to them. He began by explaining that Sam was a bird; the rest followed swiftly with Hugo's flow of tears growing. Sam was burned in a fire, whipped, stabbed, poisoned. . . . He reached the part about Sam leaving him on Somnium. "What happened, Mom? He said you called animal control?"

Mary gave a confused look, then her eyes and mouth gaped. "That was Sam?" Her shout thundered throughout the room before she covered her mouth, and tears welled. "No . . . no, no, no! Please! Don't tell me I stuffed my son in that cage!" she demanded, but Hugo only looked down in response. He didn't know what to think; only how Sam must've felt stole his thoughts.

Mary struggled to keep standing, and Bipp quickly supported her by holding her hand. "I'm a terrible mother! I knew I saw Sam's eyes in that creature! I just never would have thought–" She fell on her hands and knees with tears soaking the carpet beneath her. "What happened to him? Is he safe now?" she begged Hugo to tell her.

Hugo set the soup on the bedside cupboard; he lost his appetite as his tingling chest pain returned. "I don't know for sure what happened to him. But he blamed himself for what happened to me on Somnium and . . . he tried to . . . remove himself, thinking I would be better without him." Hugo grabbed the blankets tight, and his teeth gnashed. "I don't know what I should do. I don't think I can go back to him. I told him how I felt, but I'm unsure that was enough. What am I doing wrong? How can I help him? Should I just leave him alone?"

He began to shake. "I-I love him, and hearing that he hates himself is the worst thing I've ever felt." His heart began to race. "I . . . I want to help him live; I want to help him be happy and help him through being sad–" he wheezed and grasped the base of his throat.

Bipp instantly ran to him and hugged him tight, trying to calm him. "Don't worry. You are the greatest brother he could have asked for. You did nothing wrong, and neither did he. . . . If he still thinks he's a burden after all the kind things you say to him, then he's not hearing it."

Hugo paused for a second, but he wasn't calming down.

"When I was a child, that abusive farmer would have me work for others on rare occasions. They said I was the hardest worker they'd ever seen. And do you know what happened to those words? They went right over my head. . . . I didn't believe them. After many years of that farmer telling me I was flowery and more valuable dead, someone telling me that I was amazing to work with seemed like a joke or pity to make me feel better. I did consider it for a moment, but it never lasted. Because after so long of listening to the farmer, his words became mine. And I kept telling myself that I was useless. . . . The way I see you and Sam, is that you are water, and Sam is a vase with a hole at the bottom. Your kind words may stay in for a moment, but they all leak from that hole."

Hugo looked up at Bipp.

"Right now, you've done all you can—just rest. The only thing that can help Sam now, is if he learns to love himself. Then, and only then, will he hear your words and keep them close to his heart, sealing that leak."

As Hugo felt Bipp's soft arms around him, his heart slowed. He tried thinking of how to get back to Sam, but the only thing that sparked his mind was George telling him to retrace his steps. His eyelid drooped as his forehead met Bipp's chest. "How can I help him learn to love himself?"

Before Bipp could open his mouth, Hugo went limp and sagged against him into the exhausting ocean of sleep. Bipp then smiled and rested Hugo back against the bed. "Keep on filling that vase until you've flooded the galaxy. . . . Just like you did with me."

*Chapter 21*
# REKINDLED

Mary simply stared at Bipp, who cradled and rested Hugo's head against his puffy pillow. He even brushed a few dangling copper hairs from over Hugo's eye so he could see the light better when he woke.

"H-How do you know that? Sam's hard to figure out, even for Hugo," she asked to distract herself. Hearing all that news about Sam had left her heartbroken, completely blaming herself for Sam wanting to die, especially after the birdcage misunderstanding. She sniffled and wiped her eyes before standing with a severe wobble, trying to recover.

Bipp carefully helped her up, and after ensuring she was okay, he then took a moment to admire Hugo and tuck the blankets over his shoulders. "Well, I've spent most of my life alone. Everything Sam seems to be feeling, I've felt at least once. . . . But I didn't have a Hugo. So, I spent several years talking to myself, wondering about every little possible question. Why don't I have any friends? Why do I feel so horrible just for existing? Should I change who I am, so others will accept me? What should I strive to do with my life? . . . I guess you could say, I studied my own philosophies . . . trying to figure out who

I am and who I want to be." Bipp turned to Mary with a smile. "I figured some out over time. And now I have Hugo to help me solve the rest, so I'm great. . . . But right now, Hugo needs someone to help him, to be his rock. And I'll gladly take on the responsibility." He looked back at Hugo with a smile and a mind full of wonders for the future. "Who knows, maybe we can build a mountain."

Mary looked at Hugo, then back at Bipp with a warm feeling rising in her chest along with a deep breath. "Bipp, what does Hugo mean to you?" Mary asked, but with a strange tone that Bipp didn't quite understand.

"H-He's very special to me. He's the first creature who was ever kind to me and liked me for who I am, even though I had a . . . *difficult* past. He even liked me enough to call me family, after we only met a couple days prior. . . . I'd like to return that same affection. I want to show him how wonderful he is. He's still just a regular creature, so he has downs like anyone. And I want to help be the hope he needs to keep moving up through those downs." Bipp never left his sight of Hugo, who slept soundly through their conversation. The deep breaths Hugo pushed from his nose sank Bipp's ears and shoulders into a sea of calm, knowing he was alright.

"Do you . . . love him?"

Bipp's ears pierced the sky, and his eyes shot from Hugo to her. "I—uh. . . ." He stepped away from her.

She had her face down; she was shy about her words, but dead honest. "You and Hugo are quite the pair. And I'd go as far as to say you alone support him more than Andrew or I support each other, and that's saying something."

Bipp became dead still.

"If you're willing to be that kind to my son, and willing to take such good care of him like you have, well, instead of being his brother, I could give you my blessing for being with him on a more, romantic scale if you wish. . . . I know I just met you, and you're a rabbit creature. But I can tell you two have something strong going on." She smiled and laughed a little to help calm Bipp. "I just want my boys to find love, and you're the first person he's ever brought home, so I know he likes you," she chuckled.

"Well, I . . ." Bipp's silver cheeks ripened as he twiddled his thumbs. His eyes shyly moved to the loose, silver flower over Hugo's wrist. "Heh, do I give off a romantic vibe?" He tried to sound sarcastic.

"To be honest, I don't know for certain. That would be between you and Hugo. . . . Sure, I'm his mom, and I've had a front-row seat every day to who he is, so I know him better than anybody. . . . And I don't love him just because I'm his mom, I love him because I see things in him that are worthy of love. . . . So my question to you would be, what do you see in him that makes you look at him like that?" She paused with a smile as Bipp suddenly stared at the floor in deep thought, intentionally away from Hugo.

"And don't try to hide it. You teleported into my living room with him completely naked, then didn't hesitate to sleep in the same bed with him, weirdly close I might add. I know, one wasn't your fault, and I told you to lay next to him. But then, as you held him, you watched Hugo with so much care and smiled in a way that told me you love being with him more than you love anything else. And since I'm his mom, I have a superpower and can sense this kind of thing, especially when it's so apparent it would be harder to hide an elephant in this tiny room." She chuckled a little to calm Bipp's obvious worry again. "And the passion you show when making soup for him and knitting that new scarf alone tells me you have feelings for him."

"Heh," he tried to mirror her humor, but it only came out as a heave of nervous breath.

"You know . . . since you're not from Earth, there is no 'paperwork' available to adopt you. . . . So we can just go right ahead with you being his brother. . . . But, I get the feeling you don't want that." She shyly looked Bipp in those nervous, jade eyes. "Because I get the feeling you accidentally fell in love with him."

"B-But–!" Bipp hesitated with a sideward glance out the window and a long pause afterward. He rubbed his chest and grabbed the sweater's knitting tight before taking a deep breath. "You're right. . . ." He closed his eyes. "Hugo is . . . unique. And I . . . do *like* him . . . a lot." He peeked at Hugo, hoping he didn't hear him. And when Hugo subtly snored from his sleep, Bipp's shoulders and ears sank with a sigh of relief. "But . . ." he grimaced, "it's not what you think. Hugo . . . doesn't see love like that. . . ." Bipp waved his hands to excuse his words. "And thank you for the offer. It means a lot that you think I'm worthy of being with–"

Mary raised her hand to pause him once more. "Just because he doesn't see love like that, doesn't mean you can't tell him how you feel, especially if we're about to 'adopt' you."

Bipp stepped back and looked at the door.

"Unless . . . there's something more going on here." Mary stepped closer to him with a sharp squint at those nervous eyes.

Bipp looked away with his rising cheeks warmer than he could handle. He quickly rubbed them to hide the apparent blush, but it helped little.

"I see the worry in your eyes whenever you talk about how you feel. But trust me, if you told him, he would accept you for who you really are. . . . And by the way you talk about him, he's earned your respect and then some, so why keep it a secret—does he not deserve to know?"

After a long pause of Bipp staring at his toes gripping the carpet and his arms wrapped over his lower chest, Mary still came to him, and to his surprise, she hugged him. "It's okay. . . . Whatever's going on, I'll be there for you and Hugo. . . . You may keep the Atlas name if you wish, and I'll treat you like family, especially because you've kept such good care of him and helped him return home. I definitely owe you at least one. And know, I won't make anything official until you know for certain it's what you want. You only need to tell me, and I will help you. . . ."

Bipp couldn't look at her. He opened his mouth to speak, but he couldn't—at least, not those words. "T-Thank you. . . . And don't worry, I'm sure he'll find love like that eventually. In fact, there's another dragon I've been hinting him toward. She's amazing . . . heh." He winked awkwardly, chuckled, but new tears welled from his eyes.

"Bipp. . . ." She rested her hand behind his tense head and gently guided him over her shoulder to lean on.

Bipp tensed up entirely, took one look back at her compassionate eyes, then gently pushed her away with his shaking hands. "I-I'm sorry, Mo–" He slapped shut his mouth with the veil of his hands and squinted at the door again for a possible escape.

Mary slowly took one of Bipp's arms and held his hand. "You're okay. Don't be scared. You may call me Mom if you want. Just tell me what you're feeling; it's not that hard, is it?"

He took a long moment to calm his heavy breaths. "I-I'm going to continue my earlier topic. . . ." He peeked back at Mary, only to see her gifting him with a heartwarming smile and an accepting nod. But something about her eyes showed slight disappointment.

"Uhhh . . . I've come to think Hugo sees love differently. He's not a normal creature who falls in love, shares a kiss, then gets married or whatever. I feel like he's a bit more genuine than that. Almost like he knows what the real definition of love is. . . . I'm just trying to figure it out and maybe see love the way he does. Because he . . . is who I aspire to be like—loving, kind, gentle yet strong in a good way, and heck, maybe even a bit weird. So, I apologize if I may seem . . . attracted to Hugo like that. I swear, I'm only trying to change my stars to a better path."

Mary paused for a moment and stared at the rabbit. But then, she hugged Bipp again, tight enough to squeeze the air from his lungs. "You'll fit right into this crazy family. Just know, whatever weighs you down, you're not alone; you can go to anyone in the Atlas family for help. If you couldn't tell already, we are a very open family, and we'll accept you no matter what sinks you. And just know, your difficult past doesn't define who you are now."

She let go and gently rested her hand on his chest. "Even *those* scars don't cover your story."

Bipp blushed again. "How did you–"

"Like I said, I'm a mom; I see everything that goes on in this house, especially when you tug at your new sweaters to hide yourself more. You're just like Andrew with hats. . . . But don't you worry. Love makes everyone do bizarre things here and there. Even I became shy about my larger body when I started liking Andrew. But when I told him that I liked him, my body wasn't even a blink in his thoughts." She smiled and returned to the tight hug. "Though I am still a bit self-conscious about it. But Andrew and I are working on our self-perception together, especially now that he has those burn scars over his face. In fact, you should talk to him about it."

Bipp paused with a blush and a glance to the side before resting his cheek on her shoulder. "T-Thank you, Mrs. Atlas," Bipp wheezed before Mary shyly let go. He instantly heaved with his back bent and hands over his thighs. "This family is full of huggers, isn't it?"

Mary chuckled and waved her hand to excuse the silly question. "I don't know what will happen in the future. But, please, if I could have one request. . . . Make sure my boys, this includes you now, are safe. Sam in particular needs the most guidance, being the youngest."

Bipp lightly patted his cheeks to stop the tears that snuck from him. "Right. I promise I will not let anything wrong happen to them. And let me add, that promise is one I intend to keep with my life." He took a deep sniffle, but smiled.

Mary flicked him on the chest. "You don't need to be sacrificing yourself! Just help them, ya weirdo!" Mary and Bipp both chuckled, then they sat on Sam's bed. "Just for fun, let's talk about you. What does Bipp Atlas wish more than anything, apart from the topic of this family?"

One of Bipp's ears twitched as he thought. Then, he sighed with relief at the new topic. "What I really want . . . that doesn't involve this family, is for our worlds to become one. I promised Hugo that I'd bring Earth and Somnium together. And I have unlimited ideas for how creatures on my planet could help your species, and your species could teach us so many things. I would love to map out wherever we are in space and maybe start a modest garden somewhere. Creatures would come, share what we discovered, add to the galactic map, and eat soup together. Maybe start space travel between our two neighboring planets." Bipp smiled and tapped his foot on the base of the book pile. "I could finish these. Some of them explain how things such as space travel could be possible." Bipp's ears drooped. "But I fear that fantasy may only exist in a perfect world and would take a long time to accomplish. . . . So, for now . . . I think I'd like to stay here, learn as much as I can, and maybe with your human technology, I can eventually bring more creatures over here. . . . But I don't know what the future holds. . . . So if Hugo still wants to go back to Somnium for Sam, could I take these books and a few of these Earth maps with me?"

Mary chuckled. "I think Hugo would need to answer that."

"Sure, you can have them," Hugo murmured. Both Mary and Bipp flinched and looked at Hugo, who slowly began to sit up. "College has . . . traumatized me to a point where I don't think I'll need those again. And besides, you seem far more interested in the more sciencey-discovery stuff than I ever was. I just liked the stars," Hugo chuckled. "And once you've read them, I have lots of questions about Somnium's . . . *physics* that I'd like to talk with you about, if you don't mind."

Bipp bowed to Hugo. "Thank you . . . for the books." He looked up at Hugo with a nervous smile. "Heh, when did you wake?"

"When you said something about joining planets. Why?"

Bipp shyly rubbed the back of his neck. "No reason."

Hugo squinted at Bipp before he shrugged. "I have made a decision though." Mary and Bipp looked at Hugo quizzically.

"I might know a way back to Sam. If it works, then I will think about it further. If it doesn't work, then we will stay on Earth. I want to make the final decision, knowing if we can even get to him or not."

"Okay . . . if you wish. . . . But, how would we get back to Somnium?" Bipp nearly sighed as his hands sank into the plush bed beneath him.

Hugo looked up at the ceiling in thought. "Well, we first traveled there with George's door ability. But I'd like to check George's office before we decide. He said to retrace my steps to find where I belong, and that phrase is bizarre, even for George. He even mentioned the college."

"You're going back based on what Apotheosis told you?" Bipp chuckled, wondering if Hugo was serious.

Hugo shrugged. "It's the best I got."

Bipp looked around the room, especially taking notice of Sam's Saurian figurines. He couldn't help but pick one up and admire it after wiping some dust from the velociraptor's head, which bore dark feathers along its entire spine.

"That's Din. . . . Sam's childhood favorite. Those memories are ones I hope to never forget; though I doubt Sam remembers much of him." Hugo looked at the star pattern across his blanket with his mind delving deep into a daydream. "It's strange to think how much we change."

Bipp sighed again with a subtle sink to his face; then, he set the figure down. "Let's get going. I'll pack these books and–" He looked at Hugo. "Do you need any help getting up and whatnot?"

Hugo lifted the blankets from his body, and as the room's air met his delicate, surprisingly naked skin, he shivered and quickly threw the blankets back over himself. "Uh, yeah. Could you get me some clothes?" he asked with his face turning ghost pale.

"Welp, you two do what you need to do. I'll be . . . elsewhere." Mary left the room to give them some privacy. But she left with an obvious wink to Hugo.

"Mom!" Hugo's cheeks blushed before he heard Mary chuckle down the hall.

Bipp watched *that* event unfold. But he only smiled with a subtle chuckle from his nose. He then leaned down near the pile of books and raised an emerald-green scarf of incredible length. "I knitted this while you were asleep. I tried to make it the color of Sam's eyes, so no matter what planet you're on, part of him will always be with you. . . . This time, no metal, just a rough material that's common on Earth and somewhat immune to fire according to Mary. It's really warm, and. . . ." Bipp froze for a minute. "It's too big for you now. . . ." Bipp looked down at it, folded in his arms. "Should I cut it?"

Hugo smiled. "No, it's perfect. Thank you for making it. But uh, could I get some pants as well . . . and–" Hugo stopped as he stared out the window, through the gaps in the curtain. White fluffy flakes swayed down peacefully with little wind. Hugo's heart warmed. He always liked the snow on Earth, for it meant many months of the brightest ground, even at night. But at this time, it made him think of how long he was on Somnium. "And maybe a sweater."

"Alright?" Bipp said, still confused about how *formal* humans were regarding clothing. Bipp was always overdressed compared to other creatures on Somnium just for wearing pants and a cloak to cover his scars. He set the emerald scarf over Hugo's shoulders, then searched through the nearby dresser.

*So, I've been gone for almost three months. . . . I was right about Sam's birthday. And I guess I expected time to be slower on Somnium due to that orange supergiant's mass, but that was just a farfetched guess based on something I learned at college.* Hugo scoffed at himself. *Wow–*

"You're quite the nerd, Hugo," Bipp interrupted.

"What?" Hugo looked at Bipp as he pulled out a pair of cartoon, yellow, starry pajama pants, which Bipp thought were soft and rather funny based on how he rubbed them and nearly laughed.

"I might use this design for my maps. I've been thinking about new ways of drawing the stars anyway, and I kinda like this."

Hugo couldn't help but smile a little.

Bipp then pulled out a green knitted sweater, similar to what he was wearing, but more 'Hugo' sized. "Is this good?" Bipp laid the clothes on the bed but paused as he looked at Hugo. He was still shaking, not a lot, but enough for Bipp to notice. "Here." Bipp took up the sweater, brought it over Hugo's head, and tugged it to his stomach.

"Bipp, go get Mary; I'll take care of the rest. Thank you."

Bipp looked curiously at Hugo before doing so. Hugo threw on the pajama pants and sat up, observing the snow.

"What is it?" Mary ran into the room with Bipp.

"Bipp said I was gone almost three months. . . . Is that true?" Hugo begged to know if he wasn't crazy.

"Yup, almost three months."

"Okay." He took a deep breath. "And how long ago did you see Sam?"

"More than . . . two months ago."

Hugo's head and eye drooped. "I wasn't even gone two

weeks." He paused and thought of how Sam spent two months alone with Dr. George. Hugo stood, then awkwardly wrapped the scarf over his shoulders multiple times. "I'm sorry for worrying you for so long, Mom."

Mary fixed Hugo's sweater, tugging all the wrinkles to help him look cuter. "You're fine, Hugo. None of this is your or Sam's fault." Before she could help Hugo stand, Bipp stood before them.

"Eat your soup first," Bipp commanded, surprising Hugo and Mary. "You haven't eaten in a while, and if we find a way to go back, Apotheosis will probably try to kill us. So eat up; you need the energy. Also, we worked really hard on it. Hope you like it." Mary looked at Bipp with a concerned raise of her eyebrow as Hugo agreed and took up the bowl. He quickly ate, then tried to stand. But he wasn't used to walking on two feet. Even his muscle memory seemed tampered with, so simply rising from the bed was met with wobbling limbs.

"Here." Mary and Bipp took the soup bowl and helped Hugo walk, each supporting him with an arm.

Just as they neared the kitchen, the sound of wheels crunching along the snowy driveway flicked Bipp's ears. "I'll tell Andrew to keep the car going." Bipp and Mary rested Hugo on a dining chair, then Bipp excused himself.

"So, what is Apotheosis, and why does it want to kill you?" Mary asked with a worrisome combination of firm and patient.

Hugo lowered his head. "Apotheosis is the president of our college, Dr. George. He's apparently a powerful monster that killed thousands. But it's strange. He likes Sam; I think it has something to do with his soul, but after watching George, I think there might be something more, like he's almost preparing him for something. . . . It doesn't matter though, unless my plan works," Hugo sighed.

"You don't sound very motivated to go back there."

Hugo's head lowered farther. "I'm still thinking about it—what I should do if we *can* go back? What do I say to Sam?"

Bipp ran into the kitchen, holding a backpack from Hugo's early school days. "Could I borrow this to carry the books in?" he asked with his face low, thinking he may be overstaying his welcome.

Hugo looked at the bag and remembered those days with a shiver. "Sure, you can keep it."

Bipp bowed instantly. "Thank you!" He then ran back into Hugo's room to gather as many books as the bag could fit.

Mary grabbed the soup pot. "Well, if you are doing something dangerous like facing a monster, I'm glad he's with you," she chuckled, but her eyes spelled great concern. "Can you walk?"

Hugo stood and tested his legs, promptly leaning against Mary. "Yeah, just need to get used to it." They walked to the garage, but once Mary reached for the doorknob, a quick shout came with the sounds of rumbled movement.

"Oh, right. . . . While you were gone, and we went searching for you, nobody was here to keep the house alive, so we have a little mouse problem. And your father is . . . well . . ." She opened the door to Andrew, who stood on the car's hood with his legs and arms ready to jump to the ceiling.

As they creaked open the door, Andrew swiftly turned to them with his eyes showing an apparent fear under the shade of his navy-blue cap. "Hugo! What happened to you? Is everything alright?" Andrew begged to know as he watched Mary practically carry him.

"He's not taking it too well," Mary whispered with a giggle.

"Did you see another cute mouse, honey?"

"Yes! I really don't think these catchers work! Once we release them, they just come right back here! We need to get the lethal–" Andrew froze as Mary eyed him, as if she was telling him to watch his next words.

He sighed. "Okay. . . . But if this persists, then I'd like to suggest moving. . . . Can you help me with the one in the catcher now?"

Mary smiled and helped Hugo in the car before she helped Andrew. He asked what they were doing in the garage, and as they waited for Bipp, Mary explained the situation to her best ability. Then, as Bipp hopped into the back seat next to Hugo, Andrew's eyes grew. "Wait . . . Sam tried to– . . . h-hold on a second." He looked away with his body shaking, found a trash can, and emptied his stomach into it. He didn't look so good after that. "A-And you're trying to go back there?" he exclaimed, begging to know everything.

"We're just seeing if it's possible; Hugo will make the final decision then," Bipp explained, setting the overly stuffed backpack, enveloped by his cloak, on the seat between him and Hugo.

Everyone could see Andrew's shaking fingertips bite into his palms. He wanted to say something, but gulped it down. "Okay . . . but I'm driving," he said. They watched him nearly march to the driver's seat as they nervously sat in, then Andrew reluctantly began the drive. "I'm not sure how to think about this." He gripped the steering wheel tight. "Why did this have to happen? Why Sam of all people? He'd never hurt a fly! And–" He tried to wipe the tears, so he could see the road. Mary quickly helped him hold the wheel. He pressed the gas pedal harder, trying to get to Sam as promptly as possible. But once they almost flew off the road, Mary held his shoulder to calm him down. He slowed down, understanding Mary's eyes, but he still exceeded every speed limit. "What's going on with this family? Other planets, alien animals, how are we even going to explain the rabbit when we arrive at the college?" Andrew asked, swimming with more questions than he was asking.

These questions scrambled Hugo's mind further.

"If I want humans and the creatures of Somnium to become one, I think they should see me how I am. I mean, you all know me. What's the difference if other humans see me as well? Are they not used to other species?"

Mary shrugged at that, knowing that hiding him would be a struggle. Bipp was very noticeable, especially wearing her oversized green sweater and bearing those massive ears that bent against the car's ceiling.

"I like your idea, Bipp. . . . I especially love your dream of mapping where we are in space and starting a modest garden somewhere. . . ." Hugo was looking out the window with his palm under his chin. Everyone seemed to pause. "If I can't go back to Sam . . . I promise I will help you achieve every last bit of it."

"You . . . love my dream? . . ." Bipp asked so quietly, their human ears didn't hear. He thought for a moment, rubbed his cheeks, and curled his fingers into fists. For a reason unknown to him, he didn't like Hugo admitting defeat for returning to Sam. "You will see him again. *That* is my promise to you. It may not be today or this year, but it will happen. I'll even help you build a rocket ship that soars to the edge of the universe if it means finding him." Bipp stated, staring right at Hugo, hoping that helped him feel better.

Andrew took several minutes to calm down before he patted his hand inside the passenger cubby, then pulled out a thin picture book.

"Here's that sign language book you wanted; it's a little worn. But it was the only one in the library."

"Thank you!" Bipp took it in his hands and promptly began reading it.

"Did you check out that book, Mary?" Andrew asked softly. "Your name was on the return card."

"Yup. Sam asked for it about a year ago when we visited there. He said that since he was bad at talking to people, maybe he would be better at signing to people instead. He was so cute and excited when he received it. Though he was timid about reading it with us around."

Hugo glanced at Mary and Andrew before resuming his thoughts out the window.

As the drive went, Bipp showed what he read by making hand signs. And rarely, to cool his brain, he switched his attention to every detail of the car, how fast the trees went by, how warm it was considering the winter cold; it all delved him in amazement and wonder of human technology.

Hugo spent the entire ride staring at the snow. . . . *Sam . . . the thought of you being alone. . . .* "W-Why does my chest hurt?"

Mary turned back and watched Hugo rub his chest, hoping the pain would disappear. But this pain was deeper than even his scars had to show, and it stung like a knife slowly inching in with every thought. *What happens if you never know love? I just . . . hope you see . . . that I am here, and . . . I really do love you.*

Mary wanted to reach out to Hugo, but just as she reached out her hand, Hugo looked at her. She froze at *that* watery eye.

Once Mary learned about Sam being the bird and how

she felt by looking at his eyes then, she now studied her son's eyes, never to make that mistake again. And with Hugo's eye, she was scared. Hugo looked out the window for the rest of the trip, not caring much about what Bipp and Mary were doing staring at him. They both wanted to help, but first, they needed to know if returning to Sam was possible.

Bipp looked down with a sorrowful expression.

They eventually arrived at the college campus and parked in front of their old dorm. "Wait." Bipp instantly sprang from the car and gaped at the castle, which was stained from age with a brownish-gray tint to its walls and bore five spires to pierce the snowy clouds. There were even some blue jay mascot banners that caught his attention. "I get it now. . . . This is why you two were acting weird on Zenith. It is very similar to that library." He looked at Hugo, who stood from the car. He was shivering from the year's early cold. Bipp grabbed his backpack and ran to Hugo. He quickly tucked the scarf tighter around him and stood shoulder to shoulder with an arm wrapped around him, hoping to warm him. They walked along the stairs, and at the top was the building's bulletin board with the Atlas family's before-college photo pinned to it. Sam and Hugo were circled, and beneath the photo had a phone number and a large label that read 'missing.'

Bipp looked at Hugo, wondering how he would react. But Hugo simply removed the notice and wiped the snow from Sam's face. Seeing Sam so happy made Hugo feel weightless. *This memory.* He loved it, and he loved seeing everyone together like that. "We may need to update our family photo once this is all over." Hugo nudged Bipp, who then gave an uncertain smile to the photo.

"Oh, that," Mary said once she caught sight of what Hugo

held. "We printed out so many of those, but–" She reached into her pocket and pulled out several photos. "Andrew copied the original, so each of us could have one." She handed one to Hugo, but she leaned close as she got to Bipp. "Don't worry; we'll make an updated one." She smiled and handed a copy to Bipp.

Andrew carried the soup along the shoveled, quartz steps to the main door as they finished their memory lane. Hugo tucked the photo in his scarf, and Bipp in his backpack, before they prepared for what the students might think of Bipp. There weren't many students due to the snow keeping them indoors. So once they opened the central, twenty-foot-tall doors. . . let's just say being sneaky was far out the window.

*We should've used the back door.* Hugo quickly thought, but it was too late.

Of about thirty people in that grand hall, more than twenty instantly stared at Bipp as the cold wind whistled past his back and cracked the massive curtains forward. The crowd froze for what seemed like many minutes. But eventually, the Atlas family began to walk down the hall. A few brave students walked to him and said comments like, "nice costume, a little late for Halloween don't ya think?" or simply, "What are you supposed to be?" Bipp answered patiently, which each human needed. But even with his simple answers, they either didn't believe him or were so weirded out by him that they left the scene. That is, except for one.

There was a strong, burly man walking in their opposite direction, until he saw Hugo, who walked behind Bipp. "Wait, Hugo!"

Hugo paused for a second, then turned before his eyelid stretched apart. It was Brian, his and Sam's roommate. "You.

. . ." He stepped away; even Bipp showed concern from such a strong individual.

"It's okay." Brian raised his hands and walked straight to Hugo. "Look, man, I'm sorry for before. I didn't know that kid was your little brother. And when you yelled that he was . . . I guess I lost it." He folded his arms and eyed Hugo with a smile. "Sorry about chasing you after that. . . . You're cool in my book, man. Anyone who hits me that hard for family gets my respect." His broad shoulders sank in a sigh. "I'm sorry if I was the reason you left college. Are you coming back next semester? Because I can save you and your brother a room with me if you like?"

One of the professors approached Bipp.

"Oh. . . . Thank you for the offer, but you weren't the reason I left. . . . If everything works out, I'll ask Sam what he thinks. He was the one more interested in college." He began to walk away.

"I noticed the search flyers a while ago, and I began looking with my friends until we thought you were both dead." He reached into his backpack pocket and pulled out a pair of plastic, rectangle glasses. "The old man who gives confusing life lessons every sentence gave this to me when he caught me searching his office."

Hugo's legs froze as he glanced back at him.

"He said to give them to you the moment I saw you. . . . He was kinda weird. Weirder than Sam by a longshot."

Hugo nearly ran back to him and took up the glasses, recognizing them instantly. "These are Sam's. . . . And you're saying Dr. George gave them to you?"

Brian nodded with a hum.

Hugo bowed slightly. "Thank you for this. . . . Thank you."

He raised his head and looked at Brian, who bore a smile.

"Weirdo, why are you bowing to me?"

Hugo blushed; he didn't even realize he was doing it.

"Brian!" Shouted a dense voice without any concern for the other ears in the echoed hall. Everyone watched an older man with lots of arm hair march to Brian. "You're late for practice! If you keep this up, you will be too weak to keep the scholarship! And we both know you're not smart enough to get through college any other way!"

"Yes, Dad. I'll–"

"Yes, who?"

"Yes, Sir. I'll get on it; I was just giving back this guy's–"

"Enough of your excuses; now run."

"Yes, Sir."

With a firm grip on his dagger, this conversation instantly got Bipp's attention.

Before Brian could turn around, Andrew reached up and tapped the older man on the shoulder. "Pardon me, I know I have no right entering your family affairs, but I don't think that's how you should speak to your son."

Brian froze and gawked at Andrew, who tucked his cap a little more over his face.

"What?" The older man froze, turned, and loomed over Andrew, who was a third of the man's size. The man scanned Andrew from his big round glasses to the burn marks across his face and to the soup he held.

"Your son is obviously trying hard. I mean, he's the strongest person I've seen in real life! I-I suggest cheering him on rather than telling him to do better than impossible. And especially support him if he's helping people."

Bipp smiled at Andrew and resumed his conversation with

the professor.

The old man quickly began to snicker. "Come, Brian, let's get going to practice and leave these . . ." He looked at Bipp, who looked back at him with a quick glare. "Weirdos." He turned and left with Brian, but as they went, Brian turned to the Atlas family and mouthed, 'thank you.'

Hugo smiled a little. *He's. . . actually not bad. . . . far better than my first roommate. Maybe if we return, I'll take him up on that offer to room with him. It may take a bit to convince Sam though. . . . And I'm pretty sure Bipp would want to join us.* He looked at Bipp. *I wonder what he would study.*

Mary stared at Andrew with a smile as he and Hugo continued down the hall. Bipp sighed and slid his dagger back into its sheath. The professor still yelled at him and threatened to call security for wearing a suspicious mask on school grounds and carrying a dagger. "It's my face!" With the fed-up rise of his arms, Bipp retreated quickly and caught up to the Atlas family. "I think we should hurry. That man didn't seem to like me," Bipp whispered to Hugo.

But luckily, they made it to Dr. George's office without much further turbulence. Bipp sighed at the door. "That could've gone better."

Mary patted him on the shoulder. "Don't worry. . . . People take time to understand certain things. It actually went much smoother than I anticipated," she chuckled slightly and looked at Andrew. "And the way you talked to that man . . . I thought I was the crazy one."

Andrew blushed and fixed his tilted glasses. "Heh, thank you," he chuckled shyly. He was never much for talking about himself, especially after a compliment. But times must've changed for him to speak to a stranger as he did.

Hugo tucked the glasses in the side pocket of Bipp's backpack, then opened the door with a slow twist of the knob. He went inside, then froze. "No. . . ." Hugo's spine curled low, and his mouth sank open.

"What is it?" Bipp and Mary asked simultaneously. Hugo collapsed into the desk chair, staring at the familiar wooden door to Somnium, left open with a leathery shoe.

"That means–" Bipp started.

"I-I could've come back to Sam this whole time! How long has this been here?" Hugo yelled with his elbows on the desk and his hands over his head. He needed to think about this. It was getting too serious for his comfort. "Okay, so we can go back. But what if I go back and he kills himself? What if I can't save him? What can I do? I'm just his brother, and I don't know anything," he told himself. Everyone wanted to help him, but it was a problem unlike any of them had witnessed before. "I can stay here, help Bipp with his dreams while we go flying together, and Sam will get what he thinks he wants. . . ."

"They're your dreams too," Bipp murmured shyly.

"If I go . . . I can maybe talk to Sam–" Hugo shook his head. "But I've told him everything already! What can I do? I don't want to give up on him!" Hugo wept; his tears and snot tapped against the wooden table. "I hate this! I hate this so much! I don't want him to feel like my words are for pity or fake. I just want to show him that I love him and help him love himself!" Hugo's head hurt as he stared at the table. "I was too late. I should've told him how I felt the moment I–" He grunted. "If I am the reason he feels like he should end his life, then I failed." Hugo folded his arms and wept onto the table.

"The only way you can truly fail is if you stop caring. And I'd say you care a great deal," Bipp said subconsciously as he peeked into the stone brick room, stepping over the shoe. "Did Apotheosis leave his foot cover here on purpose?" Bipp asked himself. There wasn't much in the room except a wooden table that held two remaining vials of burbling liquid, a cracked quartz altar, and another door with the second shoe against it. The room was cramped, especially once Mary and Andrew walked in. A single wall torch emitted a flickering, dim blue flame about to be hushed by the gentle air swirling from the doorway. Mary couldn't help but notice the swaths of ebony hair over some clothes, and at the other end, a pair of khaki pants and a blue shirt were shredded apart.

Bipp's head tilted in thought at the other door. "He definitely did this on purpose."

Andrew set the soup on the stone table, then peeked open the other door. He gasped at the sight of the Glowshroom Forest, bearing countless skyscraper trees. Then he found that his eyes were stuck to such beauty. The tall sun cast dancing shadows from the rustling tree leaves, and giant glowing mushrooms of many colors brought light to those shadows, revealing the golden floor of fallen autumn leaves.

Andrew coughed a little before pulling the neck of his shirt over his nose. "What the–" He coughed more before stepping away from the door.

Mary raised her shirt over her nose too as she and Bipp peeked out the door.

Bipp gasped. "That's my house!" He pointed to his modest, mossy, loosely-boarded cabin near a distant tree in a beam of open sunlight.

Mary and Andrew looked at Bipp. "That's your–" Andrew peeked at the cabin from over Mary's shoulder, spotting the many mushrooms and other leafy greens decorating the roof.

Hugo then lumbered into the room. He looked around until his eyes met the familiar vials of clear liquid. "Guys. . . . What should I do? I can't make this decision." They all turned to look at Hugo. He admitted defeat as his body nearly dropped. He didn't want to stand anymore. He needed answers, but didn't know how to get them.

"I say no," Andrew said before Bipp and Mary stared at him.

"May I ask why?" Hugo murmured.

"Because I don't want to see you get hurt! I mean, look at you! Your left eye is gone, and you have a massive scar on your chest! You can't even breathe out there! I'm sorry, but this is becoming too much for me to handle! We can't lose you again! We spent months thinking our sons were dead! Do you know what that's like?" Andrew took a few breaths. Mary stood shocked. "No! I'm sorry, but it's too dangerous!" He paused as Mary held his trembling hand. "I-I'm so sorry for all of this happening to us. If only I were a better father, I would've known that bird was Sam. Then, maybe we wouldn't be in this mess!" He could hardly keep it together, weeping as he spoke. "I know I'm a bit hard on myself . . . but I can't help but feel that this is all my fault. . . . Please, Hugo. . . . I love you and Sam with all my heart, and I want the world for you both. But I don't think my heart can take letting you go, knowing what dangers are out there. There has to be another way to bring Sam home! There has to be!"

Bipp stepped forward. "I-I agree," he said with his head and eyes down. "Like I said before, Sam wanted this to protect you. And you have so many scars already, almost as much as me. . . . I . . . I think, if you go back, and you get hurt, you'll hurt Sam more than ever. I know it's confusing, because he isn't in the safest scenarios, but I know it will only get worse, especially if we show up: two creatures without a soul ability; heck, we don't even know what to say to Sam. Like you said, you've told him and showed him in many ways that you love him, so now he knows. And he's smart enough to predict what you're willing to do for that love. . . . And it's scary to think what could happen to you. . . . So please, for Sam, for me, for Andrew and Mary, and even Ventus' last sacrifice to bring me here, stay here where it's safe and live a happy life." He squinted at the floor with his rising cheeks swelling with his discomfort. "But please, just know, you're not alone. No matter your decision, I'm with you, and happy to be so. . . . And don't worry, we'll find a way to fill Sam's vase eventually." Bipp closed his eyes, as if he expected Hugo to hate him for giving such an opinion. "I'm sorry."

Hugo looked up at Bipp after that and almost reached out his hand to him. *Bipp. . . .*

Mary glanced at Bipp for a second before she walked to Hugo and cradled his cheeks within her gentle palms. But Hugo felt a slight tremble with her fingertips. "We love you, Hugo, and like Bipp said, we are with you. But you don't have to strain yourself anymore. We all love Sam and have always wanted to help him. That's why you went to college and asked to be homeschooled with him, right? . . . If you can't decide, we'll simply walk back to the car and go home. We'll call professionals or make a plan to bring Sam home eventually." She hated that last sentence with a quick frown at herself. She wanted to say something more, wanting to save Sam as quickly as possible. But what could they possibly do? "I'm so sorry, Hugo." She hugged him tight enough to break his spine, and tears ran down her round cheeks fast enough to soak his shoulder. "I want to help. I-If there is anything I can do, let me know, and it will be done without hesitation."

*Protect him and love him more than anything in the world.*

Hugo glanced behind him. He could've sworn he heard the lady's voice again. But nobody was there. And then, he couldn't resist his drifting mind. His lone eye passed Mary to the vials in the corner; two were still full. In that instant, his breaths grew heavy as a numbing tingle flowed through his body. His heart pumped so fast he could feel it pound his fingertips.

Mary slowly and messily released Hugo from the hug and looked to where Hugo's eye drifted. "Hey, what's on your mind?" She sniffled mightily.

"I-I don't know. I–"

At this moment, his heart felt warm, and his body took control as he walked to the vials. Without his permission, his fingers gripped the cold plastic and raised one from the slot.

*What just happened?* He blinked.

His heartbeat rippled the fluid inside, as he then turned his head to the three of them, whose eyes showed concern for what he was about to do. "I'm sorry. . . . Just know that I am grateful for your advice, and I love that you're here to help me with this. . . . But . . . I can't help it. He's hurting now more than ever, and I just . . . need to be there, so he's not alone." He sniffled with his nose stinging, and he looked at the vial. *I'll never be given a chance at a normal life again. . . . But for you . . . it's worth it.* With much hesitation, Hugo tilted the vial over his mouth and let it pour between his lips. Then, before half of it was gone, he set it back in the slot. His throat, then chest, burned, not just from the juice, but from the pure weight of his decision yanking at his heart.

"Wait . . . what are you–" Bipp paused as Hugo took off his

sweater. Sadly, it was too late for his pajama pants as a large tail slithered down his pant leg and ripped out from his waist.

"I'm sorry, Bipp. I know how much you wanted to stay here," Hugo growled from his expanding throat and elongating neck.

"What the?" Andrew yelled, watching his son's body grow longer and longer.

Bipp couldn't suppress his amazement. "Oh . . . it's fine; just do what you need to do." He picked up Hugo's starry pajama pants and tightly tucked them into his backpack.

Ash-white horns sprouted, honey and ruby scales replaced his skin, snowy fur grew along his back, and a colossal snout pushed from his face. Hugo adjusted the scarf over his neck as it simply shifted over his expanding shoulders. His ears flicked into enormous triangles, and his feet and hands tripled in size before the blue light in the room danced off his shining scales like a disco ball. His pink, forked tongue slithered past his lips, and his tail thunked against the wall and grew around the room's circumference. Once the heat faded from his growing neck, he gulped in the crowded air.

"That's slightly easier the second time," Hugo panted, holding his thumping chest with his huge hand and looking down at his lengthy body covering most of the room. He had to press his shoulder and thigh against the wall to give his family enough space to move.

Both Mary and Andrew were speechless with an apparent shiver at the sight of Hugo. But as he looked at them with his familiar, kind smile, they relaxed a little, knowing he was there.

Hugo then stepped from the door and onto the soft forest soil with a crack of dry leaves. He breathed in deep through his snout, smelling every slight scent of the world. The delicious, distinct aroma of the glowshrooms, the cozy autumn scent of dry leaves, the flickering sun's warmth against his broad snout; how he missed this. The warmth, the senses, all things he never truly appreciated until now. But something ached in his chest; the weight of his choice pulled his heart to his stomach, for he knew the calamity if it were the wrong one. With the finishing flip of the scarf over his neck, he looked back into the room with everyone still staring at him; then his chest really began to hurt. "I'll try to get back soon. Keep this door open as long as you can. . . . Hopefully, I'll bring Sam home too." He bobbed his head for Bipp to follow him, but only if he wanted to. "I love you," he said worriedly to Mary and Andrew. But before he left, his welling eye caught Mary's attention.

"This shouldn't surprise me. . . . Hugo's soul and ability to fly are connected to Sam somehow anyway. So no wonder he can't help but go back to him. . . . But why am I feeling–" Bipp murmured to himself and scratched his chest. "What the?" He looked at his chest.

"Bipp," Mary began.

"They'll be okay. . . Just you see. I'll make sure of it." He looked at Mary with a smile, but tears soaked his cheeks from his closed eyes, then he grunted with his teeth peeking from his lips. "One day, we'll have peace. One day, we can be together as a family. . . . Just you see." Bipp collapsed on his hands and knees, gulping for air.

"Bipp!" Mary was just about to help him up before he stuck out his hand to block her.

He grasped his chest tight, grimacing. "I'm . . . such a liar. . . . I didn't want to stay on Earth just to learn more technologies. . . . I-I also *really* wanted to spend more time with you three. . . . I'm . . . not good with goodbyes. Nor have I ever liked anyone as much as you three," Bipp growled, grabbed his thigh, and tried to get up. "And ... the reason I didn't hesitate to sleep in the same bed as Hugo ... is because ... I wanted you to be proud of me for helping your son. And he's afraid of being alone, so I thought if I held him close, he would feel better.... I swear I would never do something he or you wouldn't agree to. ..."

Bipp slowly stood with his legs wobbling, and he grabbed the soup along with his backpack. "But I thought it was okay to sleep with him like that, because just a few days ago, he slept on my chest to feel better while we sailed to Dawn...." He bowed to them, rubbing his chest. "Please forgive me if I overdid anything; I will never do it again if you request so."

All the heat in his body rushed to his cheeks as he looked down with his ears over his eyes. But then, he looked at Hugo, and just for a second, every silver hair across his body sparkled like someone threw glitter all over him. Mary and Andrew blinked with curiosity furrowing their eyebrows. "I'm sorry for lying. I'm just not used to feeling like this; it's a little discomforting for me, heh." He rubbed his chest in a circular motion with a fist to apologize in sign language, similar to how Luna once showed him. "Oh, your sweater...."

"Keep it. It looks much cuter on you anyway," Mary said with a shy wave of her hand. "But please tell me ... what are you feeling?"

Bipp smiled. "Thank you so much. I'll ... never forget this. . .." He bowed deeper with a mighty sniffle, then raised his head with a worrisome glance to them with his eyes reddening. "I really hope to see you two again, and maybe, if I come back, the five of us can make some more of that mint chocolate." He slowly turned around and hopped from the room; then he turned to look at them one final time. He sniffled, took a deep breath, gave a fake smile, and then walked after Hugo before grimacing and holding his chest. "What's going on with me?" he growled under his breath.

Mary and Andrew stood there for a few moments, digesting the seriousness of the situation. Both had hoped that Hugo and Bipp were joking in some weird way. But seeing all that . . . shook their bones.

"Andrew . . . I want you to stay here, or at home, wherever you think is right. Please . . . wait for us," Mary commanded softly.

"Wait, what do you mean? Where are you going?"

Mary looked back at the one-and-a-half vials remaining. "In all my years, I have never seen Hugo so worried about anything. Even in the most stressful situations, he was always calm and thoughtful. . . . But this made him cry, even go to near panic when he just grabbed that vial like he wasn't thinking. . . . This situation with Sam is *dire*, especially if he's acting like that. So he needs all the help he can get. Plus, I need to make it up to Sam for not recognizing him when he needed me most." Mary walked up and plucked Hugo's remaining half vial from the slot.

"Wait! Don't do this! Hugo's at least been here before! You would be going in blind! Plus, you don't know what that juice will do to you! It turned him into a dragon, and maybe Sam into that bird! Just think about this . . . please."

Mary paused at his words, then looked at him with a smile. "I've always admired how you want to keep everyone safe. . . . But if Hugo and Bipp were serious and spared no detail. . . . I'm going to help them." She paused and looked at the beautiful world past the door. "I will never abandon my boys again. I don't care what I turn into, so long as I am there for them."

Andrew grabbed Mary's arm and paused. He looked at the lone vial still on the rack, then at the floor. "What can I do to be a better parent for them? . . . I know Hugo's growing up, but I just don't think I'm ready to see him as an adult, especially if he's making those unsafe choices. . . . To me, he's still my little boy, and I want to protect him and guide him to the best future."

Mary smiled at him in a way that raised his eyebrows with worry. "I guess we both still have something to learn as parents." She winked and guided Andrew's hand from her arm even as he looked at her with a thousand questions wishing to stall her hand. "Don't worry; nobody's perfect."

Andrew sucked in through his teeth and grimaced as Mary raised her arm and gulped down the clear liquid. "Oh no."

## Chapter 22
## STARLIGHT

Bipp arrived at the Atlas household, promptly resting the soup and backpack through the window on an inside table. He then swapped his new sweater for his torn cloak. He didn't want to damage it where they were going, so he folded it nicely and laid it beside the soup. "I'll be back for you three," Bipp said to the soup, backpack, and sweater before looking at the candles on the windowsill. One had shrunken down to the melted wax with barely a flicker on the wick, but the other was snuffed out completely. "How are you still burning?" He thoughtfully squinted at it with a smirk and tilted a fresh candle into the one remaining before it caught flame. He set it in place, then ran after Hugo.

Hugo didn't waste any time as he sprinted through the woods, mapping the quickest way to King's Garden in his head. Instead of sprinting ahead, Bipp stayed behind Hugo, simply thinking. He was filled with such joy from meeting Mary and Andrew that the mountainous roots could not slow him down. But the thoughts on his mind were like an anchor. Along their trip, he never let Hugo out of sight; he made sure of it.

They cut around Petal and eventually arrived on the road to

Rafflesia, where tiny flakes of ash dotted the edging grass and mushrooms. Before they knew it, the ground crunched from the depth of the ash beneath their feet. When they passed the last tree of the forest, the ground quaked with every ten steps they ran, stumbling Hugo to the ground a few times.

Bipp's ears rose to their apex, and he squinted in thought. "Impossible, are they still–" He closed his mouth and sprinted over the hill to the sight of Anzu, Ella, Ventus, and Luna still at war with George. "But we were gone for nearly two days! How–" Bipp froze for a minute. "Hugo was talking about time earlier." He looked back to Hugo, then back toward the forest, thinking about the candle. "I'll ask more about that later."

Hugo ran to the hill's top and looked at George, who stood in front of Sam. He was protecting him from Anzu's assault. But before either of them could step down the hill, George's fiery white eyes turned to them. "Ah, it's about time you two got here. Did you enjoy your family visit?" he asked in a way that sank a heavy venom into Hugo and Bipp. "Though you two did arrive a bit earlier than expected," he whispered and looked at the ground. "It seems our time has been cut short. . . . Perhaps my hint was too understandable."

Sam's heart sank when he turned his head to look at them. "No. . . . You were safe. You had a chance at a normal life. . . . Why did you come back?" he thought aloud, then limped to George. "Please, don't hurt him! H-He must have hit his head on something and doesn't know what he's getting into!"

George chuckled. "Oh, Sam. He knows exactly what he's doing, and he cares too much about you to accept your offer." George turned his body to Hugo. "And don't worry, he's grown on me. I'll try my best not to hurt him."

"Hugo!" Ventus yelled, surprised. His white and blue feathers were stained red from his blood and scruffy to say the least. He stood between Anzu and George with his wings spread apart to protect him. But just by how his wings bent and lungs swallowed, he was just about done for. "You idiot! You had a chance to survive this! What are you doing back?"

Hugo ignored Ventus for a moment as he sucked in through his snout. "Geoooorrge!" he shouted, grabbing every creature's eyesight. The dark flames around George shook Hugo down to his bones. But to save Sam, he knew he needed to do more than face this fear; he needed to cut it up and eat it, just like Bipp and his pumpkin.

"Yes, Hugo?" George said with a smooth and formal tone. The creatures around him were now used to his polite demeanor, but something about him still had them on edge.

"Let me talk with Sam!" he shouted once more. But his vigor died when George's fruity chuckle met his ears.

"Oh, Hugo. Like I said before, I have no power over Sam. Everything he does is by his will alone. If you wish to speak with him–" George turned around and extended his arm to Sam, "you must ask *him*."

Everyone's attention was now on Sam.

"Sam?" Hugo said with his hand out to him, hoping, praying Sam would take it. After many seconds of silence, Hugo walked to Ventus alongside Bipp, still with his hand out, never breaking sight of Sam.

But Sam lowered his head in shame. He didn't know what to do. He wanted to yell at Hugo for being an idiot for returning; he also wanted to stick with George to never be a burden. And a tiny part of him wanted them to go home together. It was tearing him apart to the point he hardly moved. "Y-Yes, Mom?" Sam blushed, hard enough to burn his cheeks. He didn't move an inch. *Why! Why do I keep calling him that? In front of everyone too! It's so weird! I've never had this problem before!* "H-Hugo," he corrected himself. *Good. . . . But he probably hates me for calling him that.*

After a few moments, Bipp looked at Hugo, who began shaking. "Oh no," Bipp murmured.

*That was the best I had? Just take my hand and leave with me?* He wanted to slap himself in the face. *What can I say to him? What can I do? He's right there!* Hugo's mind clashed with each thought until his tongue slithered out from his lips' loose grip. "I, uhh, was wondering, is there a way I could help you love yourself? Or maybe, is there anything I can do to help you feel free enough to talk to me about wanting to die?" He paused for a second to think. "Please, just know you don't have to be alone through this. I *want* to be there with you," he said with a wince, unsure how Sam would respond.

But Sam froze with a blink, and he looked down. He felt a strong wind yank each feather. But he didn't care much about that as Hugo's questions spun his mind. *Love myself? . . . Why would he want that?* He looked at all the creatures staring at him before looking back down. *I guess I could talk to him about it, but not with all these creatures around, just me and him.* He looked at Hugo's kind eye, and a smile almost broke across his beak.

*It would be selfish to love yourself. You are an anchor around everyone's throat, and nothing you can do will fix it. You should crawl back to the filth you belong to, knowing that you should never know love. You don't even deserve food; why should you deserve love?*

Even George saw Sam's eyes suddenly sink and his working leg now struggle to keep the appearance that he could stand. If the pressure of all eyes weren't keeping him pinned, he would've collapsed.

"Oh, what a shame," George said before Hugo reached Ventus, Ella, and Anzu.

Luna and Bipp were standing behind them, knowing they couldn't fare much in a soul battle. George smiled as he stared at the eight of them. "Finally, everyone is together: Earth, air, water, and fire." He finished, looking above Hugo with a particular grin.

"Hugo is not fire!" A voice rumbled the valley and ceased all thoughts in shock.

"What?" They turned to the eastern forest, and every mouth gaped. However, George was still smiling.

Just as Hugo and Sam turned their heads, dense clouds that blocked the darkening sky were shoved farther than the horizon could reach by a pair of colossal sapphire wings.

They suddenly squinted from the howling storm of golden leaves and ash nicking their cheeks. Ventus and Sam were forced to the ground before their feathers took flight from such a force. It took them a second to realize what could possibly carry those wings. But once everyone saw the body, their jaws hit the ground with their knees. It was a dragon, whose gorgeous sapphire body and wings blocked every star in the night sky. The fading sun had no chance to warm them, for her shadow covered more than even clouds dared to dream.

Sam trembled in bone-chilling fear. *I'm dead.*

The dragon landed with a planet-cracking thud that popped and rang Hugo's ears; even George wobbled a little.

"I am," the dragon said with her wings wide apart, glaring at George with her colossal snout pointed at him. Hugo gawked up at her with his pupil shrunken in shock; he wasn't even tall enough to see the top of her fingers, for her body easily compared to the two dragons that formed mountains on Dawn. Even Luna stood mouth and eyes agape at the creature.

"Right on schedule," George said with a volume for only Sam to hear. But the colossal dragon could certainly hear it, as her ears were the size of an ocean's trench and pointed right at him as he spoke. "A little bigger than assumed in my prophecy, but not bad. . . . I suppose this means it is almost time."

"Who . . ." Bipp and Ventus both gawked up with their necks aching. Just the beauty of her long cloud-like fur wisping along the mountain range of her spine and tail was enough for them to pass out, not to mention her breathtaking sapphire eyes.

George squinted for a second and curiously patted his chest. "Now that everyone's here– . . ." He paused, then seemed to lurch forward with a heavy gulp. "Come on. Not now," he murmured.

Sam looked at him before worry flooded his fiery face.

"You all need to run," George growled before a pool of shadow crept from him to everyone's feet. Not even flowers could be seen. The only light that dared exist was found in their shadows, as if George was a dark sun.

Hugo's heart began to curse him by pumping fear into his skull. He trembled and backed away before the dragon above them roared an azure solar flare straight from her mouth with ear-popping volume. Luna quickly stood in front of everyone to block the heat from such a force, and Ella eased its heat by summoning several bubbles from the nearby plants.

Then, the dragon stopped with George standing over Sam to protect him. Sam looked up at George's smiling face. "Your family is quite something," he panted as the surrounding shadow vanished under the blue flames wisping in the grass.

"Sorry! I-I didn't think it would shoot out like that! Is everyone okay?" The dragon stepped toward Sam with great concern showing from her beautiful eyes.

Hugo's eye furrowed in thought. *She . . . sounds familiar.*

"What's going on, Mr. George? What was all that just then, telling us to run?" Sam's head spun. He looked at Hugo for comfort, who nearly had his eye shut from the weight of fear. Sam then looked up at the sapphire dragon, and what a mistake that was on his poor little heart.

"False alarm, nothing to concern yourself with right now," he chuckled and turned toward the dragon. "I'm impressed you know how to breathe fire already."

She ignored him and looked down at Hugo. "It's okay, Hugo; I won't let the darkness get to you."

Hugo's ears now twitched upon hearing that gentle voice. He slowly looked up at her. And once it settled in his head, his body came to a calm yet horrified stillness. *Wait . . .* "MOM?"

Hugo felt light-headed after that roar.

The dragon gave him a large smile, then glared at George. "I will not make the same mistake twice of letting you two feel alone. . . . Although, my fire didn't kill him. Why?" she asked.

Bipp's mouth fell open, and he pointed at Mary with his wobbling hand. "I . . . love her."

Sam was so shaken with fear that he barely heard a word the dragon spoke. Its voice brought a familiar warmth to his chest, but he couldn't put his feather on why. *I need to get out of here! This thing's going to kill me!*

"Imagine the most powerful creature, then multiply it by infinity," Anzu growled. "But he seems to care a lot about Sam, probably since he has the soul of time. So I've been trying to attack him or get him to do something with his soul. If we kill him, things may work out like two-hundred years ago. But, if Sam uses his time soul, this would be easy."

Mary was just about to smack Anzu with her tail for talking about hurting Sam, but it was too late.

"I'm sorry, Sam, but I'm running out of time." Anzu subtly raised his hand at Sam. George then watched the ground as if he saw what Anzu was doing. In a flash, he grabbed Sam and threw him to the side before two stone spikes pierced the ground and impaled George. Sam's eyes showed true panic. Instantly, he tried to fly away. But with no practice, he barely made it off the ground. Ventus raised his wings and summoned a gust of wind, slamming Sam hard against the ground.

"Stop hurting him!" Hugo yelled at Anzu and Ventus.

George walked through the spikes as if he was a ghost. "Your fight is with me." Before anyone could react, George raised his hand to the sky with his fiery eyes glaring at Anzu and Ventus.

Then, a hair-shifting boom pierced the sound barrier and snapped the air over their heads. And within an instant, an object smacked into George's hand with a ground-cracking thud, pushing dirt and debris away from a new crater around him. When the dust cleared, George was gripping the obsidian sword with a white-wrapped handle. Before anyone could think, black fire crept from George's hand to the tip of the sword . . . and it continued to grow longer and longer until the flaming sword nearly reached ten feet long.

Bipp instantly looked to the stars, trying to spot where the sword came from. "Yellow star, third to the left of the moon, mid-autumn, evening. . . . Got you." He squinted. "Wait . . . is that in *our* galaxy?"

But Luna's eyes snapped open at the sword. Her fangs gnashed before Ventus looked at her. "That's *your* sword?" Before Ventus could turn back to face George, Luna opened her mouth and shot fire from her throat at George. It crackled and burned like a rocket lifting off the ground. She dug her claws into the dirt to keep her place as the sheer thrust of her fire pierced the air with enough force to fly.

*Wow,* Hugo mused, staring at her.

But George simply held up the sword, deflected the fire with a firm swing that shoved the air around them, and within a blink, he appeared before Anzu.

Anzu barely had time to react before George aimed the sword dead center at his chest. "No, Snow, stop this. Don't–" George whispered before he thrust the sword deep through Anzu with loud cracks from his suddenly breaking ribs. Anzu's breath wheezed out as the lengthy blade pushed in with George's every step. Its tip erupted out his back with a loud snap of his spine, then a pool of blood suddenly soaked his white shirt. Anzu stood still in shock, staring down at the blade in his chest before he began trembling in horror.

"N-No, please—I–"

George yanked out the sword and thrust his gloved hand deep into the new opening in Anzu's chest. He grabbed the dinosaur's heart and dug his shoeless toes into the dirt before closing his eyes.

After everyone escaped the shock of seeing Anzu stabbed, they hastily pushed at George with wind, water, and fire. Before Luna's flame accidentally burned Anzu, George let go of his heart, allowing Anzu to finally collapse. He twitched and choked on his blood with the hole through his chest gushing.

George spun around to see if Sam was okay, but before he

could look at Sam, he nearly fell to his knees with his bloody hands trembling. "I couldn't stop it. . . ." George thought aloud to himself, staring at his shaking hands. "He didn't have to die, Snow. We could've searched for the soul without doing that. . . . But . . . you're right. Even with his soul . . ." he looked at the ground, "we couldn't find it." He paused before looking at Sam. "But I won't give up, not after coming so far. There has to be a way to help these creatures without you possessing Sam."

"No. . . . Not this again," Sam wheezed with his eyes wide and his head going numb. As he recovered from that body slam, he watched Anzu's pool of blood slither around the flowers. *Don't pass out. Just breathe. . . . You can do something. Just because you saw this as a child doesn't mean–* He closed his eyes with the heavy popping of his eardrums.

*Nothing can help the dinosaur. Your visions will always come true in some manner, for you are past and future incarnate, and what you see is final.*

"Shut uup–" Sam vomited. His chest was on fire, and his stomach forced him to feel the pain from the ground slam with no fat to cushion. He rubbed his chest and quickly felt two broken ribs sinking under the pressure of his wing. He begged his leg to stand. "I want to help them." He pushed off the ground with a sharp grimace and yelp. Then he forced his trembling leg to stand straight and nearly screamed. He wasn't strong enough for this, he needed food, but he believed he had to earn it first. He glared at George and raised a wing to him and Anzu. *Just focus on the past, what I saw, what I heard and felt. . . .*

At that moment, George froze and looked down at his chest. "What the?" His surprised tone shocked everyone. And as his old skin showed and the dark fire around him vanished inch by inch from his face to his neck, his eyebrows furrowed in thought.

Sam heaved each breath, trying to focus amongst the trembling pains scattered throughout his body.

George winced, then looked back at Sam with a thoughtful squint. "Sam?"

"I-It's okay, Mr. George, I know you're still there. . . . Please, once I get that demon out of you, let's just leave, go back to your house, and work on my soul some more." Sam smiled at George, but boy was his heart skipping every beat as everyone looked at him.

He closed his eyes and thought aloud to himself to calm down. "Today, you each begin your adventures. You may have an adventure with your closest friends, but each experience will be different—some good, some perhaps bad. Every adventure comes with its ups and downs, but once you are down, you can only go up. And once you are up, you can always go higher. So never give up. And remember, dusk always occurs before dawn," he grumbled, trying to focus.

George smiled mightily at Sam.

"What?" Ella squinted hard. It was subtle and slow, but Anzu's blood retreated from the grass and back into him.

George looked at his body; the fire was sinking down his chest. He then looked at Anzu, recovering from the verge of death. "This is unexpected. . . . I thought he would've–" he whispered, then hacked and wheezed with sudden coughs. Once everyone looked at him, he tried to catch his breath. But it took a moment before he even stood straight and looked back at Sam.

"Is he . . . okay?" Ventus asked before everyone began asking the same question.

"If you can take this fire away, then I'll do as you ask and go home. . . . But if I were you, I would focus on the dinosaur." George grimaced.

"Hey, you! Are you sick?" Ventus yelled at George. But George simply ignored him for the time.

Sam shut his eyes once more. "I don't know if I can help Anzu! But if I help you, maybe we can help him together! Just take my hand, remember?" he shouted to keep the voice out, for he felt his head numbing as each second passed. But even his volume couldn't keep *her* out.

*Where was this when your mother needed you? Why do you care for that lizard more?*

*I don't! I just–*

*You hated your mother, didn't you?*

"Aaaaaaahh! Shut up! SHUT UP! Get out of my head!" Sam roared and pressed his wings against his temples before ripping out his head feathers.

The fire crawled back over George, and blood seeped from Anzu. "Snow, enough. He doesn't deserve such torment." George took a moment to look back at Anzu.

Ella and Ventus promptly tried to help. She stabilized the blood with her water ability, and Ventus dried out the openings in his wounds. Both of them were in tears. But Ventus still eyed George with a curious glare.

"I commend him for trying to help us both. . . ." George looked back at Sam, who collapsed from the instant exhaustion of listening to that voice. "If only we had more time."

"Please, Anzu, you can make it. Just hold on!" Ella begged. Anzu looked at the clouds above and raised a hand to Zenith, making its orbital round.

"I . . . can't hold it anymore."

Ella and Ventus looked at Zenith. Ventus gasped at its

sight. "Wait."

"He spends half his energy holding it, Ventus! He can't wait anymore!"

Ventus stared at Anzu. "What if we drop it on Apotheosis?" He thought some more as everyone looked at him. "Something's wrong with that creature. He has a weakness he's not spilling. If we begin to drop it, Apotheosis will protect Sam. . . . Ella, can you keep the blood in Sam's body still?"

"That is a stupid idea. Apotheosis is much more likely to survive that than we are." Ella looked back at Anzu. "And besides, I refuse to take someone's freedom like that." She looked at Anzu's blood. "That was my mother's weapon."

Ventus growled. "Idiot. We won't actually drop it, just pretend until the last second. A falling island will certainly distract Apotheosis long enough for us to do something about Sam; whether that be taking him away or killing him is up to whoever. I'm out of any other ideas, and I don't hear a plan from anyone else." He scoffed as nobody looked at him. "Whatever. I'll distract him until Anzu is ready." He watched Anzu choke up some blood, and he quickly reached out his wing to help, but then turned around with a suppressed grunt. "Sorry, Anzu, just hold on a little longer." He looked at Bipp, Luna, and Hugo. "You three, attack Sam."

He looked up at Mary. "And you!" He froze when she looked down at him with her kind, fiery eyes. "Do what you wish," Ventus said with his legs instantly wobbling with the weight of telling *that* creature what to do. "Does everyone understand?" Ventus asked. Nobody immediately disagreed with the plan, but there were many uncertain thoughts.

"Don't worry, Anzu; I'll keep your body working, just–"

Anzu held Ella's hand. "If I perish, I want you to have my

soul."

Ventus' eyes welled once he heard that.

Ella pressed her hand firmly against his chest. "Shut up! I will never let you die!"

Anzu chuckled. "I will never be *really* gone. If you take my soul, I will be with you forever." Ella sobbed as Ventus initiated his plan by launching himself toward George.

"How are we doing, Sam?" George asked, feeling Sam's body for injuries. George felt the two broken ribs and a broken knee, luckily on his bad leg. "Alright, let me heal you up, then I want you to hide somewhere again; this is getting danger–"

Ventus summoned a gust of wind and sucked Sam from George's grasp, stumbling him through the flowers. "You're with me now, idiot!"

George growled and turned around, stabbing the sword firmly into the ground. And once he let it go, the fire around it snuffed out; the white cloth handle remained unburnt. Ventus quickly sucked the air from around him and shot sand in his eyes. He danced around the vacuum, blasting rocks toward George.

Mary looked down at Hugo, knowing he didn't want to go along with Ventus' plan to attack Sam. "It's okay, Hugo; let me handle this. I won't lay a claw on Sam." She smirked, thinking she was rather clever using the word *claw* there. She ran up to George and simply punched him with her island-sized fist. The impact and the surprising speed of it knocked the wind out of George. The punch's force pushed Ventus away, but he stabilized in the wind, gawking at the crater she left. The sword landed right next to Luna, who then squinted in thought.

But the fun thing is, Mary didn't stop there. She punched and punched again until the hole was as deep as her elbow.

Then, she blasted the hole with a roar of her blue fire.

Bipp and everyone else simply gawked at the event. He looked at Hugo with eyes ignited in amazement. "Dragons are breathtakingly curious." He couldn't restrict his grin.

As the dirt beneath their feet became hot from her fire, George flew up from the hole and grabbed Mary by the snout. Smiling, he pulled her off her feet and took her into the sky, far above the clouds. "I applaud you, Mary, your soul meets my expectations of you. . . . I'm glad I fled your house when Andrew called for you."

Mary's eyes snapped open. "You!" she roared. To George's surprise, her snout ignited and blasted two fire beams onto him. He let go, and she fell. But she opened her wings with a cloud-pushing hurricane of a flap and cracked the planet upon her mighty landing.

Bipp gawked at her with a million words he wished to cheer. Mary glanced down at him with a smile and a wink, instantly forcing his legs to leap to the skies with cheers.

Ventus quickly advanced on Sam and raised his wing to do the final blow.

Sam looked up at him with his pupils shrunken in fear. His heart stopped, and his breath ceased at the view of Ventus' eyes speaking the word: death.

George closed his eyes. "This is a bit more problematic than I anticipated. . . ." He looked at Ventus, just about to swing his wing through Sam's neck. "Fine then. . . . *Starlight*."

Hugo's fur stood and tingled. He instinctively looked at the sun and moon vanishing into darkness. Now, the planet relied on only the light of the stars. But Hugo's eye widened as the stars began to move. His stomach twisted with worry slithering through his innards.

Ventus swung down his wing as fast he could, but a beam of many colors shot down at the speed of light, singeing the side of his beak. Ventus screamed and leapt onto Sam before the barrage of Apotheosis began.

"Get under me, all of you!" Mary demanded with haste, raising her wings over her body as a shield.

Ella carried Anzu by the water in him, Luna grabbed her sword in her mouth, and everyone but Ventus, Sam, and George ran beneath Mary before every star in the sky shot down with all colors imaginable. Within a second, the valley was drowning in blinding beams of starlight. Mary grimaced as she took most of the impact. Her knees and elbows bent as the repeated lasers punching her back nearly forced her to bow to George. The barrage ended fast, but after a wince, Mary simply shook it off and unfolded her wings. There were many charred marks and a little blood, but nothing she couldn't handle. She promptly looked beneath her to see if everyone was okay.

"She's going to be a problem, isn't she?" George said with a smile. "I didn't expect her to be *this* much stronger than Dusk and Dawn."

Hugo looked up. The sun and moon returned among the gas nebulas, but all the stars were gone, as if George cursed the sky by forbidding all starlight. He trembled from the fear of darkness crawling over his scales as George descended.

George looked at Sam, then smirked a little. Ventus was on top of Sam, knowing George wouldn't hurt him with such an attack.

Ventus rolled off Sam's body, gasping for air with his eyes wide. He touched the side of his beak where it burned, wincing from such a tender wound. "You're a smart bird." George landed next to Ventus. "But you need reminding that *I* am your enemy. Sam is the opposite."

Bipp peeked up, observing the valley and the thousands of small craters that now took its place.

Ventus gnashed his beak. "Stop playing with us! I know you can kill us all!" Ventus stood, wiping the soot from his pants. From blood loss and a hopeless fight, he was losing it. "That's it! I'm not playing games anymore!" Ventus roared, but George showed no favorable response except removing the dark fire.

"I agree." George wiped the blood from the edge of his lips and lumbered toward Ventus, who took many steps back, unsure how to interpret George's words.

"A-Agree with what?"

"I will no longer play games with you. You want the real thing. . . . So I'll begin by taking what's most important to you."

Ventus scoffed, still stepping away from George. If birds could sweat, Ventus would be soaked. "I-Idiot, I don't have anything! I don't even own this body anymore!"

George smiled and pointed at his own head.

Ventus' eyes grew: The weight of terror sank his heart, and his backward steps hastened. "No . . . not that." Ventus' terrified voice barely left his beak before he summoned a gust of wind to take him away. But George simply increased the gravity and pulled him down. "Nooo!" Ventus screamed. His talons hit the ground, and he collapsed on his face. Even his wings were too heavy to lift.

"Don't mind me, just making a few permanent adjustments," George said, leaning down with his hand extended toward Ventus.

"Stop! Please! I'll do anything! Take my wings! Take my soul! Just not my mind!" he choked on the amount of wild begging he gave. He glanced at Hugo or Bipp to help him, but they tended to Mary and Anzu. Ventus felt abandoned. Save the broken or help the healthy. An impossible riddle to get right during war, but he just hoped those he deemed his friends would show him a speck of attention in this moment of need. "Please...."

Then, George's warm, wrinkly fingers rubbed through his head feathers.

He screamed till his throat dried, then his head simply felt lighter. As his eyes slowly rolled back, he knew he would never be the same if he let go. But before he could hold on, the darkness took him without any friction.

# Chapter 23
# MOONLIGHT

Hugo ran to Mary's grimacing face. "Are you alright, Mom?"

She tanked the starlight attack like a champ, but her fangs gnashed with her eyes squinted shut. "I'm fine, really. Though it feels like I laid on hot coals for a minute there." A few tears escaped the tight grip of her eyelids.

Hugo watched her and couldn't hold back the tears. "Bipp, check her back!"

Bipp sprinted up a hill and gasped at the sight. From the back of her neck to the end of her tail lay a landscape of damage amongst her tree-tall fur. "She took it all," Bipp said, gawking. Her wings had many-colored singe marks, and many of her scales had fallen off. But it wasn't as bad as they expected. Since each scale was a hardened shield, they absorbed most of the damage.

"I'll be fine; just give me a moment." She tried to stay still as she stood, for any movement she gave shook the ground with a mighty quake.

"Please, Mom, just lie down. You've helped more than any of us thought possible."

Luna ran to Bipp, grabbed his hand, and led him to Anzu. "What are you doing?" Bipp asked. Luna pointed at him and Anzu, then placed her hand on Bipp's chest with a few more gestures.

"My soul?" He squinted, still learning her language in the early stages. Unfortunately, the distance between Earth's and Somnium's sign languages was considerable, especially because Luna had large hands with only four fingers, and she almost always used one arm to keep her lengthy body balanced. She even had the sword in her mouth, which didn't help. It was even more distracting as white fire now inched along the sword.

Hugo observed those around him, especially Anzu and Mary. "That was only the beginning, wasn't it?" He looked at Ventus, who had George kneeling near his unconscious body with a hand crowning his skull.

Sam shyly limped to George with his wings grasping his stomach from the lingering pain of Ventus' ground slap. But little did he know, half the pain was simply starvation. "I-Is it over?" he whispered, trying not to gain anyone's attention.

George smiled and raised Ventus by the head feathers to meet eye to eye. "Almost, but there are a few things I need to do before the end of this."

Sam looked Ventus right in the face, and his ribs yanked down his chest with a sudden feeling. "C-Can I help him? Maybe if you wake him up, we can convince him we don't mean harm, right?" Sam knew it was a stupid request, especially after all that had happened. Little to nothing could make up for what they had done to their home. And he liked Anzu and wanted to end the violence as quickly as possible to help him.

George chuckled. "As you wish." He simply looked at Ventus, whose eyes then snapped open. He instantly screamed and flapped at George, who then let go and watched Ventus hit the ground and gulp in the air around him.

"Did he take my mind? Let's see; my name is Ventus Libertas, my Zenith flight record is fifty-two seconds from end to end; I've read over a thousand books from the royal library and can still name them all, and I think I'm afraid of love. . . . I'm rude to creatures to keep them away from me. . . . I just don't want to experience the pain of loss again. But this family is so persistent that I–" He slapped his wings against his beak to shut it. His eyes showed more fear than ever before, as if a long-buried volcano was about to erupt from his planet's crust. Sam looked at the sad creature with a blink. Even Bipp gave a glance and a flick of his large ears.

Ventus suddenly held his head with a squinting grimace, then slowly looked up at Sam and George. "W-What did you take from me? . . . A-And what's this profound thumping in my skull?"

Before Sam could speak, George raised a finger to him. "One second, Sam." He stepped closer to Ventus, who frantically crawled away on his back. "Let me tell you some hard advice. . . . There is always the pain of heartbreak that comes with the cost of love, through death, through breakup, betrayal, or simply letting go. . . . And let's not forget rejection." George looked at Bipp, whose shoulders rose in an embarrassed discomfort as he shyly looked away.

"How does he know about that?" Bipp whispered to himself.

George looked back at Ventus. "Heartbreak is the most agonizing pain; trust me, I've experienced the worst of it too, but love is the greatest reward, and our time without love is doubtful to be called a life." He coughed a little. "If you want to grow, open your heart, then experience life how it's meant to be enjoyed."

Ventus looked away in deep thought; his eyes brought a certain sadness to Sam.

George cradled the blue jay's beak and helped him look him in the eyes. "With that arrogant and confident mask you wear, you limit yourself. . . . I want you to know before we continue that you are one of my favorites among the Atlas family, and I want you to be happy in life."

Ventus tilted his head in confusion.

"You are smart, I will not deny you that, but I think you are distracted with the dream of being the hero on that academy door, even though its memory has long run cold in the minds of many. . . . You used to have a dream of being Anzu's librarian, so you could show your best friend a better life. What happened to that dream?"

Ventus' beak shook agape with the breaths of his voice unable to make a sound.

George stood with a sigh. "I don't think love is what you fear, at least, not entirely. . . . I think you're more afraid of failure, because every time you do fail, you are reminded of the love you lost and may lose again if you open your heart. . . ." He sighed, looking at Ventus' speechless, teary expression.

"Pardon me for saving this part for last, but the times you hid from Exos in the royal library, reading all those books, trying to be better than the giant birds for your friend, inspired me to create a college on my planet. You became the school's symbol, and your inspiration is depicted throughout the halls. You are more than enough for any academy door, because I wouldn't have just any bird on my college banners." He smiled.

"So, I think it's time to let those false dreams go, because by trying to achieve such, you neglected areas of life that I think you would find more joy in. . . . You'll see what I mean in a few moments. Just . . . think about it. Use your . . . mind."

With a final, confusing smile to Ventus, George turned away and gestured to Sam to continue, who inched closer to Ventus during that speech.

"Who . . . are you?" That was all Ventus could think to respond as his eye twitched with the heavy tilt of his spinning head.

"Hey," Sam interrupted.

"H-Hello?" Ventus scooted farther from them while slowly raising his wing behind his back.

"I wanted to say sorry for all the trouble we've caused. If you'd forgive us for just a second, we could maybe help you and your friends."

George gave a cough, then a heavy hack. Sam and Ventus flinched as George grabbed his knees, and blood splatted on the dirt near his shoes.

"Mr. George?" Sam reached his wing to him before George led it aside.

"Sorry, Sam. I was hoping we had a little more time than this." He wiped the blood from his mouth onto his already-bloody sleeve.

Sam completely forgot about Ventus and stared at George. "What do you mean? A-Are you okay?"

"I'm fine. It's just . . . certain events aren't happening the exact way I anticipated."

Sam squinted at George with every cell in his brain spinning. He rubbed his chest with his wing and let out a long and slow exhale. "Mr. George, d-did you take my mom's cancer?" A feeling like cool air rushed through his feathers. It began to feel like each feather stabbed deeper into Sam's skin. But once he felt the warm flow of blood sink from every pore, Sam's eyes snapped awake. Ventus then slapped his wings together, and Sam grunted as if a million swords were shoved into him.

George simply sighed as Ventus smiled. Then, he sucked all the air from around George, including the air from his lungs. "You idiots–" Ventus instantly choked, and blood splatted onto the ground from his beak. "What the?"

"I was hoping this future wouldn't show. . . . But it seems like it couldn't be helped. . . . The tiny choices we make are sometimes the most impactful," George murmured to himself.

Ventus lost his grip on the air. George casually walked to Sam and observed the countless bleeding holes. Sam fell onto the ground, gasping for air that his punctured lungs couldn't grasp.

"He just wanted to help you." George glared at Ventus, who still coughed, but was getting better. "You've doomed yourself." Ventus looked up at him, then froze at *those* snowy eyes.

"Moonlight."

Ventus' heart gave up when he heard that word. He was so afraid that even his lungs seemed to go still. "That word . . ." Ventus creaked his eyes to Luna, who dropped her flaming sword from her gaping mouth and stared at George with her ears high. Both creatures felt their hearts hang the weight of a thousand anchors.

Ventus looked back at George, who tended to Sam. Then, Ventus bowed to the deity before him. "Not this power. . . . I'm sorry. I-I–" Ventus couldn't find the words anymore. He didn't think himself worthy of speaking before George now. He was nothing.

As Ventus begged, the moon sank closer to the planet until it consumed the entire sky around them like a grand canopy. The shadow of Somnium didn't exist on the moon, as every amethyst inch was brighter than the now-fading sun. Ventus' horrified face met the ground, for that was all he could do now: pray to the god for any form of mercy. Everyone looked up as moonlight warmed their heads, then they all gawked at the sheer size of the moon.

Hugo's neck shrank down with his wobbling shoulders. To him, the moon was growing fast enough to crash into the planet.

"Is this another attack? H-How can we block that?" Bipp yelled. Luna grabbed Bipp. "What the—What are you doing?" Bipp asked. She grabbed Bipp's hand and placed it on Anzu, then his other hand over his own chest. Luna then tried desperately to describe what to do. "You want Anzu . . . to protect us?" Luna nodded in haste, but she wasn't content with that answer. She then tried to speak with her mouth to help him understand, but only air escaped her throat.

Anzu was so weak that he could barely raise his eyelids. But he tried to do all he could to help. The loose dirt around them slowly formed a wall. But it collapsed instantly.

Luna grabbed Bipp's hands again to ensure they were firm against Anzu and his own chest. "I don't know how to use my soul!" Bipp's voice sounded more and more worried as the moonlight shone brighter, now feeling hotter than a midday sun. Luna began to breathe heavily, and Bipp could hear her heart pounding her ribs with the intent to break them.

Anzu grabbed onto Ella's hand. "Let me go. . . . Take my soul." Those words barely left his mouth in a whisper.

"No! I won't do that! Please Anzu! Don't give up!" Ella begged.

Anzu guided her hand to his chest. "We can win. Take my soul, let go of Zenith, and with ground and water together, *you* will have the power to save this planet."

"You idiot! Not now! Not after all we've been through! I want to start a life with you! Don't you see! I was just about to ask you to marry me before all this happened!" She paused to gulp in enough air to feed her thumping heart. "I will *never* let you go. . . ."

Anzu's eyes peeked open a little more, and he smiled. "Well, in that case . . ." He unveiled his fingers to the bracelet with diamonds, rubies, and even limestone swirling in infinite patterns. "Let's pretend none of this happened. And we're back at the castle, looking at the bright future . . . together." He heaved his final breaths. "Sorry we skipped the soul companionship."

Bipp instantly looked at Hugo with a nervous wince. As Hugo still tended to Mary with all of his focus, Bipp sighed with relief. "I'll tell you . . . when my stupid fear no longer controls me," he whispered to himself.

Mary's mammoth ears flicked, and she glanced at Bipp with a squint.

Ella was drowning in tears and snot as she removed the daisy flower from her hair. "We didn't skip anything. . . . I've been waiting for this moment since you gave me this." She sucked in a messy sniffle. "So, Anzu, will you be my soulmate?"

"Y-Yeah." He could barely nod, but he did just enough for Ella to smile. Then, Anzu couldn't help but smile with her. "Before we do this . . . the reason I fell in love with you wasn't due to your immeasurable beauty, or your fantastic smile, but your precious kindness and grace that made my anger seem nonexistent. . . . If you could gift this old dinosaur with one last thing, it would be to never stop being you." He struggled to put the bracelet on her and wheezed for air the second it met her right wrist.

Ella admired it with a smile, then reached into her dress pocket and pulled out a sea-shell bracelet with so many shells carved and polished with images of their memories together that the fishing net holding it together was hardly noticeable. "Your anger is nothing to be ashamed of. In fact, I always thought it was cute and brave the way you expressed how you felt. . . ." She sniffled. "You're my best friend; I love your smile, your understanding cinnamon eyes, and your strange ability to cheer me up and make me laugh. I even love your big, cute dinosaur head that you're so self-conscious about. . . . I love everything that makes you . . . you." She wept, trying to lighten the mood as she slid the bracelet over his left hand. Now it was official according to Somnium culture. "And I don't want you to go."

"Ouch, my head isn't *that* big . . . is it?" Anzu jokingly smiled at her, appreciative that she said all those things. "I will never go, for I will love you forever, right here." He reached up and pressed his small, velociraptor hand against her chest.

With his last drop of life, Anzu leaned up; Ella met him the rest of the way, and they kissed.

It was messy from all the tears and snot everywhere, especially from Anzu's bigger nose, but that didn't cross their minds.

Ella felt something refreshing and invigorating enter her chest, like a space she didn't know existed was filled with a cradling warmth just before the loud pats of Anzu's heart went silent, and he collapsed. She slowly opened her eyes to Anzu, who lay there with eyes like black pearls. Ella's ears sprung to their apex at the last hope of hearing his heartbeat. But such a grace never came.

It was hard to tell with all the tears flooding from Ella, but her left eye was no longer an ocean blue, but a cinnamon brown. After she wiped her face rid of tears, she rested her hand on Anzu, just to feel his big, soft, leathery face one last time. Her eyes squinted in thought before she rested her hand over her chest. Then, she smiled.

Without further hesitation, she raised her hand to Zenith. And before anyone could react, the air around them moved with the sudden shift of Zenith losing its orbit. "Get next to me," she commanded with a sniffle, hardly able to contain herself. Then she stood and walked toward Mary while wiping her face with the sleeves of her dress. Everyone in their group did so, apart from Ventus. She took hold of the water in his body and pulled him next to her.

"T-Thank you," Ventus said, so ashamed and scared to even look up from his bow.

Ella straightened her fingers, and suddenly, four triangle stones pierced the ground and tipped over into a colossal pyramid that covered even Mary. Then, with the simple raise of her arm, Hugo heard the walls shift and pound from the outside. And almost in an instant, everything went dark.

Mary blew a whisper of blue fire next to Hugo. He looked up at her as she smiled at him.

Ella nearly collapsed from the sorrow and pain of losing her best friend, but after a moment of staggering, she surprisingly smiled once she closed her eyes, doing *the thing*. Her arms then moved swiftly without hesitation, as if Anzu was helping her through every movement, every feeling, scent, and thought, like he gently held and guided her arms on that ocean beach, never to leave her side.

But then, a thunderous boom numbed their ears and rattled their bones as the ground began to quake. "You don't happen to mind if I stay here?" That voice forced chills up their spines. Ella, Luna, and Bipp turned to George, who stood right next to them with a smile that impaled them with fear.

Before anyone could react, George simply looked at the top of the pyramid. Then, the stone walls cracked, and the pyramid's apex sank with a landslide of rubble. The amethyst moonlight pierced through the cracks and holes with beams of fire that scorched the inner walls.

"Nooo!" Ella swung her arms wildly. She tried to rebuild the pyramid before the light could reach them. But it all happened so fast. In a last-ditch effort, Bipp grabbed onto George.

The nano-second moonlight hit the dirt, each particle of light exploded with loud bursts of flame. Great explosions booming over every inch shattered the pyramid into a million pieces. The attack struck everyone inside. With nowhere to hide, nothing to block, they all took what remained of the moonlight attack, but it was more than enough to evaporate them.

## Chapter 24
# SNUFFED OUT

All was silent but the sizzling ebony ground. Steam wisped from the hot dirt and curled into the dark sky. Hugo squinted open his eye to the new world around him. He didn't even have the strength to look away from the warm ground his cheek pressed against. His heart thumped so much, he worried he might be dying. But as the moments passed, and his breaths calmed, he shifted his head to look at the crater he found himself in. The grass, the flowers, and the trees were all gone and replaced by air smelling like smoke and rotten eggs. The crater's surrounding wall was so vast and tall, Hugo couldn't think of a way out without a rocket ship. A constant stream of water from the distant river delta gushed into the crater and soaked the dirt around Hugo into thick mud. But his snout twitched with the stench of iron; it yanked his eye to Mary, who lay beside him with her wing blanketing him. Hugo's heart stung as he saw the many holes in her wings. He had a few burn marks across his lengthy body, but she saved him from the worst of it.

"Hu-go," Mary murmured.

His heart fell from his chest, and his legs instantly found the painful, panicked energy to stand and limp to her face.

"Good, you're alright." Her voice made Hugo think she was dying; it was brittle and far too soft for even the calmest whisper from a mouth that big. "Maybe Andrew was right. . . . We should've stayed home," she coughed with a smile.

Hugo began to weep as he nudged his snout against hers, just to feel his mother's subtle breaths and ensure she was alive. "I'm so sorry, Mom. This is all my fault."

"Hey, Hugo," Bipp murmured, limping toward Hugo. His fur was burnt black from George's fire. "I-I think I'm done adventuring for a while," he joked, then collapsed at Hugo's feet.

"Bipp!" Hugo yelled and instantly searched him for wounds. He surprisingly didn't have many apart from the burns, but it was apparent he had a lot of pain tolerance not to be screaming right now.

"You killed him," Ella said under her breath. She stood with her whole body shaking. Her once daisy fur was now gray from the ash and burns; her long ocean dress was mostly burned away, and the left side of her body seemed to hang by her bone joints. But she raised her right arm to Zenith and looked at Anzu's bracelet as it sank near her elbow with much of her fur burned away. "He was holding back; he was kind enough to hope you would stop. . . . Well, allow me to show you the power of a planet," she growled all of that. But then, she paused with a quick squint. "Wow . . . so that's how you felt," she spoke to herself before slowly looking at her chest. She scoffed with a hum and smirk, then rested her hand just over her heart. "Oh Anzu . . . let's use that anger properly, shall we?" She smiled at George, then threw her arm down.

A roaring push of wind shouted from the heavens as Zenith instantly dropped through the atmosphere faster than gravity could fathom. Clouds shot away before thousands of bird silhouettes scattered from above.

George coughed and grabbed his knees once more. His breaths were heavy, and they wheezed through his throat like a rusty flute. He glanced back at Sam to make sure he was alright after that, and he was. He had left Sam under a barrier made from part of his fire. It was a perfect shield—so dark, moonlight feared it. Some of the fire wisped through Sam. It seemed to breathe for him and stop the bleeding, but even to Sam's best effort, he couldn't move a toe.

"How long do you have?" Sam tried to yell, but it hardly wheezed from his throat.

George smiled. "I could never deceive those eyes for long." He turned away from Sam to hide his face. "I would guess . . . ten minutes before the cancer wins. . . . Do you hate me?"

"No. . . . I could never hate you, Grandpa. I just wish I could've done more to help you. And I wish you would've given it to me, so through my death, our family hopefully wouldn't have to see that cursed disease again. We helped my mom get rid of it . . . but I would've loved to help you too."

George smirked with a scoff through his nose, but a few tears welled in his eyes.

Hugo observed the results of the attack. Luna was lying on the ground, hopefully just unconscious. Ventus lay on his stomach; all his feathers were charred so much, he almost looked like Sam. And if he wasn't dead already, he wasn't getting up soon. Bipp . . . well Bipp was fine, just exhausted and a bit toasty.

George turned to Ella with her shaking knees struggling to support her. "You seem to be adjusted to his soul already . . . a real connection." George smiled.

"Hugo . . . help her. It's up to you two," Mary murmured.

Hugo turned to Mary. He was so nervous about fighting George that his fingers and toes gripped deep into the mud. "But, Mom, that figure is–"

"I know who he is . . . Bipp told me about your fear of the dark and being alone. . . . But you have to be brave, Hugo. If you want to help Sam, your passion needs to be stronger than your fear. I believe in you." Her eyes squinted closed from the apparent pain and exhaustion.

Hugo turned to George and shriveled upon seeing the black fire. His body was trembling, begging him not to go anywhere near that monster. So to help himself, he looked at Sam, who lay there with wisps of dark fire weaving his wounds shut. Hugo gulped, then he took a hesitant step forward.

Ella formed mountains to stab George. She cracked the planet open to send him to the fiery hells below. She shot lava at him like the planet was her cannon and ripped the fluids out from his skin. As Ella threw everything she had at George, the ground shook more than a hundred earthquakes.

But George easily dodged or survived them all. But he did have to move Sam a few times from her wide-scale attacks.

Hugo's legs could barely stand, but with the world shaking, he couldn't even lie down without getting nauseous. "G-George," Hugo murmured nervously with his eye closed.

George raised his hand to Ella, requesting her to cease. Ella, of course, didn't care what he had to say. But she played along to catch her breath with swords of water and stone forming individually within her tight grasps. "Yes, Hugo?" George asked and turned off the fire in an attempt to settle Hugo.

"C-Can you please stop? E-Everyone's getting really hurt," Hugo asked in the politest way he could.

George laughed at him, but that laughter quickly wheezed

into a heavy collection of coughs.

Ella raised her stone sword-held hand carefully.

George took a moment to recover and wipe the blood from his lip. "Oh, Hugo . . . you really are the most curious of all the creatures."

George lumbered heavy and sluggish steps closer to him until Hugo was about to pass out. And even then, he flowed his warm fingers through the hair between Hugo's ears. "To you, so much has happened already. And for that, I apologize." He knelt in front of Hugo to help him look him in the eyes. But Hugo kept his eye closed as if his life depended on it. "If you wait a little longer, the bloodshed will be over. And if Sam wants to, he and the rest of your family can go home, as if none of this had happened."

That offer tempted Hugo. *The rest of my family, huh*? With the instinctive flick of his forked tongue to George's parchment and sawdust scent, he thoughtfully opened his mouth. "C-Can I adopt all of them? Then, we can all go back to Earth, and you can have whatever you want with this planet."

George laughed at Hugo again without coughing, and this time, it worried Hugo.

"I like the way you think, and I wish it were that easy. But no, I don't think that's an option. And besides, we're almost finished here. If all your friends stay down, they will live, that I promise you."

Suddenly, a sound of gagging and choking twitched Hugo's ears. George turned around, but he only sighed. "So, the final choice has been made, . . ." George said to himself with a final, searchful glance at the ground, then lumbered to Sam, who had many spikes of stone and water impaled through him. "I guess nobody in Rafflesia had a soul ability to fix all this. . . ." he whispered, then coughed with a splat of blood skimming his lower lip. "Snow . . . I know what you plan to do to him once I die. . . . Just, if I could have one request. . . . Give him a final exam. Let him choose. Let him show that he is stronger than me, strong enough to overcome you. Don't force him into it . . . and if he doesn't want you, let it be so. . . ." He looked to the heavens and squinted at Zenith in thought. "I'm sorry, Sam, we've run out of time. . . . I was never worthy enough to be your guide. But hopefully, I have set you on the path to find who will bring out your light."

"It's finished," Ella said with a sigh. "He can't survive that." George glared at Ella with eyes that reflected the screams of her death. But to her surprise, he didn't kill her; he just returned to Sam.

Sam's eyes drooped as his fearful little heart felt colder with every draining pat. "You have to hold on, Sam, just for a few more seconds. It's almost over." George whispered with his hands over his feathery torso.

But even with so many wounds, Sam felt nothing but fear pumping his heart at the last hope to survive. George removed every spike, then quickly filled in the holes. But beneath Sam's skin, he felt cold and wet. Like his dying heart pumped out whatever it could in a final attempt to keep him alive. Sam gasped and held his blood-soaked chest. He was familiar with the feeling of death, but this scared him. "I just wanted to help," he murmured before his lungs gave up. His beak opened and closed with the last attempt to breathe, but it strangely felt good, like one less thing to worry about.

"You will. . . . But sadly, from now on, you'll have to carry our dreams on your shoulders alone."

George peeked at Zenith, covering the sky and rocketing

closer every second. He whispered to himself for just one second with the quick stroke of his frosty beard, then left Sam to his demise and turned to Bipp. To Ella's and Hugo's discomfort, he smiled and lumbered toward him.

Hugo, however, nervously stood between them. "I won't let you hurt Bipp. He's done playing your game, and besides, you said if he stayed down, you wouldn't hurt him." George actually stopped at Hugo and looked at him with a kind smile.

"I'm sorry, Hugo." Before anyone knew it, George grabbed Hugo by the right horn and smashed his left cheek against the ground . . . over and over.

Bipp watched it all. Every time Hugo's face hit the rocky dirt, Bipp felt the familiar whip sting across his chest. "No . . ." Bipp whispered, wincing every time Hugo's face hit the ground. "If you felt . . . the pain you give to creatures," Bipp winced once more with fresh blood trickling from his left ear.

George stopped and smiled, but a few tears escaped his eyes and twinkled the evening sunlight on his cheeks.

"Then you would stop, right? We just have to understand each other." Bipp stood. He looked at Hugo's unconscious face, and his chest stung more than any whip could offer.

George charged back his arm for good measure, ready to smash Hugo's skull through the rocks below.

Bipp's chest hurt so much that he grabbed its fur and leaned forward, about to scream.

"There he is," George said before each hair of Bipp's silver fur mirrored all the colors around him. His body glittered so brightly, George squinted. And before anyone could blink, Bipp roared, and a massive beam of amethyst moonlight shot and expanded from every hair on his chest like a rocket thrust. The front of his cloak burned away with each thread vanishing in the moonlight.

George blocked the beam with both arms, but his feet slid back on the loose dirt. "This growing family really is something," George grunted and smirked while he stood his ground. But then he sighed and looked at Sam, whose eyelids sank. "Thus concludes the prophecy of my end. . . . Remember me, but don't repeat my history no matter how much it wants to resurface. Know to forge your own upon mine, learning from my mistakes and victories. That's how we grow into creatures bigger than you or I can fathom. . . . And if you still don't see your value . . . look around you, and witness the mountains and valleys you move," he murmured as a black flame sprouted from his old shoes and spidered along the ground to Sam. Then Bipp's beam of moonlight crackled and burned George's old skin easier than paper.

"W-What?" Sam breathed, barely able to hear George with everything going on. His eardrums rang; his legs and wings were way colder than his chest. And darkness slowly surrounded his vision with George right in the center.

George grimaced at Hugo and his friends. Zenith was mere seconds away from crushing Somnium.

The black fire began to form a dome around Sam as he choked blood on himself. "P-Please. Grandpa, don't go. We can still help everyone together. Just take my wing," he murmured with a raspy voice just before his eyes closed.

"I'm sorry, little one. But my chance for helping has come to an end."

Sam tried to raise his wing to George, but before he knew it, the black fire blocked him with a growing canopy of flame.

"I've given you the seeds and have no more advice for the future we all chose; so thusly, you've completed my history class. Now just hold on a little longer, and ace that final exam," George said with a smile at Sam. But as his skin charred black and flaked away from Bipp's scorching moonlight, it was impossible to tell if that was a smile. "Goodbye, Saiai."

Then, Sam's heart slammed into his stomach as he heard George collapse without a final breath to give warning. Wisps of smoke curled from his bones, and the pushed air from Zenith brushed his dry, burnt, flaky body toward the horizon. At that moment, the canopy of dark fire sealed Sam away without a flicker of light to be seen.

Ella pulled her friends close, then cut off Bipp's beam of moonlight with walls made of granite and diamond. Bipp gasped as she formed another pyramid over them. His fur whispered light through each hair's tip and moved calmer than ripples in a puddle. "What was that?" Bipp looked at his chest. The front of his cloak was charred black on either side. And now, the many scars among his white and silver fur were displayed to all who would look at him. Bipp blushed and tried to hide his scars by tugging the sides of his cloak inward. He began to heave with every breath before slapping himself in the face. He needed to focus on more important matters, if Hugo was alright. But, just as he sprinted at him, Zenith punched Somnium.

## *Chapter* 25
# BRIGHTEST LIGHT

The only thing Hugo felt was his blood pumping against dirt and rocks. He gasped through his snout the second he woke from shock, but dirt filled his throat instead of air. He moved his arms, ready to dig for his life, but once he gave up that space, dirt collapsed and packed tighter against him. Then, he could feel his stinging lungs begging for air like gravel was ripping them to shreds: he heard his chest thump at the dirt, hoping to give him room. He choked and gagged just before he heard a precious voice.

"Quick! Pull him out!" shouted the muffled voice of Bipp before something tugged Hugo's tail.

Hugo was yanked into an open, dust-lingering cave. His throat tensed up before he vomited and gagged his lungs free from the mud packed within him.

"You're okay; just hold still a moment."

Never before had Hugo been so happy to hear that rabbit's voice. And as the soft thumb of Bipp wiped the teary mud from over his eye, Hugo felt a calm flutter of butterflies dance in his chest with the free yet dusty air now filling his throat.

"Here." Ella's soothing voice melted Hugo further; then he

felt the dry, scratchy rocks and sand lift from his scales and fur with the cool cavern air to replace it.

He opened his eye to Bipp's soft, silver hand and the dark underground beyond.

"Do you hear anyone else?" Ella asked with haste.

Bipp backed away from Hugo with his ears high and twitching with every breath Hugo gulped. But a strange and repetitive burst of air squinted Bipp's eyes as he listened.

"Yeah! I think Luna's over there!" Bipp pointed a few feet from Hugo.

A beam of light shone from a hole in the ceiling and hit many dust particles on the way down. It enveloped Bipp's fur and sparkled every hair like a disco ball. Hugo wouldn't dare look away from him. For one, he was too in shock to look anywhere else, and two, he simply liked the soft look of him in this rocky cave, even if he did wear his burnt, shredded cloak like an apron to cover his front.

After a few calming breaths, Hugo looked at Ella, who especially looked beautiful with her arctic fur dancing along with specks of sand glittering in the light.

Hugo's ears twitched as rocks clacked and sand shifted right beside him. Before his eye, Luna was yanked from the dirt. She too gulped for air and gripped her chest to ensure she was still beating.

When she emptied her throat of mud, and Ella graced her scales by lifting rocks off her, she coughed for a moment, then blew a wisp of white fire for everyone to see well. And once their eyes adjusted to the light, they all spotted Mary's sapphire, colossal snout pushing dust around with her deep breaths. Ella dug her toes into the dirt and raised her palms to Mary. She pushed at the air with a grunt, and with it, the dirt was removed from Mary's nose to her neck, allowing her to relax her chin onto the ground.

"Thank you," Mary heaved, far too hurt and exhausted to open her eyes. "Are my boys alright? I know I heard Bipp."

Hugo quickly scanned the cave for Sam and sucked through his snout for the scent of blueberries or burnt chicken. But not even a whiff of Sam flared Hugo's snout. "Sam. . . ." Hugo sank his head against the dirt. He peeked up through the hole in the hope of seeing stars. But there wasn't even moonlight to grace the sky with light. Only a warm sunset of orange and pink ripples beneath the puffy spread of clouds shone through that hole. His forked tongue flicked out with the yearning desperation for even a speck of starlight.

"Got you." Ella raised her arms before Ventus was yanked from the adjacent wall of rocks and dirt with a few scratches along his wings. Everyone watched him, expecting him to move or scoff at them for saving him last, but he didn't move, nor did he breathe. Ella instantly threw back her arms, yanking the dirt from his throat in a long trail of brown sludge. Bipp ran to him and pressed his ear on his chest before Ventus brushed him across the opposite ear. "Get off me."

Bipp promptly did so.

"Okay . . . That's everyone," Ella sighed with relief, counting the five with her finger. Once she lowered her arm, she sat beside Hugo with her back bent, and she folded her arms over her face and knees.

"I beg your pardon, Mrs. arctic fox, but that's not everyone," Mary murmured.

Ella's spine rose and sank when she sighed with a deep breath. "I don't feel his heartbeat against the dirt," she sighed again. "It's possible he didn't make it."

Bipp looked at Hugo, who still searched for just one star.

Hugo's throat stung with his snout beginning to ooze snot onto his lips. He was about to cry, but he didn't want to. He didn't want to even think that Sam could be gone.

Ella looked up as Hugo began to tremble with the struggling floodgate about to burst. She rubbed her face free from dust, then looked up at the hole. "Come on. I'll bring us up. Maybe he's just not in the ground."

Before Hugo could look at her, she dug her toes into the ground, then raised her right arm. Then, to everyone's surprise, she smiled a little. "This is going to be a lot easier without Zenith."

The ground beneath them instantly trembled before the tiny hole in the ceiling ripped open with an ear-popping crack. Suddenly, the setting sun gifted the walls with warm light, and even Mary began to rise from the planet's crust with a massive stone platform beneath their feet. Hugo watched in amazement as the many rock layers passed them faster than he could count, as if they were on a colossal elevator.

Ella slowed their ascent as they neared the top. And just over the hole's ridge came the tips of castles and mountains of rubble. Mary shook the hills from her back, and she sucked in so much air, Hugo's fur rose to meet her snout.

Bipp's eyes welled as he saw that the once beautiful city was now part of the ash and rubble of King's Garden.

Mary struggled to spot Rafflesia through all the dust as she peeked over the mountainous rubble. Zenith had perfectly fit into the crater caused by George's moonlight attack.

Bipp took out his lined paper and the pencil he brought from Earth, then added a few things. "Like the two mountain peaks, now we have the two destroyed cities. Surprisingly, the only big city left is the tower of memory, unless you count Cactus Bay in the far south," he murmured.

Hugo took a moment to see the world around him: no stars, no moon, destroyed cities, and an ash-buried field around them. *Is this . . . my fault? Should I have just stayed home with Bipp?* He looked at Mary, so beautiful and majestic. And he looked at Bipp, just happy to be alive and by his side. He then sighed and looked to the east, where he last saw Sam. "I'll search there for him."

"I'm coming with you of course," Bipp said quickly, looking at his cloaked chest and rubbing it. "Maybe I'll ask Luna more about my soul ability later," he murmured with a smile he couldn't suppress. He looked at Luna, who heard him with the twitch of her ears, but she was done for the day and just lay there in thought.

"I'll meet up with you in a bit. Just give me a second to feel my back again," Mary said.

Hugo nodded worriedly before he limped off with a final glance back to ensure everyone was well.

Sam wasn't alone. No matter how much his body numbed, and the dead silence rang his eardrums, he couldn't escape the feeling of being imprisoned by a thousand watching eyes. The dark fire that once cloaked George, canopied over Sam's still body with many wisps of heat and cracks of malice. But he could not feel or hear any of it. A thick layer of his dried blood shielded his feathers, and as his wheezing breaths slowly failed to keep him awake, one question spun in his mind.

*Why did Grandpa do all this, when he could've just killed me?*

*It was all for you, the useless anchor.*

The voice sank Sam closer to death, nearly fusing his back with the boulder he lay against as he almost gave up living right then.

*Why? Please, just tell me why would anyone do all that . . . for me.*

*He made the mistake of loving you. . . . That old fool held on to you and tried to swim up. But with such an anchor to pull him down, drowning was inevitable. . . . You were an even bigger fool to try and gain the old man's acceptance. Nobody will ever accept you. . . . Time was his weakness—You were his weakness, his anchor, his burden, his sorrow. He could predict the future, but he allowed this one to show for a reason beyond even me. He actually loved you so much and wanted to uncover your nonexistent potential that he eradicated an entire city, just for the hope of finding a soul similar to yours . . . to undo all that he did and to help everyone without killing you. He was willing to do whatever it took to help, and you were the hope. But funny thing, hope . . . it doesn't exist when it's the most useless pest on the planet. He felt everyone's pain as they died. He wept, and all you did was ponder if he was a monster. Everyone suffered, all because of you, the real monster.*

The dark fire opened the canopy from the top and shrank to a young flame beside his head. Sam's eyes met the instant results of his actions: Rubble shifted and clacked as buildings gave in to gravity, the sandy wind shot at anything that stood in its path, and the sky showed not even a twinkle of a single star or the faint amethyst moonlight that had always been. Sam hated himself, believing everything the fire spoke, that all this was his fault.

*You and the old man shared the same goal, to help others more than you or he could fathom, but you weren't ready in his foolish opinion. And now that he's gone and your time is up, it's your choice. Die and remove the anchor from everyone, or live and drown everyone who remains. . . . Again, I can kill you faster than a blink, easier than a breath, end all this pain, all you must do is ask. But, before you die, you must give me your soul.*

Before Sam could respond, something significant blocked the sunset from his feathers, and surprisingly, it made him warmer in its shadow. For a second, he didn't recognize the silhouette. But once it pressed its ear against Sam's heart, he saw the glimmer of Hugo's white fur. *Do you want me to die?*

*I would love it if you died, and so would everyone else. But the old man limited me with one of his tricks. I cannot help you end this pain unless you give permission.*

"He's not breathing! And I can barely hear his heart!" Hugo screamed to Bipp, but Sam couldn't hear him.

*I don't want to die, because it'll make Hugo sad. I want him to be happy, but . . . would he learn to forget about me? His life would be easier without the anchor pulling him down, and he has many friends supporting him. So, if I were gone, he would eventually be okay.*

Sam's heart stopped, and his breaths became silent. While Bipp held Sam's head up, Hugo gripped his hands over Sam's chest and shoved down repeatedly. Sam's ribs snapped with every push, but at this point, Sam was gone. Only one thing could save him.

*This is it. Do you want to accept my offer and die, or reject it and live?*

Hugo soaked his feathered chest in tears and snot while he shot Sam with those powerful cannon arms; Bipp blew into his beak, both hoping he would live.

*I want my family to be happy. . . . I want them to know that I love them more than anything. And I want to be helpful to those around me. . . . Whichever choice allows those three things, I want it.*

*Not a direct answer, but I understand completely,* the fire said in a suspicious tone before the young flame beside his head crept into his feathers, then crawled into his beak.

"What the?" Bipp said, instantly stopping the mouth-to-mouth. He stood and backed away. "Uh, Hugo, we should get out of here."

"No! Not until he's okay!" Just as he said that, Sam's eyes opened with flames whiter than snow. Each raven feather wisped like swaying tree leaves before the black fire crept from their stems and coated Sam in a beautiful whispering flame. His wounds vanished, but he couldn't tell, for the soothing, warm fire conquered all his pain.

Sam blinked a few times to get a feel for it. With his new eyes, he could see everything the universe had. Stars from half the universe away were as bright and vivid as a firefly a few inches from his face. He even watched individual light particles race to Somnium from their sources. But space would never look the same after that starlight attack, draining all light from the stars. Some would take a thousand lifetimes to return to Somnium, but luckily for Hugo, a few nearby planets still shone like stars in such darkness.

He also saw the moon. The rocket-like thrust of that moonlight attack shot it far from orbit, so far from Somnium that he doubted it would ever return. He could see his bedroom, how tidy his bed was for if he ever returned, and with a few of Bipp's silver hairs laying within the threads of the dinosaur-themed comforter. He saw how the galaxy spiraled in perfect harmony with each celestial object. But then, a subtle, quick pinch shocked his body and forced him to wince.

He slowly sat up. Overall, he had never felt better in his life. And to his astonishment, he could move both his legs and all his toes. He wanted to stand to test it out, but Hugo caught his sight before he could move any further.

Hugo stared at him with apparent fear trembling his body.

"Hey, Hugo." Sam stood, then saw a black ink slowly pool from his feet and onto the dirt; it was so dark, it consumed any light daring to touch it. Hugo took a step back. "Wait! I'm sorry, I'll just–" Sam patted his body. "How do I turn this thing off?"

*You're mine now. And it's about time I turned you off.*

Sam froze at those words.

"I'm here, Sam. H-How are you feeling?" Hugo asked with his eye closed. His heart pounded so fast in fear that he couldn't look at Sam anymore without passing out. But he cared about him enough to force himself to stay.

The fire around Sam began to get hotter and hotter with every passing second. And the darkness pooling from him reached Hugo's retreating feet and hands.

"Shut up about me. Just, uh, how are you doing?" Sam looked around his entire body, looking for an off switch. *Come on, what are you doing, fire? I just want to talk to him, but not like this!*

Sam suddenly grimaced and tried to hide the pinching pain, but it was relentless, never giving him a chance to breathe.

"Never mind." Sam then carefully walked to Hugo. "Just don't look at me, alright?" He stood before Hugo. "Can you smell me, hear me?" Sam asked, trying to comfort Hugo with *the thing*.

But Hugo shook his head. "You don't smell like burnt

chicken or blueberries anymore. . . . A-And I can't even hear your heartbeat. . . . I-I know your still there, but–"

"But I am your nightmare . . . aren't I?"

*Fill the vase.* The voice of a kind lady whispered behind Hugo.

Hugo's ears twitched, and he looked back again. But like before, nobody was there. *What is that?* He paused with a blink, then turned and bowed his head to Sam.

"I'm sorry, I–" Hugo peeked open his eye and fought with all his might to see Sam. But when the white fire vanquished Sam's familiar green eyes, and the intense heat dried Hugo's vision, his head went numb, and his legs weakened. "You don't have to change yourself. Please, just give me some time to get used to it, and I promise I'll be able to look at you again without fear." His body was shaking in horror. *Come on! He needs to feel it! He's going to hate himself even more if I can't even look at him!*

At this moment, the pain of the fire grew so intense that Sam couldn't open his beak without screaming. It was hard for Hugo to see what Sam was feeling under that colorless fire, but once Sam collapsed on his wings and knees, Hugo saw, and he definitely heard. Cries of sheer agony squeezed through the cracks of Sam's bone-grinding beak. Even drips and strands of saliva shot with the breath of his screams.

*You aren't as strong as the old man, and even he couldn't stop me from killing that Saurian.*

"You . . . killed Anzu?"

Hugo took a step closer with his eye begging to look away from him. "Sam?"

"Run! I can't hold it!" Sam forced his eyes to look at Hugo, who had tears flowing from him.

*Fire, stop this! How do I turn you off?*

"Here, let me help–"

"No! I don't want you to help me!" Sam roared; he didn't mean to sound so aggressive, but with his pain, he was surprised he didn't bite off his tongue. But as Sam saw Hugo take a step closer to him, there was only one thing he could think to do.

"I hate you, Hugo! I-I never want you to see me again! Please!" Sam lied through his gnashing beak with his eyes squinted shut. His skin felt as if it were melting. In the back of his mind came the dream he had of the black fire roaring and melting him down into a puddle. "I will never stop hurting you! You need to go away and never look back!"

Hugo growled at himself. Part of him wanted to listen and respect Sam's request, but as Sam wept, Hugo couldn't help but step closer. "I can do this . . . I can do this." He breathed in and out with deep heaves. Then, he forced his eye on him. *That is Sam. . . .* he told himself, but the fire around Sam forced him into fear. *That's my little brother! . . .* He closed his eye and begged himself to remember Sam's bright emerald eyes. *Sam is here, right beside me.* He breathed once more, opened his eye, saw the fire, and instantly shut it. His heart thumped into his head with the echoing image of Sam's fire burning in his eye. "Sam . . ." Hugo said and wobbled closer.

"Go awaaaay!" Sam yelled at the ground, hoping Hugo would run and be safe from what he felt was coming.

Hugo walked around Sam until the entire length of his body formed many circles.

Then, from Sam's boiling flesh, he felt something smooth and surprisingly cold press against his back.

Hugo raised Sam and cradled him against his chest where

he lay. "You're going to be okay . . . just take a breath, and focus on you. Forget about me, please. Allow yourself to live in the present and let go of the future."

*You're hurting him.* Like someone's lips pressed against his ear, the fire spoke so loud that Sam could barely hear Hugo. He didn't want to listen to the voice, but its words made him worry. Hugo's embrace did help him shift his focus from the pain. But he couldn't help but look at Hugo's scales; some melted, while others were so burnt they turned black.

"Can you close your eyes for me?"

Sam looked up at Hugo's face, and to his surprise, Hugo's eye was already closed. Tears still came from him, and he was trembling in fear, but he still held him close.

*He . . . can't even look at me anymore.*

"It's okay, Sam. I can take this for a moment; just close your eyes and allow yourself to sink against me."

Sam looked at Hugo's charred scales again, then closed his eyes. To his discomfort, the feeling of burning that he felt now was the same feeling of the elk shoving him into the splintery fire.

The fire grew more and more, but the dark pool seemed to pause. Sam's wings wrapped around and squeezed Hugo tight. And as Hugo's lungs expanded his chest, Sam's wings spread apart with him. And in this moment of silence, Sam felt and heard Hugo's heart thump against his cheek.

Hugo gently placed his hand on the back of Sam's head before Sam closed his eyes. "Now, keep your head on my chest, and breathe with me. We can calm down and do *the thing* together."

Bipp had his mouth open as he stared at a few embers leaving Hugo's fur. "That dragon. . . ."

"He's still alive?" Ella shouted as she came over a hill of rubble.

Sam grimaced at the distracting noise of her voice and the following noise of shifting rubble under her steps. The fire around Sam grew quickly as each rock clacked. Hugo too grimaced at that intense heat. Even his dragon hide couldn't sustain it much longer, especially if it kept growing.

Bipp turned to her and gestured for her to lower her voice.

Ella paused at Bipp's request, then looked at Hugo and Sam. The fire was apparent and almost rose to the height of Hugo's ember-swishing fur; together they formed a like image of space with many stars. She watched Hugo's fangs peek under his rising lips as the pain pierced his tolerance.

"Is he still a threat?" she whispered. But little did they know, no secrets were safe from the fire; with it, Sam could hear the breaths of an insect, but only when the voice in his head lay dormant.

Sam gnashed his beak and opened his eyes to Ella. "If I'm a threat, then why are you still talking? Wouldn't you be dead?"

After hearing *that voice* from Sam, Hugo opened his eye and let go. He didn't want to, but his legs forced him to step back.

"No, wait, Hugo. I didn't mean–"

Ella stepped forth, and Sam stared at her with a vile squint. The fire resumed its magmic conquest over his skin. And little did he see, the fire that engulfed his body was rising in temperature and size.

"I'm talking to you out of respect for Hugo. If he weren't willing to try with you, I would've had to drop the moon on you." She squinted at the black sky with only the hue of the late, fading sunset to color it. "If I could find it."

*She's trying to make you a burden again. . . . Kill her.*

Sam grabbed his head; the voice came loud, for when it spoke, the sides of his head went numb. The mouth of the voice poisoned his brain with a wet, pointed tongue to sting his eardrums with venom. *No, I won't do that! I told you I wanted to help! Not this!* His wings shook from the fight to keep control of his body. But he felt his toes twitching on their own, as if they waited for him to slip from his focus.

*Then you will never be helpful.*

Sadly, those words were all it took. At this moment, the black fire exploded from around Sam. Hugo leapt in front of Bipp and Ella before the fire could evaporate them. Its heat burned through Hugo's scales, and its force smacked him and his friends into the rubble.

Hugo screeched and wrangled his body while gripping the dirt. It felt like someone was pressing a freshly-used pan on his side.

Bipp instantly looped around him to see the damage. Most of the scales on his left side were black, melted, and fused into his flesh. His new scarf was especially burnt, but still able to hang from his neck with the remaining threads. "Ella! Get water on him now!" He let Hugo grab onto his left hand and squeeze as hard as he wanted. But Bipp regretted doing so, for Hugo's grip quickly broke some bones.

"There isn't any! He just burnt away the clouds! I'll need a moment to gather some from the ocean!" She flew from between the rubble and Hugo with spherical rocks under the pads of her feet.

The fire grew faster; its height doubled Sam's, and its width nearly crowned the boulder he stood on. Then, the fire over his eyes blazed with such heat, Sam screamed and collapsed to his knees. Before anyone noticed, the black pool covered every bit of ground they could see.

"Stooop iiit!" Sam roared and wrangled in such agony, he slammed his back and head against the rock in the hope of knocking himself out. But at that moment, he felt his left knee bend with the gentle rise of his foot before his talons pierced the boulder and dug deep, deeper than the length of his leg, tenfold. He could feel layers of rock slide past his ankle at unfathomable speeds.

Ella flew just over Hugo with rocks circling her. "This is it, Sam. . . . If you don't control this, I will have to fight you. . . . But I know you're fragile and sometimes kind. So I would like to think you can be saved. Just lower the fire, and maybe we can help y–"

"Go away, please! If you try to save me, you'll all die!" Sam then yanked out Luna's sword, gripped tightly within his toes. The sword instantly caught fire and grew so long, it impaled a nearby building. He tried to drop it, but even with his greatest efforts, he couldn't move a single toe.

*Stop this, fire! What are you doing?*

"What's going on?" Mary spoke and walked with heavy thuds over many fallen buildings.

Sam's eyes snapped open at the sight of the creature, and he looked back at the sword once more. *No, no, no! Don't hurt it. I . . . won't let you–*

". . . . This fight is far from over," Ella murmured.

Sam looked at Ella as two spheres of rock lay spinning on her palms; she was ready to get violent.

*You need to kill them.*

Sam forced his body to turn his back to them. *No! This isn't what I want! I told you I want them to be happy!*

Mary carefully stepped forward with a smile. "Sam? Is that you?" Even though she tried to be gentle, the ground shook with every step she took.

The tremors shook Sam from what little grasp he had on his thoughts. He looked back and up at the intimidating creature, who stared at him with a familiar, warm smile.

Without permission, his right toes curled slightly and rose from the ground. He tried his best to control his movements, but it seemed impossible, like his brain had a new, more assertive, co-pilot.

*This is your last chance before things go bad. You are too weak to help anyone. Give me your soul, and you won't be a burden. Give me your soul, and they live the happy lives you wish for.*

Sam looked up at Hugo, whose fangs gnashed and cheeks scrunched to his closed eye.

*If that's your definition of happy, then no . . . you can't have my soul, just let me heal him–*

Sam's curled toes knocked on the rock.

George's door instantly appeared before the sword. Its extending flames roared around the door. He grunted as he begged his leg to move the sword away; he screeched in agony at the simple hope of dropping the sword. But as saliva shot from his throat and dripped from his beak after his attempts, he felt his chest sink with the horror of what was about to happen. With haste, Sam looked back at Ella.

"I changed my mind. Kill me! Do it now!"

Ella didn't know how to respond to that.

*I won't open that door if–*

*Shut up! You are not in control here! You will never get my soul! Especially when I'm so close to helping them. Just give me a chance!*

*Your death would've helped them.*

The door creaked open, and Mary grunted.

Sam veered his head to the door, and his pupils shrank at the horror of seeing the dragon's blue chest gushing blood out the door. He felt it all through the blade's hilt: It poked through her scales like a pencil through paper, blood singed and boiled against the sword's heat as it shoved through the hastened pounding of her heart, the awful crunch and snap of her spine attempting to suppress the extending fire.

Sam was speechless, frozen, and terrified. He couldn't look anymore. But to his regret, he couldn't shut his eyes.

And at this moment, the fire spouting from the sword vanished with the door and left a tiny hole compared to her colossal body.

Mary's eyes gave a curious squint before her throat hunched her head forward. With a gulp and a gasp, she looked at Hugo and smiled. "I . . . think I'm ok–" Blood vomited from her throat with a suppressed splash through her teeth. "Heh–" She smiled again with her head swaying to and fro until her legs submitted to gravity, and she fell with a mighty thud onto the nearby buildings and rubble. Everyone on the planet felt her hit the ground. Hugo looked up at her through debris and dust that had burst from beneath her with an upward plume.

A numb silence with ears ringing and hearts thumping hushed everyone's mind.

"No. . . . Noooooooo!" Hugo roared so loud, Bipp's ears rang louder. Hugo let go of Bipp, who curled his fingers with a wince to make sure he was alright after that grip. Hugo forced his body to stand, grimaced, and could barely extend his wobbling legs fully.

"S-Sam," Mary wheezed.

*Why does she sound so familiar? . . . She kinda sounds like Mom, but much louder.* Sam squinted open his eyes, looking right at the dragon's sapphire eyes. "How do you know my name?" Sam asked, but Mary's head quickly numbed. So she said the first thing that came to her mind.

*T-Through the rumbling storm and the long cold night*
*you will find . . . w-warmth in my open arms.*
*Like your heroes who fall, you will rise with them all*
*And you will see how high you'll fly.*
*The sun will rise, and the night will set,*
*and you will see your brightest light.*
*My strong, and brave, Saiai.*

Sam turned pale. And his eyes lit agape with his beak. His knees struck the rock, but that bone-shattering pain barely brought a blink to his eyes, nor did the fire around him make him wince anymore, for the pain in his stomach and chest . . . burned beyond pain. It burned so much he wanted—no, needed someone to rip out his heart as it slowly dawned on him through a mix of doubt what he had done. "No. . . ." His toes finally relaxed, and the sword rolled from his grasp.

"Don't let anyone say that you don't deserve love."

Hugo sprinted to her despite his body begging him to collapse. "Just hold on, Mom! I can fix this!" Hugo screamed before roaring fire on Mary's stomach, trying to burn shut the wound.

"It's okay, boys, I'm. . . fine, really. I don't . . . feel it. . . ." Her eyes drooped. "Wow, I'm tired—heh. . . . Can you two be strong for each other, just for a moment? Don't blame yourselves, please . . . don't. . . . I'm . . . going to take a quick nap, and then . . . we can go home. I love you both more than you could possibly understand. . . . My precious boys. . . ." Mary's eyes closed, and her wheezing breath slowed.

Sam was dead still. He didn't even feel his tears sinking from his eyes. But he felt something worse than death. . . . He felt . . . curious. But not in the speechless, indescribable type of curious common on Somnium. This curious was a feeling and a thought a creature should never have to suffer through. There was a numb, stinging horror across his skin and in his deepest flesh, but it wasn't enough to extinguish what burned inside. "No . . ." he said again, for it was the only word he could think of. He hoped this was all a disgusting lie. But as he watched Hugo desperately try to seal the wound with snot and tears sinking from his face like a waterfall, Sam's vase finally . . . shattered. . . .

*I killed her. . . .*

Bipp and Ella only watched the horror of the event unfold. Sam made no noise or movements. And at this moment, the family photo that once lay tucked in Hugo's scarf, caught Mary's breath and curled through the burnt fabric before sliding under Sam's toe.

Sam barely had the will to look at it, but once it caught his eye, it snagged his pupils and forced him to stare. The photo they took as a family, the last time they were all happy before he decided to go to college. The edges began to burn in the black fire, so Sam moved his foot and hoped it wouldn't fly away.

"Ella, Bipp! Please, find Ventus! He knows a doctor who used to live near here!" Hugo begged.

But nobody wanted to move as they watched Sam. To them, Sam appeared to be void of any emotion, but they all knew he was drowning in it.

He knelt there, eyes wide, beak closed, silently staring.

Then, something swelled his chest with horrific, burning pain as the picture flew away with Mary's fleeing breath. He reached out his wing and grabbed the photo, but it instantly burned in his grasp.

He couldn't hold back the monster anymore.

Hugo's mind raced with anything he could do. *Maybe I can give her CPR, but she's too big! . . . Maybe I can find that doctor, but I don't want to leave her! . . . Maybe . . . I should've–* He looked up at Mary's once-plump cheeks sink down. *Should I have let go of Sam? And stayed–*

Air left her mouth and pushed Hugo's fur back, but no air came back in. Hugo instantly veered around, trying to find anything to help as his heart raced with sudden panic.

"I'm sorry, Mom! I-I should've just stayed home!" Hugo cried. *I killed her! She was just trying to keep me safe! But I'm so stupid; I didn't think–* He vomited and tried to heave in and out as much air as possible to keep his screaming, aching heart from exploding.

At this moment, the planet's ground and remaining clouds went dark. Sam unhinged his beak and screeched to the sky with a beam of black fire shooting from his throat, piercing many layers of the atmosphere like a needle through fabric. This was a cry, a plea to release all he felt, all he had buried inside him. The rock beneath his talons cracked and crumbled under the sheer thrust of his raven-like screech.

Then, within a blink, he appeared before Mary. The air cradled Sam as if the laws of gravity no longer applied to him. Her heart still beat, but she was losing the battle with a beat slower than the gentle taps of Sam's cane. He rested his wings on her snout and screeched with a sound that would tear anyone's throat. He tried to go back; he begged the universe to take her back only a few seconds.

The world flashed around them as Sam thought of the past. Buildings were restored, the burns and dirt vanished from Bipp, but every time, Mary remained with her eyes closed and her warmth fading. "GO BACK!" Sam demanded the heavens. "I don't care if you hate me for the rest of my life. Just go baaack!" Miles of Zenith, including the royal library, vanished, replaced by an empty grass field. Then, a white fire flashed and instantly faded around Sam's dark fire.

In that instant, to everyone's comfort, Mary returned to when she was a human. The new, empty space sucked them closer to her for a moment. But when they caught their wits, they saw her: curly copper hair, big arms, and jolly cheeks that lightened everyone's hearts. A smile barely had time to form across Sam and Hugo's mouths before Mary began to choke. She grabbed her throat and wheezed. Her lips instantly became purple as she collapsed.

"Nooo!" Sam yelled, quickly grabbing onto her. But even his most gentle touch scorched her skin. "Ahhh! I'm sorry!" He retreated many feet away from her. Even his lungs heaved as they raced air in and out like a train engine.

Hugo grabbed Mary and tried to breathe for her, but she gagged once Hugo's mouth met hers.

Sam punched the rock with his foot, hoping to summon George's door to Earth. But when the rock split in half from his pounding and no door came, he wept. "Noooooo!" The white light flickered around Sam once again. Clouds formed over Sam and darkened like coal. "Just one second! That's all she needs! A dragon without that wound!"

Then, before anyone could blink, Mary turned back into a massive dragon, sending air, rubble, and dust-like bullets around her expanded mass. Hugo and Sam were shoved back by her. When Hugo's ears rose at the sound of her tornado-spawning breaths, Sam looked up and saw the wound, still fresh and gushing with her forthcoming death.

Sam's heart finally stopped, and his pupils shrank. "I still can't . . . control it." He desperately looked at Hugo. *Maybe if we hold hands like with George and me—*

*Give me your soul; then I can save her. Even if you held everyone's hands on this continent, you would only pull them down with you and burn them, for you are the useless anchor, and if you continue this path, you will decide how she dies: as the mother you loved or the dragon you feared.*

Sam looked at his mom. His breaths grew heavier than Hugo's, and his heartbeat shook his body enough to quake the ground he stood on. Then, above all else, his head felt numb enough to pass out. *I guess . . . in the end . . . I couldn't be helpful and strong like you.* He looked back at Hugo through a blur of tears. *I hope me going away makes our family happy. . . . Just know . . . I loved you all so, so much. . . . And thank you, for letting me be a part of your memory.* He filled his lungs with a deep and final breath. *It's not about me. . . . It's not about me.*

*Goodbye, the only light I've ever known. . . .*

"Take it! Take all of me if you must! Please, save her!"

Hugo's ears rose at those words as a sudden shift in the air whispered eerily through his fur, and he looked back at Sam. *What did he just do?*

Sam reached his wing to her with his head sinking and his vision darkening around her. "You'll be okay, Mom . . ." he whispered, then splashed into the unconscious world with a hard thwack against a rock. And at this moment, the white fire over his eyes blackened like the rest of him.

Hugo ignored Sam and resumed back to Mary. But Mary was unresponsive, and her chest continued to gush with blood. His tears and snot soaked her in the messiest way possible. "Mom . . ." he wept with his head now pressed against her bloody chest. All he wanted to do was to feel her heartbeat one final time.

"He wanted her wellbeing more than anything. . . ."

Hugo opened his eye at that voice. It sounded like Sam's but much calmer, firm, and altogether . . . warm, especially to the sensitive fur against Hugo's eardrums. And with the upward twitch of his ears, he heard the sharp snap of fire crackle from Sam.

"I'm so sorry, Sam. . . . I didn't know she would come. I tried. I–"

"It's a pity she has to die."

It was at this moment when Hugo froze stiff, and his heart melted with a sinking anchor tugging it down. With his head pressed against Mary's chest, he felt her body shift with a loud, squishy noise.

"Run, Hugo."

Hugo's ears forced his eye to look at Mary just as Sam yanked out a sapphire orb from Mary's bleeding chest. He felt a particular heat weigh his stomach and slither up his neck.

"Put that back," Hugo commanded with his pupil shrinking and the familiar warmth of fire tickling his uvula.

Sam ignored Hugo and opened his beak to the orb.

Sam paused as his body shifted to the sheer force of Hugo's hand gripping around his stomach. Hugo loomed over Sam with fire dripping from the tight gaps in his grinding fangs. With that eye, it was apparent he no longer saw his brother in that body. "Where is Sam?"

"Saiai's light is gone," Apotheosis spoke.

Hugo felt a snap in his chest, he couldn't explain the sinking feeling, but the creature at the mercy of his grasp chilled his blood enough for him to shake from his scales in fear. And just as Sam pressed the blue orb into his chest, allowing it to vanish into the black fire, Hugo roared a beam of fire onto Sam. To Hugo, his beam of fire was not one for combat, but a cry to keep his brother and mom alive. But he suppressed it. He needed to save them, but how could he bring himself to hurt Sam? Once he stopped, and only a river of tears left his body, all he saw left of Sam was the black fire whispering over his cute beak.

"Please . . . let them go," Hugo wept and let go with his hands trembling. He felt his head go light and his eye droop. *No! Don't pass out! I just . . . I need to . . . protect them and love them more than–*

It was at this moment, when Sam exploded with a white flame. Its outward force threw Hugo back near Bipp. This scorched Hugo, for this fire was hotter than any star. The flame wasn't really white, but a shimmering light of an actual divine being as wisps of green, blue, red, and all other colors curled with the flame's light.

As Hugo never broke sight from Sam, he saw the white flames and the colors of the universe and heard them scream in the hope of escaping Sam. The wisps of white flames looked like hands, grabbing at the air, begging for life. And Sam was like a black hole, consuming all light without resistance or mercy. Even the sunlight's hue over the horizon warped and sucked into Sam's darkness. Hugo tilted his head, and the warp moved with his perception. With Sam's body, so skinny and small, enveloped in black fire, the white flame around him formed an eye with him as the pupil.

Hugo looked back at Bipp with more than fear paralyzing his tongue. "W-W-We need to r-run," he stammered horribly, but Bipp's ears heard him clear enough. He didn't want to leave Sam and Mary, but it was their only chance to survive.

Bipp breathed while staring at Apotheosis. "It's okay. . . . I'll distract him." He stood and withdrew his ebony dagger with the ruby embedded in the pommel. "Ella, help Hugo and the others escape to my house; I don't think I'll be needing it anymore."

"No. . . . We're all making it back; just wait a moment if you can," she grunted as she closed her eyes and raised her arms to their apex. To the sensitive touch of Bipp's toes, he could feel the ground begin to shake.

Apotheosis stepped forth. Heat ebbed closer with every inch, scorching and evaporating anything within an arm's reach. Even the ground beneath him vanished in flames as he walked without the need for a floor. Ella looked to Hugo, whose feet seemed stuck to the ground as he tried to pull. Shaking her head rid of the deathly feeling of Sam overwhelming her, she sprinted to Hugo and grabbed his tail. "Come on!" She pulled, but Hugo wasn't moving, nor could he move if he tried. The sight of that dark figure, and the words he spoke about Sam being dead, were enough to kill him outright. His family had disappeared before his eyes, *and it was all my fault.*

"I'm so sorry." All Hugo did and could do, was weep.

"You're next, dragon."

Apotheosis raised his wings, and Hugo rose from the ground with them. Ella dangled for a moment before letting go and attempting to pull Hugo with the mud on his feet or the water in his stomach, but Apotheosis was too strong. Before Hugo could blink, Apotheosis flipped Hugo over, his belly facing the sky. "To think, this isn't my wish. Saiai was the one who wished for you never to see him again. . . . In a way, he wished for you to hate him, so you'd stay away." To Hugo's ears, Apotheosis growled and whimpered those words. Then, with some hesitation, he rotated his wings down.

"Sam! Wait! I– aaaa– AAAHHHHH!" Hugo's long spine snapped like a tree branch in an instant crack and crunch. Ella and Bipp's ears sank with the horror of his bones snapping and cracking. Hugo screeched until his throat bled and wore out until his poor neck emitted only dry grunts, unable to be heard over his bones. When the final part of his spine gave up with a snap, and the back of his head met the base of his tail, his eye rolled back, and his head felt beyond numb.

"Noooo!" Apotheosis screamed, then paused for a second. To Hugo, it sounded just like Sam. But to his light head, he could barely think about it as his eye just about forced itself into the blurry darkness ebbing around his sight.

Apotheosis dropped him without mercy and let him smack on the ground, head and tail first. Hugo flopped along the ground, trying to run from that monster. "Get away!" Hugo wheezed, but his tail and legs refused to move, forcing him to pull his lengthy body through the dirt with his foreclaws.

Bipp was so horrified by the sight, he couldn't move, let alone allow himself the grace of looking away. He simply stood with his hands over his mouth.

"Heeelp!" Hugo screamed and flopped, trying to move with his cheek sliding against the ground. He had no control of his spine and barely his neck, nor did he feel much below his shoulders. Then, Apotheosis hovered down and consumed his sight. Hugo grimaced from that heat. It inched closer and grew hotter with every eerie second the fire crackled around Sam's body.

Bipp wept. He couldn't help but feel the horrors of what Hugo felt as he watched. He knew he didn't stand a chance against Apotheosis, but he had to try. "I promised Mary that I'd protect us." He took a deep breath. "Just one final kill."

"Now you understand. . . . Sam didn't want you in his life." Apotheosis raised his foot near Hugo's right eye. "Now join your fellow dragons."

Bipp stomped forth with a thunderous thud, instinctively pointing his ebony dagger at Apotheosis. "Stop it! I will never let you–" he yelled, but trembled horribly.

Before Bipp could gasp, the white fire around Apotheosis blinked.

Apotheosis then appeared centimeters behind him, rising his back fur in a thousand goosebumps as his jade pupils shrunk in horror. Bipp swung his arm back, fast enough to cut through Sam's neck. But the dagger just wisped through Sam as if he was nothing more than a flame. "No. . . ." Bipp's eyes snapped awake, and he looked at the dagger. "Mom?"

Apotheosis grabbed him by the throat with his left foot and repeatedly bashed his head against a stone until he stopped moving. Blood gushed from the many new openings along his head as not even a twitch jerked his quiet body.

"Noooooo! Biiiip!" Hugo roared.

Apotheosis resumed to Hugo, who screeched as he felt the sudden heat and sharp talons on Sam's toes stretch open his eyelid.

"Goodbye, brother," Apotheosis growled and dug his blistering talons deep around Hugo's remaining eye.

Hugo screamed and tried to get away. But with his last seconds of sight, he paused as he saw the subtle sparkle of water drops tap the ground beside his snout. He looked up to the sky and saw that the water had come from the dark figure looming over him, but the most drops steamed away before they dripped from those fiery eyes. Then, from under Apostheosis' growling, a faint whimper rose Hugo's ears. *Sam's still there. . . .* He tried to get up, just to talk to him once more. But a force unknown to him, like a false gravity, pinned him against the ground, unable to resist the monster. "Saaam! I'm going to help you! Just hold on!"

Then, his ears instinctively rose as the ground shook with a growing roar from the horizon. The ocean had arrived, rushing like an army of chariots, splashing like whips to their horses.

"We're getting out of here!" Ella shouted, hoping Hugo heard her.

Apotheosis hesitated with a sniffle and grunt, then yanked out Hugo's eye with a bloody tug and snap before all went dark. "Let the eye of the galaxy shut."

Hugo's heart thumped, and that was all he could hear or feel. The more he thought about it, the faster his heart pumped. He couldn't feel the ground nor the air roll past his teeth; even more so, he couldn't tell if he was awake anymore. The darkness had won . . . for it was all Hugo could see. His white fur wisped upward like tiny hands hoping for the surface's air, but the weight of the deep depths found its pull and consumed him until his final breath bubbled past his teeth to the heavenly stars just out of reach.

*I'm . . . so sorry. Many people were hurt beyond recovery; some . . . even lost their light. But the light you see in him hasn't vanished yet, has it?*

*When I met you, I didn't see this happening. I didn't see Sa-*

*iai having such a massive hole in his vase that this much water would splash out. . . . I thought . . . having you and your growing family . . . would prevent even the slightest crack. I was wrong. . . . But now that your eyes are shut, you can at least hear me better, and you can easily feel me in your heart. . . . Maybe, I can help you truly see. I did promise I'd check if everything's alright after Dawn, didn't I?*

A warm giggle tickled the weightless fur in Hugo's ears.

*You grew up to be something more than I expected, not just a friend, nor the brother he needed, but perhaps . . . something completely unique.*

There was dead silence, but Hugo's chest warmed, like the dark, cold galaxy around him had a bright core to warm all the long star trails around him.

*Your fears have caged you long enough. Come, let's help you break free . . . and let's get our son back.*

*To be concluded in Book Three:*
*Curious Souls...*

**Luke Sheehan** *found joy in writing at a young age when he disobeyed his English teacher and wrote funny stories instead. He spends his free time stargazing on clear nights and practicing flight to help find the adventures Hugo dreams about. To learn more about Luke and the future of the Curious series, visit him online at starrow. org*

Made in the USA
Monee, IL
01 April 2023

a7ca89ff-3432-4504-81c0-b859b158e05fR01